THE MAN IN BLACK

A GOTHIC GHOST ROMANCE

STEFFANIE HOLMES

BACCHANALIA HOUSE

THE MAN IN BLACK

CROOKSHOLLOW GOTHIC ROMANCE, BOOK 4

Revised Second Edition
containing bonus content

Steffanie Holmes

Want free books, exclusive giveaways and exclusive sneak peeks at upcoming Steffanie Holmes paranormal romance books? Sign up for the mailing list to get the scoop.

ISBN: 978-0-9951302-5-8

✸ Created with Vellum

PROLOGUE

ERIC

I woke up inside the floor.

That whole concept was weird. For starters, to say *I woke up* wasn't quite accurate. I don't really remember how my eyes came to be open, or indeed what had closed them in the first place. My consciousness seemed to rise up from within me, like a diver emerging from the depths. I had been swimming in the murky water, and then, suddenly, I was exposed to the sunlight again.

But being inside the floor ... that part was accurate. I could see beams running along either side of my head, and a giant horizontal void strung with glimmering spider webs. My body seemed to emanate light, for around me I could make out the scratches of rodents against the wood, and the electrical cables winding through the space, but deeper into the floor was all blackness.

The first thing I did was look down at my hands. As a musician, my hands meant everything to me. They were the instruments through which I channelled my thoughts and moods. They looked the same as always; long, strong fingers, the distinctive calluses around the pads marking me as a violinist. They might've been a little paler than usual, but nothing to be worried about.

Now that I knew my hands were okay, I had to figure where I was and how I'd managed to get stuck inside the floor. I took a deep breath, and fell.

I cried out as I dropped through the ceiling, flailing my arms to catch something, anything, to prevent me falling on my back and hurting myself. I watched the chandelier on the ceiling hurtling away from me as I plummeted through the air. Only I didn't land. I fell right into the floor and kept going, passing through a basement, then plunging through a wooden floor into a crawl space, and finally into the dirt below. A worm crawled in front of my face.

And that was when panic seized me. *Is the house falling down? Was it an earthquake? How had I ended up down here?* I opened my mouth to scream, but then clamped it shut again, realising that I'd just fill it with dirt, and then I wouldn't be able to breathe …

But I shouldn't be able to breathe anyway. I'm buried in the dirt beneath a house. I should be suffocating.

The worm inched across my vision.

What is going on?

I tried to move my arms, and found it quite easy. I held my hands in front of me, watching the way the dirt fell through them, as if my hands weren't really there at all. I waved my finger at the worm, and my finger passed right through its body. The worm continued its travels, oblivious to my presence.

This was no natural disaster. Something was seriously wrong with me.

I lifted my hands over my head, and as I did so, my body shot up again. My head popped out from the dirt, but before I could get a good look at the crawlspace, I found myself in the basement. I brought my hands down again, and that stopped my descent. My body still seemed to be emanating a slight glow, and I could see some of the objects piled around me. Old toys, stacks of books, a couple of microwaves. Boxes labelled with loopy handwriting. Something about the stuff looked vaguely familiar, but I couldn't place it …

I pointed my hands toward the basement steps, and, without moving my feet, I flew toward them. But instead of hitting the wooden stairs, I flew through them, feeling only a faint tingle in my limbs as I passed through the solid staircase.

Okay, so that explains why I'd fallen into the dirt. I didn't seem to be able to touch anything anymore. I needed to get to a hospital, maybe they had a pill to fix translucency. I stretched one arm out in front of me, and used it a bit like a conductor to direct my hovering body. I floated up the staircase, flew through the door, and ended up in a very familiar kitchen.

Dark oak benches, grey marble tops, delicate china cups lined up in the dresser, a collection of ceramic cats crowding the windowsill. I'd recognise those cats anywhere. *I'm in my mother's house.* That was why it felt so familiar, despite the strangeness with my body. And now I was levitating in my mother's kitchen. I floated over the counter and sat near the chandelier, gazing down at the old-fashioned gas-fired stove that she'd used to over-boil every vegetable until it ceased to be anything but an unpalatable brown goo. I'd never seen a kitchen from this angle before. It looked strange, otherworldly, like the deck of a spacecraft.

From my vantage point, I noticed several things. I noticed that the ceramic cat collection my mother kept on the windowsill was out of order. My mother was very particular about those sorts of things, so the fact that the orange cat was not next to its mate and the striped cat was on the end instead of being near the middle was a little disturbing.

I also noticed the body on the floor.

It was a woman, wearing a floral dress and frilled apron. A cupboard was open beside her, and a wheelchair was on the floor behind her, tipped on its side. She'd bent down to get something – a cupboard was open – and hadn't got up again. The woman lay sprawled on her back, her face staring up at me, double-chin held proudly aloft, eyes wide and unblinking, skin a strange mottled colour.

It was my mother, and she was dead.

I knew I should feel some emotion, some sense of sadness or loss at discovering her demise, but I did not. I felt oddly detached from the whole situation, as if I were watching a movie, instead of something in real life.

My mother is dead.

She'd been a bitter and hard woman, and had shown little love toward me. "You're just like your father, a useless dreamer!" she would scream at me when I came home from my music lessons. I'd left her as soon as I was old enough to live on my own, and I only came to visit her out of obligation. In recent years, she'd developed Alzheimer's, and oddly, the disease had actually brought us closer. She seemed convinced I was a seven-year-old boy again, and that Dad would be home any moment. She couldn't seem to remember that in her eyes, I was the spawn of my father; the ungrateful, lazy folk musician who'd left us twenty years ago. Instead, she wanted to bake cookies and play soldiers with me.

But now she was dead.

A woman dressed in a nurse's whites bent over the body, her eyes wide with fear and shock. She reached down and lifted up my mother's wrist, pressing her fingers against the skin to feel for a pulse. "Oh no, oh no," she kept mumbling as she tried to puff air into my mother's lungs. But it was no use. The nurse's saliva dripped onto my mother's floral dress.

The nurse looked up, straight up at me. Our eyes met for a moment, and then she looked away, completely oblivious to my hovering presence. She reached for the phone on the wall and dialled a number, her tone businesslike as she described the scene to the person on the other end.

She hadn't seen me. I was floating *right above her,* and she'd looked straight at me and hadn't seen me. I was a student of the macabre, a gothic rock musician. I knew what that meant.

I was dead, too. But now I was a ghost, a floating, see-through ghost. And of all the places I could've chosen to haunt, I'd ended up in *my mother's house.*

The train rattled through the countryside, hurtling past rolling hills and fluffy sheep that leapt back from the tracks in terror, like little clouds scurrying across the landscape. I stared out the window, my lips stretched in an epic pout that glared back at me in my reflection, while my fingers tapped out an angry text message.

I can't believe I have to go to hicksville for two whole weeks.

No parties, no raves, no cocktails. Did they even have a *pub* in Crookshollow? How was I going to get through two weeks without setting foot inside a pub?

Just because I'm the only one who doesn't have a spouse, or kids, or a pet helicopter that needs walking, they chose to send me away. What about my life? What about my commitments? I had tickets to the biggest house party of the year, and instead of shaking my arse on the floor with Cindy, I'm going to be plonking it on some dead lady's sofa. No thank you.

And worst of all, my banishment to hicksville couldn't have come at a worse time. This was the crucial weekend for Operation Shag Damon. I had finally been making progress with Damon Sputnik, the spunky Russian DJ who was lighting up the London dance scene right now. I had been in love with Damon ever since I first saw him behind the decks, his shaved head bobbing along with the beat, his thick muscles bulging from beneath his fluorescent vest. I even had a poster of him at home, his shirtless body decorated with a prowling tiger tattoo. I had such a weakness for tattooed men. I kept the poster on the inside door of my closet so that, on the slim chance I ever did get lucky with Damon and was able to bring him back to my place, he wouldn't see it and think I was some kind of crazy stalker.

That, and my landlord didn't want anything hung on the walls.

The truth is, I'd never in a million years have gone after a guy like Damon, but after things ended with my last boyfriend, Joel, I hadn't exactly been putting myself out there the way a single nearly-30 gal should. So my pal Cindy has been pushing me to get off my arse (and to stop feeding it Wagon Wheels and Hobnobs, but that's another story) and go after someone. So of course I walked straight into a club and fell for Damon, the most unattainable guy I could possibly have chosen.

Over the last six months, most of my weekends had been occupied with getting Damon to notice me. It had become a kind of project for me, and like everything else in my life, I attacked it with all the determination and cunning I could muster. I bought him drinks. I stood right down in front when he did his DJ sets. I was always the first person to like his social media posts. On Cindy's advice, I got some special contact lenses for clubbing so I could leave my glasses at home, and I squeezed my not-unsubstantial arse into tiny skirts and hot pants in an attempt to lure him with the promise of flesh. I'd even offered to hand out flyers for his parties at other events, which earned me a lifetime ban from Vortex and The Crib down in Chelsea. Apparently handing out flyers for a competing gig was frowned upon in the scene. Now I knew.

Despite Operation Shag Damon moving at a rollicking pace, Damon barely seemed to register my existence. I couldn't find any shorter skirts on the high street, so apart from abandoning clothing altogether and just waddling around naked, I was running out of ideas. I was just starting to give up hope, and then *last weekend* happened.

Last weekend. The thought of it still made me smile and my chest flutter with excitement. I'd been hanging out in my usual spot near the stage during Damon's set. He finished spinning, and as he came off stage, he tossed me his sweaty towel. I caught it and draped it over my shoulder, and he'd grinned and grabbed me, pulling my body hard against his, and shoved his tongue down my throat.

Our passionate snogging session in front of a blaring speaker stack definitely stood out as one of the highlights of my life. But I'm pretty sure Damon was so blazed, it was unlikely he even remembered my name, or the piece of paper with my number on that I'd shoved into the pocket of his jeans. He certainly hadn't called it.

That was why going to *this* weekend's party was so important —I had to make him fall for me before he got distracted by another, thinner, more-interesting girl.—

But of course I couldn't tell Clyde any of this. As far as my boss was concerned, I was just a plump, mousy junior lawyer who ate takeout every day for lunch and didn't look like a supermodel squeezed into a size-0 Marc Jacobs suit. And that was exactly why Clyde called me into his office after lunch today. "Baxter!" he barked, tossing a thick file across his desk. "Do you listen to the news?"

"What news?"

"*The* news, you know. The *news* news. The shit that happens in the world outside of this firm."

I didn't miss a beat. "Nothing much of interest happens outside this firm, sir."

"Atta girl," Clyde said in his most condescending tone. "Anyway, it seems that another celebrity death hit the headlines this week. That famous violinist, Eric Marshell, was killed in a car accident."

"I hadn't heard that." I didn't pay much attention to the music world outside of the London club scene, but even I'd heard of Eric Marshell, the dashing rock violinist with his black jeans and leather jacket and smouldering good looks who was single-handedly making classical music cool again. "Were you a fan?"

Clyde snorted. "My wife was. She went to his show in London last week with all her girlfriends. She even has a poster of him hanging on the wall above our bed. Imagine fucking your wife while that man's gargantuan face stares down at you?"

"That's …" I couldn't find an appropriate adjective. I was too busy trying to mentally block out the image of my boss going at it with his wife.

"Well, shit happens, whether you hear about it or not. So, Marshell's dead, but that's of little concern to me. What *is* of concern to me is the fact that his elderly mother, Alice Marshell, was found in her house, dead from a heart attack not long after her son's untimely demise. It looks as if the son was actually on the way to see her when his car went off the road."

"That's interesting." It wasn't, but I wasn't sure what I was expected to say.

"It is to you." Clyde tossed a thin black file across the desk. "Alice Marshell is a client of ours, with quite substantial holdings. Most of her files are from before we went fully online with the system, so it's a bit of a paperwork nightmare. Eric was her only child, and there's no husband or other family named in the will, so with Eric gone, dividing up her assets suddenly got a lot more complicated. Unfortunately, she's been infirm for the last five years, and we have very little of her relevant paperwork here. Someone will have to go down to her home right away and put everything in order before the usual bloodsucking relatives start to swoop in. And I've decided that someone is you."

"Me?" Inwardly, I groaned. Occasionally, in situations like this, the firm needed to send a lawyer out to a client's home to go through their paperwork and execute the will. Most of our clients were older, and sometimes they had no one left by the time they passed on, so it was our job to figure out what they had, sell off what assets needed to be sold, and place the money where it needed to go. Everyone who'd done it hated it, and usually fobbed it off onto a junior lawyer. As an intern, I'd done one such sojourn two years ago, for a dead duke on the Isle of Skye. I'd snuck Joel up, and we polished off the old duke's wine cellar and had wild sex in the hunting room. But this time around, I had no boyfriend and no desire whatsoever to leave London for whatever shithole this old lady lived in.

"Of course I mean you." Clyde stared at me, nudging the file closer to me with his pudgy fingers. "You're the only person available to leave today. The senior lawyers all have families, Bob is entertaining clients on his yacht, and Lila has plans all weekend that can't be cancelled."

Of course she does. She has plans to fuck your brains out while your wife is at the opera.

Clyde Greyson was a notorious womaniser—he'd slept with most of the women in the office, many of them *in* the office. I had to be careful opening up supply closets in case I accidentally saw something I couldn't unsee. But Clyde had never once approached *me* with the offer to visit a supply closet. Privately, he'd told Lila that "chubby girls" weren't his type—a slip the bitch had been delighted to spread all over the office when she came back from their most recent weekend dalliance.

If I had a boyfriend or a kid or a size-0 arse, this wouldn't be happening to me. I racked my brain for an excuse, any possible reason I couldn't go. "But sir ... I have tickets to an event this weekend, and ... I have to feed my cat ... and um, water my peace lily, and my parents are coming down from Leeds, and—"

"I play golf with your father, remember? Your parents live in Chelsea."

Damn. "Right, yes, of course. But I do have these tickets for a party—I mean, an *opera* on Saturday. I can't go to Crookshollow, wherever that is—"

"It's only a few hours from London on the train. It's a lovely little village; the wife and I went for a weekend getaway once. They have a bit of a gimmick with having burned the most witches in England. It's Halloween there all year round. You'll love it."

"It sounds delightful," I said, in a voice that implied it sounded anything but.

"You'll only be gone a couple of weeks, and of course, we'll reimburse you all your expenses and these opera tickets of yours. Look at it as a holiday in the country."

I hate the country.

But I didn't say anything. I had a lot of thoughts in the offices of Greyson, Smithe & Hanley that I didn't say, mostly because apart from the people I worked with, I actually liked my job, and didn't want to lose it.

I'd always been kind of weirdly fascinated with death, and how different people deal with it. As a teenager, this manifested in a weird goth phase where I read a lot of Poe, wore a lot of black lipstick, and basically frightened several years off my conservative lawyer parents' lives. At university, I gravitated more to estate law than criminal defence, which was what all the cool kids did. The way people divided up their estates said a lot about who they were in life, and what they considered important. In death and wills, the truth is always revealed.

But my interest did not extend to giving up the next two weeks of my life to living in the middle of nowhere while Damon Sputnik partied on without me. My heart sank as my exciting weekend of Operation Shag Damon dissipated before my eyes. I forced a smile, knowing there was no way I could get out of it. "Of course, sir."

"Excellent. Go home and pack your things. Janice has already booked you a train. It leaves at four. Do a good job on this, Baxter, and there might be something in it for you." Clyde winked. "Maybe even a something with its own office."

An office. It was the dream of every junior lawyer to eventually move up the ranks and acquire one of the sought-after private spaces on the second floor. I'd been passed over twice for promotion—beat out by two obnoxious size 0s—and Clyde knew that I was itching to move up and prove to my father that I was successful. He knew that by dangling that carrot in front of me, he could count on my cooperation. The guy may have been pushing seventy, but he was still slick (he *was* a lawyer, after all).

And that was how I found myself slumped against a rattling window on a Friday evening, clutching the stub of my one-way train ticket to Crookshollow, nowheresville, Middlesex. Population: 11,056 people, 35,000 sheep.

Delightful.

My phone beeped. The businessman sitting across from me shuffled his paper and frowned. I pushed my black-rimmed glasses up my nose and glared right back. *What do you expect, buddy? I don't have a carrier pigeon in my Kate Spade bag ready to fly messages home to my friends.* I pulled my phone out of my jacket and checked the message.

It was Cindy, texting to see if we were still on for club-hopping tonight. Cindy and I had been friends since our university days. We'd met at the student pub. I'd been stood up on a date and she'd been dumped by her boyfriend, and we bonded over our mutual heartaches and several G&Ts. Our friendship was mutually beneficial: I helped her study and pass her exams; she introduced me to the London underground club scene and the excitement of picking up random strangers from the dance floor.

Now I worked at the law firm and Cindy was in advertising, but we still danced every weekend like we had in college. Cindy had just heard about a rave going down at an abandoned warehouse in Camden. *Damon's going to be there.* My stomach churned with jealousy as I texted back to say I couldn't come, and that I wouldn't be going to Damon's party on Saturday, either.

I knew that, at age 29, I was probably too old for clubbing, but after 60-plus-hour weeks pushing paper around my desk and sucking up to Clyde so he wouldn't overlook me for advancement for another year, I needed to let my hair down and go a little crazy. And a club—with its pounding music and wild lights —was the perfect antidote. I could float in an ocean of bodies and be part of the group, part of the "in" crowd. It sure beat standing in the lunchroom by myself, sipping coffee while all of the skinny associates giggled together in the corner.

Cindy texted back, *Bummer! I'll give Tanya your ticket and keep an eye on Damon for you. I'll make sure his hands don't wander.*

I sighed, and replaced my phone in my pocket. Grabbing my bag out from under my seat, I pulled out my sketchbook. I balanced it on my knees, frowning out the window at the lush, green landscape as I flipped open a page and doodled a gnarled, twisted tree, the roots knotted up, the way my stomach felt right now at the thought of what Damon might get up to this weekend without me. I added a snake curling around the trunk, wondering how the design would look as it wound its way up my spine.

I had decided to get a tattoo before my 30th birthday—an enormous piece that covered my back and maybe my shoulders, too. No one at work would need to know it was there—it wasn't as if any of the male partners were clamouring to sleep with me— but in my party clothes, it would stand out. It would mark me as special. And in a club full of perfect size 0s with perky breasts and stomachs full of E, Elinor the dull lawyer had to do *something* to stand out.

I'd always been a good artist, and had even thought about going to art school at one point. But my father—a high-profile defence attorney, and my mother—a law clerk, had drilled that dream right out of me. My parents would never approve of a tattoo. They didn't think body art fit with the corporate image—

the blank drone with perfectly coiffed hair that they saw as the only way to get ahead in life. When I was a kid, my teachers would hold up my drawings in class, but all my parents ever wanted to know was how my grades were.

"Why are you doodling?" my mother would scold me. "Go and do something useful, like read a book or your homework." "There's a reason I've never met a rich artist," my dad was fond of saying. "It's a dead-end career, Elinor. Just work hard at school and forget about your little scribbles."

Of course, even if I'd pointed out the hundreds of successful artists hanging in the Tate Modern, my dad never would have changed his mind. Instead, because I always wanted to please them, I hid my journals and tattoo magazines under my bed. I did my homework and got good grades and went to the same law school my father attended. I graduated with honours, and started my career in a prestigious London firm.

But as I fumbled my way through law school, only half-interested in the work, I watched the art and drama students with envy as they raced around the campus with facial piercings, vintage clothes and beautiful tattoos, yelling "Give me a location!" and looking so excited about the future. But of course, they were all probably living on the streets now, whereas I had a job at Greyson, Smithe & Hanley, a nice salary, and an apartment in trendy Camden that only housed a small population of cockroaches. I had even snogged Damon Sputnik. I didn't have a right to complain about my life.

The tattoo was going to be my one concession to my creative side—my secret rebellion against my sensible, pre-planned life of law offices and beige clothing and boring men. But I was determined that I was going to draw the piece myself, and it had to be just right. My friend Tanya had recently hooked up with a tattoo artist and during a particularly drunken party, convinced him to ink some cherry blossoms on her ribcage. They were nice enough, and considering the artist was off his face at the time, only a *little* crooked. *I could have done better than that*, I couldn't help but think every time I saw those droopy blossoms.

But when it came to my own tattoo, I just couldn't decide on what I wanted. My 30th birthday was fast approaching, and I'd have to make a decision soon. I'd filled an entire sketchbook with ideas, but nothing seemed right. Nothing was good enough, *me* enough, to be permanently etched into my skin.

Maybe nothing seems right because your body isn't right, I thought to myself, my stomach churning with loathing. I hated the way I looked right now. I'd always been on the chubby side, but ever since I'd started working at the law firm, I had no time or energy for eating healthily. My gym membership card had sunk to the bottom of my bag, along with twenty Snickers wrappers and a dried-up lipstick. I'd gained a couple of extra pounds, and every time I looked at myself in the mirror, I heard my mother's voice in my head, reminding me that fat girls didn't attract good husbands.

So when I thought about actually having to take off my shirt and lie down in front of a hot, shirtless tattoo artist, (because in my head tattoo artists are always large, muscular, shirtless dudes), my stomach churned even harder. I was supposed to be two dress sizes smaller when I turned 30, but then, if I was two sizes smaller, maybe I wouldn't need the tattoo.

At least I'll have plenty of time to work on my drawings while I'm in Crookshollow, but the thought brought me no comfort. So instead, I put my sketchpad away, jammed my iPod earbuds into my ears, and stared out the window, listening to Damon's latest album and figuring out how I could rescue the situation. *How should I play it when I see him again? Aloof and cool, or enthusiastic and flirty? What should I wear?*

If only I didn't have to go to Crookshollow. But it's only two weeks, and then I'll be back to my life like nothing had changed. Nothing can happen in two weeks, right?

~

THE TRAIN PULLED in at a tiny platform. The weather had taken a turn, and it was pouring down outside, the wind pushing the rain underneath the awnings and pelting the waiting passengers with wet misery. I stepped off the train and glanced up and down the platform, but couldn't see anyone holding a sign for me. It figured that the firm's local contact ran on *country* time. *This weekend is off to a fantastic start.* I pulled the lapels of my jacket up around my neck, and dragged my suitcase toward the parking lot.

The situation in the car park was no less dire. There was only a thin covered walkway around the station entrance, and it had already been claimed by what looked like a horde of elderly American tourists, judging by the flags pinned to their camera bags and the volume at which they were complaining. I was just debating whether I should grab a taxi or call Clyde's secretary to find out what was going on, when I noticed someone running across the platform towards me. "Mrs. Baxter? Mrs. Baxter?" It was a short, roundish old man in a grey trench coat, his black umbrella fluttering in the wind. He extended his hand toward me, his smile friendly, but I noticed he didn't offer to share his umbrella.

"It's *Miss* Baxter," I corrected him, yet another thing my mother enjoyed reminding me I hadn't yet accomplished—finding a husband. Was the whole world determined to remind me how crappy my life was this week?

"Oh, my apologies." His hand was still hanging out there in mid-air, his smile frozen. I reached out and shook it quickly, forcing myself not to jerk away from its cold, clammy touch. My escort had a round face, beady eyes hidden behind thick, tortoise-shell glasses pushed up his nose, and thin white-grey hair that was balding on top. He wore trousers and a threadbare cardigan. He glanced at me nervously, biting his lower lip. "I'm Duncan McLain. I am ... *was,* I should say ... a close friend of the Marshell family. I've been taking care of Ms. Marshell's home and affairs while she was infirm, and I'm the executor of her will. I've got a cab waiting for us. I can take your bag if you like."

"I can manage." I pulled out the handle on the suitcase and followed him across the parking lot. I had just successfully navigated the heavy case over the kerb when someone passing the other way accidentally kicked it. The case slipped into a puddle and sent a spray of cold water up my legs. I gritted my teeth, feeling the icy water soak through my thick stockings, but kept going.

By the time I reached Duncan's cab, the rain had reduced my pristine suit to a soggy mess. My feet squelched in my new flats. I allowed Duncan to play the chivalrous man and wrestle my suitcase into the boot, while I clambered into the backseat of the cab and begged the driver to turn the heat up. We pulled out of the parking lot, and I got my first look at Crookshollow.

It looked like every other small English village I'd ever visited; a mixture of faded terraced housing, quaint cottages and ghastly concrete office blocks. A few big box stores and a skate park dotted the area around the station, but as we neared the centre of town, the buildings got more pleasant—mock-Tudor shopfronts bumping against ultra-modern apartments, and more quaint cottages and wisteria-covered walls. Street signs drawn in loopy handwriting, old-fashioned street lamps hanging over long pedestrian malls.

"Sorry about the cab ride," said Duncan. "Your office organised a car for you, but there's been a mix-up at the rental place, and they won't have one available for another couple of days. But don't worry, everything in Crookshollow is within walking distance, provided you like to walk."

"Great," I grunted in reply.

Duncan took my staring out the window as an interest in the town, so he launched into a monologue about the history of Crookshollow. Apparently, the town had been one of the national centres for pagan worship until witch frenzy had hit and the witch hunters had come in and cleaned the place up, burning more than 200 witches right in the town square. On any other day I might've found this lecture fascinating, but I was too tired and cranky from the train ride to care.

I tuned out Duncan's historical lecture, and focused on the strange array of stores lining the main street of the village. Crystal shops, tarot readers, even an occult bookstore. *This is ridiculous. Where am I—Salem?*

"Don't mind all the magical shops," said Duncan. "It's just our little theme. You know, for the tourists. Now that we're not burning witches anymore, the supernatural around here is kind of an attraction. You know, 'Welcome to Crookshollow: Come for the Burnings—Stay for the Fabulous Mince Pies.'" He chuckled at his own lame joke.

"Where is the house?" I spied a delicious-looking bakery, the window filled with chocolate sculptures and cakes piled high with cream. The sign read *Bewitching Bites* in loopy handwritten lettering. My stomach rumbled. All I'd had to eat since breakfast was a greasy mince pie and disappointing coffee at King's Cross, but that was a few hours ago, and it was getting close to dinnertime.

"Not far from here. Don't be fooled by her shabby exterior, the house is quite beautiful inside. Alice just didn't see the point in paying to upkeep the gardens when she never went outside to enjoy them."

The cab pulled up an oak-lined driveway. The approach would once have been grand and stately, but was now overgrown and wild. Weeds peeked out from the flowerbeds, creeping across the concrete drive, which was grubby with mould and grime. The lawn had gone to seed, the tall stalks swaying in the breeze, some patches as high as my waist. I saw statues toppled over, ornamental ponds green with algae, trellis arches sagging under the weight of their burden. Everything was choked with creeping weeds. Even though Alice Marshell was supposed to be rich, she clearly hadn't hired a gardener in the last five years. I could see why Duncan was so quick to absolve himself of responsibility for it.

"Here we are then," said Duncan, as we pulled up in front of the house. "Welcome to Marshell House."

I opened the door and climbed out in the rain, staring up at that towering facade. It wasn't a house in the true sense of the word, but a crumbling Victorian gothic mansion right out of a Wes Craven film. Built from dark brick and black-stained wood, Marshell House seemed to rise up out of the earth like a Lovecraftian beast. Two hexagonal turrets flanked the central section, the peaked roofs penetrating the cloudy sky above. A porch stretched along the front of the house, the gothic arches giving the appearance of a grinning row of teeth ready to devour anyone who dared enter. Two round stained-glass windows decorated with a multi-pointed star formed the focal point of each turret, like eyes glaring down at me. The house's shadow fell over me, and a shiver ran through my body. Was it a chill from the cold weather, or something different?

Duncan was going on about history again. "… and Marshell House is one of the newest homes in the area," he explained. "The land was originally part of a much larger estate, but the family that owned it ran into some trouble back in the 1700s and sold off most of their land. Alice's grandfather purchased it and built the home in the Gothic Revival style—"

"While that's all *fascinating*," I said, crossing my arms over my sodden coat, trying to keep what little warmth was left inside of me, "I am soaked through. Can we please get inside?"

"Oh! Of course, I'm so sorry." Duncan lifted a set of old-fashioned keys from his pocket, crossed under the ornate porch arch, and fitted one into the door. "There are only two keys to the front door," he explained. "I've got one back at my office, and this is the second set, which I'm giving to you. All the other keys on this ring also belong to the house, although I'm not quite sure what all of them unlock just yet. The police have finished their investigation, so you don't need to worry about disturbing anything, and I've left some of the council files on the house in the office for you, in case you need them."

"Thank you." Duncan pushed the door open, and I dashed inside.

One quick glance around the entrance hall was all I needed to know that this house had the same Wes Craven vibe both inside and out.

Duncan pushed my sodden suitcase through after me. He stood on the stoop, his beady eyes regarding me with concern. I clamped my mouth shut, forcing my face to look impassive. But it was too late. Duncan must've noticed my concern.

"Are you sure you don't want to stay in a hotel? You will be all alone in this large house. I could have my office arrange—"

"No, thanks." While the idea of a hotel suite complete with Jacuzzi tub did appeal, I wanted to get the job done as quickly as possible so I could get back to London and rescue Operation Shag Damon. If I stayed in this creepy house, I'd probably never sleep, which meant the work would be finished in half the time.

"Well, just call me if you change your mind."

"I will. Bye, Duncan." I tried to shut the door, anxious to escape the rain and get out of my sodden clothes. But he was still standing there, looking all needy and concerned.

"Do you need me to show you where everything is? I know this house pretty well—"

"That's fine. If I need any help, I'll call. I promise." I forced a smile. Finally, Duncan stepped back, gave me a jaunty wave, and walked back to the car. I pushed the door shut behind him. The wind caught it, slamming it with a loud *CRASH* that rattled the walls in the entranceway. The sound echoed through the large, empty house.

I flicked on a light, revealing even more of the large entrance hall decorated in an old-fashioned style. My teeth chattering, I yanked off my jacket and pulled open my suitcase. Finding my largest, warmest jumper, I pulled it on, balling my hands into fists inside the sleeves in an attempt to warm my numb fingers. That taken care of, I took a better look around my temporary home.

The front hall was decorated like a Victorian museum, the kind of style an old woman might think of as timeless, but was really perennially ugly. On the wallpaper, naked cherubim stared at me from fluffy clouds, their wide eyes following me as I moved deeper into the house. A heavy coat rack stood in the corner, and a sideboard stood between two uncomfortable-looking chairs, each upholstered in faded floral fabric. I set the keyring down on the sideboard next to a porcelain statue of a grinning cat, and moved across the hall. The floorboards creaked ominously beneath my feet.

The only sound was the squelch of my shoes against the rug and the slow *tick-tick-tick* of a grandfather clock somewhere in an adjacent room. The house seemed heavy, the walls groaning under the weight of all that solid oak and richly patterned fabric. I stood in the first doorway and peered into the next room. It was some kind of receiving room, with more uncomfortable chairs placed around a Rococo-style coffee table. Faded prints depicting various naval battles adorned the walls, as well as cameo portraits of old, stuffy-looking people. I stopped in front of a large one above the fireplace—of a grim-faced woman dressed in heavy brocade, her eyes a beautiful rich blue. They stared straight ahead, almost following me as I moved across the room. *Alice Marshell,* I guessed.

On another wall hung a portrait of a young man, his handsome face set like stone. Black ringlets streamed down the sides of his face, and his black jacket and trousers faded into the shadowy background of the painting. In his hand, he held a battered violin, resting it against the side of his neck. The artist had taken great pains to depict his fingers holding the neck of the instrument. I guessed that must be Eric Marshell, the famous rock star.

Beyond this room, I could see a dining room with a long table, still set for dinner, and another sitting room, this time in a drab green hue.

This house could be really cool, if it was updated a bit, I thought, my gaze landing on the high ceilings, ornate chandeliers, and large, arched windows. *I wonder what will happen to it now that the old woman and her son are both gone—*

The staircase creaked. I whirled around, my heart clattering against my chest. It sounded like someone descending the stairs.

"Hello?" I called out, my voice wavering. *Great, now the intruder knows you're scared.*

Another creak. It was definitely coming from the top of the stairs. I scanned the landing, but all I could see up there were shadows. I took a step back into the entrance hall, searching for something I could use as a weapon. But there was nothing except that cat statue, which would probably do more damage if it were a real cat.

What are you doing? Don't be ridiculous. Of course it wasn't someone walking around up there. This is an empty house. You're here because this is an empty house. You're just scaring yourself.

But I couldn't shake the feeling that someone, or *something*, was staring back at me from the landing at the top of the stairs. I felt weirdly self-conscious, as if the eyes in those portraits were following my every move. I didn't want to stand in the large, open hall anymore, so I darted across into the room on the bottom floor of the turret, slamming the door shut behind me. I fumbled along the wall for the light switch and flicked it on.

Even with the two dusty chandeliers lit up, the room was shrouded in darkness. The bay windows were obscured by thick red velvet drapes. But apart from its gloominess, this room wasn't actually too bad. Heavy oak bookshelves lined one of the walls, crammed with dusty volumes bound in black leather. A large desk dominated the space, but there was no computer in sight, only a typewriter set aside, and a stack of black leather ledger books. In front of the windows were two overstuffed chairs, a small table containing a chessboard set between them. There was even a fireplace along one wall, and a small stack of wood in the basket beside it. The room reminded me of a cosy writer's study or professor's office, the kind of room you saw in movies where secrets were hidden and puzzles were solved. I liked it instantly.

I moved behind the large oak desk and jiggled one of the drawers, but it wouldn't budge. Locked, most likely. That wouldn't be a problem—these old desks were easy enough to break into. I'd deal with that later. For now, I needed warmth. The house clearly had no central heating, and despite the heavy drapes, the air was bitterly cold.

I got to work setting the fire. There was no way I would live in this house for a fortnight without some kind of heating. Once I had some decent flames roaring, I opened the door to the hall, grabbed my laptop, and dumped it on the desk.

Back in the hall, I felt foolish for being scared. Sure, the house was a little creepy, but it was just because it was old and enormous and someone has recently died inside.

A board creaked upstairs. My heart started pounding furiously. *You're being ridiculous. Stop listening for ghosts and get your things unpacked so you can get to work. The sooner you finish the catalogue of Ms. Marshell's assets, the sooner you can get back to your life.*

Swallowing my fear, I grabbed the handle of my suitcase and started hauling it up the stairs.

ERIC

I heard the front door creak open, and I watched from the top of the stairs as Duncan entered the house, followed by a brown-haired woman of such stunning beauty, I thought for a moment I must've have imagined her. Even in flat shoes, she towered over Duncan, and her sodden suit clung to every curve of her body, accentuating her womanly figure. She flicked strands of matted hair from her heart-shaped face, her intelligent hazel eyes surveying the hall from behind a pair of cute black-rimmed glasses.

The brown-haired beauty pursed her bow-shaped lips as she took in my mother's decor. Duncan dropped the keys into her hand, and scurried back outside. They had a brief conversation through the crack in the door, and then the beauty shut the door on Duncan, a wise decision if ever I'd seen one. Even though he'd been a good friend to my mother ever since my father left us, and he'd looked after her when I moved to London and she got sick, I'd always had a bad feeling about that man. I realised then that I should've moved closer and listened to their conversation, but I'd been so preoccupied watching *her* that it hadn't even occurred to me.

Who is this remarkable woman, and what is she doing in my house?

It's not your house, I reminded myself. *I'm pretty sure dead men can't own property.*

While I'm haunting it, I feel entirely justified in calling it my own, I retorted inwardly. I'd been stuck alone in the house for eight days now, and eight days was a very long time without anyone to talk to. When I'd been alive, eight days of peace and quiet would have been a welcome holiday. Eight days away from the squabbling of my band and the stress of the road. Eight days without being harassed for autographs in the street, or hounded by interviewers for the most private details of my life. It sounded like heaven ... in theory.

But now, I was desperate to get out, to figure out what was going on, and if I could somehow reverse my current poltergeist status. I was going crazy here by myself. I couldn't even turn the TV on or listen to a record. I'd taken to having conversations with myself, although they usually turned into arguments—I can be one stubborn asshole, even when I'm fighting with myself.

I stood in the shadows at the top of the landing, watching the woman peel off her sodden jacket. Underneath, she wore a nude-coloured blouse, perfectly tailored to accentuate her pear-shaped figure and her plump breasts. Now, though, it clung to her skin, practically see-through, revealing the lace of her black bra and her nipples, standing hard as rocks from the cold.

I groaned, and I felt my cock swell as blood rushed toward it. *That* was an interesting sensation. *I didn't know ghosts could get hard.* It certainly hadn't happened to me in all the days since I'd been a ghost. There was no blood to rush there, after all, so it was only the lingering, familiar sensation of arousal. Apparently, it didn't matter, because when I glanced down at my crotch, there was my cock standing proud, jerking at the sight of this beautiful woman's nipples as they jutted out from her blouse.

I turned away, embarrassed. It felt wrong to stare at her like that, when she didn't know I was there. I may be dead now, but I could still be a gentleman. I counted to ten inside my head, picturing my mother in her nightgown—the most unsexy image accessible to me—and waited for my arousal to flop. Then I floated back to peek again. The woman had covered herself in a large wool sweater and was standing with her back to me, looking into the receiving room and giving me a nice view of the curve of her back and her arse. I floated across the landing, wondering what she was doing in the house with a suitcase. *Did she buy the place? But that doesn't make sense. It would take a long time for the lawyers to sort the estate out, especially since I was gone, too—*

I set my foot down on the top stair, and the floorboard creaked loudly.

I leapt back into the shadows just as the woman looked up. My non-heart thundered in my chest. I stared down at my foot, hovering a few inches above the faded floral carpet. I bent down and tried to rest it on the floor again. But it was the same as it had been the past eight days—my foot sank right through the floor as if it weren't there at all.

But how—

I had *felt* the floorboard beneath my feet. Not the ghostly tingling that usually accompanied my nonexistent body passing through solid objects, but an actual, solid surface. I'd leaned my weight on that board, and it had *creaked*. I hadn't imagined it. The woman peered up at the staircase, searching for the source of the creak. She hadn't imagined it, either.

I'm a ghost, I don't have weight, so how did that happen?

It could just be a coincidence, I raged back at myself. *This house is old. It creaks. It just happened to have a senior moment right when you put your foot down. Maybe the sensation was your mind tricking you, because more than anything you wish you were alive so you could go down and talk to that woman—*

Maybe ... but I wasn't so sure. I had to pay even closer attention to my sexy intruder. I floated out to the edge of the railing and locked down.

The woman had grabbed her briefcase and was stashing it in Mother's office. I heard her curse as she tried to light the fire. I started to think about going down to see what she was up to, but she appeared again and dragged her suitcase up the stairs, muttering something under her breath.

I slid back into the wall as she dragged it past me, so that just my eyes and nose were in the upper landing, as if I were part of one of my mother's horrid nautical prints. Even though I knew the woman couldn't see me, I felt perverse standing right out in the open around her. Besides, I hadn't been a ghost long enough to know if I was invisible to absolutely everybody, and I didn't want to test the theory by having the hottest woman I'd ever seen fall down the stairs.

The girl flung open the door to the master bedroom. She took one look at Mother's flowery suite and shook her head. "Yuck, no thank you." She moved on to the next door. My old bedroom.

I hadn't been inside my room since I'd become a ghost. I still had a lot of bad memories from living in this house, and particularly from that room. I didn't want to spend my post-death time dwelling on them. But if the hazel-eyed beauty was going in there, than so was I. I moved through the wall cavity—a family of mice scurrying between the framing alongside me—and came out in front of the vanity unit in my bathroom. I stood in front of the mirror, staring at the reflection of the wall behind me, an empty room where my own body should have been. Ghosts, it seemed, didn't warrant a reflection.

"Ghosts Without Reflections" would make an awesome song title. I closed my eyes, searching for the first few notes of a melody. Slow, haunting, melancholy. *If only I could still hold an instrument ...*

I heard the thud of the door hitting the stopper, and opened my eyes to see my new houseguest throw her suitcase down on my bed. The room was exactly as I remember it the day I left— brass bed-ends polished to a high sheen, my few toys hidden away in an oak chest at the foot, threadbare blankets covering the bed, an embroidered alphabet sampler on the wall above the tallboy. I noticed the framed picture of my father I kept beside the bed was gone. Briefly, I wondered if whoever cleaned the room had found my stack of music magazines under the bed. I bet my mother had had them burned.

It was strange to see this woman walking through the space that had once been so intimate to me, a prison of my mother's making. I watched from the bathroom, frozen, as the woman walked across to the window, her hands running over the heavy velvet drapes that obscured the round, stained-glass window. She peered through, but it was impossible to see anything through the coloured glass.

Instead, she turned to the window on the other wall and stared down into the backyard below, filled with overgrown garden beds and trees that had gone wild, and down the back, the gleaming marble edifice of our family mausoleum, and an old well obscured in the hedgerow, the crumbling capstone pulled across the opening. The woman sighed heavily, and turned back to the bed. She picked through her suitcase for some fresh clothes and a toiletry bag. She pulled a towel from the stack on the tallboy, and headed for the bathroom.

I heard her gasp, and I leapt back into the wall. Had she seen me? Or was she gasping at the hideous Blythe doll my mother had sat in the chair in the corner of the room? I couldn't be sure. I peered through the soap dispenser as the woman entered the bathroom and stood in front of the mirror, sweeping her matted hair off her face and peering at her reflection in the mirror. She frowned. *Why is she frowning?* I couldn't see a pimple or a wrinkle or any other reason for a woman like that to be frowning.

The woman reached into the shower, and turned on the water. I heard the gurgle of the ancient heater clicking on. While she waited for the water to heat, the woman scrambled through her toiletries, lining up bottles of shampoo and body lotion along the edge of the bath. Then, she stepped out of her sodden skirt, and peeled off her shirt, revealing round, perfect breasts trussed up in a black lace bra, and a pair of matching panties that accentuated her buxom hips.

Now that erection was pressing against my *trousers-that-weren't-really-there* with urgency again, but I didn't feel turned on anymore. I just felt dirty, like a pervert, spying on her without her knowledge. I sank back into the wall and waited in the hall until I heard her switch off the water. I gave her five minutes to put her clothes on, and then I floated back through the wall to see what she did next. I didn't like spying, but if I wanted answers, I didn't have a choice.

She glanced around the room nervously as she stepped out of the bathroom. Had she seen me before? Was that possible? She certainly looked like she was looking for a shadow, but neither the woman from Duncan's company who found my mother's body, nor the ambulance, nor the police, nor even Duncan himself when he'd come to inspect the house had seen me, even when I wafted right in front of them. The mail lady had looked right through the window at me when she shoved my mother's catalogues through the slot, and hadn't seen me. So how could this woman?

I remembered my foot on the stairs, and I stayed hidden inside the wall, just in case it was true. I had to figure out why she was there before I revealed myself to her. Ghosts couldn't be too careful these days. For all I know, she could be here to exorcise the house and send me on into whatever bleak void awaited me.

The woman must have decided the room was safe. She started to unpack her suitcase, folding her clothes and placing them neatly into one of my old drawers. She tossed a pile of my clothes —t-shirts and jeans I'd worn as a kid—onto the chair in the corner, so they hid the Blythe doll's face. I smiled, remembering how as a kid I used to cover up that doll's face with a black t-shirt every night so she wouldn't stare at me while I slept.

Next, Hazel Eyes dumped her bag out on the bed and arranged

her things on the nightstand—in seconds, it was cluttered with makeup brushes, a paperback novel, and an iPod dock. So she was staying a while, then. But why?

After emptying her suitcase, the woman went back downstairs. I followed her at a distance, sticking to the walls. In the study, she pulled at all the desk drawers, one by one. They were all locked. Mother kept all of her things locked away tight.

Next, the woman pulled out a laptop, plugged it in, and booted it up. While she waited for it to load, she dumped a second bag out on the desk beside her. There were four chocolate bars inside, and she grabbed one and opened it, lying back in the chair by the fire, her face relaxing as her lips slid over the candy. While she was distracted, I floated over from the wall behind her desk and inspected her open card case—Elinor Baxter, Estate Lawyer. So she was here to take care of Mother's will. Not an exorcist, a lawyer.

Well, Elinor Baxter, welcome to my home. I hope you make yourself comfortable.

Very comfortable indeed.

After dumping my stuff in a room upstairs (complete with creepy doll and strange children's drawings pinned up on the walls—at least I was certain it wasn't the old lady's bedroom. Sleeping where the dead woman had slept totally freaked me out), I returned to the study. As I descended the steps, the upstairs landing creaked loudly.

First the creaks, then that strange shadow in your bathroom ... if I didn't know better, I'd swear this was the opening sequence to a horror film. I hope I'm the plucky virgin heroine, and not the doomed slutty victim destined to die in a disgusting and creative way.

Judging by the amount of sex you've had in the last year, I'd say you'd be a shoo-in for the virgin.

I shook my head, trying to ignore Devil's Advocate Elinor—that loud voice inside my head that always asked too many questions and had a quippy answer for everything that I never said aloud. I needed to rid myself of the unsettled feeling in my gut. *It's just an old house with creaks and drafts. You're used to living in a modern apartment. It's natural that it would freak you out a bit.*

My stomach rumbled. *Ah,* finally a problem I could fix. I went to the kitchen to survey the dinner options. The sight that greeted me made my head spin. This kitchen was old. Really *old*. The oven was one of those imposing, gas-fired devices that looked more like it tortured heretics than grilled cheese. The only thing cluttering the marble bench tops were cow-shaped jars for sugar and tea. A row of ceramic cat figurines lined the windowsill. I peered under the sink. Where was the dishwasher?

This house has no dishwasher. I am going to have to wash my own dishes. What the hell has Clyde set me up for? I am a lawyer, for fuck's sake, I shouldn't have to rough it like this.

I pulled open all the drawers and cupboards, greeting each new find with horror. There was no espresso machine, no Vitamix. I couldn't even find a toaster. How would I make daiquiris without a blender? I wished I'd thought to bring mine from home.

Thankfully, someone had thought to clean out the refrigerator, so instead of several days worth of the old woman's rotting groceries, all that remained inside were two blocks of butter and a bottle of tonic water. *Brilliant.* Even though I was starving, a girl cannot exist on water and butter alone.

I would have to go grocery shopping at some point. But right now, I had the company credit card burning a hole in my pocket. Without a car, going out wasn't really an option (I wasn't much of a walker), so I whipped out my phone and scanned through the Crookshollow listings for a restaurant that delivered. *Pete's Pizza.* That would be perfect. My stomach gurgled in happy anticipation as I imagined a Hawaiian pizza all to myself, piping hot and dripping with melted cheese and BBQ sauce. I hit Pete's number and raised the phone to my ear.

"Pete's Pizza," a youth with a cracking voice answered.

"Yes, I'd like a large Hawaiian pizza, with extra BBQ sauce, please. And a side of chips. Do you do garlic bread?"

"We sure do. Normal or cheesy?"

"I'm feeling gluttonous tonight. Give me the cheesy garlic." *It's on you, Clyde. I hope you remember to buy me an extra-wide desk chair for that office you're giving me.* "And a large bottle of Coke." I'd spied a liquor cabinet in the other room. Hopefully that contained some whisky. Or vodka, or anything I could mix to make a sugary alcoholic drink, I wasn't fussy. With pizza and booze, I could almost pretend that being stuck in this house for two weeks was going to be fun. *Almost.*

"Your total is seventeen pounds-fifty."

"That's fine. I'll pay by credit card. Delivery to Blossom Road, number 22—"

"Twenty-two Blossom Road?" The voice on the other end sounded incredulous. "But isn't that the Marshell house?"

"Yes, that's the Marshell House. Now, what's the delivery time? I'm pretty hungry, so—"

"Is this a joke? Because it's a pretty lame joke."

"This isn't a joke." I was starting to feel desperate. "I am staying in the Marshell House. I'm a lawyer—"

"Look, I don't get paid enough to deal with this shit. Have a NICE evening." The phone went dead.

He hung up. I tore the phone from my ear and tossed it on the kitchen table. *He was the maker of the garlic cheesy bread, and he hung up. The bastard.*

My stomach practically howled with hunger. My mouth was wet with the promise of cheesy garlic bread. And my stomach and my mouth would not be denied.

There was nothing else to do. I was going to have to venture into town, on foot, in the rain, and find something to eat. *This is Clyde's secretary's fault for booking my car at some hicktown chop-shop. What kind of rental company doesn't have any cars available?* I thought bitterly, hating this stupid town more and more with every passing minute.

It was too far into the main street to visit Bewitching Bites, that little bakery I'd seen from the cab. I'd have to try my luck at the little row of shops on the corner of Blossom Road. I glanced out the window. The wind had picked up, brushing the trees against the windows, scraping the branches along the glass.

Behind, I could see black clouds rolling in, swallowing the grey. As if this rain wasn't miserable enough, a full-blown storm was on its way.

I dug my winter coat out of my suitcase and pulled it on, adding a hat and gloves for good measure. I grabbed a flowery umbrella from the stack in the hall, and stepped out into the madness, pulling the door shut behind me.

Immediately, the wind whipped through the porch, grabbing my Rick Owens knitted hat and flinging it away. "Fine!" I snapped to the weather gods. "You can keep it!" It was a scratchy hat anyway.

I popped the umbrella and made a beeline down the drive, running across the concrete, my ballet flats sliding against the grimy surface and my hair whipping madly around my face. When I reached the end of the drive, I turned left. As I did, the wind grabbed the umbrella and gave it a defiant tug, pulling the ancient frame inside out and snapping two of the ribs.

By the time I collapsed through the door of the dairy/takeaway shop, my shoes were squelching, my hair was plastered to my face, and the umbrella had been turned inside out so many times it was more like some piece of modern sculpture—*Umbrella Revisited.* The blue-haired old woman at the counter glanced up and clucked in sympathy.

I grabbed a basket and started filling it with every conceivable item of delicious, edible comfort food. Crisps, salsa, bite-sized chocolate bars, salted cashew nuts … *mmmm, salted cashew nuts. I'd better get two of those.* I glanced down at my basket—I had a diabetic coma in there. I could see why *Cosmo* magazine recommended never going shopping on an empty stomach. But this was an emergency.

"Is this all, dearie?" The woman asked as she rung up my purchases.

"Give me one fish and some chips." I panted, staring at the

takeaway menu behind her head, my stomach growling with agreement. "And don't be stingy with the vinegar."

"I wouldn't dare," Blue Hair smiled. "Are you having some friends over tonight?" She pointed to my family-sized bag of crisps.

"Oh, sure. Yeah, we're having a quiet one inside tonight, just watching movies with the girls, you know." I handed her the firm's credit card. "How long for the chips?"

"Five minutes, dearie. Can you wait that long?"

"Sure. I've got nuts." I punched in the number and took my receipt. "Does anywhere around here sell alcohol?"

"There's an off-licence on the other side of the tattoo parlour, although you young ladies should remember that you don't need alcohol to have a good time." Blue Hair handed me my bag. "You don't look like you're from around here."

I took in the woman's paisley pinafore and severe bun, and nodded. "I'm from London," I said, swiping at a strand of hair that was plastered to my cheek. "I'm just up here for a couple of weeks to, you know, get out of the city."

"Well, Miss London, you take care in that weather tonight. Perhaps next time you'll think twice before heading out without a hat."

As I walked down to the off-licence, I stopped in front of the tattoo parlour and peered inside. The sign read Resurrection Ink. In the window were large posters depicting several complex tattoo designs—intricate medina drawn entirely with dots, black-and-white tribal work that curled elegantly around the shoulders, and an enormous chest piece on a man's toned, muscled torso, depicting an unfurling dragon, its scales gleaming. Its mouth was open, and it had been coloured in such a way that it seemed almost three dimensional, as if it was bursting forth from the man's sculpted pec. *What a joke. As if there'd be any decent artists in a town like this. It's probably a front for a local pot ring.* But my eye kept being drawn back to the curling dragon, its emerald gaze seeming to follow me as I moved past.

At the off-licence, I grabbed a bottle of whisky and two bottles of wine (thank God for expense accounts), went back to grab my chips, and started back toward the house. By now, the black clouds had rolled overhead, and the rain was coming down in sheets, blown sideways by the whipping wind. I tossed the useless umbrella into a rubbish bin, pulled my coat tight around my neck, put my head down, and ran.

Wind pounded against my body, and I had to fight for every step. I ploughed onward, screwing up my face against the frigid assault. The warmth of my chips pressed against my stomach, reminding me there was light at the end of the tunnel. Finally, after what seemed like an age, I reached the gate of the house, raced up the drive, across the porch, and grabbed the door handle. *Where did I stash the keys?* I patted my coat pockets. *No keys.*

"Great. Just fucking brilliant." I mumbled. I put down my grocery bags and checked my pockets again. *Nothing.* Had I even grabbed them on the way out? *Shit.* I cupped my fingers over my eyes and peered in through the hall window. Yes, there was the old keyring, right on the table in the entrance hall, where I'd left it.

"Fuck," I whispered, my teeth clattering together. Now that I was standing still, the wind still assailing me, I was beginning to get *really* cold.

I peered through the window again, rapping against it with my fingers, wondering if I was going to have to break it. I could call Duncan to come over … no, that wouldn't work. My mobile phone was charging on the desk in the office. Besides, I'd be a popsicle by the time he got here. There was a cherub statue near the bottom of the steps. If I threw that through one of the windows and then reached through and unlocked the door … it would make a mess, but at least I'd be out of the cold. I didn't really fancy stepping out from the relative shelter of the porch to grab the statue, but it was looking as though it might be necessary.

One last time, I grabbed the door handle and jiggled it. Out of the corner of my eye, I saw something flash past the hall window. A black shadow moving as quick as lightning. *That was what I saw in the bathroom before.* Fear clenched in my chest. I leapt away from the door, twisting the handle spasmodically as I did so.

The door fell open, and I stumbled backward. The wind caught me and spun me around, and I caught my heel on the front door stoop and tripped forward. I sailed across the hall and landed in a heap at the foot of the stairs. The wind grabbed the door and slammed it shut behind me.

I sat up, searching the hall for the shadow. Of course I couldn't see it anywhere. *It doesn't make any sense. The door was locked. I heard it click when I left the house. I'm sure I did. I tugged on it pretty hard, and it wouldn't budge. How did it manage to fall open just now?*

Maybe the bolt was old? Maybe I broke it somehow ...

I locked the door, then tried the handle. It wouldn't budge. The lock still worked fine. So what had happened? Did it have something to do with that shadow—

Snap out of it, Elinor. It was nothing, probably the lights flickering in this stupid old house. You are freaking yourself out over nothing because you don't want to be here.

My stomach rumbled, and I remembered my bags were still outside, getting saturated on the front steps. I opened the door and pulled them inside, careful to jam the door open with my foot so I wouldn't have any more surprises.

Inside, I pulled off my soaking coat, and went to the kitchen and unpacked my groceries. The dairy had had frozen pizza, and after discovering to my delight that the stove had been converted to work on gas, I popped open the box, pushed the Hawaiian pizza out onto a baking tray, and pulled open a can of pineapple and added a ton of extra slices, then squirted a generous swirl of BBQ sauce on top. I slid the whole thing in the oven. One of the advantages of being single was adding whatever additional pizza toppings I liked. *About the only advantage to being single, but hey, a girl takes what she can get.*

While the pizza was cooking, I poured myself a whisky and coke (with a particularly generous slosh of whisky), and took this —and my fish and chips—into the study, which was getting mighty toasty now that the fire was roaring away nicely. I pulled open the package and stuffed several sticks of potato happiness into my mouth. *Oh, that is good.*

As I sat and munched and dried off and stared into the flames, my mind went back to the strangeness with the door. I remembered jiggling the lock, feeling the bolt stuck. It wasn't moving. And then, the next time I turned the lock, it opened with ease. Why? How?

ERIC

*W*hat the fuck was that?

I flew back into the wall cavity, and stared down at my hands. They looked just the same as they always did. Long fingers with hard calluses on the tips from the tough strings of my violin. They looked as solid as ever to me, but I knew from the past eight days that whenever I tried to touch something, my hands fell right through it. No part of my body could touch anything else, not even the floor. It had taken me two full days of concentrating just to learn how to control my floating enough so I didn't sink back into the basement every time I turned around. Yesterday I'd spent seven hours trying to pick up a piece of lint off the hall curtains. The lint never budged.

And yet, when I'd seen Elinor trapped outside and trembling from the cold, I'd touched the lock—actually *touched* it—and managed to push it aside for her.

How is that even possible?

One thing was for certain. Whoever this woman was, she was useful to have around. Useful, and beautiful.

I knew I had to find a way to communicate with her. If being around her made me able to touch things—even if it was some-

41

thing as tiny as a lock—then she might be the only person who could help me get out of this wretched house.

Elinor moved through the house, humming to herself as she fixed a pizza and poured herself a drink. Her hair was dripping wet again, but she didn't seem to mind. I watched her from behind the stairs as she sank gratefully into one of the overstuffed chairs by the study fire, and lifted her glass to her lips. I hated hiding in the corner where she couldn't see me. But I didn't want to frighten her away. She was my only hope. I had to wait for the right moment to reveal myself.

So I watched. I watched her drop her prim-and-proper lady routine and scoff down her vinegar-soaked chips with gusto, followed by three slices of pizza. I watched her stare at her open laptop with distress, and then watched her pull out her mobile and dial someone's number. A boyfriend? I couldn't explain why that thought made my stomach twist with anger.

I was a ghost. I was dead. It wasn't as if I had a chance with her. I didn't want to be involved with her, I just needed her to help me. So it was none of my business who she was calling. *Was it?*

I sank back into the shadows, not wanting to find out more than I wanted to know about my new houseguest, and yet, not able to stop myself from listening in.

ELINOR

$\mathcal{I}$ was too wigged out by the front door incident to start work that evening. Instead, I pulled my phone out and called Cindy.

"Ellie, guuuuurl!" Cindy answered, sounding about as gangster as a cartoon character. "How is life in smallville?"

"About what you'd expect," I said, taking another gulp of my drink. At least I felt satisfyingly full now, thanks to the chips and pizza. "I'm staying in a place that makes the House of Usher seem like a sleek modernist cube."

"The House of Usher? That sounds like a cigarette brand." Cindy had majored in film at university, but had scraped by in her classes while spending every spare minute partying. She was great fun, but she didn't share my love of reading. She would often mock me about being a book nerd. I would retaliate by peppering my conversation with references to my favourite gothic novels. It wasn't much of a thing, but it was *our* thing.

"It's Poe." I smiled at Cindy's ignorance. It still weirded me out that my friend didn't share my love of dark literature, or any kind of literature for that matter. I couldn't imagine *not* reading. If you don't read, how do you spend stormy winter evenings? What do you do on your beach holiday when the water is too cold to swim? How do you pass the time on the tube? Cindy was an account manager at a major London advertising firm. She was still thin and blonde and gorgeous and always the life of the party, but she still didn't read. "It's a crumbling old place, the kind of house that would have the lead role in a horror film. It's a little bit scary being here by myself, actually. I keep hearing things and—"

"Oooh, is it haunted? Are you seeing white sheets everywhere? Is a ghostie all up in your grill?"

"Stop talking like that," I laughed. "You sound ridiculous. It's just a strange old house, is all. Are you still going to the party tonight?"

"Of course. You know I never miss a chance to get my groove on. It's going to be a good one, I think. Do you want me to keep an eye on Damon for you? I can even do a bit of sabotage if I see him with another hottie."

"Thanks, Cindy, you're a pal. Maybe you could even slip him my number, tell him to call me if he remembers me from the other week. You know, work your magic."

"For you, my love, I'll perform a little hocus-pocus."

"I appreciate it. Listen, I'm going to be stuck up here for a couple of weeks. I was wondering if maybe you'd like to come and stay next weekend? Take a day off work, come out on the train, help me drink a bunch of expensive piss on Clyde's tab, and just have a girls' weekend. We haven't done that in ages."

"That sounds amazing, doll. But getting away is going to be tough. We've got a huge project due at work, and I'm not sure if I'll be able to swing a day off, let alone leave town for the week-end. Plus, there's that huge trance festival next Saturday night, and I don't want to miss it."

"Oh." My stomach sank. I'd forgotten about the trance fest. Two weekends in a row I'd be missing out on the fun. "That's okay. If you can't get away—"

"I want to, Ellie, you know I do. I'll get back to you, okay?"

"Of course." I struggled to keep the disappointment out of my voice. I wished, just this once, that Cindy could pull some strings for me. "I understand. It's no big deal. Just let me know."

"Listen, Bia-tch. I've got to roll. Tanya's here to pick me up. I'll text you tomorrow and let you know how things go tonight."

"Bye, Cindy. Have fun." I hung up, and flung my phone on to the desk in frustration. It skidded over the edge and clattered against the floor, the back popping off and the battery bouncing under the desk.

THAT NIGHT, I slept fitfully. I couldn't seem to settle. The bed I'd chosen appeared soft and warm, but appearances, as I discovered, could be deceiving. Sharp corners poked at me from an object stored underneath, ensuring that whichever way I turned brought forth some new agony. I made a mental note to call Clyde in the morning and ask if a new mattress could be charged to the company account.

Unlike my flat in London, which backed onto busy railway tracks and was pressed up hard against the wall of a couple who liked to throw things when they argued, which was most nights, Marshell House was quiet. *Too* quiet. I felt strangely aware of myself, as if someone was watching me, carefully scrutinising my every movement. But of course that was ridiculous.

When I did fall asleep, I would wake again after what felt like only a few moments, my skin clammy and my mind racing from dark dreams. I'd left the curtains open over the stained-glass window (because otherwise the room would be too dark), and the moonlight passing through the glass made strange prisms of light dance over the walls.

Finally, at quarter to five I could take no more, and pulled myself out of bed. I turned the shower on, locked and bolted the door, and stepped under the water. I yelped and leapt back as a trickle of scalding hot water came out, burning my leg. It soon faded into an ice cold stream, and as much as I fiddled with the knobs, I couldn't get anything more than a lukewarm trickle.

Weird. This shower worked fine yesterday. I hate old houses. I fumed as I pulled on my favourite pencil skirt, stockings and a fitted jacket over my shivering body, my usual work uniform. *At least I'm awake now, I guess.*

Down in the old kitchen, I boiled the kettle on the stove, and dug out an ancient tin of instant coffee from the back of the woman's cupboard. I slapped some cheese slices onto bread and put the ancient gas oven on grill, then dumped a couple of teaspoons of the amorphous black granules into my mug. I wrinkled my nose as I thought wistfully of the double shot cappuccino from the cafe across the street from the office. I'd be drinking one right now if I was in London, where I belonged. I made a mental note to buy some fancier coffee on my next trip to the store. And a coffee machine. And a blender. Clyde was going to be very sorry he left me in charge of my expenses.

That is, if they even have proper coffee in this hicktown.

Now that I had something approaching caffeine in my belly, I could get down to business. I stacked my mousetraps on a chipped china plate and settled myself down in the old woman's office. *First things first.* I plugged my iPod into my portable speaker, and turned on some house music. Now I could pretend I was getting ready for a night out with Cindy, instead of sitting in a dusty library in a crumbling old house, going through old bills and bank statements for a creepy old woman.

At least there were some advantages. In the office, I had to wear business suits and heels, and I always felt like a doughnut stuffed into cling film. All the other female lawyers were stick thin, and looked like they belonged in magazines, or at least on TV shows about slutty law firms. Here I could chill out in bare feet and eat mousetraps and listen to music, and no one could lean over my desk and thrust their fake breasts in my face while they dumped their caseload on me so they could go shag the boss in the supply cupboard.

At least here, the girls from litigation aren't making snide comments about my weight in the lunchroom.

Music sorted, I started my work. I began by finding all the files and stacks of paper in the drawers and cupboards around the library, and stacking them in one huge pile on the floor. First, I needed to sort out all the irrelevant papers, of which there would be many. Then I needed to comb through everything carefully, compiling an up-to-date database of Alice Marshell's assets, as well as any outstanding accounts and possible claims against her estate. All this had to be done before I went over everything with Duncan, the executor.

After that, I had to contact Ms. Marshell's bank, insurance companies, investment firms and other companies of interest to get final updated accounts. I had to have meetings with Duncan to make sure he understood his responsibilities. And then I probably had more boxes of papers to go through—I could expect to find some hidden under a bed, or perhaps in a dusty attic.

It was actually fun exploring the library. I scanned the book titles as I pulled files from the cupboards under the bookshelves. It was a strange mix; Confucius, T.S. Eliot, John Locke, lots of Goethe ... They were all bound in thick leather, and many had gold lettering on the spines that looked suspiciously like it might be real. I nodded my head to the music as I worked, and, for a time, I lost myself in the papers. It looked as if this severe-looking woman had led a pretty interesting life.

One of the ledger books on the desk contained a stack of old newspaper clippings talking about the search for a missing man. GEORGE MARSHELL DISAPPEARANCE REMAINS UNSOLVED, a headline read. Alice Marshell's husband, and the original owner of the property. It looked as though her husband had run off. Many journalists and experts suspected he had another family in Europe, although nothing was able to be proven. He'd left Mrs. Marshell with nothing except the house, which had been in his family for years and was mortgaged to the hilt. I flipped to the back of the folder and noticed several clippings about Eric Marshell and his band, but I decided to read those later.

In another ledger, I found an auction house record that showed Alice Marshell had sold a long list of antiques from the house shortly after her husband's disappearance. And it seemed that she'd invested the money in some speculative oil companies. Risky stuff, especially for a single mother with little else to her name, but it had paid off, and Alice Marshell had grown her little nest egg over the years until she could pay off the debt on the house.

I finished with the last of the files in the cupboards, and tried the desk drawers again. None of them would budge. I jiggled the handle, which had worked on the front door last night, but it was no good. In fact, the drawers looked remarkably solid. *Wonderful.* Now, in addition to all the other work I had to do, I'd have to search this huge, dusty house for the key. I could just get someone in to break the drawer, of course, but the desk looked pretty old and expensive and heirs tended to get a little bent out of shape when antique desks got ruined.

Sometimes these locks have a simple bolt you could push open. I grabbed a brass letter opener from the desk and slipped that in the crack between the drawer and the desk. I moved it around until I felt it connect with something metallic. But even as I jiggled it, I could tell it was hopeless. This desk was built solidly, and these drawers were designed to be secure.

"I wouldn't bother with that. She only used that drawer to hide her toffees."

My head jerked up. In the corner of the room stood a man. Quite a handsome man, actually, as criminals went. He wore a black tailored suit jacket, black shirt, and tight black trousers that accentuated his broad shoulders, thin waist and muscular frame.

He had long dark hair that fell past his shoulders, and a strand of tiny ringlets hung over one piercing eye—the iris such a deep, dark brown that it was almost black itself. A smattering of black stubble adorned his strong jaw. There was something about his face that looked familiar, but I couldn't place it. Whoever he was, he certainly wasn't supposed to be in the study.

"Who … what …" I leapt back in the chair. Because the chair was on wheels, it skidded off the mat and bumped into the bookcase behind me, sending a rather large and heavy volume of Proust's *Swann's Way* down onto my head.

"Hello," the intruder said. His voice was rich and deep, like a hot toddy on a cold day. "I'm sorry to have startled you. I'm just so pleased that you can hear me. That you can *see* me."

"What do you want?" I snapped, hiding my shock and fear behind anger. I rubbed my head. Proust had some very sharp corners.

The man in black smiled, the corners of his eyes crinkling up in a way that might have been attractive had he not been there to rob the place or murder me or possibly both. "I was going to ask you the same question," he said.

"You're the one who is breaking and entering. You don't get to ask the questions." I knelt down, not taking my eyes from him as I fumbled in my briefcase, my fingers seeking out the hidden compartment where I kept a small flick knife. When you were a lawyer who regularly dealt with death, you had to be prepared to deal a little out yourself. Not that I'd ever stabbed anyone before, but the man in black didn't know that.

He looked amused by my comments. It wasn't good when the villain was tickled by your demonstration of bravery. It meant he knew something you didn't. My fingers closed around the handle of the knife. I pulled it out and pushed it up the sleeve of my jumper, standing up and inching my way along the bookshelf away from him. If I could get to the door, maybe I could make a run for the street.

"I'm not breaking into anything. I'm the rightful owner of this house. You're the one who is sitting at my mother's desk and pulling out all her papers."

I glared at him again, and suddenly realised where I'd seen him before. His face was on the front page of the paper in Clyde's office, and the newspaper clippings in the folder, and in some of the faded photographs in the hall. He was Eric Marshell, Alice Marshell's son. He was the famous violinist who had been killed in a car accident the day before his mother died. There was no mistaking him. But if he was dead, then how—

"But that's impossible." My hand flew to my mouth. My heart pounded against my chest. "You're supposed to be dead."

"I *am* dead." To demonstrate, Eric lifted his arm, and swiped it at a lamp. Instead of clattering to the ground, the lamp remained upright, his arm passing right through the shade. He looked over at me, his cheeky grin never leaving his face.

This cannot be happening. I fell backward, my chair clattering against the hardwood floor. "Don't come near me," I breathed, backing up against the bookcase. My hands trembled as I raised the knife, holding it in front of me, the tip pointed at Eric's face.

"You can put that down," Eric said, his voice calm, yet firm. As quick as lightning, he glided across the room, and swiped his hand over the blade, his skin passing through it like air. "It's not going to do anything to me."

Even though his body was non-corporeal, his deep, gravelly voice cut right through my body, sending a shiver of delight through me. I was always a sucker for deep voices, and if you added that to Eric's tousled black hair and intense eyes …

What are you doing? Why are you looking at him like that? Who cares if he's gorgeous. He's a … a …

"How is this possible?" I asked, more to myself than to the beautiful man in front of me.

"I'm not exactly sure." Eric's hand rested in the middle of the blade. "The last thing I remember was driving from London toward Crookshollow. I was on the way to visit my mother. The next thing I knew, I was trapped in this house, and my body didn't exist anymore. I've been here for ten days now, and I've learned I can walk through walls and levitate, and float around aimlessly. But all that is pretty useless since I have no idea why I'm here, and I can't seem to leave this house."

"But what *are* you?"

"All signs point to my being a ghost. I guess technically I'm now haunting Marshell House." Eric laughed bitterly, his voice reverberating deep into my aching core. I longed to hear that voice whispering something hot against my earlobe. Goddamn, he was one sexy ghost.

Focus, Elinor. You have a real problem here. "Okay, fine. I'm going to try and be calm about this. Let's say for argument's sake you are a ghost. Have you come to hurt me?"

Eric's eyes flashed with anger. "Didn't you hear what I said? Even if I wanted to hurt you, which I don't by the way, I couldn't. I can't even pick up a pen. And even though you're living in my house without my permission, I'm not suspecting you of evildoing. I'd appreciate it if you'd extend me the same courtesy, and stop staring at me as if I'm an axe-murderer. It's rather disconcerting."

'Don't get snippy with me. I've just found out that ghosts are real. I'm trying to process here."

Eric's eyes bore into mine. He looked so real, so solid. If I hadn't seen his fingers inside the knife blade with my own eyes, I could have sworn I could reach out and touch him, stroke my hands along that handsome jaw, entwine my fingers in that wavy black hair, press my lips to that succulent mouth—

Ahem.

What are you thinking? He's dead. You're staring at a ghost and all you can think about is sex? I really *was* desperate. Why, oh why, couldn't I be in London right now, chasing after Damon, instead of here in Crookshollow talking to the world's hottest poltergeist?

"Can you please step away from me?" I managed to choke out. "I need some air."

Eric did as I asked, bowing slightly as he glided to the other side of the desk. I sucked in a few deep breaths, screwing my eyes closed. *Okay, this can't be real. Maybe the water in this stupid town is making me sick or something, and I'm just hallucinating the ghost of a dead rock star. Because that can't possibly be a ghost. Ghosts are see-through and scary and definitely not beautiful and sexy. So, when you open your eyes, he'll be gone, and everything will be okay.*

I opened my eyes. The man in black was still leaning through the desk, his face only a few inches from mine. "Boo," he said, grinning wickedly.

"Argh! That's not funny." My heart hammered against my chest.

Yup. He was definitely still there.

"Sorry." Eric gave me a sly smile. "I was just checking that you were still breathing. I thought maybe you were trying to join me in my eternal slumber."

I inched along the bookcase toward the door. "*Really* not funny. Stay away from me."

"Listen, joking aside. I really don't want to hurt you." Eric lowered his voice, which only seemed to improve the husky quality of it. "I'm only revealing myself to you now because, so far, you're the only one who's been able to see me. I think you might be able to help me. Plus, I'm going crazy being stuck in this house by myself. There's no one to talk to, and not being able to pick anything up is really limiting my ability to entertain myself."

"I've seen you …" His words hit home. "You mean, the shadow in the bathroom?"

Eric nodded. "I didn't look, I promise. I was just trying to figure out what you were doing in the house."

"By watching me in the shower?" I gaped at him, horrified at the thought of that handsome man looking at my less-than-perfect body. For some strange reason, even though the idea was repulsive, it also made my heart surge with desire. Somewhere deep inside me, part of me *liked* the idea that Eric was watching me. How fucked up was that?

Eric shook his head forcefully. "I swear on my mother's grave that I didn't look. I'm no pervert, Elinor. If a woman is naked with me, it's going to be because she was begging me to tear her clothes off."

Is that an invitation? I gulped back the salacious thought. "How do you know my name?"

"I read it from your business card. You left your case open on the desk."

"How very observant of you. And did you have something to do with the front door?"

"Yes, but that was strange. I saw you outside, all cold and wet and miserable, and somehow I was able to turn the lock. Apart from placing my foot on a stair when you first came in, it's the first thing I've been able to touch in ten days. So you can see why I'm hopeful you might be able to help me."

"Why would I want to help you?"

"Because you seem like a really nice person." Eric flashed me a brilliant smile, his dark eyes gleaming mischievously. It was the kind of smile that would have melted my heart, had he been a guy with an actual, literal pulse. Actually, scratch that, it was melting me anyway.

"I'm not as nice as I look," I shot back. "Try again."

"Fine. You'll help me because ..." Eric gestured to the papers I'd strewn out across the desk, "you're obviously from my mother's solicitor's office, here to clear up the estate. You've got a ton of work to do. A literal Mount Everest of work—my mother has money hidden *everywhere,* and she never hired an accountant, so you're on your own."

"That's my job. What's that got to do with you?"

"I can help. I can tell you where all her secret papers are kept, and the key to the locked drawer. I can tell you about the investments in Arabian oil, and the bank account in Liechtenstein, and the secret house in Santorini. In return, all I ask is that you just *try* to help me."

"Help you do what? What help do ghosts need? About the only thing you look like you could do with is a decent haircut, and I'm lousy with scissors."

Eric smirked at my remark, tucking a strand of his black hair behind his ear. "I need you to find out what happened to me. I didn't drop dead of a heart attack, Elinor. I think I've been murdered." He pointed to the local newspaper sitting on the desk, where a headline announced his tragic death from a hit-and-run collision. "I'm front-page news, but no one seems to be looking for clues. According to that article, the police think it was probably a drunk driver, but I'm not so sure. I think whoever murdered me has covered their tracks pretty well, and maybe they think they've got away with it. But I've come back from ... wherever I'm meant to be, for a reason. I don't think I can move on with my afterlife until I figure out how I died, and why."

"How did you come back? Did you see a light? What about the pearly gates?"

"I don't know anything. I can't remember my death, or even much about the days leading up to it. The last thing I remember was driving up from London to see my mother. So why has my ghost ended up in Marshell House? I didn't die here. At least, I haven't seen my body, or any bloodstains."

"Oh, God," I groaned, sinking against the bookcase. "Please don't let there be a dead body here, too."

"You're a lawyer. I thought you guys loved murder."

"That's criminal defence. I'm a probate attorney. I just do paperwork. Do I *have* to help you? Can't you just leave me alone and we call it even?"

"No can do, I'm afraid." Eric gave me a broad smile. "You're too beautiful for me to just ignore."

The wind rushed from my lungs, as if someone had punched

me in the gut. My mind reeled at his remark. People didn't usually say *that* to me, especially not incredibly attractive, suave-looking dead musicians. I wasn't the pretty one—that was Cindy, with her blonde hair and her model body and her flirtatious laugh. I was the smart one, which men usually found intimidating, or the drunk one, which men usually found hilarious in a sad kind of way.

I searched Eric's face for a sign that he was joking again, or that he was giving me a line. But his eyes met mine and held my gaze. I found myself falling into his stare, losing myself in those wide, dark pools.

This is a really bad idea. But, he's so ...

"Fine." I shrugged. "I'll do some googling for you, but that's it. And you've got to stand over there. I'm finding it hard enough to concentrate with a ghost in the room, without you being all up in my grill."

"All up in your *grill?*" Eric sneered. "Where are you from, the harsh streets of Harlem?"

I felt wounded. The ghost was mocking me. That wasn't cool. "Chelsea, actually. It's just slang. I only say it ironically. Do you want me to help you or not?"

"Of course. I'm sorry. Thank you." Eric bowed again, a strangely formal motion for a man I knew to be some kind of famous rock star.

As Eric turned away, I took a couple of moments to inspect his arse (tight and sculpted, yum). Eric floated back across the room, his black motorcycle boots hovering a few inches above the carpet as he turned back to face me. Feeling nervous with Eric's gaze on me, I slid back into the desk chair, opened up my browser, and typed in Eric's name. It didn't take long for all the headlines to start appearing:

ROCK STAR VIOLINIST DIES IN TRAGIC HIT-AND-RUN

CAR ACCIDENT TAKES OUT GOTH ROCKER

POLICE LOOKING FOR 2ND CAR IN MARSHELL WRECK

HUNDREDS BUY TICKETS TO ERIC MARSHELL'S FUNERAL

MARSHELL'S BAND TO RELEASE TRIBUTE SONG

I clicked on one of the articles. "Look at this," I said, jabbing my finger at the screen. "It looks like you were run off the road just outside of Crookshollow. The police found two sets of tracks at the scene. The other car sped off. There were no witnesses. They're looking for information about the driver, but so far nothing's come up. All they know is that it was a Golf with high-performance tires. But there's nothing in here that indicates they're treating this as a murder investigation."

"I have nothing to indicate it, either, except a gut feeling. And since I don't actually have a gut anymore, I'm going to assume this overwhelming sense of injustice is telling me something. Does the article say anything else?"

I scanned the colour image that accompanied the article. "Holy shit, your car was an absolute mess. No wonder you died."

"I can't see from over here," Eric said dryly.

"Fine. You can come a bit closer. But don't touch me or I am calling a priest to exorcise the shit out of you."

"Fair enough." Eric floated back to the desk and leaned over my shoulder. His hand hung down at his side, and his fingers fell through the desk. I stared at the stump of his arm disappearing into the wood. It was strange, but I was already used to the idea of him being a ghost. Perhaps it was all that gothic literature I read in university, but I wasn't afraid of him, not really. I was *fascinated*. I was the heroine of my own gothic tale. I just hoped mine had a happier ending than most.

"You're right," said Eric from behind me, his voice dark. "It is a real mess." I thought I detected a tremor in his voice. I glanced over and saw him staring intently at the screen, his eyes darting into every corner of the image, fixing on every detail of the accident that had taken his life.

"Oh, I'm sorry. I didn't think about … that you might not want to …" I quickly hit the BACK button. The search menu flashed up again.

'No, Elinor, it's fine. It's just a shock. I am … I *was* only 35. I didn't expect to be dealing with *this*—" with a flick of his wrist he indicated his ghostly form, "—just now. I had more music to write, more shows to play. Please, I didn't mean to frighten you." He reached out for my hand, his fingers passing through my skin. When he touched me, a fire leapt from my fingers and exploded along my arm, as if I'd just jammed my fingers into an electric socket.

I leapt back in shock, yanking my arm away from him. The ghost of his touch still played against my skin. I rubbed my fingers against my palm, but the hot, tingling sensation didn't go away. "I said not to touch me!"

'I'm sorry," Eric breathed, staring down at his own hand as if he couldn't quite understand how it was attached to his body. "Really, it was an accident. I didn't mean—"

He looked so guilty, and I felt bad for him. He had just died, after all. "It's okay." I sank back into the chair. "You just surprised me.'

'I promise I'll be more careful." Eric was still staring down at his hand, his expression unreadable. An awkward silence descended upon us.

I turned back to the screen, hoping to find something to ease the tension. "Hey, this is new." I clicked on a link to a news story that had gone live only an hour ago, squinting at the screen to read the title.

THIEVES RANSACK THE HOUSE OF ERIC MARSHELL.

Just days after the famous rock violinist was found dead in a horrific car accident, Devon police report that Marshell's country property has been broken into. The break-in occurred last night. Neighbours reported hearing a window smash, and an unfamiliar black car was spotted leaving the quiet cul-de-sac around 3am. Although several rooms in Marshell's house were trashed—with objects strewn across the floor, and furnishings and paintings slashed with a knife—it doesn't appear as if anything was taken. Police will issue a full report once they've produced an inventory of the house, but they ask if anyone has any information relating to Eric Marshell's death or this break-in, to contact them.

"That's odd," Eric said. "Why would someone break into my home?"

"All sorts of reasons," I said. "It could be completely unrelated to your death. You were quite famous, so I'm told. Perhaps it was some crazed fan wanting to sniff all your underwear, or an enterprising crook wanting to grab all the Eric Marshell possessions he could to auction off on eBay."

"But then why wasn't anything taken?"

"I'm no expert, but I've read my fair share of detective stories, so I can hazard a guess. Usually, when people break in somewhere and smash a bunch of stuff but don't take anything, it's because they're looking for something in particular. You in possession of any rare diamonds? First-edition manuscripts? Possibly magical ancient artefacts that transport anyone who touches them to another dimension?"

"Not that I'm aware of. I do have a nice record collection, with a few rare pressings, but—" Eric pointed at one of the images of a oak bookcase crowded with stacks of vinyl, "—it looks as if they haven't even touched it."

"And there's nothing else you can think of? You're not into anything illegal, are you?" Musicians were often into drugs. I found myself hoping that Eric wasn't. I couldn't bear to be around someone who did that shit, not after—

Don't think about him now, Elinor. Focus on Eric.

"Not unless classical music and expensive whisky have suddenly been outlawed. I can't think of what could be ... oh, no." Eric pointed at the screen again. "Zoom in on that picture."

"Don't get too close!"

"I won't. Please?"

I rolled the mouse closer. Eric peered at the image. It showed the damage to one of the rooms in his house. It was a kind of salon, with a vaulted ceiling and comfortable, overstuffed couches lining the walls. It was probably a really nice room when it wasn't such a mess. Oak coffee tables had been broken and flipped over, and several of the paintings on the walls were torn to shreds, their frames smashed against the ground. A grand piano stood open in one corner, the top torn off and broken into splinters.

"That's odd," Eric said.

"What's odd?"

"This is my music studio. It's not a recording studio, just a room I use to compose and play music. There's a lot more damage in here than in other rooms."

I pointed to an ornate wooden frame in the corner of the room. "Was that where you kept your violin? It's empty."

"It's supposed to be empty. I have two identical violins, so I always have a spare in case one of them needs repairs, but both of them came on tour with me."

"Are they identical?"

"They look pretty similar, but they're made of different woods and have slightly different properties. I can tell them apart, and so can most of the hardcore fans. They even have names."

"Of course they do." I rolled my eyes. "Let me guess, Romeo and Juliet?"

"Actually, Tristan and Isolde. I use Isolde for all my promo and most of the stage show, and Tristan for certain songs that require a more delicate sound. Do you think the thieves were looking for my violins? Why would they want that? They were hardly valuable instruments. I play Cremona. They're made in China. It's the same brand my father used. They're sold at every corner music store for less than 500 quid."

"Uh, hello? eBay. I told you." I glanced at the image again. "But I think you're right. I don't think they were looking for your instruments."

"Why not?"

"Look at how all that stuff is piled up on top of the stand. There's some torn papers, and broken bits of that guitar. They were still rifling through your stuff long after they saw the stand was empty. It's all a bit odd. If you were breaking into someone's house, why bother smashing all their stuff? Wouldn't you want to grab what you wanted, and run?"

Eric reached behind his head, scratching a spot behind his dark curls. "Maybe it's a revenge thing. Someone is getting me back by trashing all my stuff."

"But you're dead. What would be the point?"

Eric shrugged. "I'm out of ideas."

"Me too. I think we need to start from the very beginning. Maybe it would help if you went through what you *do* remember about your death?"

"That would be a great idea, if I could remember what happened. That's the thing about being a ghost. I can only remember certain things about ... before. I remember heading out on tour, and racing from the airport to play our last show in London. I remember being on stage, feeling the heat of the lights in my face. I remember driving up here as soon as I got off the stage to see Mother, but I don't remember why. I only remember that I felt scared."

"Well, that's something. What would you be scared of?"

"I don't know."

"Did you have your car with you at the show?"

Eric shook his head. "No, it's probably back at my home in Devon. I must've rented a car. What car did it say I was driving in the article?"

I scanned the text. "You're right. It was a Fiat, rented that evening. So you must have been desperate to get up to Crookshollow, to go rent a car specifically for that purpose."

'I've known you twenty minutes and already you've figured out more than I've managed to do in eight days."

I beamed at his praise. "Perhaps you'll remember more once we dig deeper into this."

'Yeah, maybe." Eric looked uncertain.

My phone beeped. I checked the message, thinking it might be from Cindy. She'd promised to text and tell me how last night had gone, but I hadn't heard from her. But it wasn't Cindy, it was the car rental company, informing me they had just dropped the car off at the house. That gave me an idea. I looked up another report on the car crash, and pulled up a map of Crookshollow. A few seconds later, I was on my feet. "Come with me."

I grabbed the keys to the house from the table (I was *not* going to make that mistake again), and flung open the door. Eric was still standing in the doorway to the study, watching me with a concerned look on his face. "Come on." I gestured for the door. "I haven't got all day."

"What are you doing?"

"*I'm* doing nothing. *We* are going to get your memory back."

"And how will we do that?"

"By visiting the site of your death," I said triumphantly. Eric's expression froze. "Come on, Eric. It's the only way. I don't know how many ghost stories you've read, but ghosts always have a connection to the place they died. If going there will jog your memory, it might give us more to work with."

"I don't know, Elinor. I don't think it's going to work. I don't think I can leave the house. As soon as I get close to the walls, my body is flooded with this overwhelming sensation that I need to turn back."

"You said that having me around gives you the ability to do things you couldn't normally do, like feel solid objects. So why couldn't it allow you to go outside? Just stick close to me. But not too close," I added, for good measure.

Eric didn't move.

"Are you afraid or something?"

"You're damn right I'm afraid," Eric said, his eyes boring into mine. "Would you want to see where you were killed?"

No. "Don't be a pussy. You're supposed to be some kind of badass goth superstar. Now fix your eyeliner, embrace the morbid ridiculousness of this situation, and get out here."

Eric set his mouth in a thin line, and stepped across the entrance hall toward me. He reached the threshold of the door and stopped, his face grim. His whole body tensed, and he leaned forward, pushing himself toward the door. It looked as though he were fighting against some invisible force. I stepped over the threshold, and held the door open with my hand. "Just one more step," I said.

He frowned, but raised his hand, tentatively extending his fingers across the threshold of the door. Eric's face twisted in concentration—he was trying to push through that repelling sensation to reach me. I noticed his fingers, long and thin and beautiful, the tips hardened from furious playing. Musician's hands. I bet they could play a tune on *anything* … I made a note to look up some of his music when I was alone.

Eric's fingers dangled in mid-air, and then they passed over the threshold. He gave them an experimental wiggle. His face broke into a grin.

"Hey, this is strange! I tried to float through the wall last week, and it was like coming up against a solid object. But look at this! I don't know what it is about you, Elinor, but I'm *very* glad you're here."

I turned my head as I held the door open for Eric, not wanting him to notice the heat collecting in my cheeks.

Eric stepped forward, his foot passing over the threshold and hovering a couple of inches above the porch. His grin grew wider as he moved the rest of his body across, moving to stand beside me under the porch, a black silhouette that cast no shadow on the ground. Once he was completely outside, I shut the door behind us, shoving the key in the lock and dropping the ring into my pocket. I wasn't going to forget the keys again.

"This is amazing," Eric gushed behind me. "It feels so good to be outside again. I feel all tingly—"

I turned back to him, and screamed. Something was wrong. Terribly wrong. Eric was growing faint—his body fading like the image on an old TV screen after someone turned it off. I could still make out the outline of his black suit, but through his torso, the wisteria trailing around the porch railing was clearly visible. Eric looked down at his hands. He cursed as he watched the tips fade into thin air.

"I think ..." Eric whispered, his voice weak, "I have to go ... back inside ..."

Inside, now. I fumbled with the keys in my pocket, finally managing to grab them and jam them in the lock. My heart hammered as I watched Eric's motorcycle boots vanish, followed by his shapely calves and knees. My hands shook so violently that it took me three tries before the key slipped in. "Hurry!" Eric's weak voice pleaded.

I turned the lock and flung the door open. I was so desperate to save Eric I forgot my fear of touching him, and I tried to push him back through the door. My fingers dropped right through his skin. This time, I didn't feel the sharp explosion of heat down my arms, only a weak, warm tingle, barely distinguishing his presence from the air around him.

Please be okay, I prayed silently. *Please don't disappear.*

Eric's face burst with effort. He moved slowly across the

porch, his arms circling around his head as if he were swimming through thick toffee. With every agonising step, his shape faded away, until I could barely make out the edges of his face against the dark bricks. I gripped the handle so hard my knuckles ached. *Hurry, Eric! You're almost there.*

Eric reached the door and heaved himself over the threshold, just as his face faded completely from view. I squinted my eyes to try and find him. I could only just make out the outline of his shoulders and the shadow of his face as he slumped on the floor. I dived inside after him, slamming the door shut behind me.

I collapsed against the back of the door, panting heavily, trying to slow my racing heart back to normal. I watched as slowly, bit by bit, more of Eric's body became visible. He was hunched in front of me. At first I thought his legs had disappeared for good, but then I realised that he wasn't kneeling on the floor, he was floating halfway between it.

When his colour had fully returned, Eric floated up again, so that his feet hovered on the same floor as mine. "That was close."

I rose to my feet, still leaning back against the door. I didn't quite trust myself to stand under my own weight. "I'm so sorry. That was scary, Eric."

"I know." He gazed at me intently. "I think … I nearly stopped existing. Thank you for saving me."

"I didn't save you. It was me who insisted you go outside in the first place." Guilt overwhelmed me. A hard lump clung to my throat. *You're not about to cry, are you? You barely know this guy, and it's not as if he can die. He's already dead.*

"Hey, I was willing to let you off, but you're an honest lawyer. I like that." Eric smiled. "It's okay, Elinor, really. We didn't know what would happen. Now we know."

"What *did* happen?"

"I guess I'm not allowed outside of the house. It makes sense. In all the ghost stories I've read, the ghost is confined to some specific space. Marshell House must be my boundary."

"So what are we going to do?"

Eric sighed. "I hate asking anyone for anything, but I'm getting pretty desperate. Please, could you go and have a look at the crash site?"

"Why? It's pointless without you there. The whole reason we were going was to see if you could remember anything."

"Take some pictures on your phone and bring them back, or a video if you can. Anything that might help me remember. Plus," he said, giving me a wry smile, "I can tell you're pretty clever. You can look for any clues that the police might have missed. I think you'd like that, Miss Not-a-Criminal-Lawyer."

"I'm not a detective, either."

"Ah, but this *is* a ghost story." Eric gestured to himself. "And all the best ghost stories contain beautiful amateur detectives."

"They also contain heroines in voluminous gothic gowns who end up dead at the end. I'm not sure which character one I am."

"Did you pack a voluminous gothic gown in that Prada suitcase of yours?"

I shook my head.

Then I think you'll be fine. Although," he said, grinning, "I bet you'd look stunning in a corset."

I grabbed my coat from the rack beside the door. "Fine. I need to buy a printer anyway, since your mother has no concept of twenty-first century office equipment. Will you be okay here by yourself?" I stared at Eric with concern, wondering if he was going to fade away as soon as I left.

"Oh, sure. I'm used to my own company by now." Eric gave me a tight, formal wave. Strangely sad to be leaving him, I pulled the keys from the lock and went outside, shutting the door softly behind me.

I GUESSED the people at Crookshollow Car Rentals must be as

scared of Marshell House as the Pete's Pizza's employees. They had parked my car on the street outside the open gate, and hadn't even bothered to come up to the house to give me the keys. Instead, I found an envelope with a hastily scrawled note in the letterbox. *Because that's safe.* I unlocked the little Fiat and plugged my phone in, turning on the GPS and entering King Alfred Road, the name of the street where the paper said Eric's car had crashed.

The drive took me through a neighbourhood containing even larger, older, and creepier homes, many in gothic revival or Georgian styles. I didn't know why people around here had such a problem with the Marshell house. This whole town is filled with probable haunted houses. Why were people afraid to even walk onto the property?

I snorted with laughter. I guess if people thought there were ghosts inside, they were right. Although Eric was probably the least frightening spectre I could've imagined. What was frightening was how much I liked him already, and how much I wanted to impress him by finding something useful at the wreck site.

It turned out, King Alfred Road was a country road. Stately manors and gothic mansions gave way to quaint cottages peeking out from behind dry-stone walls, and fields of puffy white sheep snacking on lush grass. After just a few miles, the houses grew even more spread out, and all I could see was miles of rolling farmland and a dense forest. What was Eric doing out here? He wouldn't come this way driving from London to Crookshollow.

The forest grew denser, and as I rounded the crest of a hill, I saw a small wooden sign reading WITCHES CEMETERY. Behind it was a field filled with crumbling tombstones, many toppled over or crumbling away. Both the earth and the trees around the graveyard were charred black, as if they'd been on fire. I wondered what had happened there. I bet if I asked Duncan, he could give me a whole history lesson on the place.

The spot where Eric had been run off the road was easy to find. Two sets of tire tracks criss-crossed the road like ley lines.

One set of tracks went straight off the right side of the road and into a ditch. The council had already righted the power pole Eric's car had wrecked.

I noticed something wrong immediately, something the papers hadn't picked up on. The tire tracks were on the other side of the road, the same side I was driving on now. Eric hadn't been driving to Crookshollow. He'd been driving *away*.

I pulled over on the verge and got out, wishing I'd paid more attention to all those crime investigation shows on the telly. Weren't detectives always looking at tire tracks and determining who had driven where and done what? How fast were they travelling? Was the driver drunk? How many greasy hamburgers had the passenger eaten that night? CSI teams could solve it all with just a glance at the tracks. But I was a probate lawyer, and it just looked like a mess of skid marks to me. I pulled out my phone and took a quick video of the road for Eric.

Next, I went over to the ditch where Eric's car had landed. The grass had been charred black and cut up in the crash, and the dirt beneath churned up by the workers who'd pulled the car out of the ditch. A dark stain blotted the earth beside the power pole. *Is that Eric's blood?* The thought made my stomach turn.

This is where he died.

It was hard to think of Eric as dead, because he was so ... animated. But I remembered the way his fingers had fallen right through me, how touching him caused a hot, unnatural energy to race through my skin. And it brought it all back, all the pain and horror of Joel's death. *Don't get attached. Because eventually he's going to be gone forever, and you'll be alone, again.*

Joel. I hadn't thought about him for ... almost a month. That was a record for me. I'd been so distracted with Operation Shag Damon that I hadn't been sad for a while. It seemed like I was getting over him. But as soon as his name entered my mind, fresh tears sprung to my eyes. *Don't think about it, Elinor. You have to concentrate, for Eric.*

So I concentrated. I bent down and started to search the ground, moving in a sweeping motion to inspect every square inch of dirt. *This is pointless,* Devil's-Advocate Elinor complained. *The police would have been over every inch of this ground. They did that when high profile people died on their turf. What do I think I am going to find that they hadn't—*

Out of the corner of my eye, I spotted a glint of metal down in the ditch. An empty drink can. The police wouldn't have bothered with that—there was probably a ton of rubbish in the ditch. *But what is that, poking out of the top* ... I peered closer. A small scrap of paper was pushed through the lip of the can. Someone must've tucked an extra bit of rubbish into the can before tossing it away. It could be nothing, but it could be ... I crouched down, aware that I was probably getting my favourite Vivienne Westwood skirt all dirty, and picked up the can. A couple of shakes and I was able to dig out the paper. It was wet from the rain, but being inside the can had probably saved it from being completely obliterated. I clasped my hand around it and, after a final glance around to ensure I hadn't missed anything, went back to the car.

Once inside I held the paper up to the light, squinting to read the tiny print. It was a ticket stub, but the name of the show had been smudged too badly to read. All I could make out were the words "Coppeli—" and ADMIT ONE. A phone number had been scrawled across the top in a messy pink pen.

It could be a clue. An actual, honest-to-goodness clue, just like in a mystery story. Eric was a musician, so if someone murdered him, there was a fair chance they were in some way related to the music industry, and would have plenty of reason to toss the scrap of a ticket stub away. Feeling a little pleased with myself, I stuffed the stub into my pocket. I started the engine and sped away, eager to get back to the house and show Eric what I'd found. It was funny how quickly I'd gotten used to the idea of having a ghost around. I wasn't even questioning my sanity. I mean, I could be hallucinating Eric, couldn't I? Maybe someone had slipped some kind of slow-release hallucinogenic into my drink last weekend. It would explain why I'd managed to conjure up a ghost that was so ridiculously attractive …

It was weird, but when I thought of it that way, Eric being a ghost trapped in the house because he couldn't cross over until he solved the mystery of his own death was actually the *most* plausible explanation for everything that had happened.

If you'd told me two days ago that I'd be hanging out with a spectre, I would've laughed in your face. But Eric was so … likeable. Arrogant, and a little stiff and formal, and his jokes were in pretty bad taste, but I could forgive a lot when my poltergeist was so damn gorgeous.

Is that why you're so keen to help him, because he's hot? Devil's Advocate Elinor sneered inside my head. *Do you think he's going to be so grateful that he's going to make sexy ghost love to you on his mother's bed? That makes no sense. First of all, he's dead. Second of all, Eric is … was … a famous musician. He had groupies lining up to share his bed every night. If he was alive, he never would've noticed a frumpy bookworm like you. And it's no different now, it's just that for some unknown reason, you're the only person who can see him.*

I'm not trying to— I started, but stopped the thought in my head. I knew better than to attempt to lie to Devil's Advocate Elinor. I was a lawyer. I was trained to spot a lie.

Even if he was alive, it could never work. And he's not alive, just like Joel isn't alive. So don't get attached to him, Elinor. Don't get involved. I'm telling you this for your own good.

"Shut up," I said to myself, as I drove back past the charred witches' cemetery and back towards the village. *Atta girl,* Devil's Advocate Elinor shot back.

*E*very minute that Elinor was away was agony to me. I hadn't realised just how desperate I'd been to have someone to talk to, and now she was gone again, the house felt so large and oppressive and empty, even more so than when I was alive. I floated aimlessly around the downstairs rooms, nervously flicking at my mother's antique vases and cat statues with my fingers and watching my skin disappear through the glaze. It was weird being nervous and not being able to touch anything. I had all this energy humming around my body, and I couldn't do anything with it.

I know how I'd like to burn it off, but ...

That was an inappropriate thought.

But I couldn't help it. Elinor was just so *tempting*. With her no-nonsense brown hair and her black-rimmed glasses and her tight skirt clinging to her gorgeous curves, she had that whole hot librarian look down to an art. I could tell just from our short conversation that she was whip-smart, and she was ready to call me on my bullshit, which I admired, although I didn't necessarily welcome it.

Back when I was alive, I'd had a lot of girls, although not as many as Allan or Pierre or the other members of my band and crew. Performing was so physically and emotionally intense for me that I preferred to drink alone afterward over making small talk with Bambi-McCockenstein or whatever that night's goth groupie's name was. But I'd definitely enjoyed more than my fair share of the world's population of beautiful women. I'd been a loser and a loner in high school, and now that people knew who I was, it was a major ego boost to see women falling over themselves just for a night with me. It was fun, and I loved the sex, but it was easy. And easy got boring after a while.

I could tell that wasn't Elinor's game. It didn't even seem as if she really knew who I was. She certainly didn't fall all over herself in front of me like my female fans. I'd have to work to win her, and I was happy to rise to the challenge.

Just thinking about her in that tight sweater, her glasses pushed down her nose, was making something rise right now.

No. Reality slammed into me with enough force to knock me back through the hall wall. My phantom erection faded into the nothingness that was my body. What was I thinking, getting all hot under the collar for Elinor? It didn't matter how I felt, I was *dead.* Elinor wasn't interested in a fling with a restless spirit. I needed to stop being distracted by my mother's sexy estate lawyer and focus on the problem at hand: how to move my soul from the living world to wherever it was supposed to go.

Luckily, as a musician who played music that *Rolling Stone* described as avant-garde-gothic-neo-folk-meets-Freddy-Mercury (try saying that three times fast), I had a strong interest in the occult and hauntings and other supernatural phenomena. Unfortunately, all my books were back at my own house, probably torn to pieces by the mystery burglar. Luckily, I was in Crookshollow, where information about the occult was never far away. Maybe I could get Elinor to go to the library—

I heard the car pull up outside. I was still feeling pretty shaken about my current situation, and in a split second, a wicked thought crossed my mind. If I was stuck like this, and I couldn't have the kind of fun I *wanted* to have with Elinor, I could at least amuse myself. I rushed through the hall, and waited behind the door while she fumbled with the keys. She was carrying a huge printed box under one arm. A few moments later, she pushed the door open, and stepped inside, calling "Eric! You won't believe what I found—"

I leapt through the door, raising my hands above my head, and yelled, "Boo!"

It was childish, but seeing Elinor's face crumple with terror, before twisting into a mock-angry scowl was well worth it. She dropped the box on the floor and tried to swipe me with her bag, but the leather sailed right through me.

"You are *three*," she snapped, entering the study and slumping down in one of the chairs.

"Oh, come on. It was funny. I'm dead. I have very little in my life right now. I'm simply trying to make lemonade."

"I'd rather have a G&T," Elinor sighed. "I can't believe I just had the life scared out of my by the ghost of a dead pop singer. For the second time today."

"Not pop-singer, *rock-violinist*. You *really* have never heard of me before?" I hadn't intended for that to come out sounding so arrogant, but I couldn't help it. I had been on the Graham Norton show, and done a lap around the *Top Gear* track. I had played sold-out shows across the world. I am ... *had been* ... practically mainstream.

Elinor shrugged. "I've heard vague rumblings. I'm not really into classical music, Eric."

"Why not?"

"It's boring."

I chortled. "That is exactly what someone who's never heard a classical piece played properly would say. What music *do* you like, since you're such an expert?"

"Just normal stuff. House and techno. Tunes you can dance to."

"Talk about boring."

"Look," Elinor dumped her bag down on the desk, and retrieved the printer box from the hall. Packaging beads rolled across the floor as she pulled out boxes and cords and instruction manuals. She seemed to be avoiding looking at me. "I've got a lot of work to get through today, and I have to get this thing set up. My boss isn't paying me to debate the merits of different musical genres with a ghost."

"Of course, you're right." I felt as if I'd said something wrong, but wasn't sure what. "So amidst your very important printer shopping expedition, did you found the place?"

I floated over to stand beside the fire, deliberately hovering a good three inches above the floor, hoping to unnerve her. Behind me, the flames roared invitingly, and I felt a pang of longing to feel their warmth on my skin again.

Elinor looked up, and gave a thin smile. "I did, and it was a good thing, too, because we were assuming something that turned out to be false. Eric, you were driving the other way."

"I don't understand."

"The pictures in the paper didn't show any landmarks, so we just assumed you were driving toward Crookshollow, but you weren't." Elinor plugged the printer in and flicked it on. "You were headed *away* from the village, and not back to London, judging by the road I found you on. If I had to guess, I'd say you were on your way to Devon."

"Is that important?" Did where I was going really matter? What mattered was that I had died, somehow, in that car. So shouldn't we be more interested in the other car, the one that had run me off into the ditch?

"Of course it's important. We're trying to reconstruct your last movements. We'd been assuming you hadn't yet arrived in Crook-shollow—"

"We were?"

"—and now we know you had already come to Crookshollow,

done whatever it was you'd come to do, and left. That could be *very* important, assuming we can figure out what you came here to do. And that's not all. I even found a clue. At least, I think it's a clue," Elinor pulled a small piece of paper from her pocket, smoothed it out against the table, and held it up so I could see it. I leaned in, peering at the tiny words on the faded ticket stub.

'It's from one of the shows on my tour," I said. "You can just make out the word "Coppelius" there. Our last album was called *Coppelius' Alchemy*, after the character in Hoffman's *Der Sandmann*. I wouldn't expect you to know it—"

"Well, *that* was condescending."

"It wasn't meant to be. I just don't know many lawyers into obscure German gothic texts, is all."

"I know Hoffman." Elinor pushed her glasses up her nose. "I wrote an essay about *Die Nachtstücke* in university, in the only non-law course I was allowed to take. Just because I have no idea who you are doesn't mean I am some kind of uncultured hack."

I was impressed that this wholesome-looking girl had heard of such an obscure piece of German literature. I just couldn't believe she hadn't heard my music.

'I didn't say you were an uncultured hack, although how you could've read Hoffman and not heard of my band confounds me. Now, back to this ticket. I couldn't be certain which particular night on the tour this came from, but I think that might be the logo of the theatre up there." I pointed to the corner of the ticket, where a faded symbol was just visible.

'I might be able to find out which theatre this is," said Elinor, lifting a blank sheet of paper off the stack by the printer. She set the ticket down on the table, pulled the lid off a fancy ink pen, and in a few strokes had drawn a pretty accurate representation of the logo.

'Hey, that's pretty good." I was impressed. If I'd tried to draw that freehand, it would've looked like a squirrel's finger-painting.

'No, it's not, but it will do the trick. Here." Elinor snapped a picture of her drawing with her phone, then plugged the image into Google Search. Within a few moments, she'd pulled up an exact match—the Usher Hall theatre in London.

"That was the last show of the tour," I exclaimed. "It was the last gig I ever did."

"This can't be a coincidence, and I think it proves that your death wasn't an accident. Whoever ran you off the road was at that show, and they threw this stub out the window as they fled the scene. Any idea whose phone number this is?"

I shook my head. "I've no idea, and the handwriting doesn't look familiar. But that might not mean anything. Who remembers phone numbers these days?"

Elinor frowned at the stub. "You're right. You only ever write down the number of someone you don't know. Everyone else you have saved in your phone. Or, in your case, you probably have a secretary who handles all your calls. Do you ever get letters, emails, packages from crazed fans?"

"Oh, all the time."

"Eric, I'm serious."

"So am I. I get stacks of that stuff. Women send me underwear. Men send me used condoms. My manager deals with it all. She probably has a list of all the particularly weird ones. I could call and—" I cleared my throat, remembering my problem. "I mean, you could probably call and ask her."

"That won't do us any good unless we know who was at that show."

"There were thousands of people there! I *am* quite popular, you know. What do you plan to do, use facial recognition software to scan every crowd image from the night and feed them through an MI5 database?"

"We could do that, if you like, but I think I know an easier way." Elinor thought for a moment. "Theatres have pretty sophisticated booking systems these days, because of all the trouble they've had with ticket scalpers. Whenever my friend Cindy and I go to shows or raves, we have to put our names on our tickets. You can't get in without an ID that matches your ticket. If we can get a list from the ticket agency of everyone in the audience that night, we can cross reference it with your secretary's list of crazies and see if any names pop."

"But how are we going to get the ticket agency to give up that list?"

Elinor sighed. "It looks like I have to do everything around here." She tapped out something on her laptop, then pulled out her mobile phone and punched in a number. As she waited for someone to pick up, she glared at me and rolled her eyes.

"My mother said never to make faces, because the wind could change and you'd get stuck like that," I said. "Besides, I can think of a much better face for you to be making."

Just as Elinor snorted in response, I heard someone's voice chirp on the other end of the phone. "Hello," Elinor cleared her throat and put on a curt, professional voice. She punched a button on the phone, switching it to speaker. "This is Elinor Baxter at the London firm Greyson, Smithe & Hanley. I have a client involved in the recent Eric Marshell case—"

"It's *so* tragic," the young woman on the other end whined. "Eric was so young, and such a talent. It's just unfair that he's dead, and crusty old pop singers like Elvis and that guy with the fugly glasses are still kicking around."

"Yes, of course. It's one of life's cruel jokes." Elinor rolled her eyes, holding her hand over her mouth to keep from laughing. "I understand you recently hosted a show on his tour?"

"O. M. G. It was *amazing*," the girl gushed. "I got to work backstage that night, and so I was right on the side of the stage during Eric's performance. He's just amazing, so intense, so self-possessed, so sexy. The way he throws himself around the stage while playing every note perfectly—"

Elinor looked up at me and rolled her eyes again. I shrugged. I couldn't help it if this girl enjoyed my performance. I mimed striking my bow against the strings, and took a little bow. Elinor covered her mouth again, but not before a little snort emerged. Her eyes panicked, she gave me a filthy look, and averted her gaze.

The girl was still going, "—and when he performed 'The Raven's Revenge', he was looking *right at me* the entire time. I thought I might die and go to heaven right there—"

"Right, well, that's very nice. But I'm going to need you to send me some records so we can proceed with our case. I just need a list of all the attendees at Eric's last concert. Preferably with contact details, if you have them."

"Do you think someone at the concert had something to do with Eric's death?"

"I'm afraid I can't disclose that information, but I can tell you that there may have been a person of interest to our investigation in the crowd that night. Will you cooperate, or do I require a court order?"

"Sure! Of course, I mean, anything for Eric."

"And, I don't need to tell you that it's very important that you don't speak about this with the press or the police." Elinor lowered her voice. "We think there might be something dodgy going on in the police department, perhaps someone there is in on it. Eric's legacy depends on us being able to conduct our investigation in secret. Do you understand?"

"Of course," the girl whispered back, clearly pleased to be made part of this covert operation to uncover the truth about my untimely death. "I'll get you what you need today."

"If I could get you to email them over, please." Elinor gave the girl an email address.

"I'll get right on this!" the girl gushed. "I'm willing to do *anything* to help. Seriously, if you need a witness to say that Eric was there that night, I can testify. I even went backstage afterward to see if I could meet him, but the man on security was running everywhere yelling into a phone, and the guy in the parking lot told me Eric left in a taxi the minute the show finished. Which was a bit disappointing because there were a bunch of us back-stage ready to meet him, but after a performance like that he probably just wanted a cup of tea and a decent sleep. He really is the greatest musician in the world, you know. I've never heard anything as deep and spiritual as *Coppelius' Alchemy*. It's just sooooo amazeba—"

Elinor hit the END CALL button with a visible expression of disgust.

"Hey!" I exclaimed. "I was listening to that."

"It's nothing you haven't heard before," she said, making a face. "Besides, I had a suspicion the word *amazeballs* was about to come out of her mouth, and I've had about all of the heart attacks I can handle for today."

"Thank you for doing that," I said. "But aren't you worried about using your company email address? Surely a high profile, prestigious law firm closely monitors all correspondence."

"Are you concerned about me, Eric Marshell?" Elinor's head snapped up, and she stared at me with a strange expression on her face.

"I don't want you to get into trouble on my account. I can't exactly march down to your office and tell your boss the reason you outright lied to a ticketing office."

"I appreciate the concern about my legal integrity, but I can handle myself, thank you. I created a new email address. It looks like a legit address, but isn't in any way linked to my firm."

"Clever."

"It's been known to happen from time to time." Elinor turned back to her laptop. "Now, I've lost the whole morning to investigating your untimely demise. Can you please leave me in peace so I can get to work on your mother's estate?"

FOR THE REST of the day, Elinor worked through my mother's

files, sorting the papers and typing information into a complex spreadsheet. Every so often she'd hold a page up to the light, frown at it, and then I'd hear the furious tapping of her deleting large sections of her work.

Initially, I left her alone to her work, and floated up to my bedroom to try to grab the handle on my ancient toy chest. After an hour of pushing my hands through my childhood possessions without actually feeling any of them, I floated back downstairs to watch Elinor work. That was much more interesting.

I hovered over a chair by the fire, sometimes offering up tidbits of information I knew about the accounts, but mostly just watching Elinor. She was quite something. The work must be tremendously boring, but she toiled away at it unceasingly, her fingers flying over the keys as she added data to her spreadsheet. Every so often, she would glance up and glare at me.

"You're distracting," she said.

"You don't look that distracted."

"Well, appearances can be deceiving. I usually type twice as fast."

"I know that's not true. If you typed any faster, you'd open up a wormhole in space. Can we put some music on?"

"Sure." Without looking up from her files, Elinor leaned over and pressed the button on her iPod. A loud crash echoed across the room, followed by a pulsing bass line that sounded more like a bodily function than a series of musical notes.

"What the fuck is that?" I growled, leaping out of my chair.

"Music," Elinor replied, her face somewhat irritated.

"That's not music. It sounds like something crawled into your speaker and died. Don't you have anything decent?"

"This is decent. It's Damon Sputnik's latest album, and it's what I like," Elinor shot back. "It's fun to dance to."

"How the fuck do you dance to this?"

"You just ... you know, dance." Elinor demonstrated in her chair, flailing her arms out to the sides and nodding her head. She looked like a chicken that had just stood in a glob of bubblegum. "It's more fun in a club full of people, though."

"That's not dancing." I floated across the room and stood in front of her desk, extending my hand toward her. "Find me a song by Ghost Symphony, and I'll show you dancing."

Elinor stared at my outstretched hand in a mixture of intrigue and disgust. "You're asking me to dance with you."

"What kind of rock star ghost would I be if I didn't try and educate you on the merits of real music? Seriously, put on 'The Hunt,' by Ghost Symphony."

"But, if I touch you, won't that make the ... weird electrical feeling come back?"

"I can deal with it if you can." In fact, I welcomed it. I don't know what had happened to Elinor when I grazed her skin earlier, but it had shocked my body in a strange and not unpleasant way, sending a pulsating warmth through my usually unfeeling limbs. I wanted to see what happened with prolonged contact.

Plus, I really wanted to watch her shimmy around the room in that figure-hugging skirt.

Elinor stared over at the pile of paperwork, then back to my hand. She sighed. "Fine." She pulled up her iTunes account and searched for the song I suggested. I resisted the urge to sigh with relief when the horrible techno racket disappeared, replaced by the opening notes of a beautiful, rich violin melody. The notes swelled, swirling to fill every corner of the study. After a few bars, the electric guitar came in. Drums began to pound, all snare and toms, powerful and hypnotic.

As Elinor placed her hand on top of mine, her porcelain skin sank into my fingers, and I felt a burst of fire shoot down my arm and through my whole body. It was so powerful and real that I leapt back, my feet sinking a foot below the floor.

Elinor looked equally shocked. Her glasses slid down her cute nose, revealing wide doe-eyes. She stared at her hand. "What is that? It was even more intense than the first time. Is it the same feeling you got when you touched the lock?"

"No. That just felt normal, like touching any old thing. This … electric thing is something completely different. Maybe it's just what happens when ghosts and real people touch." I gestured down at my legs, which were only visible above the knee, the rest of them floating in the floor below.

"It doesn't make sense. I don't know what ghosts are made of, but I don't think touching you is supposed to feel like electricity shooting through my body, is it?"

"I don't know either. Is it painful?" I felt awful that I'd hurt her.

"No." Elinor said this quietly. "It's actually kind of nice. It's intense, though."

"Shall we try again?"

"I don't know, Eric. This might be too much." Her eyes darted nervously between me and the door. She was uncomfortable. I could fix that.

"Come on," I said. "The song's almost over. You'll hardly have to dance with me at all."

I hovered back at her height, and extended my arm again. Elinor looked at it for a long time, her eyes darting between my face and my outstretched fingers. The music swirled around us, cymbals crashing and the melody swooping majestically like a falcon ready to attack. Finally, Elinor reached out with her fingers, and lightly brushed the ends against mine. The hot feeling shot through me again. But this time, I didn't pull away, and neither did she. We held our fingers together, while the strange energy pulsed outward, soaring along my arm and reaching with warm tendrils toward my chest. I felt as if my entire body were glowing.

Elinor moved her hand, so her palm lay flat against mine. It was so odd to see her fingers nestled right inside my body, and even odder to *feel* them there, not as fingers usually feel, but as a hot ball of energy, emanating heat to a steady rhythm.

It took me a few moments to realise the rhythm was Elinor's heartbeat.

I stepped forward, my hand shifting against hers, her fingers dancing inside mine. I pressed my other hand against her back, my palm sinking into her flesh. If I were alive at this moment, I would push Elinor against my body, and relish the warmth of her, the shape of her, against me. But I couldn't do that, so instead I folded myself in closer to her. The front of my jacket brushed against her chest, sending waves of pulsing heat through my whole torso.

"This is amazing," Elinor breathed, her bow-shaped lips parting slightly. I didn't trust myself to reply, so I smiled back at her. I started to sway, pushing my right hip forward, moving the warmth through her leg. Elinor sensed the movement through her skin, and she moved backward, turning her body with me. I stepped again, and again we slid across the floor, our bodies sweeping and dipping with the music.

With my next step, I pushed myself closer, bowing my head slightly, so that my face hovered inches above hers. My eyes locked on those bow lips, ripe and delicious like the first berries of spring. I could feel my spectral cock straining against my boxers, ready for action. *God, I want this woman—*

"I like the music," Elinor said. Her voice wavered. She sounded nervous. I wondered if she was speaking because she sensed what I wanted to do, and she was trying to fill the space between us, to stop me from doing something I couldn't take back.

"Mmmm ..." I shifted my fingers in her hand. The heat flickered, thrumming through my body with a quickened pace. She *was* nervous. *Interesting.*

"I love the ... distortion. The way it crackles right through my whole body," Elinor breathed. "It's almost as if the music is mirroring the sensation when we touch."

"This piece is originally written by the composer Niccolò Paganini, a Greek violinist in the early nineteenth century," I murmured. If she wanted to talk, I could at least impress her. "He was known for making liberal use of the *diabolus in musica*, the devil's tritone, which creates that haunting dissonance you hear in the piece. Of course, Paganini's composition has been sped up and updated, and accompanied by the electric guitar, bass guitar, double bass, and drums, it's quite the feat of modern gothic rock."

"Who is playing the violin in this piece?" Elinor asked, her lips barely moving, struggling to form the words.

"I am, on Isolde. Ghost Symphony is my band."

"Eric …" Elinor's face turned up to me.

I leaned closer, I could practically taste the sweetness of those berry-red lips, feel the warmth of her mouth against mine. The air between us crackled with electricity. Elinor shifted her weight against mine, falling into me as she leaned forward, her lips pursed, waiting.

I brushed my lips against hers. It was like no other kiss I'd ever experienced before. The heat leapt through my body, twisting from my mouth right through my core. I felt as though I'd swallowed a hot coal, and though it burned me deeply, it was the most delicious thing I'd ever tasted. I leaned forward, my weightless body pressed against hers, my lips parting to devour her heat as our bodies hummed with pulsing energy.

Elinor wrenched her body away from me. The spell broke. The heat fled my body, leaving me devoid, weightless and without sensation. It was like being torn from a moving vehicle and sent spiralling into the air. At least, that was how I imagined it felt. I still couldn't remember my accident.

Elinor crashed against the desk, knocking the iPod onto the floor. My violin solo cut off in mid-arpeggio as the player skidded across the rug and crashed into the hearth. The screen flickered and went black.

She was breathing heavily, and she stared at a spot past my shoulder. I noticed that her body was shaking. She gripped the desk with both hands, her knuckles white.

"What's wrong?" I took a step toward her, but she shook her head vigorously, her brown hair fanning about her face. Her glasses had slipped down her nose. She looked like she was about to burst into tears.

"I can't do it," Elinor whispered. "I'm sorry, Eric. I just can't."

I saw tears pooling in the corners of her eyes. I stepped back, holding up my hands in mock surrender. *Was this because of me? Had I really scared her this much?*

"Elinor? What's wrong?"

Elinor looked like she was about to say something, but instead she just shook her head, turned on her heel, and fled the room. Her heels clacked as she raced up the stairs, and the door to my bedroom slammed shut, shuddering through the house.

I hung my head, watching the patterns on the old rug fade in and out of focus. I couldn't believe things had gone so terribly, so quickly. *What had I done wrong?*

*H*e's dead.

I flung myself down on the bed and buried my face in the pillow. The memory of Eric's kiss still burned on my mouth. I closed my eyes, but all I could see in my mind was him leaning in, his lips brushing mine, softly at first, but then deeper. His face wasn't against mine, it was partially inside it. In that moment, he had become part of me, his body falling into mine so that we were one. The feeling was indescribable. My whole body still tingled from the shock of his touch. No kiss had ever felt like *that* before ...

He's dead. He's dead. He just kissed me, and he's dead.

It was as if I was caught in some tragic gothic novel all of my own. And I'd done it to myself. Damn my loneliness and desperation. Eric was infuriating, and cocky, and rich and famous and freakin' gorgeous, and completely out of my league, which made him *exactly* my type. I could feel myself starting to like him, *really* like him. And I liked working with him on the mystery of his death, putting my brain to work on something other than trust agreements. And I *especially* liked the way he looked at me when I made that phone call to the ticketing agency ...

But Eric was dead. I had to remember that. The very reason I was helping him find his murderer instead of doing my actual work was so that he could cross over and get to wherever dead people are supposed to get to, which was not into my arms. Eric was a fucking *ghost*—I couldn't even touch him, not really. *How would we even ...*

My cheeks flushed as my mind conjured up an image of Eric's naked body and flashed it across my vision.

No. I clamped my hands over my eyes. What was I turning into? Who was this girl who went all weak-kneed for a man she'd just met? A man who wasn't even fucking *corporeal?* I can't even touch him, and the worst part of all ... one day, I would have to say goodbye to him. *We don't have a chance to have a life together, because he's already had his life. He's gone, and I can't care about him, or else I'm going to get hurt. I'm going to fade away, just like last time ...*

No. I couldn't think about *that.* Not now. I needed to stay strong. Somehow, I was going to have to go down and face Eric, tell him that I would help him figure out what happened to him, but that was the sum-total of my role in his afterlife. I would apologise if I'd given him the impression that there could be something between us, but from now on he needed to keep his distance from me.

I rolled over and pulled my blanket over my head. *Any minute now ... I'll get up and go downstairs and talk to him. Any minute ... just as soon as I've sorted out these horrible butterflies flitting around in my stomach ...*

"Elinor?" Eric called. I peeked around the edge of my blanket, but I couldn't see him in the room anywhere. His voice sounded muffled. He was respecting the locked door, and staying in the hall. I was grateful he was such a gentleman. I didn't want him to see my eyes all puffy and my hair all rumpled. I had some standards.

"Go away," I cried.

"I'm sorry. It was my fault. I shouldn't have been so forward."

I said nothing. I didn't want to admit that I had no problem with him being forward. I just didn't like him being dead.

"Elinor ..." Eric's voice was pleading. He sounded really distressed. "Do you want to talk about it?"

Yes. I want to very much. "I want you to leave me alone, please."

Eric didn't reply. I listened hard, but couldn't hear anything. It was one of the problems of living with a ghost. You couldn't tell if he'd gone away or not.

After a few minutes of silence, I felt certain Eric had left. I pulled my glasses off and buried my face in my pillow again. This time the tears came, thick and fast, great rivers of sticky, salty water running down my cheeks. I cried for Eric, who had lost his life well before his time, and I cried for Joel, because I hadn't allowed myself to think of him for a few weeks, and I was definitely thinking about him now. And I cried for myself, because I had finally found the perfect man, a man who actually *liked* me, a man who matched me and excited me, and that had seemed so impossible after Joel ... but I couldn't be with him, because he was dead.

Everyone I fall for dies.

ERIC

You idiot. You complete and utter Neanderthal.

Listening to Elinor cry through the door was too much. I had upset her so terribly, and I felt like the world's biggest arsehole. Head pounding with frustration, I left Elinor sobbing on the bed and floated into my mother's room. I wanted to slam the door, but of course, my hand went right through the doorknob as if it weren't there at all. I settled for balling my hands into fists and slamming my head repeatedly against the wall, which wasn't nearly as satisfying as it sounds since my head would go right through the wall and into the cavity behind. The mouse that had made a nest in amongst the insulation stared at me with wide, frightened eyes every time I popped through into his domain.

You idiot, I chastised myself. *You pushed her. You always push. It's what you always do to the people you care about. You push and you push them until they leave you forever. And now she doesn't want anything to do with you.*

Elinor had been nothing but kind to me, visiting the site of my car crash and getting that list of names from the ticket agency.

And instead of thanking her sincerely, I'd pushed myself on her like a … like a … brute. Disgusting.

I couldn't seem to help myself around her. She was so … tantalising. And clever. Ever since my career had taken off, I had been surrounded by women willing to whip their clothes off in a moment in order to be with me. And that was certainly welcome. But there hadn't been a single one who challenged me intellectually. Until her.

She's read Hoffman. How many women have you met who've read Hoffman? The answer was zero.

I had to remember that a girl like Elinor wouldn't get starstruck. She was much too sensible for that. She needed time to know me and trust me before she was ready to go to bed with me. Or whatever the spectral equivalent of sex was.

I had to be patient. That's okay, I could do that. I'll give her some time to calm down. *When she emerges later, I'll apologise, and we'll start over. And I will keep my ghostly urges to myself for now.*

I hope.

One of the downsides of being the only living person in Marshell House was that even though you're upset and the only thing you want to do is hide in your room forever and not face the incredibly sexy ghost downstairs, eventually your stomach starts growling and you need to get something to eat.

It was well past dinnertime when I finally gave in to the rumbling in my stomach and decided to venture downstairs. I splashed some cold water on my face, wiping away the sticky residue of my tears. I took off my corporate clothes and pulled on my largest sweater and most unflattering pair of jeans. I didn't want to give Eric any ideas if I could help it.

Cautiously, I opened the door to my room and peered out. There was no one—dead or otherwise—in the hall. I stepped out, my foot making a loud creak as it fell on the floorboards. I tiptoed across the landing and looked over the balustrade into the entrance hall below. Nothing. No sign of Eric anywhere.

Maybe I could get to the food without having to talk to him. Maybe he was sleeping somewhere. Do ghosts sleep? I hadn't even asked him about that. I had so many questions that still remained unanswered, questions I couldn't ask now, because of the kiss. I leapt down the stairs as quickly as I could, and dashed through the receiving room into the kitchen.

I skidded to a stop. Eric was sitting at the kitchen table. Well, not sitting so much as hovering in a rough approximation of where the chair was located. His black clothing looked so out of place amongst all the flowers and cat ornaments. He gave me a friendly, lopsided grin.

"Hi," I said, waving nervously.

"Hi," he replied, his eyes warm. How did he look so relaxed, so collected? Obviously the incident before hadn't affected him that much, after all. I guess I shouldn't be surprised. He must have hundreds of girls queuing up to be with him. In fact, there were probably hundreds of freaky goth girls out there who would love to get funky with Eric the Ghost. He didn't need me, even when he was dead.

"What are you doing?" I leaned against the door frame, not sure what to do. I hadn't expected to see him sitting there.

"Oh." Eric stared glumly at a cup on the table in front of him. I recognised it as a cup I'd filled with water earlier, when I'd wanted a drink. But I'd only finished half of it. "I wanted to bring you a cup of hot tea, because you were upset, and tea always seems necessary when one is upset."

"That's sweet." My heart skipped a beat. Maybe I was wrong about the freaky goth girls.

"But of course I forgot that I can't just turn the kettle on. I read in a book once about ghosts being able to manipulate temperatures, so I thought I'd try to make tea like that. I've been staring at this water for nearly an hour and nothing has happened."

I eased myself into the chair opposite him. "It was a nice thought, anyway. Which book was that?"

Eric grinned. "*Tales from the Crypt.*"

"I used to read those, too." I grinned. "They had lots of comics in my high school library. I had to hide them from my parents, though. I have an old hardcover copy of *Great Expectations* I bought at a junk shop that I hollowed out so I could hide them inside. To this day my parents still believe Charles Dickens is my favourite author."

"I think we would've got on very well in high school," said Eric.

"Eric, I'm sorry for running away."

"It's okay. I understand."

"I'm not sure that you do."

"I was too forward. I ruined a perfectly pleasant moment."

"No … you didn't ruin anything. But you and I, we can't make something more out of this than what it is. I'm helping you so that the mystery of your death can be solved and your spirit will be able to rest, but I can't … it can't be anything more than that." I grabbed the cup of cold water and gulped it back, just to have something to do with my shaking hand. "I can't get attached to you, knowing that you're going to leave me. You're dead, Eric, and I'm just not strong enough to have a tryst with a dead guy."

As soon as the words were out of my mouth, I wanted to take them back. Eric stared at me, his eyes wide and wounded. He looked miserable. "I understand," he said, softly. "But you should know, if things were different, Elinor, I—"

I shook my head. "Don't do that. If things were different, we never would have met. And I might never have discovered how much I like the violin."

Eric's face brightened. "You enjoyed the song?"

"Very much so, it was beautiful. It actually evoked feeling, unlike the kind of music I usually listen to, which is just kind of a distraction. I hope you'll play me some more later."

"I will." Eric nodded vigorously. I dared a smile. It seemed as if we'd reached a truce of sorts. Although now that I had told him we had no chance together, and he seemed as if he would respect that, I couldn't help but feel a twinge of disappointment. I had been right all along—Eric must not have wanted me that badly, after all. He didn't really feel what I felt. He was just an oversexed rock star who's been cooped up inside with no women for days. I was the best he'd got and he was desperate to get off. It looked as if I had dodged a bullet by avoiding him.

I made myself some dinner—pasta with pesto and a mountain of parmesan cheese, and a few pieces of crusty garlic bread warmed up in that ridiculous gas oven—and took it into the study. Eric hovered over a chair by the window, his feet stretched out in front of him and his arms behind his head.

"Doesn't that get uncomfortable?" I asked him, pointing my fork at his legs.

"I don't have muscles anymore, so they can't get cramped," he said. "Do you want to play a game?"

"Huh?" I balanced my plate on my lap and ran a slice of garlic bread through the sauce, sopping up a glob of cheesy goodness.

Eric pointed to the chessboard set out on the coffee table beside him. It was covered by a thick layer of dust. "I thought we could play," he said.

"How are you going to play against me?"

"Simple. I'll tell you where to move my pieces, and you can put them in place."

"I don't know …" I looked over at my open laptop. I had intended to do some more work, to make up for what I'd missed today. And I was hoping to call Cindy before she went out for the night, get an update on Operation Shag Damon. After meeting Eric, Damon didn't seem like that much of a catch anymore, but he had one important thing going for him: he was alive.

"Come on, Elinor. You're stuck in this house with me for two weeks, at least. You might as well take advantage of my company. It's either play this with me, or spend hours texting your friend who's having all that fun in London without you."

I looked over at the stack of paperwork beside my laptop, and my phone sitting on top, then back at Eric, then back at the papers again. "Okay. Sure."

Eric looked surprised, as if he didn't really expect me to say yes. I got up from my chair, and plopped down in the seat opposite him, placing my bowl on the small table beside me. I stuffed a huge mouthful of pasta into my mouth, and indicated that he should move first.

'No, no," Eric said. "You're white, and white always opens."

'Oh, of course." I frantically tried to remember all the rules. Joel had enjoyed the occasional game, but I'd never really got into chess. I moved the pawn in front of my left rook out two spaces, and waited for Eric to point out his move.

"Knight to C6," he said.

"Huh?"

"I want you to move my knight to C6," Eric repeated.

"Which square is C6?"

Eric explained to me the algebraic notations of the board. I knew then that I was doomed to lose. He sounded like he *really* knew how to play chess.

I was right. Not ten minutes later Eric swooped his bishop across the board and declared checkmate.

"Do you want to play again?" he asked. "I'll go easy on you."

"No you won't." I soaked up the last remnants of cheesy sauce with my garlic bread. "You enjoy winning too much. I would like to know how to play better, though."

"I can teach you some things." Eric waited while I reset the board and poured myself another drink. He started to talk about the different pieces, and explain the simple strategies of the game. I had no idea there was so many layers to chess. It wasn't just random moves like I thought it was; there was some serious strategy involved. I was hooked. By the time I finished my drink, I was ready for another game.

"What was it like growing up here?" I asked, as I moved my bishop out from beside my queen, trying to dominate the centre of the board like Eric had shown me. "I mean, in this house, in this town?"

"It was hard," said Eric. "But what child's life isn't really hard in some way? My mother was a harsh woman. My father was a violinist, too. He toured the world with different philharmonic orchestras, sometimes even performing as a soloist. He played in some remarkable places, but he was gone for months at a time, and he never made much money. What money he did make he spent on tour, on absinthe and women. One day, the orchestra finished a tour in Italy, and he simply never came home. I was twelve. The only thing he left my mother was this house, which was beginning to feel more and more like a prison to me."

"Your mother was smart. I'm blown away by the way she built a fortune from nothing. There are brokers in London who don't have the skill for picking stocks that she does."

"Oh, yes. She had an incredible mind. But it was a mind twisted by jealousy and rage. She hated art, hated anything beautiful, because she could not create herself. She hated music most of all, because it reminded her of my father, and his failure as a provider and a husband. When he disappeared, she banned all music from the house. As if I didn't already resent her enough for driving my father away."

"Is that what happened?"

"I don't know. I've never been able to ask him," Eric said, his tone dark, as if he were somewhere far away. "But it looked like that to me. Whenever he came home, she would scream at him for hours about their lack of money, about his absence, his drinking, his failure. 'Why don't you get a real job?' she'd ask him over and over. But he didn't know how to do anything else. He would take me out to see concerts, or take lessons, and I would play for him, just to see him smile. He looked sad all the time, even when he played his violin. But when I played, his whole face lit up. After he left, my mother directed most of her anger toward me. I was the failure. I didn't study hard enough. I'd never amount to anything. Finally, I couldn't take it any more."

"So you left."

"As soon as I finished school, I took my father's violin—that's Isolde—from the attic, packed all my black clothes into a suitcase, and I left. I went to London, and worked at pubs, playing every-where I could on weekends, trying to make a name for myself. But it wasn't until I met Allan and we started to jam that the concept of using the violin in a traditional rock band occurred to me—"

"Allan?"

"Allan Lachlan. He's the drummer in Ghost Symphony. Allan was a regular at one of the pubs I worked at. His band played rock covers there every Friday and Saturday night. The band sucked, but Allan was amazing. We started talking, and became pretty good mates, so I suggested we have a jam. He thought I was a guitarist. The look on his face when I showed up at his bedsit with my violin case was priceless.

'But then I started playing some of his band's covers, and he just got it. Everything clicked. Suddenly, we had a sound. It was different. It was unique. We found Tom, our first guitarist, and a girl named Belinda on double bass, and we started playing at clubs down in Camden. At first it was just covers—classic pop and rock tunes redefined with our mix of classical and modern instrumen-tation. But soon I got heavily into writing music, and it was those first original songs that caught the attention of our record label. The rest is history." Eric grinned. Talking about his band made his whole face light up. It clearly meant a lot to him.

"What did your mother think of your success? Surely she must've come around to the idea that your music was a viable career."

Eric shook his head. "She never had the chance. She was diag-nosed with Alzheimer's around the time I left for my first European tour. I was still so angry with her—I didn't return to Crookshollow for four years, and by that time, it was too late. Her mind had gone back so far that she couldn't even remember that I'd left in the first place. She still thought I was a boy, and that my father was coming home. She was a very different person, kind and sweet." He laughed bitterly. "We actually grew quite close these last couple of years, as close as anyone can be to someone with dementia."

"I'm so sorry, Eric." I went to pat his hand, and then remembered what happened when I did that. Instead, I awkwardly switched to refilling my glass.

"It's not your fault. Just pray you never have to watch someone die of that horrible disease. It robbed her of her mind—her most prized possession—long before it took her life. I've come back to visit as often as I could get away, but the tour schedule makes it hard. Duncan has been looking after her, arranging all her care and managing the estate. He's been such a great help. He must be pretty upset over her death. Duncan was a friend of my father's from his school days, and he remained close to my mother after my father left."

"He didn't seem too upset when I met him yesterday."

"Oh, well, he had a pretty young thing to show around. Duncan can turn on the charm like a faucet. But enough about me." The darkness faded from Eric's eyes. "What about you, Miss Lawyer? I bet your parents are awful proud of you, with your fancy corporate suits and your impressive title."

I snorted so hard bubbles from my rum and coke went up my nose. I clamped my hand over my mouth.

"I don't think my parents know *how* to be proud," I said. "That would imply they had some kind of capability for emotion."

"Harsh," Eric said. He gestured to the board. "I demand an explanation. And while you're doing it, move my queen to C7."

I leaned over and moved his piece, then took it with my rook. He grinned, pleased that I was learning. "My parents live for achievement. Nothing will ever be good enough for them. I made dux at one of the best public schools in London, and all my dad asked was why I'd missed two questions in the mathematics exam. I was top of my class at law school, and my mother tsked because I didn't get a Rhodes scholarship. I landed my job and they were concerned that the firm wasn't high-profile enough. I could make partner at the firm and it wouldn't matter—my dad would still be pushing me to become a judge."

"That sounds tough."

I shrugged, suddenly feeling self-conscious. "They're not bad people. They always wanted the best for me."

"You are too nice. Don't defend them. Let it all out. After all, who am I going to tell?" Eric grinned wickedly. I took another gulp of my drink, and grinned back.

"You asked for it. I was never allowed to be a kid. There was no Play-Doh in my house. No swing rides or Barbie dolls. The only games I had were educational, and the only outings we went on were to museums or boring operas. I was shuffled from one expensive after-school program to another. At age four, I could speak three languages and recite pi to 100 places. I was so desperate to please them that I never complained, but I was miserable. I had no friends, and I would eat because at least food tasted good and made me feel good. At least it was something I could control. And so I got chubby, and other kids were even more horrible to me, and so I would get sad and eat, and the cycle went on. Everything I loved I had to hide from my parents— chocolate bars I'd gobble down at the bus stop, gothic novels I snuck from the library and hid inside hollowed books, notebooks filled with my drawings stashed under my bed—"

"Your drawings?"

"Yeah." My cheeks flushed an even deeper red. I stared down at the drink in my hand. "I like to draw. I am going to get a tattoo soon, and I'm trying to come up with a drawing that's good enough to be worth the pain of etching it into my flesh. But my parents thought my interest in art was frivolous, so they tried to discourage me. They probably would have got on well with your mother."

"Can you show me your work?"

"I ... I'm not sure."

"Go on." Eric gestured to the board. "It looks as if you're about to win this game. I'm in desperate need for a distraction."

"I've never shown them to anyone before. I don't think—"

"Please?"

I reached over to the desk and grabbed my sketchbook from my bag. I laid it out in front of Eric, and opened to a random page. My face burned as it fell open on a sketch of a dragon. This wasn't an eastern dragon, but a fiery European beast, the kind of dragon that unleashed fury upon unsuspecting Vikings. I'd even drawn some warriors being trampled beneath the dragon's clawed feet. In the background, a village burned.

Eric pursed his lips. He nodded at me, and I turned another page. Here was a realistic rendering of a raven I'd copied from a Victorian wildlife engraving. A single, beady eye stared up at us. I gulped. I'd spent hours on that drawing.

"The head's a bit crooked," I croaked out, scrambling to turn the page. "And the eye isn't right."

"No," Eric said. "It's perfect. These are amazing, Elinor. You have a rare gift." He studied the next drawing, a girl in a flowing gothic dress staring out of a window with a haunted expression on her face.

"They're … they're okay. I've never had any training or anything."

"Which one are you getting as a tattoo?"

"I can't decide. I like a lot of them, but nothing has jumped out as being perfect yet."

"It will. Mine came to me in a dream. I saw the image in my mind and ran down to the parlour to get someone to render it as close as possible. I was lucky my artist was so patient, because I made her redraw it eight times before we got to the actual tattooing part. It was worth every agonising hour in that chair."

"You have a tattoo?"

"Wouldn't you like to know." Eric gave me that mischievous, heart-melting grin.

We talked for hours, Eric shared more details about his crazy life as a touring musician, and after I finished a couple more drinks, I started to share more about mine. We played several games, and I even won a couple. Every time Eric smiled at me, and he smiled a lot—a deep, delicious smile—my whole body shuddered with excitement. Despite my resolve, I was still attracted to him. And what was worse, I was starting to fall for him.

It wasn't until I dragged myself to bed in the early hours of the morning, my stomach fluttering and my mind swimming with visions of Eric's smile, that I realised I had completely forgotten to call Cindy.

slept late the next morning. The sun was high in the sky, streaming through the flowered curtains that obscured the round stained-glass window, and creating a bright stripe across the bedspread. I sat up, rubbed the sleep out of my eyes, and grabbed my phone. The message icon was lit up. Cindy had sent me a message at some point in the early hours of the morning. I'd slept right through the alert. The time was 9:38 on a Sunday morning, Cindy was probably only just crashing into bed.

WHATUP BITCH? INTERESTING NIGHT. CALL ME TODAY AND I'LL FILL YOU IN.

I sent her back a smiley face and dropped my phone on top of my stack of books, sinking back into the pillows with a smile on my face. *That makes two of us,* I thought, thinking of my evening with Eric. It had been so much fun, just drinking and playing chess and talking about our lives. Eric was a good teacher, I was actually a somewhat decent player by the end of the evening. I even won the last game of the evening, which had Eric both grinning with pride and calling for a rematch.

The more I talked to Eric, the easier I found it to ignore the fluttering in my stomach. He wasn't just some hot ghost, he was actually a pretty interesting person. And he'd had a hard childhood filled with parental disappointment, which I could definitely relate to. I could picture young Eric in my mind, his hair a mess of black curls and his gaze intense as he stood alone in the music suite at the tiny Crookshollow school, playing the violin for hours as if his life depended on every note. If our paths had crossed before now, I felt certain we'd have been friends.

See? Devil's Advocate Elinor gloated. *You just needed to get over your attraction to Eric. That was what was causing all your conflicting feelings. Now that you're over it, and the two of you are just friends, you can focus on helping him solve the mystery of his death.*

Speaking of which … the idiotic girl at the London theatre should have gotten back to me with the list of names by now. I flung back the sheets and bounced out of bed. My hand poised over my "lawyer" clothes—beige and brown skirts and jackets designed to help me fit in at my conservative law firm, clothes I was now so used to wearing that I barely even owned anything else. But today was different. Today I felt … vibrant. I pulled on a pair of jeans, and a black shirt that tied with a red ribbon that I particularly liked. I stood in the bathroom and admired myself in the mirror, swinging my hips as I brushed out my brown hair and slid my glasses up my nose. The red in the shirt made my green eyes sparkle. Humming to myself, I dabbed on my usual makeup, and headed downstairs.

Eric was in the kitchen, hovering over a chair and staring at the same coffee cup filled with water again. "Any luck so far?" I asked him.

"I saw a bubble appear about an hour ago," he replied, not looking up.

I took the cup from him and dipped my finger inside. "It's still cold," I said. He sighed. I went over to fill up the kettle.

"You look gorgeous," Eric growled. He wafted across the kitchen and came to stand behind me. "I miss the tight little skirt, though."

My heart thudded against my chest. He wasn't even touching me, but I could feel that same hot energy arcing through the air between us. *I thought I was over this.*

"Eric, I said we can't do that." My words came out harsher than I intended. A flicker of something crossed Eric's face. Anger? Hurt? I couldn't be sure. But in a moment it was gone, and Eric nodded and stepped away from me.

"That's better. Now, if you let me eat my breakfast, we can get to work on your case."

Eric's eyes glinted. "Don't you have to work today?"

"I'll work this afternoon. You can even help me. It will go much quicker if you talk me through some of your mother's files."

"I can do that. In the meantime, we need to get that list of names from my manager," said Eric. "Poor Heather. She must be devastated. She's worked for me ever since my first record came out."

The kettle boiled. I poured myself a cup of tea, set down a bowl of cereal, and chopped some banana on top. Eric watched me intensely as I crunched away.

"Don't look at me like that." I frowned at him as he leaned forward to peer at the contents of my spoon. "You're making me feel all self-conscious."

"Sorry, I can't help it. You're cute, and I miss food." Eric's lips parted slightly as he watched me scoop up the last of my cereal.

"Hey, look on the bright side," I said, pushing the spoonful of milk-soaked kernels into my mouth. "At least you're stuck with your killer body for all eternity. You won't ever get fat like me."

"Don't say shit like that."

"Like what?"

"That you're fat. I don't want to hear it. It's self-deprecating and untrue and beneath you. You are clever and funny and hot as fuck, so don't spend a moment of your life thinking that bullshit even matters, because life is too precious to waste feeling sorry for yourself." Eric's eyes burned into mine. "Take it from someone who knows."

"I ..." My face burned. I didn't know what to say. I was torn between feeling giddy over the "hot as fuck" comment, and wanting to argue with him. "I didn't mean ... it's just that I *am* overweight. It's a fact. It can't be denied. I can't seem to get it together to lose the weight. And every time I'm passed over for promotion, or one of my skinny friends gets the guy and not me, I can't help but think it's because of how I look. I feel the same way now that I did in high school—I'm just the hippo."

"Elinor ..." Eric leaned across the table. "You are so much more than what you realise. And if it's the last thing I do before I depart this earth, I'm going to make you believe it."

He placed his hand over mine. The energy leapt up my arm, pushing its warmth through my body. With his other hand, Eric reached across to the cup of water, and wrapped his hand around the ceramic mug. He lifted the mug off the table.

"Argh!" I cried out. "Eric, you did it!"

"No, I didn't. You did it, Elinor. It's all you."

"Eric, I—" I stared into his eyes, losing myself in those intense orbs. *I can't do this. I can't go through what I went through with Joel again. I'm not strong enough.*

I pulled my hand away, severing the connection between us. The warmth left my body, leaving my skin tingling. The mug dropped through Eric's hand and crashed against the table, spilling the water across the surface. I grabbed the stack of papers I'd left there before the water could ruin them.

"I'm sorry!" I yelled, leaping away from the table. I lowered my head to avoid Eric's gaze.

"It's not your fault. Elinor, don't go—"

I fled into the study. I wanted to shut the door, but there didn't seem like much point. I hoped Eric got the message that I needed to be alone for a few minutes, so I could calm down. I slumped in my chair and placed the stack of papers beside me. On the top was the local newspaper, the front page headline alerting me to Eric's funeral to be held the following weekend. The article—accompanied by a picture of Eric on stage, his wild hair plastered to his face as he ran his bow across his violin so fast his fingers were a blur—covered half of the page. I flipped the paper over so I wouldn't have to see it.

I turned on my laptop. In my inbox was an email labelled NAMES FOR ERIC!!!!!!!!<3 I smiled at the girl's enthusiasm as I downloaded the file. Eric wafted in. "We should talk about this—" he begged.

I held up my hand. "I can't. I know you mean no harm, Eric, but please don't touch me again."

"But, Elinor—"

I shook my head, indicating that the conversation was over. I didn't want to think about it right now. "What's your manager's number?"

Eric called out the number, and I dialled it. I put my phone on speaker and set it down on the table, so he could hear.

"Phoenix Management. This is Heather," a crisp voice answered. She sounded young. And blonde. And like she would look fantastic in a leather corset. It was funny how you could tell these things over the phone. I thought back to Eric's comment about her being devastated, and wondered if they'd been lovers. A white-hot rage pulsed through my body as I imagined blonde, corseted Heather rolling around with Eric on a red-satin bed.

Oh yes, taunted Devil's-Advocate-Elinor. *You and Eric are* totally *just friends.*

"Hello, Heather, this is Elinor Baxter." I poured all of my skill into keeping my voice syrupy sweet. "I'm part of an ongoing investigation into Eric Marshell's death, and I understand you've been his manager for most of his career. I was wondering if—"

"Hang on a second," Heather said briskly. There was some scuffling in the background, and the sound of a door slamming shut. A few moments later Heather was back. "Sorry. It's a bit crazy around here. We've got one of those open-plan offices, and I hate it. Everyone is all up in your shit. Sooo ... you're investigating Eric's death. Are you a cop?"

"A lawyer, actually. I'm with—"

"Do you think Eric's death might've been foul play?" Heather whispered into the phone.

I paused. I didn't want to start telling people that before we had any proof, but I also knew from yesterday's call it was better to give some intrigue if you wanted cooperation without questions. I decided to opt for the vague intrigue. "It's starting to look that way, I'm sorry to have to say it. If you could—"

"You're sorry?" She laughed. "Good riddance, as far as I'm concerned."

I glanced over at Eric, who could barely conceal his shock. I read her tone instantly. Grinning despite myself, I pressed her. "Oh, what makes you say that?"

"Have you ever met him?" Heather asked.

"Oh, yes," I glanced across the room at Eric, who was staring at the floor, looking very nervous. "I've had the pleasure."

"This conversation is off the record, right? I'm not incriminating myself, am I?"

Eric made a slicing motion with his hand across his neck. Grinning, I shook my head. He could suffer. It would get him back for scaring me twice yesterday and touching my hand at breakfast. "Oh, no. We have no reason to suspect you of anything. In fact, it would be useful for the investigation to tell us anything you can about Eric. It might help us to piece together what happened."

"Very well. I've been his tour manager and press secretary for eight years. For eight years, I have done his laundry and brought him very specific brands of tonic water and hunted down a certain type of cologne. If he wants cereal at 2 in the morning, or vodka at 3 in the afternoon, I'm the one who rushes to the store. I spend weeks organising every detail of a show or an appearance, and he shows up twenty minutes late and changes everything, and everyone listens to him because he's the *artiste.* I have had to stand back and smile and do whatever he wants, or I can kiss my job goodbye.

'And then, foolishly, I start thinking, 'If I'm taking all these orders from this guy, I might as well be getting something out of it.' So I start trying to sleep with him, because hello, he's gorgeous, even if all his music is just this whiny emo bullshit. But he is too busy being Mr. Brooding Gothic Artiste to even notice me with my tits hanging out. All gloomy and melancholy, locking himself in his suite after shows, playing sad music into all hours of the night. And who is the one dealing with the hotel guests complaining about violin concertos at 4am? And for all of this, for *everything* I've put up with, does Eric Bloody Marshell leave me any part of the fortune I helped him amass in the will? No, of course not. It's all going to some bloody music charity. Eric Marshell couldn't think of anyone but himself."

'Oh, I couldn't agree more," I said, barely able to conceal the laughter that threatened to erupt from me at any moment. "Listen, about these files—"

'Just tell me what you need. I'm here to serve His Royal Gothness, even in death."

'We need to know if Eric had any fans who might've threatened him. I understand you keep a record of any disturbing correspondence."

'Yeah, we always keep the weird stuff, and Eric got a lot of weird stuff. What can I say? Goths are strange. My hip-hop clients never got vials of blood or bleached cat skulls."

'Ew." I wrinkled my nose. People really were weird.

'Yep. Yet another wonderful part of my job, opening Eric's fan mail. I'll happily send you all the letters we have on file. But don't you need a subpoena or something?"

'That's only if you refuse to give them to me, and it goes on public record." I was proud of the incredible amount of bullshit I was able to spout off without flinching. "Phoenix Management would look pretty bad if they refused to hand over vital evidence that could help solve the murder of one of their most high-profile clients."

"True." Heather paused. "Give me an email address and I'll send over a list. I warn you, though, it's a pretty long list. Eric sure attracted the crazies."

I thanked her and hung up. One look at Eric's face and I burst out laughing. "Stop!" he cried. "It's not funny."

"You said she would be devastated, and instead she's practically doing a jig," I gasped between snickers. "She *really* hates your guts, Your Royal *Gothness*."

Eric cringed. "Please try and forget you heard that name. Heather's in PR. She's good at hiding things. You don't think she could be the one who ran me off the road?"

"Unlikely. You don't go around murdering clients just because they make your life difficult. Otherwise, there'd be more lawyers in jail than out of it. Besides, she wouldn't need a ticket to your show, would she? Let's wait and see what this list looks like."

A few minutes later, an email from Phoenix Management popped up in my inbox. I downloaded the attached list—a spreadsheet over twenty pages long that consisted of names, addresses, numbers, email addresses and dates and times of attempted communications with Eric. Another file contained the contents of numerous letters and emails, as well as photographs of some rather interesting "gifts" Eric had been sent. That file I printed, picking through the correspondence as it came off the printer.

"Wow." I grinned, holding up an image of a giant rubber dildo wrapped in red ribbon. "Clearly I'm in the wrong line of work."

"This is insane. I've never seen half this stuff before." Eric frowned as I held up an image. "What is *that?*"

"I think that's a vial of blood wrapped in a ribbon of human hair," I read from the note Heather had scrawled at the bottom. "Courtesy of one Helen Manning of Chatham."

"I have no words." Eric's eyes darted over the spreadsheet. "I'm sorry, Elinor. I had no idea there were this many. It's going to take you hours to cross-reference these lists."

"Wrong." I pulled up a website, typed in my email address, uploaded both the list from the ticket agency and Heather's spreadsheet into the form, and clicked CROSS-REFERENCE. A few moments later, my inbox dinged. I opened up an email containing a file from the cross-reference engine and an advert for their premium, ad-free service.

"I am in awe." Eric bowed before me.

"The wonders of technology," I said, as I opened the file. "You're still stuck in the dark ages, Your Royal Gothness."

"Use that name one more time and the consequences will be swift and severe."

I grinned as I scanned the results of the email. According to the cross-reference, three names appeared on both lists: Adam Smith, Claude Beaulieu, and Helen Manning of the blood vial fame.

"Now all we have to do is figure out which of these three people only has half a ticket left, and who could have been in the vicinity of Crookshollow after the show that night, and we've got your potential killer."

"Well …" Eric shrugged. "Go on. I'm not exactly any help here, Elinor. It's all you."

The first thing I did was check social media. There were too many Adam Smiths to locate, but I found Claude pretty easily. Luckily, he kept his profile public, and I scanned through more than two hundred shots of him standing in the mosh pit at Eric's concert, grinning awkwardly up at his phone balanced on a selfie stick, before I found what I was looking for: Claude's post-concert scrapbook display—some blood-red paper, a few of the least blurry selfies, a mega close-up of Eric's sweat-drenched face, and his ticket, completely intact.

"We can cross Claude off the list," I said, pointing at the ticket.

Eric grinned. "You're amazing. Have I ever mentioned that?"

"Several times." The way he said that made me wish he'd mention it a few more times. My chest swelled with pride. Inside, I was grinning from ear to ear, but I had to maintain my composure, so I didn't give Eric any ideas. "Actually, could you stop? It's a bit embarrassing."

"Do you really want me to stop?"

No," I answered, and we both laughed.

"How do we track the others down?"

"This Adam Smith is going to be difficult, because his name's so common. And Helen has set all her social media accounts to private. But I'm going to check your fan forums next, and see if I can find some discussion about your last show. Maybe I can identify the final two by their posts and narrow our choice down to one."

Three hours of my life were sucked away exploring the official Ghost Symphony fan forum, an online portal off Eric's main website where fans of his work went to discuss every facet of the band's existence. It was a cesspool of crazy, populated by people analysing the lyrics to Ghost Symphony songs with the degree of fervour usually reserved for academic institutions. Others planned the outfits they would be wearing when they married Eric or Allan or one of the other band members, right down to the brand of their underthings. People discussed sightings of Eric like he was the second coming, and compared notes on concerts and events as though they were historical events on par with The Battle of Waterloo.

"Have you ever read this stuff?" I asked Eric, as I read out passages of particularly cringeworthy poetry inspired by his music.

"They say you should never google yourself," Eric replied. "And the same goes for reading what fans say about you on internet forums. If the rest of it is as bad as that poem you just read, I think I made a wise choice."

There was an entire section devoted to reviews and meetups at concerts, and that was where I concentrated my search. Someone named ASmith was a moderator on this board. I read through ASmith's posts; he had attended the concert in London and had even organised a board meetup after the show. Another thread showed a gaggle of grinning geeky and gothy types hanging out at a Camden bar. The discussion disclosed that the meetup had gone on into the early hours of the morning.

If ASmith was definitely Adam Smith—which seemed likely—and the forum information wasn't doctored to provide an alibi—possible, but unlikely—I could safely cross him off my list as a suspect. That left only one possible option. Helen Manning.

I went back to Heather's files and pulled up all the correspondence Helen had sent Eric. It started off innocently enough. She sent him a few fawning letters thanking him for his songs, and describing how they got her through some difficult times. She talked about being a loner, and not having any friends, and how kids at her school were mean to her. She must be young, fifteen or sixteen at most. The letters were dated two years previously.

Dear Eric,

I wish you would write back, just once. I am not doing so great here and I just need someone to tell me it's going to be okay. I am reading your unofficial biography right now, about that time you played a Paganini piece at your school recital, and that awful kid put superglue on your bow so that your hand stuck to it? Well, my day has been like that. Worse, in fact.

I was in art class, drawing a poster for my music project, Satanic Stardust. It was of a witch with flowing red hair. She's naked and her body is covered with tattoos. She's kneeling beside a pool in the full moon, and holding the moon in her hands. She wears a crown of stars, and a pentagram on her forehead. I was listening to your song Circe, and the image just came to me.

Anyway, this bitchy girl Stacey saw my drawing and started calling me a Satanist. Soon everyone in the room was pointing at me and laughing and yelling out "witch!" and "Satan!" Later, when I went to my locker, someone had sprayed a crude drawing of a fat girl riding a broomstick. The marker is permanent. It won't come off.

I hate them so much. I'm listening to your song, Bewitching right now, and it makes me think that as long as you are in the world, then there has to be a place for me, too. But it's getting harder to hold on to that.

Please write back.

Love, Helen

Dear Eric,

Contemplating suicide again tonight. I'm listening to Silence, *and it makes me wonder how blissful death could be. Would it be like white noise, just an eternity of sweet nothingness? That would be preferable to this hell I'm living every single day. I'd rather be nothing than the fat bitch everyone hates.*

Today, Stacey held my head into a toilet, and another girl flushed it. They tore off my Ghost Symphony violin necklace and flushed that, too. I had to go to class soaked with water and everyone knew why.

Please write back. I really need to hear from you.

Yours in silence, Helen

"Sad," I whispered.

"Yeah." Eric looked at me strangely. "I remember feeling like that."

"So do I." I'd never had my head flushed. The girls at my prestigious public school were way too concerned about breaking a nail to pull something like that. But I remember how they made me feel so small and pathetic, how they would look at me with such disdain, how they'd call me names like Hippo and Flabby, and how I wished I could be anyone but myself. I remembered dark thoughts and wishing for oblivion, because the idea of death seemed preferable to their continuing ridicule. I knew exactly what this Helen was going through. And from the sounds of it, so did Eric.

"She sounds sweet," Eric said. He looked tired, his face drawn in a sad expression. "This is the problem with being too famous. In the early days, I answered all my mail. I occasionally got letters like this, and I could say something at least mildly encouraging in return. But when we got the record deal, they gave me Heather, and it was just too easy to have her answer my mail. If I'd just sent her a letter, maybe ..."

"Don't do that," I said. "Remember, this sweet little girl could have murdered you in cold blood. There's a ton more letters here to go through."

I started reading the next letter, dated January last year.

Dear Eric,

I hate you. I hope you die. In fact, to make sure you do, I'm going to drive down to Devon (I've got my license now, not that you care), and find your house. I'm going to climb in a window when you're out, and hide under your bed. And when you get home and take off all your clothes and climb into bed, I'm going to jump out, and stab you. And then I'm going to fuck the holes I've just stabbed with my fingers. And you'll still be alive, but you'll be in agony, and you'll see my face and know that I did this to you because you didn't love me. And then I'll drag my knife across your throat, and let all your blood flow out.

I hate you!

Helen

Yikes! That was probably the letter that put her on Heather's watch list. I turned the page.

Dear Eric,

I'm sorry for my last letter. I hope you didn't read it. You have to understand that it wasn't me. It's like some demon takes over my body, and I just want to scream and yell and break shit, but I can't do that because I have to be good, so I hurt myself. And I hurt you, because you are like an extension of myself. You are the me I wish I was, wish I could be.

Please, please, please write back.

Love, Helen

The rest of the letters were like that. A mess of emotions, flipping from ecstatic to hateful to sad, often in the space of a couple of paragraphs. Helen talked about hurting herself, about contemplating suicide. But she also talked about leaving high school to study film at university, about making some friends and even finding a boyfriend. Then the boyfriend dumped her, and she'd started sending Eric gifts. First, it was a black teddy bear with a blood-red ribbon. Next, it was a beautiful purple-black crystal in a black leather bag. Heather said it reminded her of his eyes. I had to admit that she was right. Then, finally, she'd sent that vial of blood. That had been earlier this year, and Eric hadn't heard from her since.

"So we know she's a bit unstable," I said. "We're going to have to think carefully about how we handle this."

"Should you not go to the police?" Eric asked. "I mean, this girl sounds nuts."

"What happened to her being *sweet?*"

Eric jabbed his finger at the photograph of the blood vial. "That shit happened, is what."

"We can't go to the police yet. We have no real evidence. Remember that as far as the police are concerned, you were done in by a random hit-and-run. Proving pre-meditated murder is an entirely different story, and I can't do that with a ticket stub. All we know for certain is that Helen sent you some vaguely threatening letters—among many other people—and she happened to be at your concert."

"We have more than that," Eric said. He was staring down at the sheet of contact details Heather had sent me.

"What?"

"Look at her phone number."

I did. There was something about it that seemed vaguely familiar.

"The ticket," Eric said.

I picked it up and held it up to the light. He was right. The number scrawled across the top of the ticket stub was Helen Manning's. That could not be a coincidence. She had been in the car that had run Eric off the road.

We had found his murderer.

ERIC

 y murderer.

Now that I knew the person in the car that ran me off the road had also been at the concert, there was no question in my mind—my death was cold-blooded, pre-meditated murder. The realisation hit me like the opening riff of a Slayer song. I felt as though the wind had been knocked out of me, and there wasn't even any wind to knock out anymore.

Elinor wanted to figure out a plan of action immediately, but I told her to do some of her actual work. She gave me a worried look, but let me go. I think she understood I needed to be alone. I floated up the stairs to my old bedroom, and through the locked closet door. As a boy, I often hid in the darkness of the closet, away from my mother and father's arguments. I'd pretend to be an archaeologist lost in a cave, or a vampire awakening in my tomb.

I folded my legs and hovered in the stack of boxes that now occupied my special hiding spot. My fingers traced the drawings I'd made on the wallpaper—grinning skulls peeking out from the centre of flowers, black cats swiping at the fleurs-de-lis, little stick men dancing over the ivy. I couldn't feel them, of course, but I could see them, memories of a sad childhood, the fuel that later became the music my murderer had so adored.

My murderer.

This girl had followed me from the concert, and driven me off the road. She had loved my music, and she'd killed me, taken my life away, robbed me of any chance to have a future, of any chance to be with—

I buried my head in my hands, relieved to feel their solidness against my skin. My cheeks felt wet, and it was then I realised I was crying.

It was a strange realisation, not just because I didn't realise ghosts could cry. Eric Marshell didn't cry. I hadn't cried since I was a little boy. These tears felt odd; heavy and bitter against my non-existent skin. I wasn't sad. I was angry. I'd been robbed of the most precious gift I had, and I could never have back what was taken.

Time passed in a vacuum. I'm not certain how long I sat in that closet, hovering like a snake charmer and mourning my life. Some hours later, I heard Elinor on the staircase, calling my name. I floated into the wall and looked out at her.

"Eric, I know you're upset," she called, looking all around the landing. She couldn't see me. "I just wanted to see if I could help."

You can't help me, not unless you can find a way to bring me back from the dead.

Her eyes were red. She looked as if she'd been crying, too. Had she been crying for me? For some reason that made me even more angry. Elinor gulped, and shuffled back and forth on her feet.

"I know why you're upset," Elinor began, staring at a spot on the wall two feet to my right.

Oh, yeah? I bit back the urge to shout at her. *You've never been dead. How could you possibly know?*

"You feel as though this whole thing is pretty unfair. If you'd just been able to reach out to this girl, you might have been able to save her, and yourself. But don't you see? You *did* save her. Your music carried her through years of hell. It wasn't you who twisted her into this horrible person, Eric. She did that herself. We've all gone through terrible things. We all have that darkness that wells up from within. But we ..." She gulped again. "We don't murder people. You channelled your darkness into your music. You created songs that spoke to thousands of people about heartache and loss and made them feel whole again. You gave the world a wonderful legacy."

That was actually a pretty insightful comment. But it didn't help my foul mood. I stayed where I was. Elinor sighed, then walked slowly back down the stairs. I heard the door to the office click closed, and godawful techno music thudded from within.

I slunk back into the wall, into the safety of my closet. The darkness enveloped me, as it had as a child. But now I wasn't *in* the darkness, I was a part of it, empty and cold. For the first time since I had been a ghost, I wished not for life, but for oblivion to swallow me up, to take away this gnawing, crushing mixture of guilt and rage. The guilt was over the fact I hadn't reached out to Helen or any of my other fans who'd needed me, and the rage was for the life she had stolen from me, the life I could have had with Elinor. But it was too late.

I tried to talk to Eric on the stairs, but he wasn't answering. I couldn't blame him. Giving his potential murderer a name made the whole thing more real, more immediate. He'd been robbed of his life by this girl. He needed some time to digest that.

I went back to the study, and tried to get some work done. But my eyes kept falling on the stack of letters, on that creepy image of the blood vial. Helen Manning. How would we find her? How would we get her to confess what she did, or find enough evidence to put forward a case to the police? My mind kept turning over ideas and schemes, but although any of them would've made a great movie plot, each was too ridiculous, too farcical to actually work in real life.

My phone buzzed. It was a text from Cindy. WHERE U AT, BITCH? I realised I hadn't even called her about Damon. I'd been so distracted with Eric's ... Ericness, that I'd completely forgotten about my previous crush. But that was silly, because Damon still had that one advantage over Eric: he was alive.

I turned down my music and clicked CALL. Cindy picked up on the second ring. "Well, look who finally bothered to call."

"Hey, Cindy."

"Well, well, so you are still alive."

Her comment made me think of Eric, and I snorted bitterly. But Cindy, of course, didn't notice. "I thought maybe you'd shacked up with someone down in hicksville and that was why you went AWOL." Her voice sounded hopeful.

I was glad Cindy couldn't see my face colouring as I thought of Eric and our dance. That was way too complicated to explain. "No, nothing as exciting as that. It's just been crazy here. There's a ton of work to do. But I don't want to talk about work. Tell me all about the weekend."

"Oh, girl, it's been CAH-RAZY. Right, so I got to talking to Damon at the party on Friday. He's actually pretty cool, he's into all sorts of crazy stuff."

"Oh, yeah?" A tiny flicker of jealousy snaked across my stomach. Since when was Cindy hanging out with Damon? All we'd ever done was admire him from afar. Suddenly I wasn't there, and she was talking to him? How had things progressed so fast?

"He is experimenting growing his own tobacco, and he flies those little planes that look like they're made of cardboard. And I told him all about you and he thinks you sound great. Anyway, so he invited me to the VIP room after the show on Saturday, and since you weren't there I took Tanya and my friend Angela from work—"

Cindy spent the next hour recounting every detail of their crazy evening partying with Damon Sputnik and his friends, a bottomless tab of champagne and party pills. Damon had his driver take their limousine through the drive-thru, and it got stuck on the kerb and they had to get another driver to tow them out. My stomach twisted with envy. I wanted so badly to be at that party and in that limousine. If Clyde hadn't sent me to Crookshollow, I would've been the one partying it up with Damon Sputnik.

But then you never would have met Eric, Devil's-Advocate Elinor raged.

Exactly! I shot back at myself. *I wouldn't have met Eric, and felt so confused about everything.*

The doorbell rang, startling me out of my funk. "Cindy, I've got to go. There's someone at the door."

"Sure thing, sweetie. Call me later in the week."

"Are you still going to try and come up here next weekend?"

"Yeah, sure. I'll try." The phone clicked off. I actually felt relieved. I didn't want to hear anything else about Cindy's weekend with Damon. It made my chest feel tight, and I couldn't explain why.

I threw my phone down on the desk and got up to answer the door.

"Duncan?" I was surprised to see the elderly man on the porch. He grinned back at me from behind a large filing box.

"Hello, Ms. Baxter. How is the work going?" he asked, shifting the box from on arm to the other.

"Fine. What are you doing here? Did we have an appointment?"

"Oh, no. I was just in the neighbourhood, and thought I'd drop in to give you these files and see how you were getting on, maybe have a cup of tea." He smiled. "Relax, Elinor. That's a perfectly normal thing for people outside of London to do. I used to stop by on Alice all the time. We had our tea on the back porch."

"I really do have to get back to work—"

"I'll just stay for fifteen minutes. I promise I'll leave right after I've drained my cup. There's actually some things I need to discuss with you."

"Oh, well, sure. Come on in. I'll boil the kettle." I held the door open, and Duncan bustled inside. He headed straight into the kitchen, which struck me as odd at first. But then I remembered that he looked after Ms. Marshell while she was ill, he might feel pretty comfortable in the house. Duncan pulled his round body into one of the stools, and I filled the kettle with water and placed it on the burner.

"Alice loved tea," he said, his voice fading into wistfulness. "I used to make her at least ten cups a day."

"I'm sorry for your loss. I know you were close with the family."

Duncan closed his eyes. "We were. Alice was a very dear friend. She was heartbroken when George left her, and then Eric moving to London so soon after. It was just so unexpected. I don't think she ever really recovered."

"Eric came back and visited her, though, didn't he?"

"Only after her dementia had progressed to such a state she wasn't herself anymore," Duncan said. "He could be quite selfish, that boy. And after everything she'd done for him."

The kettle screamed. I made the tea, and handed Duncan his cup. "Should we go out onto the back porch?"

Duncan's face lit up. "After you, ma'am."

I hadn't ventured out into the back garden yet; I'd only looked down on it from my window. The porch was a lovely space, or at least it would have been when it was being cared for. A small iron table and two chairs sat under the eaves, giving a perfect view of the wild, overgrown garden beyond. Dead leaves and dirt had collected in the corners, and cobwebs were strung between the columns. Wisteria vines curled around the arches and snaked across the underside of the roof, slowly commencing their inevitable march to consume the whole house.

"I'm sorry," I said, setting down my tea on the table and slumping into the uncomfortable metal chair. "I didn't think to buy any biscuits. Or scones. This looks like the perfect porch for scones."

"Ah," Duncan lifted the top off the filing box. Inside was a small box bearing the insignia *Bewitching Bites*. He lifted the lid and revealed four perfectly-formed cupcakes, each with a different coloured icing. My mouth watered when I saw each was topped with chocolate curls or tiny marshmallows.

"You can come for tea anytime, Duncan." I reached for a cupcake.

"I'll bring some scones next time," he promised, sipping his tea.

"So, what did you want to talk to me about?"

"Um, well, as the executor of the will, I guess I just want to know what my role is. I was just wondering how far along you've gotten with Alice's accounts?"

"Not far. It's a big job. Alice was a very clever woman. She has a lot of different accounts and investments. Money is flying everywhere. It's a huge job to track it all. I've barely scratched the surface. In fact, I'm not sure I'm going to be able to get everything done in two weeks."

"Is that so? How closely do you need to go through everything? Surely the banking software is taking care of most of your work?"

"At the moment, my task is really to go through everything, sort it, and figure out exactly what Alice Marshell's estate actually owns. If I see anything fishy, I would send the papers along to our forensic accountant."

"Oh." Duncan shifted in his seat. "Is there something fishy?"

"Not so far. Why? Do you know something I don't?" I grinned at him, but he looked uncomfortable.

"No, not at all. Just making chitchat, getting some mileage out of my allotted fifteen minutes." Duncan took a bite out of his cupcake. Crumbs sprayed down the front of his shirt as he spoke. "I've been organising Alice's accounts for the last five years. I was an accountant before I retired, you know."

"I didn't know that."

Duncan tapped the box with his foot. "I've brought you all her records and tax filings. Everything in there is completely up-to-date. I figured it might be easier for you to work off than the online system. It can take some time to get your head around how it works."

"Thank you, that's very kind. You're right, it will be much easier."

"Good, I'm glad to help." Duncan took another bite, glancing around the porch and garden. "This house is really something, isn't it?"

"It's not really my taste, but it's a pretty amazing house. Was that all you wanted to talk to me about?" I cringed at my tone. Duncan was a nice old man who'd just brought me cake. I hadn't meant to sound as though I was pushing him out the door.

"Oh … I'm sorry." It took Duncan a few moments to come back from his memories. "I didn't mean to take up your time. I know you're busy. I just—"

"I apologise," I said quickly, smiling across at him. "I didn't mean to sound so abrupt. Lawyers are trained to get down to business as soon as possible. Our clients are being charged by the hour, after all."

"Of course that's perfectly understandable. I know you need to get back to work. I just wanted to run over some of the details for the funeral—"

"What funeral?"

"For Alice and Eric. I'm responsible for the arrangements for both of them, and with Eric being who he is, you can imagine the kind of turnout we're expecting. But of course I've got my own business to attend to, and I won't be able to be around every day. So I'm going to need you to let in a few people during the week, gardeners and caterers and such. I've typed up a list for you here." Duncan patted the top of the filing box. "The work will mostly be outside, so there should be minimal disruption throughout the week, although obviously Friday and Saturday are going to be quite hectic—"

"Excuse me? The funeral is going to be *here?* At the *house?"*

"Didn't your office tell you?" Duncan looked confused. "I was very clear on the phone about it."

"No, they didn't." *Damn you, Clyde.* He knew I'd never have agreed to go to Crookshollow if there was a funeral in the house. So instead he'd just neglected to tell me about it. Classy.

"Oh, well." Duncan shrugged. "I trust that won't be a problem. It just makes the most logistical sense. We can host 400 people in the garden, and as both Alice and Eric will be interred in the family mausoleum—"

I held up my hands. "It's fine. It's fine. Just let me know if there's anything you need."

"As I was saying, the caterers will be here on Thursday to inspect the facilities. They'll need to use the kitchen for most of the day Saturday. The gardeners will arrive tomorrow to start work on the garden. They shouldn't need to come into the house, unless they want to use the facilities, but don't let them out of your sight if they come in because they can be notorious …

I listened to Duncan prattle on with half an ear, hoping like hell that Eric was still upstairs hiding and hadn't just heard that he'd be playing host at his own funeral in a week's time.

Never mind Eric, Devil's Advocate Elinor snapped. *How are you going to handle it? It was only thirteen months ago that you gave the eulogy at Joel's funeral, and now you have to attend another one? For another guy you care about? What are you going to do, Elinor?*

What are you going to do?

After Duncan left, I went back to the office. I opened Duncan's box of accounts and started to go through them. He was right, he'd put everything in order, exactly as I needed it. This made my job much easier. I put on some music and got to work, and a couple of hours flew by without me noticing.

When I glanced up again, it was just beginning to get dark, the sky streaked with golden orange as the sun fell behind the overgrown hedges. I wondered how the gardeners Duncan had hired would ever manage to get the exterior looking presentable in time for the funeral.

Eric still hadn't come down. I went to the stairs and called him, but I got no reply. I made myself some dinner and ate it in the lounge, staring at the strange arrangement of account statements and fan mail and creepy photographs on my desk. This was turning out to be anything but the boring country sojourn I'd envisaged.

I picked up one of Helen's letters, reading over the words once again. What had made this girl so desperate for Eric's attention that she'd done all this? But then, I thought of Damon Sputnik, and all the scheming I'd done with Cindy over the last six months to get him to notice me. Sure, I hadn't tried to run him over, but I had thought about tripping him up, just for an excuse to talk to him. Was I really any different?

It all comes back to the music.

Eric's music. That's what all this was about, really. If I understood the music, I would understand Helen.

I grabbed my iPod off the desk, and slipped it into my pocket. It was time for some more sleuthing.

ERIC STILL HADN'T SHOWN his face. I kicked open the door to my bedroom, and told him if he was inside it was time for him to leave. Satisfied that he was too much of a gentleman to spy on me, I undressed and showered, washing away the strangeness of the day. After I finished my shower and crawled into bed, I pulled out the iPod, jammed the headphones into my ears, and typed Eric's name into the store.

You shouldn't be doing this, I cursed myself inwardly. *It's a bad idea. You'll either hate it, and Eric will be hurt, or you'll love it, and it will make you fall for him even more—*

Nonsense, Devil's Advocate Elinor scoffed. *I have to help Eric find out who killed him, and if it's Helen Manning, then listening to his music is going to help me understand her mindset better. The best detectives had an innate ability to get inside the heads of criminals, and that's all I'm trying to do here.*

Really?

Really.

Ghost Symphony's latest album, *Coppelius' Alchemy*, popped up. The front cover was an image of Eric with his back to the viewer, wearing a long leather trench coat that flapped around his body as he walked through a gloomy, gothic cemetery. His wavy black hair streamed down his back, and in his hand he clutched Isolde. The bow was strapped to his belt like a sword.

I clicked BUY NOW.

My heart pounded against my chest as I watched the little circle download. It clicked over to FINISHED, and the album art appeared in my library. I took a deep breath, and pushed PLAY.

The first notes rang out, slow and sombre in my ears. The melody drew into a deep, crushing riff, and soon I was nodding my head along. Then, Eric's bow screamed across the strings, and a piano fluttered to life, and the song kicked into three-and-a-half minutes of the most furious, distorted and fantastic music I'd ever heard.

I let out the breath I didn't even realise I'd been holding. The music swirled around me, full of malice and dread. My fingers drummed the furious beat against my thigh, and my head nodded along as I lost myself completely in this strange world of classical instruments and heavy metal abandon. I saw the track was called *Sandman*, after the legendary monster of Hoffman's story that tore out the eyes of children who didn't sleep to feed to his own children who lived on the moon. It was as if they'd brought the tale to life. Not the story, per say, but the mood, the sensations.

This music *was* Eric. It was raw and powerful. It was a glimpse into his soul. I couldn't believe the cocky, grinning ghost that had been bugging me for the last couple of days was the man who created *this.*

Now, I understood what had made Helen so obsessed with him. As the music coursed through my head, my body grew warm. I tossed and turned, trying to get comfortable, but I felt agitated, on edge. I wanted to do something, but I wasn't sure what. I imagined Eric on stage, his fit body wrapped head-to-toe in black and his dark ringlets plastered to his face by the heat of the stage lights. His fingers flew across the neck as he raced across the front of the stage, planting his feet wide apart as he pummelled the instrument with his bow. I pictured myself in the audience, hemmed in on all sides by sweaty, pulsing bodies, each one feeling the same awe and majesty as I felt. I imagined Eric finishing the last, haunting note, reaching down and grabbing my hand, pulling me on stage and sweeping me into a passionate kiss, while all around us, the crowd roared their adoration ...

I tore off the headphones, and threw them across the room. "This was a dumb idea," I said aloud. I rolled over, turned out the light, and tried to focus on sleep. But even with my eyes shut tight, I could still see Eric under the spotlight, his beautiful fingers dancing over the strings.

ERIC

I spent the night hiding in the attic with mountains of old junk and all the antique furniture that Dad had chosen and my mother therefore never wanted to see again. I hadn't seen Elinor since I'd run from the study, and I felt guilty and stupid for hiding for so long, although I couldn't figure out why I should feel that way. I hunted in through boxes and inside cupboards and under Chippendale chairs for my violin case, but I couldn't find it anywhere.

When I heard Elinor finish her morning shower and descend the stairs, I decided it was time to show myself. I felt nervous seeing her again, like a teenager trying to talk to his crush. *Don't be ridiculous, Eric. So she saw you when you were vulnerable. Big deal. It's not as if she can tell the press about it.*

I squared my shoulders and floated down the staircase. Best to pretend nothing happened. Just act like your normal, arrogant, wisecracking self.

But that was going to prove more difficult than I realised. When I entered the kitchen and sat down at the table, Elinor wouldn't even meet my eye. She stayed hunched over her laptop, her eyes scanning some website while she sipped her morning tea, deliberately angling herself away from me. The awkwardness hung in the air between us like a gallows filled with condemned men.

"You disappeared yesterday," Elinor mumbled into her cereal. "I had some things to tell you."

"I was looking for my violin," I answered. I wondered if she was expecting an explanation, or an apology. I didn't think I owed her one. It was my house, after all. I could move about it as I liked.

"Your violin? You mean Isolde?" Elinor was still avoiding my gaze. That was odd. Was she embarrassed about the things she'd said in the hallway? That must be it. She had been trying to push me away ever since I'd tried to kiss her, and she felt as if she'd revealed too much. That was fine, at least she wasn't looking at me like I was pathetic. That I could not bear.

"Yeah." I hovered inside the chair across from her, trying to place my body within her vision. "I couldn't see her in the crash pictures. It's quite a large case, so we would've seen it in the car. But she wasn't there. That means I must've left her in the house somewhere before I started driving again, although I don't know why I'd do that."

"That makes sense. Did you find her?"

"No. I haven't checked everywhere, though. It would help if I could remember where I'd put her. I hate this stupid selective memory thing."

"Could she not be back with the rest of the gear at the venue in London?"

I shook my head, a silly gesture, since she couldn't see it. "No. I probably left Tristan behind, sure. But not my father's violin. She comes with me everywhere. She must be here in the house some-where. But then, why I'd leave her here is also a mystery. Maybe you can help me look today?"

"I'm quite busy with work today," Elinor said shortly, her hair hanging over her face as she pushed her cereal into her mouth with giant gulps. Another awkward silence descended upon us, broken only by her furious chewing.

"Is something wrong?" I asked, breaking the silence. The question came out a bit sharper than I'd intended. I was starting to get annoyed at her on-off behaviour. I wasn't used to this, having to chase someone who only sometimes wanted to be chased.

"No. Everything's fine." Elinor looked up then, and I saw that her eyes were ringed with dark shadows. "I just didn't get a lot of sleep, is all."

"What did you want to tell me?"

"Oh, you're going to love it. Duncan came for tea yesterday. He informed me that we're having the funeral—yours and your mother's—here, at Marshell House, on Saturday."

"What?" I froze. My whole body went numb, and I dropped a foot through the kitchen floor before I managed to pull myself up again. "You can't be serious."

"Oh, I'm afraid I am. Duncan has made all the arrangements. There's going to be black flowers everywhere, and a big marquee out on the back lawn with a stage for live music and speeches, and a huge catered dinner, and they've sold 400 tickets to all of the most fanatical members of your fan club, so all your closest friends and family will be here to talk about how wonderful you are. And look," Elinor turned the screen on her laptop around so I could see the website she was browsing. "Tickets are starting to appear on eBay, for £250 each. There's not enough space here for all the people who want to go, Eric. *Your funeral is sold out.*"

I buried my face in my hands, my elbows sinking through the oak table. *No. This can't be happening.* As if being murdered wasn't enough, I was going to have to sit here and watch my own funeral? This was too much.

Elinor reached across the table and took my hand. The warmth flowed through my body, pulsing with the beating of her heart. That was the first time Elinor had initiated contact with me.

I looked up, and Elinor looked up too, and held my gaze.

"Don't worry," she said. "We will track down Helen Manning, and maybe you won't have to endure this. I'll make sure Duncan pays for what he's done. I won't let anyone get away with hurting you, Eric."

Her tone was so strong, so final. I nodded, feeling annoyed at myself for being sharp with her, and relieved that she was here. It felt good to have someone looking out for me. I was so used to having to take care of things myself.

The doorbell rang. Elinor sprung back as if she'd been slapped. "I'm sorry," she breathed, clutching her hand as if I had burned it. "I'll get that."

She dashed off. I floated to the window to see who it was. My chest swelled with warmth when I recognised the familiar blonde-haired figure shuffling from foot to foot as he waited on the porch.

Allan.

ELINOR

hat were you thinking? There I went again, getting close to Eric, forgetting about the barrier that stood between us. When I reached out to touch him, I hadn't even thought of the heat, or the way it made me feel. I just wanted to show comfort, to let him know that he didn't have to do this alone. But I'd broken my rule. I'd gotten too close ... *again.* I needed to be more careful if I was to escape this house with my heart still intact.

The doorbell rang again. I rushed through the house to answer it, assuming it was one of the vendors for the funeral. *Eric's funeral.* How on earth was I going to hold it together while I watched Eric's body being lowered into his grave?

Knock knock.

"Hello?" I pulled open the door. The man on the porch looked taken aback to see me standing there. He was young, close to my age, and wearing a black t-shirt with a grinning skull on it and a pair of tight black trousers with buckles along the seams. I recognised him from somewhere, but I couldn't quite place it. "H-hello?" he asked.

"You're knocking on my door, I'm supposed to be asking the questions."

"Oh, right, yes." He scratched his head. "So you own this house, then?"

"No." He waited for me to volunteer more information. I didn't.

"I … um … I was told Alice Marshell's lawyer was here. I'm a friend of her son, Eric. Actually, I'm the drummer in his band. I expect you've heard of us—"

"I'm Ms. Marshell's lawyer," I said, cutting him off. So that's why he seemed familiar – I'd seen the picture of him on Eric's website, standing toward the back of the band picture, looking staunch and sexy in black leather. I wasn't about to acknowledge that I recognised him, though. I'd had enough experience with Eric to know that if you wanted to keep the upper hand around these rock star types, you had to pretend you didn't know who they were. It unnerved them.

"Her lawyer? Really?" He sounded incredulous. "I don't believe you. You're trying to pull a fast one on me."

"Excuse me?" I pushed the door shut a couple of inches, indicating I was ready to cut the conversation short. What did this arrogant jerk want to see, my bar exam results?

"It's just that lawyers aren't usually so pretty. At least, not the ones I've met."

Oh. Despite the cheesy line, I couldn't help but grin. I was such a sucker for a bad boy. Allan-the-drummer grinned back. He was actually pretty cute, with spiked blonde hair and smooth, almost angelic features, although the steel spikes through his eyebrows and labret showed that he was no cherub. His piercing blue eyes flickered over my body, and the grin never left his face. And, a huge plus for him, he appeared to be completely, 100% alive.

"So what do you want at the house of Alice Marshell?" I asked Allan. "No offence, but if what I've heard about her is correct, she was not overly fond of either her son or his chosen profession. I'd expect she'd have stoned you at the door, but she also seemed quite proper and Debrett's etiquette tends to frown on the use of medieval tortures for unwanted houseguests."

'Relax, I'm not here to rob the place or make trouble. I'm meant to be giving a eulogy at the funeral on Saturday and thought I should scope the place out. But, I actually wanted to talk to *you*, Miss Pretty Lawyer with the ponytail and cute glasses. I have some questions about the estate."

'Flattery will get you everywhere. Come in," I said, throwing the door open.

Allan followed me through the entrance and receiving room and into the kitchen, his buckles clanging against each other with every step. I pulled my last bottle of wine out of the fridge and poured us both a glass, then led him into the floral sitting room. I saw Eric standing in the corner of the room, staring at me with a strange expression on his face. Allan followed my gaze into the corner, but his face didn't register Eric's presence. He didn't stop talking about the last tour they'd done together to mention the figure of his old friend in the corner. So that answered one of our questions. I was the only one who could see Eric.

"Wow," Allan said, glancing around the room at the faded Victorian roses and lace doilies. "This is very ... "

"Ghastly," I said, slumping into one of the chairs. "I can't imagine living in this house. Well, actually, I could, but only after some serious redecorating, and a contract with an extermination company to have all the spiders removed."

"I can't imagine *Eric* living here," Allan said, sitting down on the couch, leaning over the arm so that he was close to me. "It's so stuffy and old-fashioned, not like him at all. His place in Devon is all gleaming marble and wrought iron. Industrial goth, he liked to call it."

"I don't know," I said. "Marshell House has a bit of a vibe about it. It's a bit horror-film theatrics, you know, the crumbling gothic mansion filled with antiques, every room a tribute to the cruel, uncaring mother. I imagine that influenced his music a bit."

"I think all the free booze and women on the road had some impact, as well." Allan grinned. In the corner, Eric twisted his face into a scowl. For some reason, he wasn't happy about Allan being there.

"Tell me about him," I said, turning toward Allan so I could no longer see Eric's face. "What was it like working with him? I've never met him or even heard of him before, but spending time in this house and learning about his family life, I feel as if I'm getting to know him a bit."

"About Eric? He's remarkable. There are musicians who are into dark music because they think it's cool, or a way to get into kinky stuff with hot goth chicks, or whatever. But Eric is different. The music *is* him. He's intense to be in a band with; he doesn't laugh a lot, and he doesn't like to be told he's wrong. But he has an incredible creative mind. *Had* an incredible mind, I guess I should say." Allan gulped, looking away suddenly. Behind me, Eric snorted. Allan wiped his eyes. "Sorry, it's still sinking in, you know? We just played a show and then, a few hours later, he was dead."

"Do you know much about how he died?"

"The police told us it was a hit-and-run. They're still looking for the other driver, but they said that without any witnesses it's unlikely they will find him. It's just one of those horrible, tragic events that we all have to live with."

"So you said you wanted to talk to me about something? If it's to do with the funeral arrangements, you need to contact Duncan—"

"The jolly old dude? I've already talked to him. He was the one who sent me here, actually. I came up from London a few days early. I needed the time to collect myself, walk around this town and remember Eric before he … before I …" Allan turned away from me, took a deep breath and held it for a few moments, then let the air race out through his lips. "I came to Crookshollow once before with Eric. We stayed here at one of his friend's flats above a tattoo parlour after our first sold-out tour. It's quite a magical place. I want to kind of walk around and remember him."

"That's nice." Allan looked sick. I noticed for the first time that his blue eyes were rimmed with black shadows. He'd lost his close friend, his bandmate. No wonder he was a bit of a mess. I hurried to adjust my tone. "No, I mean it. I know firsthand how tough it is to lose someone close to you. What did you want to talk to me about?"

"Oh. It's silly."

"What?"

"I was wondering if I could have his violin."

"You what?"

"Eric's violin." Allan unfolded a piece of paper from the pocket of his pants, and spread it out on the table. "The one he calls Isolde. We have Tristan in our backline, but Isolde is missing. That's the letter from Eric's lawyer. It says he left me both violins in his will. He didn't have much family, apart from his mother, and she wouldn't have wanted it because it used to be Eric's father's instrument, so I guess it makes sense that he left it to me. It's a bit of an honour, actually. But the problem is, I can't find it anywhere. It wasn't in his house in Devon. The police didn't find it in his car after the accident, and so I was wondering if perhaps it might be here?"

I picked up the letter and scanned it. "I haven't seen it, I'm sorry. Could it have been stolen from Eric's Devon property during that break-in?"

"The police didn't seem to think so, and neither do I. He had it with him when he left the show in London, and from what the police are saying, he never got back to Devon. And besides, I've got people watching all the auction houses and websites in the country, and Isolde hasn't turned up. That instrument is probably worth a lot of money to the right buyer, especially so soon after Eric's death."

Allan looked glum. "It makes me sick to think it might be lost. I'd feel like I failed him if the first thing that happens to the violin after he's gone is it ending up in the hands of some nut-job collector."

"I'm not gone, you ungrateful shit," Eric cut in from the corner. Both Allan and I continued talking as if he weren't there.

"I'm sorry. I'd like to help you, really I would. But I'm not really able to get involved in Eric's affairs. I'm here looking after his mother's estate. If I were you, I'd go back to Eric's lawyer. As I understand it, the police are still investigating the break-in at Eric's home, so his lawyer probably hasn't even got to the stage of executing the will yet. It's possible the violin will show up."

"You're probably right. I'm just so *sure* it's here. I feel as though Eric is speaking to me from beyond the grave, telling me where to find it."

"I *am* speaking you from beyond the grave," said Eric. "And I'm telling you to fuck off."

His comment made me smirk. I tried to cover it with my hand. Thankfully, Allan was looking wistfully into the distance and didn't seem to notice. "I really wish I could be more help."

"Are you sure you haven't you seen it?"

"I'm sorry, I haven't seen any violins in the house."

"Oh, well it's a large house. Perhaps I can help you look?" He looked hopeful.

"I'm sorry, but I really can't do that. I haven't been through all the estate details yet, so I don't know which pieces of the estate belong to whom. It really wouldn't be appropriate for me to allow you to just poke around."

"Oh, of course." Allan looked so deflated, so sad, that I wished I could help him. My heart poured out to him. I'd been exactly where he was once before, mourning someone who'd been a profound influence on my life, unsure of what to cling to and how to proceed without them.

"But if you came back later this week, I'll have nearly finished my initial work, and I should've been in touch with Eric's lawyer about his mother's estate. Leave this letter with me, and I'll ask him about the violin. I want Eric's things to go to the people who'll appreciate them most."

"Really?" Allan handed over the letter, his lips curling into a dazzling smile.

"Of course. His songs meant so much to so many people." My voice caught on the last word, and I could feel my cheeks redden as I remembered listening to the Ghost Symphony album over and over and over last night.

"So you were a fan?" Allan leaned forward, his eyes boring into me. "I thought you said you hadn't heard of Ghost Symphony before."

My neck flushed with heat too, as I recalled the way Eric's music had made my whole body ache. "I've been listening to a little since I started working here. I really like the new album."

Behind me, I heard Eric's sharp intake of breath. My neck grew hotter. I *really* wished I hadn't said that.

"It was the best work Eric's ever done," Allan said. "It was an honour to be a part of it. I just can't ... believe ... it's the last—" He looked away again. "I'm sorry. It's just so hard to believe that he's gone."

I placed my hand on Allan's shoulder. His skin felt warm to touch. His shoulders shuddered. *Poor guy.* It was strange to see someone who looked so tough being vulnerable. Eric's death must have really got to him.

"I'm sorry," Allan said, burying his face in his hands. "We've barely even met, and here I am ..."

"Hey, don't worry about it," I said, smiling.

"You've very kind," Allan said. "You are the first hot lawyer I've ever met who is also kind."

Behind me, Eric snorted.

"Maybe that's what I'll call my practice when I open up my

own firm," I said. "The Hot Kind Lawyers. I'm sure we'll soon be the most in-demand firm in London."

Allan stood up. "I don't want to take up any more of your time. I've dealt with lawyers myself, so I know how much it's worth."

"Don't worry about it. I'm sorry I couldn't be more help."

"You've been more than helpful. I'll come by and see you later in the week," he said. "That is … if you don't mind. I would really love to find that violin."

"Um … sure. Of course I don't mind. I'm sure Eric would have wanted you to have it."

"Not anymore," said Eric from the corner.

Allan beamed. "Thank you, Elinor. But there is one more thing before I go. I'd be a fool if I left before asking, would you like to go out for dinner with me?"

"Would I …" My heart thumped against my chest. *He's asking me out.* Behind me, Eric made a strangled noise.

"I'm in town for a few more days," Allan said. "I could swing by tomorrow night, and take you to dinner. Do you like Greek food? Eric took me to this great place when we were here. If it's still open, I bet you'd love it."

I opened my mouth to answer him, but no sound came out. I just couldn't believe this was happening. I was being *asked out.* This never happened to me. I hadn't been on a date for more than eight months. And that last prospect had been a man from an online chatroom who turned out to have excellent Photoshop skills, because I'd never met a person who looked less like his profile picture. He was also a truck driver with the IQ of a walnut. There was not a second date.

"I don't know if I've ever really *had* Greek food, but I'd love to," I heard myself saying, before I could even stop to think about how crazy this was. I could feel Eric's eyes boring into the back of my skull. *I'm sorry, Eric. But this guy is cute and nice and interesting, and he's alive. I could have a future with him. At the very least, I can have dinner with him.*

"Okay, awesome!" Allan flashed me with a wide, toothy grin. I showed him to the door, and we exchanged phone numbers. Allan said he'd pick me up at 7pm tomorrow. I watched him walk back down the driveway, admiring the way his tight arse looked in his tight black jeans.

I shut the door and walked back into the house, feeling as though I were floating. *I have a date.*

My good mood came crashing down when I saw Eric standing in the centre of the living room, surrounded by the rose-covered furniture. He face looked as red as the garish flowers.

"You're going out with Allan!" he roared.

"Yes." I squared back my shoulders. "Why shouldn't I?"

The question stopped Eric short. He started to say something, but then stopped, his mouth hanging open, and his eyes blazing with fire.

"Because," he said defiantly, "Allan is notorious. He's got no interest in you as a person. All he sees is a pair of tits and a chance to get his hands down your knickers. He played you like my violin, Elinor. Which, by the way, I do not recall leaving to him *at all.*"

I jabbed my finger at the paper on the table. "I have a letter from your lawyer that suggests otherwise. And you know you're having trouble remembering what happened before your death. What is with you, Eric? That's a fine way to talk about your friend. You saw how upset he was. He is in mourning for you. I think he just wants someone to talk to."

"I don't want you to go." Eric was leaning so close to me that I could feel the energy surging between our bodies.

"You have no right to request anything of me," I shot back. "You don't own me."

"Don't go, Elinor. Please." Eric switched to pleading, but I wasn't buying it. I folded my arms across my chest.

"Try and stop me," I shot back.

Eric recoiled, as if he'd been slapped. His face crumpled with hurt.

"I'm sorry, Eric—" I stepped forward, reaching out for him. I expected him to recoil away, but instead, he lunged at me, and pressed himself against my body.

The heat rushed through me, and all thoughts of Allan flew from my mind. Eric pressed his mouth to mine, and the energy flowed through me, hotter than ever. I arched my back and pressed myself against him, falling into him. My lips opened into his, and I explored the heat with my tongue.

Eric pushed back again. His body felt solid. He had a *mass.*

What's happening?

Eric pulled away. We both stared down between us, at our two bodies, touching. "Whoa," he breathed.

"Yeah, whoa." How was this possible? Eric was corporeal. He had a form. How had this happened? "We're touching, Eric."

"I know." A wide smile spread across his face. In all the days I'd known him, I don't think he'd ever looked as handsome. "It's the most incredible feeling. I don't think anything in my entire life ever felt as good as this moment right here."

I held up my hand. Eric pressed his palm against mine. It didn't feel quite like skin; it had an elasticity to it, as if it was made of rubber. But my palm rested against his, instead of falling through it. Eric knitted his fingers through mine, while the energy pulsed between our bodies.

I started to say something, but Eric pressed his lips against mine again. They felt solid, too, but not moist. They had a kind of soft elasticity about them, as though I were kissing the skin of a bubble. It was strange, but not unpleasant. The heat emanating from Eric made the experience deliciously intense. I revelled in the sensation of actually touching him, running my hands all over his body, feeling my fingers tingle with fire as they grazed against his flesh.

"Why is this happening?" I murmured against him.

"I don't know, and I don't care." His lips sought mine with increasing urgency.

"But shouldn't we—"

"I have wanted you from the moment you walked through that door," Eric growled. "Don't waste the opportunity we've been given with questions."

I started to protest, but Eric covered my mouth in kisses, and I lost myself again, giving over to the desire surging through me. We were pressed so close that the whole front of my body hummed with warmth. My heart pounded against my chest. I wrapped my hands around his neck, sinking my fingers into his thick, luscious curls, and pulled his face closer.

Kissing Eric felt so good. It felt like the best thing I'd done in ages. His tongue against mine was like devouring the most delicious hot curry, all sweet and buttery. My whole body hummed with an ache I hadn't felt in so long. I was wanted. I was desired. And I desired him back, more than I cared to admit. Even though my mind was screaming that this was a bad idea, my whole body screamed for him, and my body was winning.

Fuck it, Devil's Advocate Elinor said. *For once in your life, do something because you want to, and damn the consequences.*

Okay then, if you insist.

Eric's hands were everywhere, running over my shoulders, down my arms, entwined in my hair, pressing against the small of my back. I grabbed handfuls of his hair in my fingers, enjoying the way it felt so normal, so real. The heat of his body burned against my hands.

Just as I was ready to make a move toward the couch, Eric pulled away, breathing hard.

"What?" I panted, my lips moist. "What's wrong?" The heat of him was a ghost against my skin. *Did I do something wrong? Please don't let him change his mind! I want this so bad ...*

"Take off your shirt," Eric commanded.

"Excuse me?"

"Please, Elinor. I can't do it." He held up his fingers, and I could see that they were still strange and rubbery. He couldn't really grip anything, certainly not well enough to remove clothing.

My heart pounded against my chest. I was standing on the precipice of something enormous. Did I really want to do this? I looked up into Eric's blazing eyes, his intense expression, his muscled shoulders pulling against his black jacket. Yes. I knew it was a bad idea, that we were doomed for heartache, but in that moment, I needed him so bad I didn't care.

I took a deep breath, and grabbed the corners of my shirt. The fabric felt heavy in my hands, as if it was weighted down by something invisible. I pulled it up, over my head, and flung it on to the rose-covered couch. Eric sucked in a breath. He stepped forward again, his hands grazing my hips. His fingertips laid a trail of fire across my belly. I reached behind and unhooked my bra, letting it fall to the floor. My breasts—grateful to be free of their shackles—bounced free.

It had been so long since I'd been naked in front of someone, and I'd spent so much time feeling self-conscious about my weight, that I should have felt nervous. But Eric's expression as he stared at me carried no malice or disgust, only an intense desire. It made me feel strong, and beautiful. Eric moved his hands from my hips over my stomach and across my naked breasts, his fingertips swirling the nipples. The heat pulsed inside me, becoming part of me.

"You are so beautiful," Eric whispered, as he bent in to kiss my neck.

I whimpered as his lips touched my skin once more, sending an arc of fire through my body. Eric bent down further, and placed his mouth against my hard, round nipple. I gasped as his tongue wrapped around that sensitive bud. The sensation was so hard to explain, it wasn't wet, but a sharp sucking, almost like a vacuum. With the heat of his mouth, the experience was intense. I moaned against him, digging my nails into his rubbery skin as he sucked. Heat radiated out from my breast, encasing my chest in fire.

Eric pressed his hands into the small of my back, holding me closer while he sucked and licked at my nipple. First one, then the other. An ache flared between my legs, growing more and more urgent. I wanted him to move lower, but he seemed content to tease and tempt me.

'You're so fucking gorgeous," he murmured, his tongue flicking over my sensitive areolae. I moaned in reply.

We stumbled backward across the rug. I felt my arse rest against the edge of the couch, and I lay back, pulling my body on to the cushions. I didn't feel self-conscious at all as I lay down before him, revealing my whole body to him while he stared down at me with those smouldering rock star eyes. The look on his face said he was pleased with what he saw.

Eric climbed on top of me, his body warm and pliant as he folded himself around me, smothering my mouth in kisses once more. I moaned as he ran his hands down my thighs, causing my skin to tingle. He kissed a trail of fire across my stomach, then nibbled a line up the inside of my thigh, first one, then the other. He touched me everywhere, except where I burned for him most.

I growled in frustration as the ache grew into an all-consuming throb. Eric laughed, low in his throat. He hovered above me for a few moments, staring down at me with that cat-ate-the-canary smirk that made him so deliciously irritating. Just as I was about to force his head down for him, he lowered himself down to my mound, and pressed his lips against me, letting the warmth of his mouth spread out across my skin. I gazed down at him and he stared right back, his eyes locked on mine, as he pressed his tongue against my swollen clit.

The touch was a flame burning bright, and I was the candle that waited to burn. His tongue worked me like a machine, running over that special spot with a furious rhythm, as if I were another instrument he was attempting to master. All the while, he used his fingers to twist and squeeze my nipples.

Eric's black curls fell over his face as he licked my most intimate places. His tongue slid inside my folds, and he used my own wetness to make up for the saliva he couldn't seem to produce. I arched my back, pushing myself closer, desperate for more of him. Eric responded by pulling away, lightening his touch so that only the tip of his tongue flicked across my clit.

Oh, that is cruel. Eric dug his fingers into my thighs, pushing me down into the couch. Now that I wasn't moving, he attacked me with his tongue, swirling it around and around until the ache inside of me became another fire, burning hot and ready to consume me. Just as I thought I would explode, Eric pulled away, rising a few inches above me and grinning wickedly at me, his brown eyes blazing. The urge faded, and he bent down on me once more. I pounded my fists against the couch in frustration as once more he drove me to the edge, then pulled away before I could climax.

Eric did this again and again, driving me to the edge of pleasure, then stopping, denying me the orgasm my body was so desperate to unleash.

The fire inside me grew and grew, the flames tearing through my stomach and licking along my arms. It consumed my legs, my breasts, my torso. It burned so brightly that when Eric pulled back, it didn't quench the flames.

When the fire reached my brain, my world exploded. It was as if my body turned into a white hot ball of flames, rolling through a dark forest consuming everything in its path. I ceased to be a person. I was a ball of bright light, a being of pure energy. My ears rang with a strange, humming rhythm.

Vaguely, in the distance, I heard someone screaming. A woman. Is that me? Am I screaming? I couldn't tell. All I knew was the fire.

My vision blurred, and slowly, the room came into focus once more. I sank into the cushions, waiting for the feeling to come back into my legs. Eric leaned over me, a giant, cocky grin on his face.

"Whoa," I murmured.

"Careful," he warned. "You're going to give me a big head."

"And we wouldn't want that. But don't worry." I grinned back. "It was okay."

"Okay?" He cocked his head to the side. "Just okay?"

"Yeah, you know, not quite what I expected from a world famous, bad-boy rock star. Maybe death has made you a little rusty," I said, faking a yawn. "But it's a good start."

"A little rusty, am I? Then get up."

I tried to, but my arms and legs were so wobbly, I couldn't hold myself upright. I flopped back onto the cushions. Eric chuckled, and I laughed too.

"Fine, I lied. I can't feel my legs."

"Good," Eric growled. "Then you're exactly how I want you. Now, let me show you how bad I can be."

He bent over me again, pressing his whole weight down on top of me. It felt odd, not heavy like other guys, but slightly buoyant, as if he might float away at any moment. His lips sought mine, and his tongue slipped inside my mouth, entwining together with mine. I reached up with my arms and traced my fingers over his shoulders, no longer freaked out by the strange, rubbery feel of his skin.

Eric leaned back, and slid off his jacket. Underneath, I saw for the first time that his shirt wasn't simply black, it was flecked with a red thread that glowed in the light, like speckles of blood. He unbuttoned it deftly, his rubbery fingers having no trouble with his own buttons, and slid it over his shoulders.

I gasped when I saw his torso. I hadn't imagined that under those sombre black clothes was such a taut, chiselled body. His shoulders bulged with muscle, and his chest narrowed into a trim waist. A beautiful dragon tattoo encircled his pectorals and ribs, its scales seemed to shimmer in the fading light, so that it almost appeared to move. The design looked vaguely familiar. *It's the tattoo in the window of Resurrection Ink. Eric's chest is on that poster.*

Eric's jeans bulged. I reached forward and threaded my fingers through his belt loops, pulling him back on top of me. I fumbled with the zipper while he ran his fingers through my hair. The ache was returning to my body. I was ready for this.

I pulled down Eric's tight jeans and he stepped out of them, revealing muscled thighs and a pair of black boxers. His cock stood erect through the thin fabric, and I almost gasped again at the size of it. I'd never been with a man that huge before. Gingerly this time, I pulled the waistband down, my lips and my pussy wet with anticipation.

Eric was even bigger than I imagined. His cock stood proud, the tip curled up slightly and purple with anticipation. I stared at it, gape-mouthed, wondering how it was ever going to fit inside me. Was it wobbly and rubbery, like the rest of his skin? Curious now, I reached down to touch it, wrapping my hand around the shaft and stroking it slowly, glad to feel that it was hard and solid, just as it should be. Eric closed his eyes, moaning softly as I stroked him.

With my free hand, I pushed his shoulder back so that he fell against the arm of the couch. I pulled myself onto my knees and leaned over, pulling his cock into my mouth. Usually I hated going down on guys, hated the way they pushed my head around, forcing me to go harder, faster, how they yelled stupid shit as they came, trying to demean me. But seeing that cock made me hunger for it. I wanted to please Eric. I wanted to see him writhe in ecstasy, the way I had done only minutes before.

My mouth slid down Eric's shaft, not even coming close to taking in his whole length. The skin still had a slight hint of that weird rubberiness, but it was hardly noticeable. My lips wrapped around his shaft, and I began to stroke slowly, using my hand to work the rest of his length. Eric twined his fingers through my hair and moaned.

I loved the sound of his voice, growling softly as I worked him up and down, my tongue sliding over every inch of him.

"Elinor ..." he moaned. "You have to stop—"

But I didn't want to stop. I was having too much fun. I increased my speed, my hand and mouth moving in unison, my tongue slapping against the tip every time I withdrew. I tried to take him back further into my throat, enjoying the way he filled my mouth completely. I could feel him starting to harden in my hand, getting closer to—

Eric grabbed my shoulders with both hands, and tore me away. I was so shocked that he'd found the strength to do that, that I barely noticed when he laid me back against the couch and used his knees to push my legs apart. His body pressed against mine, heavy and reassuring, that fire burning against my skin, and the air around us sizzling with energy.

"Eric, are you sure about this? We're not being safe."

"I'm pretty sure you can't get pregnant from a ghost." Eric grinned, his eyes sparkling.

"But ..." I was just about to ask if we could really do this, when Eric pushed himself inside of me, and the words flew from my mouth.

His length slid inside of me, filling me completely. We lay there together, not moving, just enjoying the closeness of our bodies together, of the red-hot fire heating up inside of us, the invisible flames swirling all around, enveloping us completely. Eric's eyes bore into mine, the black irises invisible against those dark pools.

Finally, after my body felt ready to explode from craving, Eric started to move inside me. He began slowly with long, deliberate strokes. I was wet enough for both of us, and the sensation was exquisite, like rubbing against silk.

Eric's mouth found mine and his tongue probed intensely, his kisses stealing my breath. His curls flopped against my cheeks, the ends tickling my sensitive skin. Soon, he could no longer restrain himself, and he began to thrust harder. I rose up to meet him, thrusting back with my hips, driving him deeper, wanting all of his length inside of me. It had been so long, and it felt *so* good. The way he filled me completely, our bodies melding perfectly together.

The heat clawed at my body, and finally overwhelmed me. I came against against him, my walls contracting around his cock, tightening as the orgasm ripped through me. My vision faded, and the world turned into white, bright heat.

Eric pumped faster, his whole body tensed, his muscles taut. Nearly all the rubberiness had left him, and as he pumped into me he felt like a normal man. Normal, but not ordinary, for no man had ever been so beautiful, or made me feel so good. All around us, the energy swirled, creating a cocoon of white hot light that encased us, protecting us, giving us this moment to share.

A third orgasm tore through me, my walls closing around Eric's cock, milking him, dragging each thrust from him. Eric's shoulders tensed around me, the muscles straining against his desire as he fought to hold on a little longer.

My body quivered with desire, and I wrapped my legs around him, pulling him in closer. With a final, shuddering thrust, Eric came inside me, his face contorting as he shuddered against me, and then went still, his spent body draped over mine.

"Whoa," Eric said, his eyelids heavy.

"Yeah. Whoa." Those exact words described how I felt at that moment.

Eric rolled off me, pushing his back against the couch. He pulled me into his arms, rolling me on to my side so that he enveloped me in his heat. As his skin touched mine, I realised that the rubberiness of it had returned, as if he were fading back from a solid form into … what he was. I almost didn't mind the odd bounciness of it as his fingers lightly traced a line over my thigh and across my breasts.

But now that it was over, my mind took control of my body once again. And my mind had questions, and clarifications, and many deep-rooted concerns about what just happened. "Eric, I don't know what happened here, but—"

"Elinor." His voice sounded desperate. "Please put that brilliant mind to rest for a few more moments. We'll talk about this later, I promise. We will sit down and really get to grips with what it all means. But for now, can I please enjoy the one beautiful moment I've had since I died?"

I nodded, and closed my eyes, relaxing into his warmth. Yes, I could give him that.

ERIC

*E*linor snuggled up against me, her body still warm and slick with sweat. Her eyes were closed, and the steady rise and fall of her body told me she'd drifted off to sleep. The fact that she trusted me enough to fall asleep in my arms made my new, solid body ache with joy. I could feel her warmth mingling with my own, the fog of heat surrounding us like a comforting cocoon. I wanted nothing more than to remain inside that cocoon forever.

I glanced out the window. The sun was beginning to set, casting long stripes of red and purple across the sky. How long had we been lying here? It must've been hours. *Maybe this was like a Cinderella thing. I get until the stroke of midnight, and then I turn back into a ghost.*

I knew there was no way I would sleep. I hadn't slept for ten days now, and right now I had too many incredible memories to replay in my mind, over and over. I would never grow tired of recalling the way Elinor writhed beneath me as she came, or the way those luscious lips wrapped around my cock—

These memories swirled around with questions. How had she

done it? How had she made me solid? And most importantly, how long would it last?

I didn't have many answers, but one thing I knew for certain: I wasn't going to waste a moment of my afterlife waiting idly to return to my spectral form. Not when I had this hot woman lying naked beside me.

Elinor moaned, and stirred beside me. She looked so beautiful sleeping there, I almost didn't want to wake her. But I needed her awake and willing for what I wanted to do.

I leaned over and ran my fingers across her face, enjoying the smooth suppleness of her skin. It felt so good to be able to touch again, and touching a beautiful woman … even better. Elinor's eyelids fluttered open, her long lashes sticking together. "Eric?"

"I'm here, babe."

"So it wasn't a dream?"

I grinned. "That was one hell of a dream."

Elinor leaned up and pressed her mouth to mine, her body melting against me like butter on hot pancakes. She cupped my cheeks with her hands, pulling my face closer to hers, her fingers reaching up and running through my hair, tugging at the ringlets.

Our kiss heated up, tongues running against each other, lips opening to devour. The smell of her swirled around me, a soft, fruity perfume mixed with sweat and sleep and her own unique scent. I drank in the joy of it, the joy of sensation, of feeling alive, of her body wrapping itself around me, opening up to me.

Suddenly, fear overwhelmed me, sucking out all the joy that swelled in my chest. Whatever had made my body solid, made me able to feel her and caress her in this way, would be taken away again. And I would be left with the memory of her, raw and real because it was so brief. I kissed Elinor with more urgency, longing to commit every touch, every sensation to memory.

I flipped Elinor over so that she was on her stomach, and those plump round cheeks were presented to me. I wanted to take my time, to savour this moment, but the panic made me crazy. I needed to have her, now, while I still had the chance.

I climbed up behind Elinor, straddling her body and squeezing her arse, enjoying the way her body shuddered under my touch. I grabbed her hips and yanked her back, impaling her on my cock with one solid thrust. I sighed as I slid into her warmth, enjoying her gasp of pleasure as my shaft touched at her this new angle.

I began to thrust into her, slowly at first, but then the fear and desire melded together inside of me, and I came at her with a ferocious passion. Elinor rose up to meet me, pushing back against every thrust. Her fingers clutched at the couch as she fought for purchase, and she made little mewling sounds in her throat as I drove her closer to orgasm.

Her back arched, as I thrust harder and deeper, wanting to drive her to orgasm. Her warmth enveloped my cock, sending a hot flame of desire through my whole body. My thighs slapped against hers as I dug my fingers into her soft skin and pulled her back against me.

Elinor glanced back over her shoulder, and her body began to shake. I felt her contract against me as she came around my cock. Seeing that beautiful face, her mouth open in ecstasy, her bow-lips moaning my name, sent me over the edge. My body shuddered with the force of my orgasm, and I cried out as I pumped into her. Elinor's muscles clenched tighter, closing around me and milking me for everything I had.

When at last I was spent, I collapsed against the couch, relishing the way the upholstery scratched my bare skin. I never thought I'd be so glad to feel that horrid fabric, but it reminded me that I was solid, I was corporeal, and I was lying here next to the most incredible woman I'd ever met.

Elinor lay facing me, one arm cradled under her head, the other draped across her round, full breasts, her fingers lightly running down my arm. She blinked slowly, as if she was trying to see if I was still there when she opened her eyes.

I pulled Elinor toward me and turned her over, pressing her back against my stomach, relishing the way her body fit so snugly against mine. She sighed as she pulled my arms across her chest, wrapping them around her like a scarf against the chill.

"I'm sorry," I whispered in her ear. "I didn't mean to be a pig. I'm just terrified that any moment I'm going to fall through the couch, and this will be over, and I'll never be able to touch you again."

"Don't be sorry," she told me. "Just be ready again soon."

"Your wish is my command." I murmured against her earlobe, smothering her face in kisses.

ELINOR

I woke hours later, wrapped in a thin throw rug from the sofa, my back warm from Eric's touch. The curtains were still open, but the sky outside was dark, the moon illuminating a pale rectangular shadow across the flowered rug. Eric's arms hung through my body, leaving a heat spot through the centre of my chest. Or perhaps that was my heart, beating a mile a minute now that I could fully contemplate what we'd done.

What we'd done, indeed. We had done it so many times, in so many positions. I never knew it was possible to have such fantastic sex for so long. I'd lost count of the number of orgasms I'd had. There wasn't an inch of me Eric hadn't ravished with his fingers or his tongue or his cock. We had been desperate, trying in vain to sate our lust for each other before he was once again a shade. But now the magic had worn off. He was Eric the ghost again, and I could no longer touch him. Our night of pleasure was over, and we had to face the cold reality.

I sat up and gazed down at Eric's sleeping face, his eyes closed, his body relaxed and serene as he floated half inside the couch. And that was when it finally hit me. The enormity of what I'd done slammed into me like a freight train.

What have I done? Fear clung to me like a damp, icy blanket. I was involved with a dead guy. I wasn't just physically involved. If I was honest with myself, (and lawyers always are—it's the only way we can lie to so many other people), I liked him. I *really* liked him. In fact, I was dangerously close to falling completely, head-over-heels in love with Eric Marshell. I was setting myself up for the ultimate heartache.

You were already involved, Devil's Advocate Elinor shot back. *You'd already fallen for him, because you're an idiot. But at least you got the most incredible fuck you've ever had out of it.*

I leaned over and grabbed my phone off the table. The clock read 3:37am. The message icon glowed. I clicked on it. Allan had texted me yesterday evening, not long after he'd left the house. He was excited to pick me up for dinner at seven tomorrow. Or rather, tonight. My stomach turned. I felt sick. I pulled my body out from Eric's warmth, and starting to scramble around for my clothing. Just staring down at my naked body made me feel filthy. I'd slept with a *ghost.* I was a pervert, a freak. I should be locked up.

"Where are you going in such a hurry?" Eric asked from the couch, his voice husky.

"I have to go." I pulled my shirt over my head with such violence that a button pinged off and bounced across the floor.

"Come back to me, Elinor. It's still dark. We've got plenty of time before the sun comes up."

"No." I squeezed my eyes shut, so I couldn't see him lying here, his naked body beautiful in the moonlight as he hovered half inside the couch. I tugged my jeans over my feet. "I can't do this, Eric."

"You're running away, again?" His voice sounded sharper.

"Look at you!" I screeched, my voice jumping up two octaves. Eric glanced down and saw his torso disappearing through the rose-covered cushions. His expression said it all.

"I'm sure it's just temporary," Eric said, giving me a weak smile.

Rage flooded me—an anger born of the fear I felt at the possibility of caring for him. "I *said* I couldn't do this. I gave you very specific instructions not to come near me, not to touch me, and you disobeyed. And now look what's happened. We shouldn't have done this, Eric, and you know it."

"Hey, don't you *dare* try to make out as if I took advantage of you," Eric snapped back. He shot out of the couch and stood up to his full height, his feet hovering a few inches above the floor and his broad shoulders looming over me. The dragon on his tattoo seemed to undulate, its scales shimmering in the pale moonlight. "You were just as into it as I was. Or were you just so weak after you tenth orgasm you couldn't push a weightless ghost off you? I don't exactly buy it."

'Fuck you, Eric. You know what I meant." My hands clenched into fists at my sides. My stomach felt heavy with a great lump of pain and rage. His words cut through me like a blade.

'No, fuck *you*, Elinor. This is getting ridiculous. I may be a ghost, but I have feelings. You're hot and then you're cold. You want me and then you pull away. After what happened here, I thought—"

"Well, you thought wrong." I grabbed my bra and underwear from under the end table and angrily balled them up as I turned to leave.

"Fine," Eric yelled. "Run away again. I don't care."

I whirled back around to face him. "You can't care. You're dead, you're dead, you're dead!" I screamed the words at his face. Eric recoiled, as if I'd slapped him. The words echoed through the empty house, filling the dark corners with their ominous tones. *Dead ... dead ... dead ...*

Dead just like Joel.

I ran upstairs and slammed the door to Eric's room. I threw myself on my bed. The mattress groaned beneath me, and my body bounced against that hard object that was stored under there. Ouch. I made a mental note to remove whatever it was before I went to sleep again.

But I couldn't move. I could still feel the lingering warmth of Eric's touch against my skin. The smell of him wafted around me. For these few short hours Eric had had a smell—aged leather and black musk and the sweat of the stage lights. He'd never had a scent before. It was intoxicating, and also horribly sad.

The thought of taking off my clothes, of showering and washing off my makeup filled me with dread. Right now I was in desperate need of some sleep. I just wanted to shut out the world and this whole stupid situation for a while. My whole body ached from tiredness and from the rigours of the night before. I kicked off my shoes, closed my eyes and waited to sleep to take me.

But it never did. My head swarmed with thoughts of Eric—his touch that set my body on fire, the hurtful things he'd said, the way he'd looked at me when he saw that I was leaving. I lay with my head in my pillow, the tears frozen on my face, for some time. The room around me grew lighter as the sun rose, but I didn't move. I didn't cry. I didn't sleep. I just lay still and tried not to think. If I thought for too long, I started to dwell on how I'd made such a mess of things.

It was only three days ago that I'd arrived in Crookshollow. Three days ago, I'd had a crush on a hot Russian DJ, a promising career at an upscale London law firm, and, so far, I hadn't needed to sleep with my disgusting boss. Now, I was living in a haunted mansion, shagging a ghost, chasing an obsessed murdering psycho fan, listening to violin rock music, and going on a date with a drummer who had more facial piercings than I had pairs of shoes. Who *was* this person I'd become? I hardly even recognised myself. I felt like a character from a movie—the one everyone is laughing at because she messed up so bad.

Except … *Allan.* He didn't know about any of this. Maybe I could salvage something there.

My date was tonight. I needed it to go well. *Really* well. I needed Allan to make me forget all about Eric and what we'd done last night and the hateful, hurtful words we'd exchanged this morning. But this was crazy. I had packed a suitcase for two weeks' bumming around an old house. I had no date-ready clothing, no decent makeup. I debated calling Cindy, but it wouldn't do any good. She'd be at work, and wouldn't be able to get back to me until the evening, long after I required her sage advice.

What did one even wear on a date with a hot, pierced drummer? At least now I had something to distract myself with. I gave up on the promise of sleep, and pulled myself out of bed. I flung all my clothes out of my suitcase, but nothing felt right. Panic was starting to settle in. I knew I was putting entirely too much pressure on this date, but I could still feel the warmth of Eric's fingers against my skin. I was dangerously close to completely losing myself for him, and I had to put a stop to that.

Yep, I was right. I had nothing but prim business suits, baggy jeans and some ratty sweaters. I needed something hot to wear. Something that didn't make me look like a boring lawyer, or a boring lawyer on her day off.

I remembered some of the funky boutiques I'd seen on the main street of Crookshollow, the racks of bright clothing hanging outside some of the crystal shops. I had hardly spent any money since I'd arrived in Crookshollow, thanks to the company credit card and the fact there was nothing to do here except talk to ghosts and solve murders. Perhaps it was time I did some shopping.

I glanced at the clock. 6:42am. Nothing would be open for another few hours. I needed something to occupy my time until then. And unfortunately, although I wanted nothing more than to hide away from Eric forever, the only thing that could distract me was my work, which was all down in the office.

I pulled a sweater over my shirt to cover against the creeping cold of the house (and also the fact that I wasn't wearing a bra and a very important button had broken), and crept out of the room and across the landing. I scanned the staircase and empty entrance hall, but couldn't see Eric anywhere. Good.

I descended the stairs slowly, wincing every time a creak echoed through the silent, still hall. Thankfully I reached the bottom without him coming out to find me. I couldn't face him again, not now. Not when it was all so fresh. I reached the door of the study, pushed it open, and slipped inside.

Once I'd shut the door, I felt better, as if I had entered a safe place. I'd spent so much time in this cosy room over the last three days, surrounded by books and warming by the fire, that it felt like a haven. A draft blew in from between the windowpanes, and I rubbed my hands together to try to keep them warm. I got the fire going, and then sat down behind the desk to do some work.

I'd been going over the accounts in Duncan's files, when I'd found one page where the numbers didn't seem to add up. The total in the account was some £400 more than the items actually listed. I decided to log in to Alice's online accounts system and see if the mistake had somehow been added by Duncan.

Duncan was right—the online accounting system was clunky and uncooperative. It took me some time to figure out how to access the right data. I pulled up the statements from the appropriate month and check out the totals. They were exactly the same. *That's odd. This system should add these up perfectly every time. I don't understand what's happening ...*

Hang on a second.

I counted the rows of transactions. There were twenty in total, for that was the amount that fit on a page. I looked again at the paper in front of me. The total was exactly the same, but when I counted, I got only nineteen entries. I counted again. Yup, I was definitely right. A row was missing from Duncan's accounts.

That's very odd.

This time, I read through the page carefully, checking every transaction against the online account. Nothing was out of the ordinary. Alice had the usual sorts of transactions—at the supermarket, the pharmacy, as well as payments to her brokerage firm, insurance, a monthly magazine subscription and some music lessons—

Music lessons.

I'd never noticed that entry on any of Duncan's accounts, but there it was in the online account system, clear as a shot of vodka, which was what I was seriously starting to think I needed as I realised what I had uncovered. *Music lessons.* It couldn't be true. Eric had told me about his mother and how much she hated music. So either Alice was secretly learning to play the piano for £200 an hour, or she was acting as a benefactor for some other poor struggling music student. Knowing what I did of Alice Marshell, neither option seemed likely. That only left one other option: someone was transacting money from her accounts without permission, and they were attempting to hide their tracks.

I hit the BACK key and flicked through the other months. Sure enough, every week, out came two transactions labelled "music lessons." Each time they were for £200 on a Tuesday and Thursday, and the transactions went back more than a year. I thumbed through each of Duncan's accounts. None of those transactions were listed. Someone had painstakingly removed every mention of these "music lessons" and then done a bit of clever formatting to prevent me from noticing.

The money was going to an organisation calling itself the Crookshollow Conservatory. I quickly googled the name, not surprised when nothing came up. Next, I checked the register of businesses in Companies House. And sure enough, the conservatory didn't come up there, either. It was a fake company, and I think I had a fair idea of who its director might be.

I remembered the way Duncan had steered our conversation out on the porch. He'd given me the tampered files and tried to dissuade me from using the online system. He'd desperately wanted to know how far I'd got on Alice's estate. I thought he was just thinking of fulfilling the obligations he had to Alice, but he was actually trying to cover up the thousands of pounds he'd stolen from her.

I have to tell Eric. The thought occurred immediately. Duncan was organising the funeral. His funeral. I didn't want the guy anywhere near the house. He had to know I'd be likely to discover his deception. Who knows what he'd do? I didn't want to talk to Eric again right now, but I didn't have a choice.

I searched the house for him, but could find no trace of my man in black. I took a flashlight and examined the cobweb-riddled corners of the basement, but he wasn't there, either. I walked around upstairs, checking in all the closets and bathrooms and guest bedrooms. I called his name, but there was no reply.

I was walking back down the hall when I noticed a skinny door next to the guest bathroom that I hadn't seen before. I thought it might be a linen cupboard, but when I opened it I found a flight of steep steps. There must be an attic. I didn't really want to go up there, but I had no choice. "Eric?" I called, moving tentatively on to the first step. "Are you up there?"

"Go away," a voice called back down. He didn't sound angry, just flat. Resigned.

I squeezed my eyes shut, trying to block out the pain that arced across my temples at the sound of his voice. "Look, I'm not here to apologise or anything. I just discovered something that I thought you should know about."

Silence.

I cleared my throat. "So, um … someone has been siphoning money out of your mother's accounts. Over £20,000 in the last year alone."

I waited. There was several moments of agonising silence, and then Eric's voice came down the stairs again. Louder this time, clearer. He sounded surprised. And annoyed. "But that's impossible. My mother is ruthless with money. She'd have caught any suspicious behaviour in an instant. You must have got it wrong."

"I didn't get it wrong," I snapped. "It's my job to discover things like this. It's only been going on since she got sick. She left the responsibility for her accounts in the hands of someone she trusted."

'Duncan?"

'I could be wrong, but I don't think I am. He came over yesterday and asked some really strange questions. He's tampered with her accounts to try to hide the transactions, and then tried to convince me to overlook the online accounts, which he couldn't mess with."

"What are you going to do about it?"

'I'm going to send all the files to our forensic accounting team, and they'll go through them and figure out exactly what's been taken. Then we'll go to the police. In the meantime, I have to convince Duncan that I'm none the wiser, so he doesn't do something stupid like skip the country." I paused. There was no answer, so I spoke again, trying to keep my voice from wavering. "That's all. I'll leave you alone now."

"Elinor, wait—" Eric called down after me, but I slammed the door and fled back down to the study.

THIS WAS the first time since I'd been at Marshell House that I'd ventured into the centre of Crookshollow. I had to admit that it was actually quite pretty, as small towns without designer boutiques and Starbucks went. The high street was clean, with wide footpaths and wooden benches set around well-kept flower beds. Several pedestrian avenues branched off it, lined with quaint shops and tiny pubs and restaurants. At one end of the street was a large modern building, built of glass and steel, that towered over the street. The Halt Institute. Who knew Crookshollow had such a modern appendage? It looked like it housed an art gallery and some other cultural things. I made a mental note to go back and check it out another day.

I found a parking space opposite the witchcraft museum, and started walking around. I caught sight of a petite girl with spiky white hair and a killer red leather jacket walking out from a vegan coffee shop. Her arms were covered in intricate, brightly-coloured tattoos. She looked like the sort of girl Allan *should* be dating. I decided to follow her and see if she could lead me to some cool shops.

Most of the shops were only just opening, so although the cafes along the high street were doing a roaring trade, and there was a line outside the door of *Bewitching Bites*, there weren't many other people about. The white-haired girl didn't seem to be in any kind of hurry. She meandered slowly down the street, occasionally sipping on her coffee or glancing in a window. I followed at a good distance, making note of the stores she paused at to come back to later.

Finally, she pulled open the door to a shop called *Astarte*, and ducked inside. *Bingo.* I stood outside and peered in the window. The store appeared to sell a huge range of items, from racks of crystals to stacks of old-looking, leather-bound books, to weird knick-knacks and—

Oh. *Wow.*

In the corner of the front window stood a mannequin wearing the most incredible dress I'd ever seen. It was black and slinky with a cowl neck, and it clung to every curve of the mannequin, before flaring out just at the knee in a flowing fish-tail skirt. The bodice was embroidered with swirling silver designs, and the row of silver swirls around the hem looked almost like tentacles rising up from the deep. The whole outfit reminded me of something Morticia Addams would wear if she were going to a fancy-dress ball. I loved it instantly, but of course, the mannequin was a size 0, so there was probably no way it would look good on me. I did see a couple of racks of clothes near the back of the store, though. If there was anything like that dress in my size, I'd be set.

I swung the door open and ducked inside. A cloying smell assailed my nostrils, and my eyes watered in the corners. I saw three incense burners on the counter. That was why. The store was much larger inside than it appeared from the street. The old Victorian shopfront had a low, dark-panelled ceiling that was obscured by new-age posters and strings of crystals and dream-catchers. Dark oak bookshelves lined each wall, crammed with books and pouches and candles of all colours and descriptions. One table displayed a range of crystal necklaces, another was stacked high with glossy books about witchcraft and candle magic. It looked like the kind of store Hermione Granger would feel perfectly at home in.

While I was standing in the doorway gaping like an idiot, the white-haired girl finished paying for her purchases and moved toward me. "Excuse me." She smiled politely as she brushed past me to get through the narrow door, leaving a trail of spicy perfume in her wake.

I was now the only customer in the store. The woman behind the counter turned to me. She was quite elderly, probably in her seventies, although the long jet-black hair that hung down her back in a single plait made her look younger. She wore several black shawls tied around her shoulders, so that it was nearly impossible to tell her real size or shape. Her nails were painted bright pink, and her eyes danced with intelligence. She fixed her gaze on me.

"I'm Clara," the old woman said. "How can I help you?"

"I'm not sure," I said. "I was wondering about that dress in your window, but I don't know if it'll be in my size—"

"Of course it is! That style of dress was practically made for your figure. Wait there and I'll fetch one for you." Clara disappeared to the back of the store, and I moved to the rack behind the window. Despite her kind words, I highly doubted that the black dress was going to look good on me. I started searching for something more flattering.

The rack was filled to bursting with dresses in all colours and sizes. But nothing grabbed me like that black dress. I fingered some silken scarves printed with spiderweb designs tied to a wooden tree. Next to the tree was a cabinet stuffed with books. I smiled as I scanned the strange titles; *The Book of Soyga, The Necronomicon, The Lesser Key of Solomon, Sexual Magick, The Ghosts of Crookshollow. Witchcraft Through the Ages, The Ghost Whisperer.* I picked one up and started flicking through it. Every page had images of ghosts and spirits from different time periods and cultures. I turned to the index, wondering if maybe one of these books could tell me something about Eric and how he had become solid last night.

Just then Clara returned with an armload of fabric. "I found a couple of others that would suit you, dear," she said, as she hung the dresses in the changing room. I put the book down and walked inside. The first dress was the shimmering black dress from the window. It was made of some slinky, clingy material. I pulled it over my head and smoothed it down, my heart beating nervously as I dared my first peek in the mirror.

I hardly recognised myself. The black made my skin look clear and creamy, the silver swirls drawing attention to my breast and hips. I did a little sashay, admiring the way the dress clung to every curve in all the right places. For the first time in years, I grinned back at my reflection. I looked like a movie starlet. Eric would *flip* when he saw it.

Don't you mean Allan? Devil's Advocate Elinor sneered.

Yes, of course. I mean Allan will love this dress. But there was no fooling myself. When I looked at myself in the mirror, I was imagining Eric's black-clad body next to mine, his beautiful fingers taking hold of me and escorting me into some music industry black tie event. But of course that could never be. A tear fell from the edge of my eye and splashed against the neckline, a tiny wet droplet against the shimmering fabric.

Quickly, I pulled off the dress and tried on the next one—a wraparound dress in a beautiful emerald green. It looked great too, but had a rather plunging neckline and short hem that I didn't think I'd feel comfortable in outside of the changing room.

And then I saw the other dress. A red so rich and intense it made me gasp. A sweetheart neckline and boned corset stitched with vines of sparkling black beads. A skirt made of multiple layers of tulle and chiffon that shimmered under the lights. It looked just like the dress the girl wore on the cover of Ghost Symphony's first album.

The skirt and corset were two separate parts, and it took me several minutes to struggle into them, and then several more minutes to fasten the corset correctly. I'd never worn a garment like that before, with laces to do up and clasps in the front. I dared a look in the mirror, gasping with delight when I saw my reflection. It fit perfectly. The corset pushed my girls up, giving me the most impressive cleavage I'd ever seen. It also pulled my waist in, without being constricting, giving my body that coveted hourglass shape. And the skirt, oh the skirt! It danced as I moved, the layers swirling around my legs, caressing my skin as they flared out around me. The red picked up flecks of light and colour, so it appeared as if flickers of flame burst from the hem. I looked like the heroine of a Del Toro film. I had no idea where I would wear a dress like that, but I knew I *had* to have it.

Neither dress was my usual style. They were too risqué, too unique for Elinor the Lawyer. You couldn't wear something like that to meet with a client or attend the firm's annual Christmas cocktail party. But being stuck here in Crookshollow was making me realise that maybe that image was not who I really was inside. Maybe the red dress was more "me" than all the beige pantsuits in my wardrobe.

My decision made, I quickly unlaced the corset and slipped

out of the skirt, put on my clothes, and exited the changing room. My heart hammered against my chest. I needed to pay for these quickly, before I changed my mind. "I'll take these," I said, handing the two dresses over. "And these books, too." I stacked two ghost books on top of my pile.

"Ah, those are two excellent and useful books if you have an interest in ghosts. Of course, as the author, I admit I carry some bias."

"You wrote these?" The woman smiled a toothy grin, and pointed to the name on the cover. *Clara Raynard.*

"That's me. Around here I'm considered somewhat of an expert on unexplained occurrences," she said. "I think you'll find chapter 13 particularly illuminating." She tapped the cover of *The Private Life of Ghosts.* "There's some information on shades that will be particularly useful for your current situation."

"What situation?"

"The Marshell House." Clara grinned. "You're the lawyer who is living there."

"How … how do you know I was staying in the Marshell House?"

"This is a small town, dear. And an old lady like me doesn't have much in her life apart from gossip." Clara leaned forward, smiling conspiratorially at me. "Duncan told me all about you, and from his description, I think you're even prettier in person."

"Oh, um. Thanks." Clara kept staring at me with that knowing smile, and I was starting to feel uneasy. She handed me back my credit card and I stuffed it into my wallet, grabbing my bags and heading for the door as fast as I could.

"I have a special interest in Marshell House," she added. I nodded, my hand on the door handle, remembering Pete's Pizza and the rental car company. "It has a bit of a reputation around here for being haunted. Many locals won't go anywhere near it. But all my investigations have revealed that the only haunting in that house was a young boy terrorised by a bitter old woman. At least, until recently. Have you seen or heard anything interesting during your stay?"

Just a hot rock star ghost who gave me the best sex of my life, I thought, my cheeks flushing. The way Clara was looking at me made me nervous, as if she could read my thoughts. "No, I mean, I don't think so. I'm not used to living in an old house. Sometimes it creaks and groans and I see shadows in the corners of the room. But I'm here to do a job. I can't let my imagination get the better of me."

"Oh, no, it's your imagination that will set you free, my dear. Sometimes instead of hiding from the shadows, we should be embracing them."

"Um, yes. Sure." I pulled the door open. "Well, goodbye. It was nice meeting you."

"Don't give him up for the grave just yet, my dear," the woman called after me as I darted into the street. "Sometimes love can endure beyond the veil of death."

I dashed back to the car, my feet pounding against the pavement as Clara's words reverberated against my skull. *Love can endure beyond the veil of death.* But how could she know ... The answer was simple: she didn't know. She couldn't know about Eric. She was just some crazy old woman who loved to ramble. But she'd written those books. A flicker of hope darted across my mind. If I'd just made love to a ghost, an old woman who read minds was definitely within the realm of possibility. I tried to push Clara's words away, but they kept nagging at my mind. I knew I had to read the chapter she'd mentioned very carefully. If there was a way to bring Eric back ...

Back at the house, Eric still wasn't anywhere to be seen. Secretly, I was grateful, because it was already past eleven and I desperately needed to get some more work done, and I was also keen to make a start on the books I'd bought. I cursed myself for not thinking of researching ghosts beforehand—maybe the books could give us both some much-needed answers.

I wanted to start poring over the books immediately, but I was already behind on my work, and I wanted to send off an email to our forensic accountant about the "music lessons" in Alice's accounts.

I made myself a stack of mousetraps and worked steadily for the next couple of hours. Around midday, the gardeners showed up to start work tearing out all the weeds and overgrown flowerbeds. They shuffled nervously on the porch and refused my invitation to come inside for some tea. At 2pm, the doorbell rang and I let the woman from the hire company around to the back garden to measure for the marquee. She too glanced nervously up at the house and got her measurements done at breakneck speed. She sped so fast out of the drive, I swear I saw smoke behind her.

At five, I told the gardeners to pack up their tools and get lost. I didn't like the idea of people hanging around the house while I was in the shower. They looked relieved when they left. This house really did seem to get to people. *If only they knew.*

I went upstairs, took a long shower, shaved my legs and armpits, plucked my eyebrows, and did all the other essential date-prep required to turn a dowdy frump like me into a vaguely attractive creature. Usually, this was the point of a date where I caught a glimpse of myself in the mirror and started to question the whole thing. *Surely this guy asked me out as a joke,* I'd think to myself. *It's a bet, or he's mad at his girlfriend and out for revenge.* But not tonight. Tonight I shimmied into my new black dress, pinned up my hair, applied some dark eye makeup and a devilish red lipstick, and did a little turn in front of the mirror. I looked good. I *felt* good … if I didn't think about Eric.

As I was teetering back down the stairs in my black heels, Eric floated past on the landing. I stopped in my tracks, surprised to see him down from the attic. Our eyes met for a moment, and his face flickered with hurt. Then he turned his head away and silently floated into a wall.

Good. That's how I liked my ghosts. Silent and sulking.

That's not what you were saying last night, Devil's Advocate Elinor reminded me.

I had some time to wait before Allan arrived, if he arrived on time, which I wasn't expecting. He was a drummer, after all. I sat in a chair by the window and picked up *The Practical Guide to Ghosts,* and started reading.

The book was all about different cultural perceptions of ghosts. What they were, how they came to be, and what kept them tethered to the world. It talked a lot about recent hauntings in Crookshollow and the rest of England, and how unlucky families had eventually banished particular spirits from their homes.

As I turned toward chapter 13, "The Ghosts Who Return," a bookmark slipped out from between the pages. It was a business card from Clara's shop. She had marked the section for me. I turned to that page and started scanning the text.

In some rare instances, it is possible that a ghost is not a ghost at all, but a soul in a temporary state of flux. The body is suspended in a deathlike state, but the mind has been so traumatised by a violent death or so incensed at an injustice that it must return in a semi-lucid form in order to put right whatever has wronged them. We call these bodiless souls "shades," for they are but a pale shade of the whole and living being.

This is nonsense. There's no such thing as souls. This is a bunch of New Age hippy-dippy mumbo jumbo. But I kept reading.

A shade usually manifests as a ghostly form resembling the living person, wearing the clothes they wore upon death, although most people will not be able to see the shade at all. Usually only those who have an emotional connection to the shade's human form will be able to see and communicate with the spirit. Shades are capable of normal speech with these representatives of the living world—whom we refer to as conduits— and a ghost hunter can use the conduit to send and receive messages.

Shades usually cannot touch or manipulate objects and may find themselves trapped within a certain dwelling or locale. Shades are exceptionally rare, and only a handful have been documented by modern ghost hunters.

A shade is tied to his/her corporeal form, even though he/she may remain separate from it for some time. Occasionally, when a particularly strong emotional state—usually anger, or fear, or love— pulls the shade back into the living world, they may manifest in a solid form. Many of the old religions record spells for sending a shade back to his/her body, but these spells have never been successfully attempted in the modern age ...

The doorbell rang, startling me out of the world of ghosts and shades and life-restoring spells. I glanced at my phone. 7pm on the dot. I replaced the bookmark and set the book on the table, torn between wanting to stay and find out more about shades and if I could somehow use the information to help Eric, and wanting to escape the house and have a great date with Allan.

The sexy drummer won out. I *was* a party girl, after all.

Allan knocked again. I checked my hair in the mirror above the fireplace, smoothed down my dress, and grabbed my bag from the table.

"Good evening." I smiled as I opened the door. Allan stood on the porch, wearing black jeans and a powdery blue shirt with the sleeves rolled up, revealing the tattoos covering his forearms. The blue set off his sparkling eyes, and his white-blonde hair was spiked in all directions. He looked gorgeous. I still couldn't believe he was my date.

"You look fantastic," he said, his eyes rolling over my whole body. I felt my cheeks flush with heat as he took in the curve of my cleavage in the clingy black dress. I wasn't used to men looking at me like that, with that hunger in their eyes. I liked it, I liked how I felt, powerful and sexy.

I glanced back into the house. I jumped when I saw Eric

standing at the top of the stairs, staring down at us with an unreadable expression on his face.

"Is something the matter?" Allan asked, peering into the house behind me. "You look like you just saw a ghost."

If only you knew. "It's nothing," I said quickly. Eric shook his head, then shrunk back into the darkness. I allowed Allan to place his hand on the small of my back and lead me down the steps. "Nothing is the matter at all."

CROOKSHOLLOW WAS SO small that Allan hadn't even bothered to drive over to pick me up. Instead, we walked toward the high street, veering off into a quaint cobbled lane lined with pubs and restaurants. Allan took me to a kitschy Greek restaurant, where a live band serenaded us with horrific folk music and the waiters kept filling up our glasses with raki, an aniseed-flavoured spirit that tasted like paint-stripper but definitely got rid of any dating nerves.

Our conversation flowed easily. Allan regaled me with tales of life on the road, and I told him about being a lawyer and some of the crazier cases the firm had worked on. As our raki was topped up for the third time, I even told Allan about my drawings, and my plans for getting a large tattoo. He explained the history of some of his own ink, and how he'd fainted the first time he went under the needle.

After a delicious dessert of *baklava* dripping with honey, Allan asked me if I'd like to go with him for a drink at a nearby pub. I was tempted, but I still felt weird about being out with Allan, as if I was somehow betraying Eric. His face flashed through my mind, stone cold as he watched me leave with Allan. The dinner was one thing, but I knew where drinks at a pub usually ended up, and I wasn't sure I was ready for that yet, not after last night.

"Not tonight," I said. "I've had way too much *raki* already." Allan looked disappointed, but took it like a gentleman. He insisted on walking me home.

Outside the restaurant, the wind had whipped up a bit. Allan held my hand as we walked back toward Marshell House. His fingers felt warm and exciting, but they didn't make fire shoot up my arm, like Eric's did. While we walked, Allan pointed out different buildings and landmarks he remembered from his visits with Eric. "Even though he was desperate to escape this place, he still had a great love for it," Allan said. "So much of who Eric is is wrapped up in Crookshollow—all the legends and history of this place."

We turned on to the corner of Blossom Road. "Hey," I exclaimed as we walked past the row of shops on the corner. "The tattoo shop is still open."

"Oh, yeah!" Allan stopped at the window. "I remember this place. This is where Eric got all his tattoos done. Bianca is one of the finest artists in the country."

Bianca? The tattoo artist was a woman. "Really?"

"Yeah. See—that's Eric right there." Allan pointed to the poster on the window of the shirtless man with a beautiful dragon winding around his ribcage. I turned my gaze away, not wanting to remember Eric's naked body.

"That's some impressive work—hey! What are you doing?" Allan pulled me toward the door.

"We're going inside." He grinned wickedly as he pushed the door open with his boot.

"No!" Panic seized my chest. I couldn't go inside a place like that. I wasn't ready. What if it was unclean? What if it was the front for a drug ring? I grabbed the nearest lamppost, my fingers gripping the wood so tight my knuckles turned white.

"Relax, Elinor. You don't have to come out with a rose on your arse. We're just going to have a look. If you want to get that big tattoo of yours one day, you really ought to actually set foot inside a tattoo shop first. What do you say?"

I stared at the black doors, open just a crack to reveal a light shining from inside. I could hear loud music blaring, and people laughing. Over that was a high buzzing sound, like a colony of hummingbirds had all come in to have Kanji symbols inked on their wings. Allan grinned, revealing his white teeth. Gulping back my fear, I released my grip on the lamppost and reached out and gripped his hand.

"Let's go," I said.

"That's my girl."

Allan led me through the doors and down a short hall. The walls and ceiling were decorated with bright-coloured graffiti art; one wall depicting cutesy zoo animals engaged in all sorts of lewd and outlandish acts. The other showed the spectrum of Norse mythology, surrounded by swirling occult symbols and constellations. At the end of the hall we entered a small, brightly lit room. Black leather sofas lined one wall, where a girl with an entire scrapyard's-worth of metal in her face sat flipping through a fashion magazine. Behind a low wall, a weedy youth lay across a black padded table, while a girl bent over his back, laughing as she ran a tattoo gun across his spine, adding flashes of shading to a beautiful pair of wings.

"Omigod," I whispered as I leaned over to stare at the wings. "Did she draw those?"

"I did," the girl said, without looking up.

I leapt back in surprise. The youth on the table laughed, but his laugh quickly turned into a wince as the woman ran the needle along his spine again.

I clamped my hand over my mouth. "Oh, I'm so sorry. I guess I didn't realise you could hear me. I hope I haven't caused you to make a mistake."

The woman looked up and grinned at me. I was surprised to see that I recognised her. She was the girl with the white pixie haircut I'd followed into Clara's shop earlier today. Up close, I could see that she was beautiful, with tiny, almost doll-like features, giant pale blue eyes, and high, movie-star cheekbones. Her neck, chest, and arms were completely covered with intricate tattoos, and her ears and nose were stuffed with all manner of metal spikes and chains. She looked completely badass.

"I'm Bianca Sinclair, and I don't make mistakes." She gave me a nod, and placed the buzzing needle back on to her client's back.

"I'm Elinor."

"Nice to meet you, Elinor. Are you looking to get something done?"

"I er …" Allan elbowed me in the arm. "Maybe. I'm not sure yet."

"Well, best to be sure, first. Or drunk. Drunk people are usually pretty sure. I just finished up a residency at a shop in Prague, and a drunk guy came in absolutely *adamant* that he wanted a SpongeBob Squarepants tattooed on his forehead. He's lucky I have a policy against inking cartoon characters." The boy on the table snorted. Bianca continued to talk to me, even as she worked on adding shading to the bones that formed the spine of the wings. "Do you live near here? I think I've seen you walking around the shops before."

"Not exactly. I actually live in London. I'm a lawyer. I'm here on an assignment for my firm."

Bianca glanced up at me with those big eyes, tilting her head to the side as she looked me up and down. "Interesting. I don't tattoo many lawyers. Plenty of defendants, but no lawyers."

"I'm just an estate lawyer, nothing as interesting as defending criminals in court. I mostly shuffle paperwork and help the relatives of dead people get their hands on free stuff."

"Don't talk like that. No one is *just* anything. I bet you had to work incredibly hard to get where you are. My mother used to say when she introduced me to her friends, 'This is Bianca. She is a professional artist.' And then people start talking to me about Picasso and I have to show them my sleeve and explain what I *really* do." Bianca laughed as she gestured to her right arm, where

Van Gogh's *Starry Night* had been exquisitely rendered across her forearm.

"Your parents are proud of you?" I clamped my hand over my mouth as Bianca laughed. "I'm sorry, that came out so bitchy. It just surprises me. My parents would probably have disowned me if I hadn't followed them into the legal field. In fact, they probably *will* disown me if they ever found out I got a tattoo."

"Oh, I admit there was a time when they were bitterly disappointed I didn't go to art school," said Bianca. "But they know me well enough to know I don't do things the conventional way. Now, my mum cuts all my work out of tattoo magazines. She has a scrapbook of press clippings and she brings it out whenever her friends are talking about their kids. It's really sweet, actually."

"She sounds like a cool mum."

"She has her moments." Bianca rolled her eyes. "So what brings a big city lawyer to little old Crookshollow?"

"I'm working for the estate of Alice Marshell."

Bianca's eyes looked sad. "I read about her death in the paper, and Eric's too, of course. It's so sad that she died within days of her son, almost as if she *sensed* he'd gone. I actually went to high school with Eric. I had such a crush on him back then."

Beside me, Allan laughed. "You wouldn't be the only one."

"Back then, I probably was. He wasn't exactly popular. A bit too thin and weedy, I think. But he always had those dark, dangerous eyes."

"And that brooding, morose personality," Allan added. Bianca grinned.

"What was he like?" I asked, ignoring Allan.

Bianca put the needle down, staring at a spot behind my head. "Eric? Oh, when school started, he was actually kind of popular. He played on the cricket team, and was a bit of a jock, although he didn't seem overly arrogant or anything. He was happy just following along with whatever his friends did.

"But then, when he turned twelve, he changed. He came back

from summer break completely dressed in black, his hair in dreadlocks. He didn't talk to anyone, stopped hanging out with his friends, and started coming down onto the football fields with my group of misfits to get stoned and talk about music. He told me his father left, and that's what made him focus on the violin as his instrument. He wanted to understand his father's mind.

"Eric won all the music competitions at school, even beating out the kids several grades above him. Eric was brilliant, he came first in all his classes, but he never had many friends, and he didn't really seem interested in making them. All he cared about was the music. The teachers called him a savant, but he never smiled when he played. I always remember that. He never smiled much at all."

"Hey, Bianca. I'm getting cold down here!" the boy on the table said.

"Sorry, Carl." Bianca shrugged, and picked up her needle again. "It's been nice talking to you, but I'd better get back to work."

Allan tugged my arm. "I should probably get you home. I'm sure Bianca would like to get back to her client."

"Oh, sure." I nodded, feeling foolish. "Well, it was nice meeting you."

"It was awesome to meet you, Elinor. Come down to the shop if you ever need to get out of that creepy old house. I'm always here. I even live upstairs. We could get coffee."

I beamed. "Thanks. I may just do that."

As we left the shop, I punched Allan playfully in the arm. He rubbed the spot, pretending to be hurt. "What was that for?"

"For taking me in there. For getting me out of the house. For making me forget about Eric's awful death for a few hours."

"Next time, keep your thanks to yourself." Allan grinned, his eyes sparkling.

We walked the rest of the distance to Marshell House in companionable silence. Allan led me up the steps to the porch. "I had a really great time tonight."

"Me too," I said. "It's been a long time since I've gone on an actual date. Usually my encounters with guys are drive-by gropings on the dance floor."

Allan laughed. "Those guys are idiots. You deserve to be treated like a lady, Elinor."

Before I could blink, Allan had closed the space between us, and his lips were pressed up against mine. All night I'd been staring at those lips, wondering what it would be like to be with him, what it would feel like to play with that tongue stud. But when Allan tried to prise my lips open and shove his tongue between my teeth, all I could think about was Eric. Kissing Allan … it felt wrong, like I was betraying Eric somehow. I closed my eyes and tried to push the thoughts away, but all I could see was Eric's face in my mind. *I wish it could be you.*

I pulled away, shaking my head. "I'm sorry. I can't—"

Allan looked confused. "Is there someone else?"

"Not exactly. I'm just—" I didn't know what to say, how to explain. "I am sort of getting over someone. I like you a lot, Allan. It just feels too soon to be kissing someone else like this."

Allan wrapped his arms around my shoulders, pressing my face against his broad, muscular shoulder. "It's okay. I won't do anything you don't want to do."

I stared down at a spot on the railing, my face growing hot with embarrassment and emotion. I felt like such an idiot. "I need to go inside now. I really am sorry."

"Please, Elinor. Forget it. Can I see you again?" Allan asked hopefully.

I looked up at his bright eyes and earnest face. "You want to see me again, after I … after I ruined our date?"

"You ruined nothing. You're worth the wait, Elinor. I have some business that will occupy me for the next couple of days, but could I be your date for the funeral on Saturday? It would be nice to have a supportive person there while I give the eulogy. I know that sounds like a really morbid date, but trust me, Eric's funeral won't be your normal prayers-and-hymns affair."

"Sure." I smiled, my hand gripping the door handle. Eric's funeral. How would I make it through that? Maybe I'd just get really, really drunk, and then everything Eric and I had done the other night would become just a dream. Maybe by Saturday, I would be over this weird thing between Eric and I.

Allan waved at me, and jogged up the drive, his black-clad frame disappearing into the darkness, so that all I could see was the bright halo of his white hair growing smaller. I sucked in a breath, willing my legs to stop shaking, and went inside.

ERIC

The attic only had two small, filthy windows that faced the front of the house, so I came down to my bedroom and watched through the round window as Elinor and Allan walked up the drive. The moonlight made his bleached hair gleam like a giant white orb. Allan leaned close to her and whispered something in her ear, and she threw her head back and laughed with abandon, her brown locks rippling down her back. I balled my hands into fists.

They disappeared under the porch, and I listened for the creak of the front door opening, but it didn't come. Of course, they were on a date. They were doing the kinds of things people on a date did on the front porch.

Allan, you bastard.

A deep rage rose up from within me, and heat coursed through my body. I lashed out with my foot, flinging a wild kick at the trunk at the foot of my old bed, desperate to let my frustration out. My foot hit the side of the trunk, sending a shooting pain up the side of my leg.

"Ow!" I grabbed for my foot, my eyes watering from the pain of the impact. I hopped on the floor while I gripped my throbbing toes, my good foot disappearing a few inches into the floorboards each time.

Hang on a second ...

I stared down at my throbbing foot. It really had happened. I'd kicked the trunk, and it had felt solid.

I took a cautious step toward the trunk, reached out with my fingers. My hand passed right through it, as though it wasn't really there. Although, of course, I was the one who wasn't really there.

So how come I felt my foot connect with the box? How come my toes were throbbing? The pain felt as real as anything I could remember. The only other thing that had felt as real to me was Elinor—

What was happening to me? Was I a ghost or wasn't I?

I wound my foot back, pulling my thigh up toward my chest. Then, releasing all of my might, I flung my leg out at the trunk. I cried out as I sailed straight through the wood, toppling over myself and landing with my head through the ceiling of the room below.

Rage bubbled up inside of me. Why did I keep getting close to something real, only to have it torn away again? Why did this stupid ability to feel objects and people keep coming and going? Why didn't I have any control over it?

You're getting all emotional, Eric. Approach this like Elinor would, with common sense. Use all that air between your ears and think. What happened differently all the times you managed to move something?

I ticked them off in my mind. I twisted the lock in the door. Elinor touched me and I lifted the cup. I kicked the chest. Elinor and I ...

I couldn't see any common element between the events, apart from the fact they all happened to me and they had all occurred since Elinor arrived in the house. But that didn't seem like enough of a connection. If Elinor and I were talking, I could ask her about it, and I bet she'd come up with an answer, but I didn't feel like talking to her right now.

Speak of the devil … I heard the front door click shut and footsteps padding up the staircase. The light in the hall clicked on. A few minutes later, Elinor appeared at the door, her face flushed from the cold, her hair a wild tangle around her face. "There you are," she said, her voice stilted, nervous. "It's good to see you downstairs again. Why are you holding your foot like that?"

"Oh, no reason." I let go of my toes. I felt a pang in my chest as I looked at her beautiful face, flushed with colour from the cold night air and whatever Allan had been doing to her. I wanted to tell her about kicking the chest, but I could hardly bear to look at her, knowing she had the scent of Allan on her lips. "How was your *date?*"

"Please, Eric. Don't be like that. It wasn't really a date. I met someone you knew tonight," she said. "Bianca Sinclair, at Resurrection Ink."

Bianca? The quiet, arty chick turned badass tattoo artist—the only other remotely interesting person to come out of Crookshollow Grammar school? "Is she still around? I would have thought she'd be running some huge shop in London or Stockholm or Berlin now. She has a rare talent."

"She said she just got back from a month guesting in Prague, but she likes her small-town roots. She's invited me to come hang out with her. Would that be okay?"

"You don't need my permission," I growled. *You didn't ask me if it was okay to go out with Allan. Because it's not okay.*

"I know, but I didn't want it to be weird for you, me hanging out with people you knew while you were—" She bit her lower lip. Damn, she looked so hot when she did that.

"You didn't think to ask me when you went on a date with my drummer."

"That was different. Allan is clearly distraught about your death. I wanted to offer support."

"And your kind of support is spreading your legs for him?"

"You're such a dick, Eric Marshell." Tears pooled in her eyes.

Elinor spun on her heel and fled the room. A few moments later, the door to the study slammed shut.

I hurled myself down the stairs, ready to go after her and apologise, but just before I could float through the door, I changed my mind. Why was I running after her? She was the one who hurt *me.*

"Fuck!" I yelled, screwing my hands into fists.

Let her sulk in there and miss out on my big news. It serves her right for taking up with Allan when she knew I ...

But whatever I told myself, I couldn't shake the horrible feeling in my stomach that actually, I *was* being a dick. I knew I should go and apologise, but I couldn't quite bring myself to do it. I pictured Elinor naked beneath me, those bow-shaped lips parted with a sigh of ecstasy. I remembered the way her body nestled so perfectly against mine. My chest ached. We could have had a chance, if Elinor hadn't rejected me for Allan.

But Elinor was right. We had no chance. That's what hurt most of all. She could have no future with me, and she wasn't the kind of girl who could just abandon herself to the moment. She needed a plan, a future, and I could give her neither. She'd made her choice, and it was Allan.

Somehow, if I was going to get her help in bringing Helen Manning to justice, I had to find a way to deal with that.

ELINOR

I could hear Eric cursing through the floor above me. I wanted to go back upstairs and assure him that I wasn't involved with Allan, but his words from earlier still stung. So I stayed in the study most of the night, drinking bourbon beside the fire, listening to Ghost Symphony through my headphones and texting Cindy about the new guy she was seeing. She wouldn't tell me much about him, but she seemed pretty smitten. When I went up to bed at 2am, Eric was nowhere to be seen. He'd probably gone back up to the attic again.

Good riddance, I told myself, although I didn't believe it.

THE NEXT DAY, Eric wasn't there when I went down for breakfast. I made some toast, poured some coffee, and read through the news headlines on my phone. There was a notice that the police had released Eric's body ready for his funeral on Saturday. They still had not located the other driver. They were calling it vehicular manslaughter, which meant they still had no idea about Helen Manning. I started to walk up the stairs to tell Eric about it,

193

but then I heard him yell some kind of curse again, and something crashed against the floor, and I decided against it.

Eric's funeral.

He was upset enough already about Allan. I shouldn't add to his distress by discussing the funeral. When his body was buried in that mausoleum and everyone came and said eulogies and there was cake, that seemed so … final. It was already Tuesday. We only had a few more days to bring Helen to justice before Eric's body was interred.

I went to the study, jammed some house music on the speakers, and worked for a few hours, but my mind wasn't on the task. I kept imagining Eric's body still and stiff in a coffin. Helen's ticket stub was lying beside me on the table, its presence reminding me that I wasn't any closer to finding the killer.

Next to the ticket stub was the letter from Eric's lawyer. Taking a deep breath, I called the number and spoke briefly with Thomas Pinchton of Pinchton & Son. He curtly confirmed that the letter was legitimate and Eric Marshell had left both Tristan and Isolde to Allan. I thanked him for his time and wished him well, although he'd hung up before I even finished my sentence.

"Die in a fire," I snapped at my silent phone. At least that cleared up Eric's ridiculous notions about Allan's motives.

Sighing, I decided it was time for a break. I sat down beside the large bay window with a cup of tea. I'd opened the heavy curtains and grey light streamed into the dark study. The gardeners were already hard at work on the front garden. A huge skip sat on the driveway, nearly overflowing with trailing weeds. One of the gardeners was wheeling an industrial-sized ride-on mower down from the back of a truck. Above their heads, I could see sunlight desperate to peek through the clouds. It might actually be a slightly nice day out there. I looked at my watch. Lunchtime. I decided to head down the road to grab a sandwich, and see if Bianca was at home.

Eric floated down the stairs just as I was pulling my coat on.

"Where are you going?" he demanded in his possessive tone.

"Out," I snapped, instantly on the defensive. *How dare he act like I owe him an explanation after the way he acted yesterday?*

"Are you going to see Allan again?"

"That's none of your goddamn business."

"Fine." Eric floated into the study, the door slamming shut behind him. I cringed at the sound. But he could be as angry as he wanted. I resisted the urge to yell something about his funeral through the closed door, but that wouldn't be right. I would wait until we made up. If we ever did.

I gathered my bag and sketchbook and went down to the corner shops. I brought some fish and chips and mushy peas from the takeaway, and headed over to the tattoo parlour. It was early, but the door was open a crack. I went inside, but the shop was shut up, a metal grate pulled down over the entrance. Next to the door, a small staircase led up to the second-storey flat. I climbed up and knocked on the door.

"Come in," a sleepy voice groaned.

I pushed open the door, not sure what I expected to see. Bianca's apartment was tiny—a small shoebox of a living room greeted me, lit by sunlight streaming in from a floor-to-ceiling window. A single bench on the back wall and a tiny table beneath a sunny window served as a kitchen. Down a short hall, I could see a bedroom, and that appeared to be the only other room in the place. But despite its size, the place was homely and colourful. Every spare inch of wall space was covered with artwork—paintings in gilded frames, sketches and scraps of paper, road signs, postcards, hubcaps, clippings from magazines, all sorts of things. Bianca's sofas were covered in ethnic blankets in stripes of red and gold, and her coffee table was a long, dark mahogany box covered with stacks of books and magazines and several candles in various stages of melting.

Bianca popped her head out from the bedroom. "Oh, Elinor!

It's great to see you. I was hoping you'd stop by. Have a seat; I'm just trying to find a jumper that isn't covered in cat fur."

"Meow!" From the back of the apartment, a cat protested its innocence. A giant ginger tomcat bounded into the living room, his nose high in the air. He rubbed up against my legs, and I gave him a rub under the chin. A few moments later, Bianca emerged, looking stunning in a pair of black leggings that laced up the sides of her legs, purple Doc Martins, and a thin black wool jumper that hung in draping layers almost to her knees, cinched around her tiny waist with a black corset belt. How I wished I could pull off an outfit like that, but then, even if I could, where would I wear it?

"I see you've met Macavity." She grinned, gesturing to the ginger cat that was happily rubbing his cheeks against my hand. "He seems to like you, which is rare."

"He probably just smells the lunch I brought," I said, pushing my glasses up my nose as I set down the box of fried happiness.

"Ah, that must be it. Thank you! I'm starving. Do you want some tea?"

"Sure."

As Bianca hunted out cups in the kitchen and pulled out the Earl Grey, I wandered around the room, admiring the artwork on the walls. Many of the sketches I recognised as Bianca's own work —they matched the style of the tattoos on display in the windows of the shop.

"You don't open the store in the mornings?" I asked, searching for something to say. Bianca was so incredibly *cool,* I felt nervous just being in her presence. What was I doing in her flat in my frumpy sweater and jeans? Why did I think I could be friends with someone so awesome?

"There's no point." Bianca pushed a steaming cup into my bands. "People don't wake up at eight in the morning and think, 'I think I'll get tattooed today.' Although I'll open up for an early appointment if a client requests it."

"Is that for protection, in case of a zombie apocalypse?" I joked, pointing to a battered-looking cricket bat leaning up against a guitar amp in the corner.

Bianca laughed. "No, I play a little with the local club on the weekends. I've got to try and do a little physical activity, otherwise I'd never see the sun."

"That's cool. Hey, is this one yours?" I pointed at a painting of a red fox sitting under the shade of a gnarled oak tree, staring out into the forest. Its snout pointed to the heavens as if it had caught the scent of something intriguing, and a glint of mischief reflected in its eyes. What stood out about the painting was the way the artist have lovingly portrayed the dappled light falling through the canopy above. It danced across the fox's fur, so that the creature almost appeared to move.

"Oh, no," Bianca said. "I'm nowhere near that good. That's an original Ryan Raynard."

"Who's he?" I asked, squinting at the sweeping brush strokes the artist had used to render the trees.

"Crookshollow's own world-renowned artist," Bianca said. "He lives in a giant manor house at the end of Holly Avenue. He used to be a total recluse, hadn't even left his house in ten years, until he met this girl, Alex Kline, a few months back. Now, they seem to be at a different event or opening or party every week. The London society pages are going crazy about them, calling them the Posh and Becks of the art world. Alex is a friend of mine, and a fine artist in her own right. We did a show at the Tunbridge Gallery in town last year. It was her first show, and she gave me this to say thanks for including her."

"Sounds wild," I exclaimed.

"Oh, you don't even know the half of it." Bianca gave me a sly smile, as if there was a whole lot more to the story she wasn't yet ready to reveal. "Perhaps you might meet them some time, if you stay in town."

"I'm only here for another week or so. Just until I finish going through Alice Marshell's things and hand the estate over to her executor." *If he isn't convicted of fraud first,* I reminded myself.

"Oh, that's a shame. I know it doesn't seem like much compared to London, but Crookshollow can be pretty wild."

"Don't worry, I know," I said. "I've met some pretty interesting characters. There was this woman in town the other day, who sold me some amazing clothes and a couple of books about ghosts—"

"Clara?"

"Yeah. From the *Astarte* shop. I saw you there once."

"I'm there all the time. I'm really into that kind of new age stuff. She can't get rid of those books fast enough. Everyone in Crookshollow has got a copy, but she's still got ten crates out the back of her shop. I hope you didn't pay more than five quid for them, because if you did, you got ripped off."

I laughed. "So you know Clara?"

"Everyone does. She's a pretty important figure in Crookshollow. She's actually Ryan's mother. She's our foremost expert on supernatural phenomena. She does tarot readings at the fair every year, and she's scarily accurate. Many people are convinced she's a witch. You *do* know that Crookshollow is the most haunted village in England?"

I laughed. "I've heard a rumour. So she's the real deal, then?"

"I don't believe in fate or hocus-pocus or any bullshit, right? I just know what I see. But I'm telling you, if Clara says it, it's probably true. Why, what did she say to you?"

"Oh, nothing. It's just about this guy—" I remembered what Clara had said in the shop the other day. *Sometimes love can endure beyond the veil of death.* Was it really possible that she knew more about my situation than I thought?

"Not Allan, your white-haired hottie from the other night?"

"No, not him. Although he did kiss me goodnight."

"Score." Bianca collapsed against the back of the sofa and sipped her tea. "I know Allan a little. He and Eric slept on my couch a few nights when they came back to Crookshollow for a visit. He's a cool guy. You know, no offence or anything, but I wouldn't have picked him as your type. We don't know each other very well, but you strike me as more of a white-shirt-and-black-tie-at-the-opera kind of girl. Not a bourbon-and-mosh-pit girl."

"That's what most people think, but I have to dress like this for my job. I live for weekends at the clubs. But I don't want to talk about myself. I'm boring. What made you decide to become a tattoo artist?"

Bianca shrugged. "I always wanted to be an artist. And when I was a teenager, I started hanging out with the bad crowd. I got my first ink at fifteen." She pointed to a grinning Cheshire cat on her arm. "Totally illegal, mind you, and not the best design. But I was dating a tattoo artist at the time, and I would hang out in the shop after school and draw on all their paper. My parents thought I was just drinking and doing drugs, which, to be fair, I was. But I was also watching these artists make a living from their art, and I wanted to as well. So I basically bugged the shop's owner incessantly until he gave me an apprenticeship."

"You learned through an apprenticeship?"

"Yeah, that's the best way. It was hard, but fun. I had to do a lot of bad tattoos before I got the hang of it. Why? Are you looking to give it a try?"

"No," I said. The word came out louder and harsher than I thought. Bianca looked at me curiously. I could feel my face growing hot. "I mean, no, thank you. I'd be too afraid of hurting someone. And don't you already have an apprentice?"

"Bobby just told me he's accepted a job at a shop in New York City, so I've got an opening." Bianca smiled. "I'm just saying, if you ever change your mind."

"Um … that's … very nice, but I already have this job. And this fancy law degree, which I should probably get some use out of—"

Bianca laughed. "Relax, Elinor. I'm not trying to get you to quit your job to live the bohemian life of a tattooist. Like I said, you don't seem like the type. Besides, you can't be a tattoo artist without having a bit of ink yourself."

"That's probably true." I handed Bianca my sketchbook. "Speaking of which, I brought this to show you."

As soon as Bianca opened the book, I regretted my decision. I wished I could snatch it back off her, but I didn't want to be rude to my new friend.

"Wow," Bianca exclaimed as she turned the page. "These are quite good."

"Yeah?" I mumbled, my cheeks burning. My stomach clenched in a tight knot.

"Absolutely. These are yours?"

I nodded glumly.

"You've got talent, girl. I particularly like this one of the gnarly tree. Or this one of the raven. Are you thinking one of these for a tattoo?"

"Yes, actually. I want something really big on my back."

"You sure you don't want to get a tiny rose on your ankle, maybe a couple of Chinese characters? A SpongeBob on your forehead? Just to get a feeling for it before you commit to a big piece?"

"I'm *sure.* Besides, I heard you don't do cartoon characters." I grinned, some of my nerves disappearing. "My problem is that I can't decide which one of these to choose."

We chatted for another hour or so. I was surprised at how easily the words flowed with Bianca. Normally, I'd feel nervous sitting beside someone so pretty and cool as her, but we just seemed to click instantly. We hugged goodbye as though we'd been friends for years.

"Are you going to be there on Saturday?" she asked.

"Where?"

"At Eric's funeral. It would be pretty hard to avoid, seems as how it's at Marshell House, but I figured you might not want to stick around with all the morose goths."

"Oh, no. I mean … er, yes. I am going to be there. Actually Allan asked me to accompany him."

"Sounds serious. He snores, by the way." Bianca grinned. "A funeral's a pretty weird place for a date, but hey, I'm not judging. He *is* the drummer in a goth band. I'll see you there, yes? We can sit at the back with your snogalicious date and tell inappropriate jokes to keep each other from tearing up."

I grinned at her use of the word *snogalicious*. "Absolutely." So it was settled, then. I'd have to attend Eric's funeral. I hoped I'd be able to hold it together. I couldn't have Bianca guessing the real reason for my fascination with Eric.

I left Bianca to open up her shop, and walked back toward Marshell House, wondering what I was going to do about Eric. Would he still be in the office after slamming the door at me this morning—

I stopped dead. A woman behind me had to swerve her pram to avoid a collision. She yelled something colourful at me, but I was too stunned to reply.

The door *slammed.*

My heart pounded against my chest. I can't believe I hadn't noticed it at the time. I'd been so angry with him I hadn't even realised. Eric had slammed the door. He'd actually become solid enough to move something in the house, something much more substantial than the door lock, and I hadn't been in contact with him. I remembered the smash I'd heard earlier that morning, of something shattering against the floor upstairs. Could Eric have moved an object and broken it? Was he becoming more solid, more real? How was that possible? What did that even mean?

I started to run. I couldn't wait to see him again, to talk to him. If Eric could touch things other than me, then that meant … I didn't know what that meant. But it had to be good, right? I had to see him.

I pulled open the door. "Eric?" I called. "Where are you?"
No answer.

The door to the study was open. I poked my head inside. No one there. "Eric?" I called again.

I heard another crash from upstairs. I vaulted the staircase two at a time, desperate to find him. "Eric, what's going on?"

He wasn't in any of the rooms. That meant he must be in the attic. I pulled the door open and crept up the staircase. I burst in the room just in time to see him fling an old wooden rocking chair across the room. I cringed as the chair smashed against a large wooden wardrobe and clattered to the floor, two of the spindles broken off.

"Eric!" I cried. He whirled around, his eyes blazing. The front of his black shirt was coated in dust from the attic furniture.

"What do you want?" he snarled.

"You're touching things," I said. "You're throwing things. What's happening to you?"

"What does it matter to *you?*" Eric shot back. "You made your choice. You've got Allan, a Ghost Symphony musician who's actually alive. What do you need me for?"

"I'm not here to talk about Allan," I said. "I came up because I heard a crash. I see you're upset, but I think I might have something to help you—" I cringed as he overturned a wooden chest. The lid flipped open and a giant stack of old photo albums and film canisters cascaded across the floor.

"It's got to be in here somewhere." Eric started fishing through another box, throwing magazines and old records in every direction.

"What?" I ducked as an ancient toaster flew past my head.

"My violin!" Eric yelled. "I need Isolde, and she's in the this house somewhere, but I can't find her. I have *nothing*, Elinor, and I'm going fucking mental. I lost my life, and I lost my family, and I lost you. That violin is the most precious thing in the world to me, and I fucking lost her, too."

"Eric, please. It will show up. But getting frustrated and

destroying things isn't going to help. If you come downstairs, I can show you these books—"

"Books? How are books going to help me? I'm dead." Eric rose up to his full height. His eyes looked sunken, haunted. His black curls hung in lank strings around his drawn features. "I'm a ghost. Books can't help me now."

"They will if they're about ghosts. I found something and I think it might—"

"Please, leave me." Eric closed his eyes. His voice was no longer angry. Now it was lifeless, defeated. That was worse. He sounded as if he had completely given up.

"I haven't abandoned you, you know. No matter what you want to believe." I was angry at him now, angry that he was hiding up here like a petulant child while I was trying to solve his murder and get his life back for him.

"I've been working and reading and investigating and asking questions and trying to figure this thing out. But what have you done, Eric? Have you given up? We have a chance ... the slimmest chance that we could be together, and I'm trying to figure out how to make it so, but you just want to sit up here and sulk and be all morose and melancholy. Well, it's pathetic, and I am through. I'm through wasting energy on a man that doesn't appreciate who I am and what I've done for him, a man who won't fight to be with me. If that's who you are, then you're not the man I thought you were."

Eric turned away from me, and stared out one of the small, low windows down into the back garden, where the marquee was being set up for Saturday. "Just go, Elinor. I don't want your help anymore. Please, just go."

Tears brimmed in my eyes. I blinked at them angrily. This was the last time I spilled tears for Eric Marshell. Without another word I turned, and fled the attic.

ERIC

*A*s soon as I heard Elinor's footsteps clattering down the stairs, I knew I'd made a huge mistake.

"Elinor, wait—" I dashed after her, but the hallway door slammed shut with a defiant clang. The sound was like a gunshot, jolting me out of my angry stupor. I paused at the top of the stairwell and listened. Her footsteps moved down the hall, down the stairs, and into the study below. I heard the door click shut and the muffled sounds of music blaring.

You're not the man I thought you were. Her words echoed inside my head. I seethed with anger, but it was because deep down, I knew she was speaking the truth. I'd enlisted Elinor to help me, and she was doing an amazing job. She'd been the one to connect Helen Manning to the ticket and the car crash. And if what she'd said before was true, she'd clearly been doing some research about my strange newfound ability to touch and manipulate objects randomly. She might've been on to something, but once again, I pushed her away instead of just listening to her. I was so convinced that everything was as bad as it could possibly be, I couldn't even believe there was a possibility we could have a chance at a happy ending.

Clearly she believed that, and Elinor wasn't the type to believe something without significant evidence in its favour. We could have had a chance, if I had just trusted her, if I had just allowed her to put that brilliant mind of hers to work.

But instead, I had been a dick, and ruined things. But this time, I wasn't sure I could fix them.

I reached out to shut the attic door, but my hand fell through the doorknob. I was a ghost once more. Downstairs, the music blared louder. I strained my ghostly ears to hear what she was playing. Something about the rhythm sounded awfully familiar.

I froze when I heard a familiar melody, ringing clearly. I know that song. I know that song because I wrote it.

Elinor was listening to Ghost Symphony. She was listening to my music. Maybe, just maybe, I had a chance after all. If I didn't fuck things up again.

I sat up in the study and worked until the early hours of the morning, the Ghost Symphony albums on repeat in the background. I lost myself in the morose lyrics and haunting melodies, and I found the hours drifted by pleasantly. Every time I got up to make a new cup of tea, Clara's ghost books stared at me from the end table. My fingers itched to turn the pages, find the section on shades, and see if there was any more information. But each time I stopped myself. I wasn't helping Eric anymore. I was done.

My resolution to stop working on Eric's case left me with a new feeling of calm. It hurt to know he was upstairs and I couldn't go to him, but it gave me a new feeling of control over my emotions. I had made all the effort, and he'd rewarded me with suspicion and jealousy. I was through with that shit. I had pulled off the Band-aid, and now I was free.

The next morning, I returned from a walk to the shops to find Duncan in the kitchen, and the house full of catering staff and florists and sound technicians and a bunch of carpenters assembling some kind of stage in the middle of the marquee. I exchanged a few awkward pleasantries with Duncan, but he was quite busy with the preparations and I didn't really want to be drawn into a discussion about Alice's estate with him, lest gave away the fact I'd discovered his little deception.

So instead, I took my tea and toast out onto the back porch, along with the paper I'd purchased from the shop. I wiped away a spider's web from the corner of the table and settled down to read the entertainment pages. There's nothing like the sordid tales of B-list celebrities and reality TV stars to make you feel better about your own life.

I was pleasantly surprised to see Damon Sputnik on the cover page. I'd been so preoccupied with Eric's drama and the fraud and the funeral and everything else going on in Crookshollow that I had barely even lusted after him. Well, it was time to make up for lost time.

In the picture, Damon was standing behind his sound desk, his face bent in concentration as he spun out a tune. He wore black jeans and a blue vest that showed off his muscular arms and bold tattoos, his freshly shaved head gleaming with sweat. I licked my lips. Damon really *was* quite attractive, with that pouty mouth, smouldering eyes and broad, muscular shoulders. He was similar to Eric in many ways—they were both musicians at the top of their chosen genres, both arrogant, both creative and petulant and both excellent kissers. But Damon Sputnik wasn't dead.

Suddenly, I couldn't wait to get back to London again to see if I had a chance with him. Maybe the easy confidence I felt around Eric would rub off on me around Damon? Maybe I'd come back a completely different person, and he'd fall at my feet? Maybe we could double-date with Cindy and her new man...

SPUTNIK'S SWEETHEART, the heading underneath Damon's picture read. MEET THE MYSTERY WOMAN WHO'S STOLEN HIS HEART. For a moment my heart fluttered as I imagined discovering an image of Damon and I locked in a passionate kiss in front of the speaker stacks. *Don't be ridiculous,*

Elinor. That was weeks ago, and guys like Damon don't stay off the market for long.

That's okay, you have other prospects, Devil's Advocate Elinor reminded me, and an image of Allan's face popped into my mind. Damn right. I didn't need Damon Sputnik … unless he needed me to help him get over his heartache when this new girl eventually dumped him, in which case I would be all over that. Idly, I turned the page to see what the paper had to say about Damon's new flame.

It was one of those collage pages from a recent gallery opening in Shoreditch. I scanned the snaps of minor celebrities and nobles no one had ever heard of partying in designer clothing and drinking strangely coloured cocktails.

There, in the bottom right corner, clinging to each other like their lives and balance depended on remaining joined, was a smiling couple. He looked absolutely badass in a white vest with DUH written across the front, his bare shoulders covered with familiar tattoos. She looked like a fairy princess in a flower crown and floaty gold dress that showed off her tanned shoulders and perfect tits. The photo caption called them the hottest couple on the club scene.

The man was Damon Sputnik. And the woman was my best friend, Cindy.

I dropped the paper with a shriek, kicking my cup over and spilling tea all down the leg of my jeans. Duncan appeared at the door of the porch, looking concerned. "What's wrong?" he asked. "Is there a spider you need me to remove?"

"No, sorry for scaring you, Duncan." I said, dabbing at my jeans with my sleeve. "I just spilled hot tea on myself, is all." Duncan looked at me sympathetically, then turned and headed back into the kitchen.

Damon and Cindy. I couldn't believe it. My heart hammered against my chest as realisation dawned on me.

Suddenly, everything Cindy had said over the last week made

perfect sense. The way she'd got herself invited out partying with Damon after the rave on Saturday, the fact she had been so sketchy about details from the night, so interested in what was going on with *me* for a change, her secrecy around her new boyfriend ... oh, God.

She was fucking Damon Sputnik, and the two of them were probably exchanging stories about the weird fat girl with the glasses who was stalking him. And all the while I was here, with Eric, and we ... after I ...

I buried my face in my hands. *I can't believe this is happening.* My best friend in the world had betrayed me. With her bombshell looks and confidence, Cindy could have any guy she wanted, but she'd chosen the one she *knew* I was after. Why? To rub my undesirability in my face? I wonder if she'd told her new beau about Operation Shag Damon, and they'd both had a nice laugh at my expense.

For six months, Cindy had been helping me scheme to get this guy. For *six months* she'd been encouraging me to talk to him and do whatever he asks, and then ... the minute I'm away, she swoops in and takes him. How long had she been planning this? How long had she been setting the putsch in motion?

My toast tasted stale in my mouth, my tea like motor oil. I threw both away, and went into the study. But I couldn't concentrate on my work, so I called Bianca.

"I can't work today," I said. "The house is chaos. Are you free? Do you want to go and do some shopping or something?"

"Sure," she said. "I've got a client at 2pm, but I'm free until then. I can show you some great places. Crookshollow is actually quite cool, for a quaint little village."

"I can't wait. I'll meet you in front of your shop in 20 minutes."

I pulled on my favourite black shirt with the red ribbon, left Duncan supervising the decoration of the marquee, and walked down the drive past the newly manicured lawns. I arrived at

Resurrection Ink just as Bianca was locking up. She looked amazing as usual, in knee-high black boots tied with thick buckles, a black tulle skirt, and a pink t-shirt that said WITCHY & BITCHY. She had put some kind of pink streaks in her white hair, making her look even more like a pixie.

"Let's go," she said, linking arms with me. I grinned at her, all thoughts of Damon and Eric forgotten for the moment. If nothing else, at least my week in Crookshollow hadn't been a total loss. I hoped Bianca and I would remain friends after I went back to London. Especially since I wasn't sure what was going to happen with Cindy ...

First, we stopped off at Bewitching Bites and snagged some warm, cheesy croissants. My mouth watered as I admired the cakes and slices in the cabinet. I couldn't help but add a couple of Chelsea buns to our order.

After we'd scarfed down our treats, Bianca took me to a tiny bookshop called *Spellbinding Books* nestled between a music store and another crystal shop. The place was amazing—four flights of winding stairs and narrow, dimly-lit rooms crammed with bookcases and overstuffed chairs. I could've spent all day in there, especially when I saw a mother cat and three kittens playing amongst the science books. There was even an entire shelf dedicated to gothic literature. I brought a stack of classics that I hadn't read since university. Daphne Du Maurier's *Rebecca*, Susan Hill's *The Woman in Black*, Henry James' *The Turn of the Screw*. Bianca laughed when I showed her my stack, and held up a grisly looking horror graphic novel she had purchased.

"I think we're going to get along just fine," she said, as she led me into a funky-looking clothing store.

For the next hour we tried on ridiculous outfits and imagined the ostentatious places we would wear them. Bianca did impressions of BBC presenters and in no time at all had both me and the sales lady laughing so hard, we cried. I walked out with a blood-red scarf and a ridiculous feathered fascinator I'd probably never wear.

"Thank you so much." I wiped tears from my eyes. "It feels good to laugh."

"It does, doesn't it? You should do it more often, Ms. Serious Lawyer." Bianca glanced at her phone. "Look at the time. I'd better be getting back."

"Yeah, me too." I had a stack of paperwork and a petulant ghost waiting for me.

We started walking back towards Blossom Road, me swinging my bags of booty and Bianca telling me a hilarious story about one of her clients. We passed by the bookstore and music shop again. An idea sparked in my mind. "Can we go in here?" I asked Bianca, pointing at the sign that read TREBLE CLEF MUSIC: CLASSICAL, ROCK, JAZZ, DJ.

"Sure," she said, raising one perfectly shaped eyebrow. She was wondering what I was up to. To be honest, I was wondering myself. Before I could change my mind, I pushed open the door and darted inside.

The shop was tiny, and instruments crowded every square inch of it. I had to duck my head to avoid hitting it on one of the acoustic guitars hanging down from the ceiling. We squeezed down a tiny aisle crowded with stacks of snare drums and racks of guitars.

"What are we looking for?" Bianca whispered behind me as I searched the racks of bass guitars.

"Why are you whispering?" I whispered back.

"Because the dude behind the counter has a crush on me, and I'm hoping he won't see us—"

"Hello!" A weedy teenage boy popped out from behind a Marshall amp. I yelped in fright and whirled away. My bag swung out and knocked over a wobbly stack of music books. Pages flew across the floor.

'Oops." My face flushed with heat. I bent down and started to pick up the books.

'Don't worry, I'll take care of it." The pimple-faced youth scrambled around after the last of the papers. He straightened up, a giant grin on his face. "Hi, Bianca."

'Hi, Ethan." She waved noncommittally.

'I'm sorry about the books," I said, my face still burning. Behind me, Bianca was stifling a giggle.

'It's no worries. It happens at least three times a day." The youth smiled at me as he stacked the books up again. "You're lucky. The last customer who came in knocked an Ibanez guitar off the wall, and he had to pay for it. Can I help you ladies with anything?" He said the last bit looking hopefully at Bianca.

'Yes, actually. I was wondering if you sold violins?"

'We sure do." Ethan led us down a cramped aisle to a wall at the back of the shop, where several models of violins, violas and other classical string instruments hung. I even saw a couple of cool carbon-fibre electric ones. "What model were you looking for?"

'I … I'm not sure," I said, whipping out my phone and pulling up Google. "It's for a friend."

'I think she's looking for a Cremona," said Bianca, giving me a strange look. "I'm not sure what model, though."

I found Eric's Wikipedia page, which listed the exact model of violin he used. I told the youth and he grinned. "Ah, the Eric Marshell special. You're in luck," he said, pointing to a plain black violin on the wall. "We've only got one of those left in stock. A lot of Ghost Symphony fans are in town for the funeral, and they've been buying them up. I've been up to my ears in lanky goth kids all week. Do you need the bow, as well?"

'Yes, thanks. Whatever type Eric used, if you happen to know." I could feel Bianca's eyes boring into the back of my head.

Ethan pulled the violin off the wall, and packed it into a box with a bow. "Do you need a case?"

"No, this will be fine, thanks."

The kid wrapped up my purchase and I handed over the company credit card. If Clyde asked me about a £500 purchase at a music shop, I'd just mention the fact that he hadn't told me I'd be working through a funeral.

"Well, there you go." Ethan pushed the box across the table to me. "I hope your *friend* likes it. And Bianca, I'm nearly ready to come in for that tat soon."

"Have you been saving your pocket money, Ethan?" Bianca smirked. His face reddened. Bianca blew him a kiss as we left.

Outside, Bianca grabbed my arm. "What are you doing?"

"I'm not sure, to be honest," I said, shifting the heavy box to my other hand. Bianca's hot-pink nails dug into my arm.

"There's something you're not telling me," she said. "Something about the Marshell House."

Phew. I couldn't even begin to explain. I was bursting to tell Bianca the truth about Eric, but I didn't want her to think I was some kind of nut-job freak. I wanted her friendship. But her eyes were boring into me. I wasn't going to get out of it without saying something. "Truthfully, I'm a little freaked out about the funeral on Saturday."

"Why? You didn't know Eric."

"True. But the last funeral I went to … it wasn't so good."

"Tell me." Bianca looked concerned. "Here, hand me that violin for a bit. You have enough to carry."

I took a deep breath, and handed her the violin. We started walking again. "I dated this guy, Joel, for three years. It was pretty serious. I was already-planning-the-wedding kind of serious. He was everything I thought I wanted—a junior lawyer at a prominent London firm, extremely worldly, quite handsome, and very socially connected. My parents loved him, and my friends thought he was great fun. I must admit I loved being on his arm at events and gala dinners. Women would stare at me enviously, and I couldn't blame them. Joel was a catch, and he could have had any woman he wanted. I just couldn't believe he'd chosen *me*."

"Ah, falling for guys whose egos are as large and unfounded as your insecurities," said Bianca. "I know the feeling well."

I grinned. "Of course, we had our problems. What couple doesn't? Joel wanted his freedom, and he'd get cagey if I asked him where he was going or who he was with. He could be erratic—ready for partying one minute, the next screaming at me because I'd shut the refrigerator too loudly." I laughed grimly. "Of course, I had such low self-esteem, I thought it was all my fault. I spent hours dreaming up ways to be the perfect girlfriend, the perfect wife."

"I think I know where this is going," Bianca said, with a knowing look. "I've dated my share of Joels, too."

I gave her a weak smile. "For your sake, I really hope not. So this was going on, but I was too ashamed to talk to my friends about it. They all saw Joel as this great catch, and I admit I wanted them to believe I had it all. I'd never been the envy of anyone before, I didn't want to lose the little bit of status I'd gained. So I kept on trying to make things work.

"But Joel kept getting worse. His mood swings became more manic than ever. And, despite earning a higher salary than me, he started having money problems. He got kicked out of his flat for non-payment of rent, and I let him move in with me. Joel didn't pay rent at my place, either, and bit by bit, he convinced me to pay all the bills and buy him clothes and then just give him cash. And I did it, I did all of it because I wanted things to work so badly.

"He started staying out all night. And the rare occasions that he did come home, his clothes were dishevelled and he smelled as if he hadn't showered in days. I'd convinced myself he was just pulling all-nighters at work to get through a difficult case, so I redoubled my efforts. I made him homemade soups, I massaged his feet, I washed his reeking clothing. I was so naïve."

"Oh, Elinor."

"And then, one evening, Joel was out and I went to bed early. I remember that I was mad at him about something. I must have fallen asleep, because I woke up to the doorbell ringing. I thought it was Joel, forgetting his keys again. But it was a police officer."

Bianca bit her lip.

"He told me Joel had been found in the bathroom of an illegal rave at a warehouse in Camden. He was dead by the time the ambulance arrived at the scene. But what was even more shocking was that the police officer told me he'd died of a cocaine overdose."

Bianca gasped. "Oh, Elinor. I'm so sorry."

I waved my hand away. Weirdly, this was the first time since Joel's death I'd been able to talk about him without tearing up. The whole event felt surreal to me, as if it had happened in a movie I'd seen.

"It's okay. It wasn't *your* fault, or my fault, either, for that matter. But it shattered me. Of course it was obvious in hindsight, but I couldn't believe he'd been hiding a serious drug habit from me. The police came and searched my house; apparently they'd been watching Joel for some time, and they had to make sure our house was clean and I wasn't involved. His firm had to hold a press conference. No one in the law circles would talk to me for six months, because of the scandal. I felt like a complete and utter idiot."

"You're not an idiot."

"Don't speak too soon." I laughed bitterly. "I haven't got to the most idiotic bit yet. Joel's parents organised this ridiculously lavish funeral with fancy French champagne and a swing band and ice sculptures shaped like Joel, as if they'd conveniently forgotten that he'd humiliated them publicly. I was struggling to hold it together. Everyone was crying and sad, and I just felt this great ball of anger welling up inside of me. If I'd died, no one would have made an ice sculpture in my image. I'd done everything I could to be a good partner to Joel, and all he'd done was pay me back in lies and deceit. Now he was the hero just because he was dead, while I was in danger of losing my job because of *his* bad decisions? I was fuming.

"Finally, it was time for the service. People were giving eulogies and talking about what a great guy Joel was and I just couldn't take it. So ..." I cringed, knowing what was next but not wanting to say it. "I stood up and said I'd like to say something. And then I laid into Joel and his drug use and horrible behaviour and all the awful things he'd done. I'd had just enough of that expensive French champagne that I thought it would be a *great* idea to set the record straight on Joel's character, but not enough wine so that I was rendered incoherent, which at least would have made the aftermath more bearable."

"Oh, God."

"Yup." My cheeks burned just remembering it. "But then halfway through my speech, I looked down at the open coffin below, and saw Joel's cold, dead face, and I broke down completely. I'd loved him, for all of his faults, and he was gone and I hated myself for it. I fell to my knees and sobbed and howled and kind of ... tore at the carpet. My friend Cindy dragged me away, but not before this delightful display was caught on camera and posted on the internet."

"Fuck." Bianca shifted the violin box again.

"Yeah. Fuck is right. So by the time I'd calmed down again, my boss Clyde was already on my case about ruining the firm's reputation. I had to take two month's forced leave just so they could recover the trust of my clients. Luckily, in our business, you don't get many repeat clients, so I was able to keep my job." I laughed ruefully.

"That's a horrific story, Elinor. But it doesn't explain this rather ungainly box I'm carrying." We'd reached the corner of Blossom Road. Bianca rested the violin on the ground and fumbled in her pocket for her keys.

I shrugged, and picked up the box. "I just ... Eric seems like ten times the man that Joel was. I feel tremendously sad that I didn't get to meet him in real life. And according to the papers his violin hasn't been found yet. I wanted to do something to honour him. Is that weird?"

"A little." Elinor laughed. "But I think it's lovely. This is definitely going to be an *interesting* funeral."

I said goodbye to Bianca outside, and walked back to Marshell House. The gardeners had done a fantastic job on the front so far. The lawns were freshly mown, all the weeds cleared away, and all the statues cleaned and set upright again. A couple of guys were standing on a scaffold in front of the master bedroom, water-blasting the house. They'd even cut back the wisteria around the porch. Now the vines looked quaint and rustic, instead of as if they were trying to consume the house. Bit by bit, Marshell House was losing its creepiness. It was actually almost quite beautiful.

Inside, I called Eric's name, but he didn't answer. He must still be up in the attic. Good. I wasn't quite sure I was ready to face him. I stared down at the violin in my arms, and my stomach clenched with nerves. What was I doing?

I had sworn just yesterday that I had given up on him. I knew we could never have a relationship. I should just give the violin to Allan, since he was so desperate to find Eric's one for himself. But I couldn't stand this ... standoff we were having. I wanted us to remain friends, if that was possible. Eric's life had been hard enough, and his afterlife even worse, and part of that was my fault. His funeral was in two days' time, and that was going to be so difficult for him to face. I had to do *something*.

I crept up the stairs, and opened the door to the attic steps. The door at the top was still closed. I took the steps slowly, wincing each time they creaked. I couldn't hear anything from the room beyond. Maybe Eric wasn't even there.

No, he was there. It was strange, but I could almost *sense* Eric's presence. In just a few short days, I had become so attuned to him that I reacted to him as if he was actually a corporeal being. I reached the door and turned the handle, pushing it inward a crack. I thought I heard him sigh from beyond the door. It was now or never.

"Eric?" I called, pushing the door inward and stepping into the room. My heart was pounding like a bass drum.

"**E**ric?" Elinor's voice punched through my thoughts.

I peeked out from behind the box of photo albums I'd been hiding behind. I could see Elinor peeking through the door, her black-rimmed glasses pushed up her nose and her hair down, framing her beautiful heart-shaped face. She looked nervous.

What could she possibly want? Only yesterday, she'd told me she was done with me. I hadn't expected to see her again for the rest of her stay. And yet there she was, looking shy and eminently fuckable. I opened my mouth to say something, to apologise. But I couldn't find the words. So I stayed silent, hidden from her view behind a huge stack of my mother's possessions.

It didn't matter, because Elinor spoke first. Her voice was firm, resolute. "I'm not here to apologise, and I don't take back anything I said. I just wanted to tell you that I got you something. A present, I guess."

A present?

She still hated my guts, but she'd got me a present?

Now I was curious. What kind of present does one even *buy* for a ghost? I tried to speak again, but again, words failed me. My chest ached when I watched her face searching the boxes for me. I wanted to run to her so badly, to wrap her up in my arms and kiss that hard, hurt expression from her face. But she was right about everything, and an apology wouldn't fix things between us. I had to accept that.

"Um ... I'll just leave it here for you. Sorry to disturb you." Elinor placed a long box on the floor, opened it up, and backed out of the room.

As soon as she was gone, I floated across the attic and stared at the object. My heart thudded against my chest. It was a violin.

Not just any violin. It was a Cremona. *My violin.* At first I thought Elinor must've found Isolde, but then I saw the clean, scratch-free body and the price tags still stuck on the neck.

Elinor had bought me a violin.

Seeing that instrument brought it all back to me, all the joy the instrument had bought to my life. I remembered playing in secret with my father during the day while my mother worked, his fingers moving mine across the strings to teach me the chords. I remembered the first songs I'd composed, back in high school when I was lost and alone, and how it had so perfectly captured my melancholy in a language that wasn't my own. I remembered playing in front of thousands of people, all screaming with ecstasy as they heard their own pain and misery and hope pouring out through the notes.

I reached down with shaking fingers, my eyes closed, hoping against hope that my strange solidness from the other night would return once more.

My fingers struck solid wood. *Yes!*

I wrapped my fingers around the neck and picked up the instrument. I rested it into my neck, breathing out as I felt the familiar weight of it against my shoulder. My fingers rubbed against the strings, and I plucked a few notes *pizzicato*, forming the notes that had become an extension of me.

I drew the bow across the strings, relishing the rich notes that rang out, echoing through the attic. I had missed this so much.

I started to play.

At first it was just scales, as my fingers sought to remind themselves what to do. But then the melody of a song called to me, and I launched into it with a passion as powerful as the time I performed for the Queen. This song was not one of Ghost Symphony's hits, in fact, it wasn't even finished yet. I'd written it shortly before I died, and it was to be released on our next album. It was a song of longing, of a life that had been unfairly taken, played with wrenching, dissonant solos and intense libretto. I'd written it for my father but, as my fingers stretched over the fingerboard, and my arm drew the bow with fierce conviction, I realised I'd also written it for myself.

Giddy with pleasure, I turned through the attic, my body sweeping with the notes as I danced to a tune that represented my life, to the joyful embracing of all my sorrow. My whole mind became one with the music—I no longer saw, heard, or felt anything that was outside. All that existed was the song, the melody.

The last, lingering notes faded into silence, and my body trembled as I came back to the real world again. When I lowered the violin, I heard the faint sound of someone clapping.

My heart skipped a beat. I realised that Elinor hadn't left after all. She was on the other side of the door, in the stairwell, listening to me play. She had heard everything. She had heard the song of my heart.

"Eric, that was beautiful." Elinor's voice sounded muffled, husky, as if she'd been crying. I peered through the open crack in the door, but couldn't see her. She must be right at the bottom of the stairwell.

"I wrote it for my father," I said into the empty stairwell. "It's the best piece of music I've ever written. We were going to record it on the next Ghost Symphony album, but I guess that won't happen now."

Silence. I waited for several moments, but Elinor didn't say anything else. I was just wondering if she'd already left, when she suddenly stammered. "I ... I'm glad you enjoyed the violin. I have to go."

"Okay."

I heard her footsteps sprint down the hall. She was gone.

"Thank you," I whispered, into the darkness of the attic. The violin fell from my hand and clattered to the floor. I reached down to pick it up, but my fingers fell right through it. I was a ghost once more.

$\mathcal{I}$ sat beside the window in the study and stared out, trying to kid myself that I wasn't listening hard to hear if Eric was playing his violin upstairs. All I could hear was the chirping of birds in the flower garden below the window and the ominous ticking of the grandfather clock in the hallway.

My phone rang. I was expecting a call from the forensic accountant, so I pulled it to my ear and said in my business tone, "Elinor Baxter speaking."

'Is that any tone to take with your best friend in the whole world?"

'Cindy?" The sound of her voice startled me out of my Eric-focused stupor. What could *she* be calling about? Was it to tell me the truth about how she'd stolen Damon from me?

'Hey, girl! What's up? Seen any more ghosts lately?"

I knew I was supposed to laugh, but all I could manage was a hollow cough. "It's fine, actually. I quite like it up here. Nice and quiet."

'I hope you've at least been getting out of that house. There must be a pub in that town you could check out. Or a knitting circle, that might be more your scene."

Cindy was teasing, but I didn't feel much like laughing. "I have been going out, *actually.* I met this cool girl named Bianca. She's a tattoo artist, and we're becoming good friends. And I've even managed to wrangle a date for this weekend."

"What?" Cindy screeched. I held the phone away from my ear, my mood growing fouler with every passing second. *You don't have to sound so surprised.*

"Yeah. Allan Lachlan, the drummer from Ghost Symphony. He's hot, actually much hotter than Damon. And his music is better." I grinned, imagining Cindy squirming on the other end.

"Oh, so Operation Shag Damon is over, then?" asked Cindy. I detected a hint of hopefulness in her voice.

"No way." I wasn't going to let her off that easily. "I'm just enjoying a fun distraction. But as soon as I get back to London it's going to be all about that sexy Russian DJ again. So what's the plan for this weekend? Can you do some more Damon reconnaissance for me?"

"Actually, that's what I'm calling you about. Remember last week you mentioned having me up at the house for the weekend? Well, I've actually got some good news for you. It turns out work got given some tickets to a weird goth funeral this weekend, and they were wondering if anyone wanted them. I noticed that the name of the house was identical to the house you've been banished to, and Doug agreed to give me the weekend off to attend …. and since I know how much you wanted me to come …"

"You mean, you're coming to Crookshollow?" I tried to keep the panic out of my voice. I'd completely forgotten that I'd practically begged Cindy to come spend the weekend when I first got here, but that was before everything else had happened. How was I going to survive the funeral without letting on to her? How was I going to hide Eric's presence from her?

"Yeah, and I was wondering if we might be able to stay in one of the rooms in that enormous haunted house of yours? It would save us paying for a hotel. It looks like weird goths have booked out every place in town."

"Us?" My stomach sank.

"Yeah." Cindy paused. "That new guy I was telling you about? It's pretty serious. I basically haven't left his bed since the weekend. Anyway, between all the mind-blowing sex, I've been telling him all about you and he's super keen to meet you and see this crazy old house. So I'm bringing him up, if that's okay?"

"You mean your mystery guy who you haven't told me a thing about?" *Is this really happening to me? Is my life really this cruel?*

"I'm sorry. I just … you've been so sad lately, I didn't want to make you feel bad."

Oh, yeah, because stealing my crush out from underneath me is totally the way to make me feel great about myself. You're a real pal, Cindy. "Look, you're my best friend. You should tell me if something big happens in your life. I'm happy because you're happy. So tell me about the guy. Where did you meet him, exactly?"

"Er … at Damon's party last weekend," Cindy said, her voice sounding strange, far away. "Listen, Ellie, I have to go. But I'll fill you in on all the details this weekend, I promise. I just want you to keep an open mind when you meet him, okay? Give me time to explain everything first."

"Why? Does he have some kind of disfigurement?" *Like that he's fucked in the head?*

"Haha. No, seriously. Just promise you'll wait for me to tell you the whole story before you judge him, okay?"

"Okay, sure."

"Cool! I'll see you on Saturday, then! I can't wait to meet your new guy."

I hung up, then threw my phone down on the chess board in disgust. Little marble chess pieces scattered everywhere.

So Cindy was coming to Crookshollow, and bringing Damon Sputnik with her. The weirdest thing was, I wasn't at all surprised. Of course Cindy would think it was perfectly alright to double-cross me and then bring the guy along to what was supposed to be our all-girls weekend.

Of course she would think that if she apologised, it would make everything fine. Why would she expect anything else? That had always worked before. At university, she would abandon me at parties to go off with guys, or say she'd meet me somewhere but then not show up because she'd got a better offer. And I'd just let her do it, because that's what best friends are for.

But I was starting to realise that maybe I was tired of letting people just walk all over me. That wasn't the way things had to be. I couldn't imagine Bianca blowing me off just because some guy waved his crotch at her. In fact, I think Bianca would probably laugh in the guy's face.

I glanced over at the ghost books stacked on the table, briefly entertaining the idea of opening them again. But I shook it off. *Let Eric sort out his own problems. If he wants my help, he can come to me and apologise. This is the new Elinor Baxter, and I'm not doing shit for anyone else without a little appreciation.*

From now on, I was looking out for number one.

I WAS on hold with the Liechtenstein bank where Alice Marshell had one of her accounts when I heard Eric calling my name from upstairs. At first I ignored him, because the New Elinor Baxter didn't go running just because someone commanded her presence. But after a while his begging became insistent, and the Lichtenstein hold music was annoying, so I cradled the phone against my shoulder and walked upstairs.

"Where are you?" I called out.

"In my bedroom!" Eric called back. "Hurry. I found something!"

I bolted up the stairs two at a time, panting as I pushed through the door to Eric's old bedroom, the one I'd been sleeping in ever since I arrived. He was kneeling beside the bed, his black jeans and shirt covered with a layer of dust, and his dark ringlets hanging over his face, staring at a long, black wooden box he'd pulled out from beneath it.

"Eric …" I stood in the doorway, folding one arm across my chest, the other holding tightly to my phone. The hold music still droned on. *If he thinks I'm going to help him with anything, then he's going to be sorely disappointed.*

He glanced up, and recoiled when he saw my expression. "You are upset," he said simply.

"Not upset. Just miffed. I was very clear, Eric. I'm not going to help you any longer—"

"Elinor, I'm sorry."

Eric blurted the words out, his face screwed up as though saying them was somehow painful to him. He blinked, watching my face for a reaction. When I gave him none, he continued.

"You were right about everything, and I'm sorry. You were very clear about your boundaries, and I pushed you into something more because I was so desperate for a connection to the real world. I let you do all the work tracking down my killer, and I barely even thanked you for it. And, most importantly, I'm sorry about the way I treated you over Allan. I can be pretty protective of the things that matter most to me, but I have to learn that I don't have a claim on you." Eric looked pained. "Will you accept my apology? Can we please … be friends?"

I sighed. On my shoulder, the hold music continued to warble on. "I'm sorry, too. I may have overreacted about some things. On the surface, I've adjusted quite well to learning of the existence of a ghost, but in reality, I'm having a harder time with it than I think even I realise. There wasn't a textbook in law school about handling an estate with a ghost attached to it, and there's some things you don't know about me that are making me extra sensitive. I think I just needed a bit of space to clear my head, and I've had it now, and I'm ready to be friends … if that's what you want to call it."

In a second, Eric was on his feet and standing in front of me, his eyes gazing intently into mine. He held out his hand, his fingers outstretched toward me. "To friendship."

"To friendship," I reached out to shake his hand, but my fingers fell through him. The familiar buzzing heat arched up my arm.

"Sorry," Eric stared down at his hand in dismay. "I can't seem to control when it comes and goes."

"I know. But we might be able to change that. I have some books downstairs about ghosts. They talk about a kind of spirit called a shade. Shades are different from ghosts because a ghost is just the shadow of someone who lived in the past marking a place, whereas a shade is the spirit of a person that's left its body prematurely, usually during tragic and untimely deaths. I think that's what you could be."

"A shade?" Eric blinked. "Could this help me?"

"Maybe. There are spells, apparently, that can return a shade to its body. Of course, I'm not one to believe in witchcraft, but I didn't really believe in ghosts either, and that didn't stop you scaring the shit out of me."

"Oh yeah." Eric grinned mischievously. I hadn't seen that grin since the night we'd … It was great to see it again. "I did do that, didn't I?"

"You sure did." I dared a faint smile back at him.

"So what are these spells? How do we do them?"

"I don't know. The book doesn't say, and even if it did, I'm not sure they'd be any use. I'm not a witch. I did meet someone the other day who might be able to help."

"It wasn't Clara Raynard, was it?"

"Yes, it was Clara. She really *is* famous around these parts. I will go and see her today if I can, and find out what we have to do. In the meantime, what can I help you with?"

"My solidness has been more and more frequent." Eric's eyes looked wild with joy. "I can't figure out why, or how, but after I played that song on the violin, I felt this weird, tremendous pull toward my old bedroom. Suddenly, I couldn't wait to see what was in here, but I couldn't figure out why I was feeling this way. I wondered if it was the house trying to tell me something, the same way it doesn't want me to leave the walls. So I came down here and I sat on the bed." Eric's eyes darted from me to the case. "I had actually become *solid* enough to sit on the covers. But the bed felt unusually hard, like there was something pushed underneath that was wedged against the springs."

I nodded, remembering the aches in my back from the lumps. "I've been meaning to look at what was under there. I just felt weird about snooping through your things."

"You're a lawyer, isn't that your job?"

"For the last time, I am not *that* kind of lawyer."

"It's a shame, because you could've pulled this out for me days ago and saved a ton of effort. It's taken me three hours of back-breaking labour to pull it out this far." Eric flexed his biceps. "My fingers are solid one moment, then fade to ghostly the next."

"What is it?" I stared at the short wooden box.

"Elinor, it's my violin case. My *real* violin case."

"But that doesn't make any sense," I said, kneeling down beside him. "Why would it be here?"

"I must have left Isolde here after I visited Mother. But I don't understand why I would've done that. It's not as if I ever came back here unless I could help it."

"No, I mean, we already knew it was probably in the house, because if a thief had taken it then it would have appeared on eBay by now. Maybe you were planning to stay for some reason? Maybe she wanted to borrow—"

Eric waved his hands impatiently. "Deduce later, Sherlock. Please just open it!"

"Fine." I pulled the case up on to the bed. It was lighter than I expected, but I guess a violin is largely air. "This is locked. Where's the key?"

"It was in my pocket when I died. I was never without it."

"Oh." Disappointment surged through me. That meant the police probably had it. But then I remembered the envelope of keys Duncan had given me. He'd said they were all the keys for the house that Eric had, so maybe … I skipped downstairs, retrieved the envelope from the hall table, and returned with it, dumping the keys out on the bed.

"That's it!" Eric pointed a finger at a small silver key on the edge of the bed. I pushed it into the lock of the case, turned it, and flipped open the lid.

"Oh my God," I breathed.

I stared down in horror, my knees growing weak. I couldn't believe what I was looking at.

That was no violin inside the case.

*E*linor's face had gone pale. She brought her hand to her mouth, and I saw that her fingers were trembling. Her eyes changed from delight to terror as she stared down at the contents of my case.

I peered around her, wondering what had struck her so. Isolde was old, certainly, and a little beaten up—certainly in a more shabby state than the new one she'd bought me—but nothing worthy of such a terrified gasp. Perhaps she had broken in transit …

No. Oh, no.

I stared down at the contents of the case, and I felt my own body surge with fear. There was no violin inside. Instead, nestled in the velvet lining, were bags and bags of white powder. Every inch of the case was filled with them.

My entire violin case was stuffed with cocaine.

I floated back, reeling. My body was so shocked it slipped through the floor, burying me half in the room below. Elinor turned to me, her hand still over her mouth. "What is this? Is this what I think it is?"

"I don't understand." I pulled myself up through the floor and peered down at the wooden frame, the familiar scratches around the rim, my father's name etched into the veneer along the outer edge. It was my case all right. But why was it filled with drugs? I'd packed away my violin myself backstage after the London show. I remembered laying the instrument into the velvet cushion. I'd locked the case and dropped the key into my pocket, and shortly afterward I was dead. It hadn't been opened since that night, so where had this cocaine come from?

"Eric," Elinor's voice was tight, strained. "Say something."

"Where's my violin? I don't understand. How—"

Elinor slammed the case shut. "So this isn't yours?"

"Of course not. Elinor. I'd never touch the stuff."

"This isn't a personal stash, Eric. This amount of cocaine is worth *millions*. The only person who'd have a use for this much coke would be a dealer. So what's going on? Is this the real truth? You were part of a drug ring, and you smuggled this lot out of Prague after your tour, and you were meant to make the drop in London? But then you got greedy and decided you wanted all the profit for yourself. So you took the goods and ran for home, stashing the case here until you could sell it. But your buyer got wind of your plan, and ran you off the road to get the stuff back. Am I getting warm here?"

I snorted in laughter. The whole concept of me being a drug trafficker was so ridiculous, I couldn't even contemplate how she could've come up with that scenario. Elinor stared at me in horror, as if my laughter was somehow incriminating me. The smile froze on my face. She was serious. She actually thought this coke was *mine*.

"Elinor, what—"

"I *trusted* you," she whispered.

"This isn't mine. I've never touched the stuff in my entire life. I'm a fucking rock star. I have all the money and groupies I need, and I earned them *legally*. Why would I need the hassle of being a fucking drug lord?"

"You tell me, Eric. You seem to have a story for every possible situation."

"Why can't you believe me?" I couldn't understand her. Why was she so adamant on believing this was mine?

"Of course I can't believe you. Here you are, making me trust you, making me think you were this great, tortured artist. And all along, this is what you've been doing." Her eyes filled with tears. "This shit goes to *children,* Eric. Young, innocent kids who don't know what the fuck they're doing. It destroys lives. Don't you get that? Don't you care?"

"Of course I fucking care. That's why I'm trying to tell you that this isn't mine."

"Don't lie to me!" Her voice sounded high, hysterical. "It's yours, it's yours. It explains everything."

No, Eric, don't get angry. If you get angry, she is going to leave again. But I could feel the rage rising inside of me. After everything we'd done together, after all the time we'd spent together, I thought we had a connection. I thought she understood me. But she didn't. "Why would you just automatically assume this is mine? Do you think so little of me that the only possible explanation that fits all the facts in your fucked-up Sherlock Holmes scenario is that I must be a scumbag drug dealer? What happened to everything you said to me the other night? Or is that just the lawyer in you talking, all the lies to get what you wanted?"

Nice one, Eric. Way to listen to yourself.

Elinor's cheeks flushed red. Her face crumpled with pain. I wanted to reach out and hold her, but I couldn't take those words back.

"I don't care what you think of me," she hissed through her teeth. "Or the fucking *hypocrisy* of accusing me of lying when you've so obviously been lying through your teeth to me. The facts speak for themselves. The drugs are in your case. A case you repeatedly talked about being fiercely protective of, a case you carried all over the world." Elinor shook her head angrily. I could see the wheels turning in her brilliant mind, putting all of the pieces together, and coming up with something so completely plausible, but so completely wrong. "And, of course, you're a celebrity. No one at the airport is going to give you a second glance. You could use your tour schedule as a front for meeting your dealers—"

"Shut up! Just fucking shut up!" I yelled, jamming my hands over my ears. Elinor froze, mid sentence.

"Don't ever speak to me again," she hissed. Then she turned on her heel, and stormed from the room.

I fled the room, tears streaming down my cheeks. I ran down the stairs, and slammed the door of the study shut behind me, the sound a mirror of Eric's action from earlier that day. I'd been so excited to make up with him, and all this time he—

All this time he was a drug dealer. He was the fucking scum of the earth.

Just thinking about it made my body boil with rage.

Some small part of me wanted to cling to what I'd thought we had, to the possibility that maybe Eric was innocent. That maybe this Helen Manning had set him up. Maybe that was her plan for revenge all along, to have Eric arrested as a drug dealer, his reputation ruined and his career taking a nosedive. *Maybe you should go back, let Eric explain—*

I shook my head angrily, pounding the pillow with my fist. What was there to explain? Helen Manning was a depressed teenager. She was not a criminal mastermind able to get her hands on a motherload of coke. Eric had the connections, the money, the alibi. He was trying to be special, to be some kind of idol, but he was just like every other guy. He didn't care who he hurt.

I squeezed my eyes shut, trying to halt the tears that threatened to overwhelm me. *It's Joel all over again.* I remembered the same pleading look in his eyes when I'd found part of his stash hidden behind the toilet. "It was just a one-time thing, babe," he'd said. "I've given up, I swear." I wanted so badly to believe that it was true that I just accepted his bullshit. I'd ignored all the signs, and then it was too late.

Joel was dead. Eric was dead. It was too similar. Too much of a coincidence. The only common factor was me. How do I attract these douchebags?

My chest tightened in fear as I realised that Eric's actions had also placed me in grave danger. At some point, the people Eric had been working for would come looking for their drugs. This much coke just doesn't disappear. I needed to deal with the very real fact that I had hundreds of pounds of class A drugs in my possession.

But not right now. Right now, I needed a stiff drink.

"WHAT'S WRONG?" Bianca asked as she slid into the stool beside me. "You look awful."

"Thanks." I frowned into the bottom of my second pint glass. After discovering Eric's secret stash, I'd texted Bianca immediately and asked her to meet me for a drink. I didn't really trust myself to drink alone at that point. She'd been with a client and had to wait until she finished, so she told me to meet her at the Tir Na Nog, an Irish pub down a hidden alleyway not far from Clara's shop. Bianca was running twenty minutes late, but that was okay, because the barman was very friendly and quite nice to look at, and I'd already managed to drown two pints and a small bowl of crisps.

"I mean, you look upset. Did something happen?"

"I don't want to talk about it," I growled, pushing my glass across the table towards her. "I want to do one thing, and one thing only: get shitfaced and forget about it."

"Is that really a good idea? I mean, don't you need to work with sensitive legal documents tomorrow? Do you really want to do that hungover?"

"Who are you, my mother? No, you're not, so stop with the third degree and make with the next round." I'd never in a million years have talked to anyone back in London like that, especially not someone who was a new friend and about a hundred times cooler than I could ever hope to be. But I had an overload of sass ever since I'd arrived in Crookshollow, and I knew Bianca wouldn't mind. I was right—Bianca grinned, and darted off to the bar, returning a few moments later with two overflowing pints.

"I always thought you'd be more of a wine drinker." She grinned as she sucked the foam off her drink.

I took a huge gulp, enjoying the faint buzz of oblivion that was starting to encroach on the corners of my mind. "Usually, I am. But I haven't had a wine kind of day. I've had a drown-my-sorrows-in-ten-pints kind of day. How are you? Hopefully better than me?"

"I'm fine. My client is very happy with the tiger I painstakingly drew on his left arse cheek. He's going to come back next week with his girlfriend so she can get a leprechaun on her shoulder blade. Imagine that? Four years at art school and I was never taught how to draw a leprechaun. I spent twenty minutes googling leprechaun images before I left to meet you, and you wouldn't *believe* the stuff that came up. People are *weird* ..."

Bianca started talking about something related she'd seen on the internet, and I tried to listen, nodding along at the appropriate moments. But my mind had returned to Eric. I just couldn't believe that after all his earnest speeches and sweet acts, he'd been a drug dealing scumbag. He'd completely fooled me with his smooth talk and his brooding, artistic temperament. I thought he was the perfect guy. And that said more about me than it did about him. Am I really such a poor judge of character that I hadn't seen through all his bullshit?

"… and don't you think it's bloody disgusting?"

"What is?" I snapped out of my internal dialogue.

Bianca tapped the screen on her phone and shoved it across the table towards me. I could see it was an eBay listing. I shook my head.

"It's one thing to talk about kinky related-related internet searches, but it's quite another thing to see the results of such a search." I pushed the phone back across the table. "I don't want to be put off my beer."

"We're not talking about leprechauns, anymore, Elinor." Bianca tapped the phone back towards me. "And no judgement, but I think after this pint, you might need to slow down a little."

I glowered at her in mock defiance, took a swig of my drink, and stared down at the phone. It was a listing for a violin. It wasn't even a particularly nice-looking violin. The picture was grainy, and I could see that the front of the instrument was covered with scratches. Then I looked at the price.

"Whoa, is it made of some sort of rare wood or something?" I wondered who on earth would bid on such a shabby-looking instrument for £12,345.

"That's Eric's second violin. He called it Tristan. Someone put it on eBay. Can you believe it? I bet it was the same people who trashed his house down in Devon."

"Yeah." *Eric's violin.* Although I was supposed to not be thinking about him, I stared at the picture with renewed interest. It was Eric, all right. The trader had put up images of Eric at concerts playing the exact instrument. No wonder people were going crazy over it.

I thought Allan had that violin? Why is he selling it on eBay? My head is spinning. I can't think about this now. I must remember to ask Allan later ...

No. I shook my head violently. *I'm not thinking about Eric any longer. I don't care where his stupid violin ends up.* I pushed the phone across the table with more force than I'd intended. Bianca lunged and managed to catch it before it sailed off the edge.

"Sorry," I mumbled, but I had broken the spell. I was supposed to be getting over Eric. I was not going to help a drug dealer solve his murder. And that was final. I tossed my head back and drowned the rest of my pint.

"It's fine." Bianca watched me slam my empty glass down with a concerned look on her face. "So, what's really going on, Elinor? Why do you get so weird every time I mention Eric's name?"

"It's nothing, really." My brain seemed to float inside my skull. I felt oddly detached from my body, as if I had to push my thoughts really hard to make them exit my mouth as words. Perhaps Bianca was right, and I should slow down. It wasn't even dark outside yet.

"It is not nothing. You're acting ... well, you're acting as if you're in love with him. Which is impossible, since he's dead. Hence my line of inquiry."

I leaned forward, barely noticing when my elbow hit my empty glass and knocked it over. "Bianca, if I told you something and it was really weird ... I'm talking *The Addams Family*-level kooky here. What would you say?"

"I live in Crookshollow. I've seen too many strange things and heard too many ghost stories to be a sceptic." Bianca leaned on her elbows so her face was only inches from mine. "What is it?" she whispered.

"Eric is a ghost," I whispered back. "He's haunting Marshell House. And I was ... well, I was falling in love with him. Until I found out he was a drug dealer."

Bianca stared at me for several moments, not speaking. Then she snorted. Then her snorts turned into some weird, high-pitched squeal. Her face turned red as she struggled to hold in the full extent of her mirth. The couple at the next table eyed us curiously as Bianca made strange, strangling noises in her throat, before collapsing on the table in a ball of shuddering, tear-streaked laughter.

"What?" I glowered at her shaking form. "What's so funny?"

"I'm sorry, Elinor," Bianca gasped. "It's just … that drink must have really gone to your head. I mean, Eric being a ghost I could *almost* believe, but then you said you were in love with him, and I just … you two are so different. And then you said he was a spectral drug-dealer … and … I cannot even … it sounds like a cheesy *Tales from the Crypt* plot."

"Yeah," I grinned weakly. "It does."

"Oh God," Bianca wiped the tears from her eyes with her napkin. "I'm going to remember that one for a while. Eric Marshell a drug dealer. Now I've heard everything. I think we need another round, and this time, I'm getting you some orange juice."

I watched from the attic window as Elinor returned home in a taxi. The moonlight shone on her silky brown hair, so that it glowed like a halo around her heart-shaped face. The time on the grandfather clock in the corner of the attic read 2:57. She was grinning stupidly as she paid the driver and skipped in a crooked line down the driveway. She fell over her own shoe and collapsed into a heap, but instead of cursing she just broke into unadulterated giggles as she struggled to her feet and readjusted her crooked glasses.

She was drunk. Gloriously, hopelessly, dangerously drunk. I wondered where she'd been to get in such a state. Had she been out with Allan?

It's none of your business if she's with Allan, I thought bitterly. *She's made it clear that she doesn't want anything to do with you.*

The front door slammed. I heard heavy footsteps on the stairs. Even though I knew I should leave her alone, something in my belly flared up. I *had* to see her. I flew through the door of the attic and down the steps, pausing in the shadows of the hall as I watched Elinor stumble across the landing toward my old bedroom.

She really was a mess. Her cheeks were flushed red from the cold air and the alcohol. Her eye makeup was smudged in dark streaks across her face. Her clothes clung to her gorgeous curves, plastered there by sweat and sticky spilt drinks. There was a beer coaster stuck to her elbow.

I longed to lurch myself into the hallway after her, to speak with her, to try again to convince her I wasn't this evil person. But another part of me, the part that had spent too much of his life chasing after the approval of others, hated Elinor for betraying me like this. She hadn't even wanted to listen to me, she just automatically jumped to a conclusion. The wrong conclusion. Why should I have to convince her of anything? Shouldn't she know me well enough by now?

I watched Elinor crash against the bedroom door. It fell open and she sprawled across the floor, again exploding into uncontrollable giggles.

"Eric," she hiccupped. "You're still here?"

"Of course I'm still here. I can't exactly go anywhere," I said.

"I … drink … I am drink …"

"Yes, you're very drunk. And I can't help you into the shower, I'm sorry." I tested my fingers on the door. They bounced slightly against the wood, but then fell through.

"… s okay …" Elinor stumbled to her feet, steadying herself against the wall and staring at me with sparkling eyes. "I can manage."

But she couldn't. She took three steps and then fell down again. Her knee made a hard SMACK as it hit the polished wood floor. "Owie." Elinor rolled over and clutched her knee. "I have owie. Kiss it better."

"I can't." I was starting to feel desperate. I hovered over Elinor, my body screaming to touch her. She was so close, I could feel the heat rising off her. She formed her lips into a surprised O, and my pants tightened around my growing erection. I tested my fingers against the wall. This time, they didn't sink through, but hit the wall with satisfying solidness. *What is she doing to me?*

Did I love her? Did I hate her? Why did she have to roll around on the floor like that, her hair fanning her face like a halo, her top slipping down and revealing the edge of her supple breast?

She's drunk. She doesn't know what she's doing. You have to be the gentleman.

I groaned as I reached down and grabbed Elinor under the arms. When my fingers touched her, she shuddered with delight. The warmth rippled through my body, depriving me of all rational thought. *Hold on, Eric. Keep your cool.* I tried desperately to send a message from my brain to my cock, which was already bouncing eagerly against my waistband. *You can't do anything with her now.*

As I pulled Elinor to her feet, she fell against me, leaning all her weight against my body. Luckily, I was solid by now, so she didn't fall through. Instead, the heat surged between us, and the air around crackled with electricity. I looked down at those heavy-lidded eyes and those pursed, bow-shaped lips and it took all the self-control I could muster not to throw her against the bed and tear off her clothes.

Elinor thrust her head up towards me. I turned mine to the side so fast I wrenched something in my neck. But it was no good. Elinor was determined. She gabbed the sides of my head with both her hands, threading her fingers through my hair in a way that drove me crazy, pulled my head back to face her, and thrust her tongue into my mouth.

This kiss was different than any we'd shared before. It was wild, untamed, out of control. It was a kiss that spoke of dark lust and a delicious night to follow. It ignited my whole body, so I ceased to be human, but instead became a ball of flame.

I pulled away. Elinor stared up at me, her lips not even an inch from mine. "What's wrong?"

"This isn't right," I said, my words coming out hoarse. It took all my self-control to hold her upright without throwing myself at her. "I have to get you to bed."

"I was mad at somebody ..." she murmured, her breath touching my lips.

"You were mad at me ..." I whispered back. "But I don't understand why."

Elinor lurched away from me, her face crumpling with pain, as if she'd been slapped. *She's remembering why.* I cursed myself for reminding her. "I am. I am. I hate you, Eric. I hate you for being like him. For being just the same as him. A dead, deadbeat loser. *I hate you!*"

I took a step towards her, my hands raised in supplication. "Like who? You made a mistake. We can talk about this—"

"Get out!" Elinor screamed, her face contorting into something ugly, terrified. She reached down and grabbed her shoe from her foot, and hurled it at me. It sailed right through my body and clattered against the wall behind. She raised the other shoe and threw it at my head. I felt a strange whisper of it passing through my body before joining its mate on the floor.

"Fine," I snarled at her, while she looked for something else to throw. "I only came down here to see if I could help you, anyway. You threw yourself at *me.* So if I'm a dead, deadbeat loser, what does that make you, Elinor? *What does that make you?*"

She screamed incoherently, and the sound was a knife twisting in my gut. I'd said something wrong, really wrong. I'd torn something from her that could not be replaced. I knew that even if Elinor remembered nothing else about tonight in the morning, she would remember what I'd said, and she would hate me forever for it.

I had broken whatever it was that we had. It could never be repaired again. I turned and floated from the room as fast as I could, her screams following me as I flew up the stairs and through the attic door.

I floated around in circles, listening to Elinor's cries rising up through the stairwell. Her pain was intense, palpable, consuming her whole body and mind. It had poisoned her against me. I realised then what I should have realised before, if I hadn't been such a self-centred idiot. There was something secret in Elinor's past that was preventing her from believing me. That's why she said, "I hate you for being like him."

It wasn't about me, which meant I could have fixed everything with her, but now it was too late. White hot rage filled my head, pressing against my skull. I was furious at Elinor, for projecting upon me all her insecurities about someone else. But mostly, I was furious at myself.

The rage came in waves. Sometimes, I was overcome with it, and I would hunch over, clutching my hands into fists, my body shaking with uncontrollable fury. And then it would ebb away, leaving me hollow, devoid of emotion, an unfeeling, unwanted ghost of a man.

I stared at the new violin in the corner. A new song swirled around inside me, a melody that encompassed everything I had experienced since I'd become a ghost and met this remarkable woman. It was a song of ultimate longing, the song of a love that could never be.

I reached down and plucked at the strings, my fingers passing through them without connecting. I couldn't take the song within my head and turn it into music. I couldn't do the one thing that kept me sane, that kept my rage and pain and anger from overwhelming me.

It's no use. I glared down at the instrument with a mixture of longing and revulsion. Even if I *could* pick up my violin, I couldn't play the song. I couldn't let myself be vulnerable like that. Because the song was for *her,* and she would not listen. She would not see.

The song would remain trapped inside me forever, the same way I was trapped inside this house, inside this life-that-was-not-life, forever.

ELINOR

My head is made of agony.

ELINOR

I want to die.

I am never drinking again.

ELINOR

I stayed in bed most of the following day. People pounded on the door downstairs, wanting to get in to prepare for the funeral on Saturday, but I ignored them. The clamour of the workers assembling the marquee outside was like a freight train running through my brain.

Bianca came to visit at lunchtime. She bounded into my room and jumped on the bed beside me. Her weight caused the springs to bounce and my stomach to lurch aggressively. "Go away," I moaned.

"That's no way to talk to your favourite drinking buddy," she cooed. "Not after I scaled a tree and climbed in the bathroom window when you didn't answer the door. Besides, I brought hangover food."

I watched, bleary-eyed, as she set down a bag of goodies on my nightstand. A bottle of sports drink, a huge box of painkillers, and a warm, delicious-smelling parcel of fish and chips.

"Uuuuuuurggh." I did my best impression of a zombie shuffling toward the promise of human flesh as I reached for the chips. My stomach rumbled. I'd been so busy feeling sorry for myself, I hadn't realised how hungry I was.

"Drink some of this first." Bianca handed me the sports drink. "It will replenish your electrolytes."

I glared at her as I accepted the bottle and slowly sipped the raspberry-flavoured liquid. Bianca looked stunning in a white tank top with some band's illegible name scrawled across the front, a black lace mini-skirt and combat boots. Her pixie hair was freshly styled and her makeup perfectly applied. Why was she not lying in a pool of her own sweat and vomit, like I was? "Why are you so chipper?" I demanded between sips.

"Because I stopped drinking after three pints, and you went on to do five more." Bianca grinned.

"Oh." I reached for a chip and stuffed it into my mouth. There was a horrible moment when I swallowed and it seemed as if it was about to come back up, but the warm potato settled nicely in my stomach. I tried another.

"Yes, and then you started doing shots with an Irish bloke. And then you challenged everyone in the bar to an arm-wrestling match. You even won two rounds. The Irish guy was very impressed, by the way. He left you his number." She held up a crumpled napkin that was lying on top of my bag.

"Delightful." I managed several chips in a row. I already felt a lot better.

"Oh, but that's not all. At one point you jumped up on a table and—"

Bianca was interrupted by a great crash from above. I covered my ears as the sound of something heavy and wooden hitting the floor reverberated through my distraught skull. Bianca yelped and leapt off the bed.

"Yikes, what was that?" Bianca stared at the ceiling as if she were afraid it might come down on her. Something else crashed against the floor directly above us, shattering into pieces. *That sounded expensive.*

"Rats," I mumbled.

"Those must be some pretty impressive rats," Bianca mused,

giving me a strange look.

"Yeah, they're fucking ridiculous. I'm trying to get exterminators in, but my boss doesn't consider that a legitimate expense." Bianca looked like she wanted to say something else, but I pulled myself out of bed and stood on shaking legs on the floor. My head spun madly, and my stomach lurched, but it was time for me to face the light of day. I had work to do.

"Elinor, are you sure—"

"I'm going to take a shower," I mumbled, stumbling toward the bathroom. I wasn't even sure if I'd be able to stand up in the shower of my own accord, but I had to do *something* to avoid a conversation about Eric and last night. "Make some tea and I'll see you downstairs in twenty minutes."

WHILE I SHOWERED, I could hear Eric pacing the length of the attic. Occasionally, he hurled something across the room. Luckily, with all the noise of the work crew outside and downstairs, I didn't think anyone would notice.

I wanted to shout at him, *Why are you doing this? Can't you just slink off quietly into the night like the scumbag you are?* My whole night was pretty fuzzy, but the things Eric had said to me replayed over and over in my mind like a broken record. The kiss kept replaying, too. Why had I thrown myself at him like that? The whole thing made me feel sick.

Why did he have to keep being here, rubbing my face in my own failure to fall in love with anyone decent?

Fuck him. He's not my problem. He's made that perfectly clear. It's time to forget Eric Marshell, once and for all.

After I pulled some fresh jeans and a white shirt over my clean body, I felt a lot better. I swallowed two pills to stop the throbbing in my temples, and went downstairs. I wasn't even off the staircase when Bianca pushed a hot cup of tea into my hand. "The kitchen is filled with cream cakes," she said, holding up a tea towel with two delicious-looking cakes on top. "I snagged us a couple. The folk at Bewitching Bites sure went crazy for this shindig."

"Oooh, are those from Bewitching Bites?" I licked my lips. I was in danger of becoming seriously addicted to that bakery.

"Yeah. It's the best place in town. They do all the events around here. When I opened my tattoo studio, they made these amazing Turkish Delight cupcakes with hand-piped tattoo designs in chocolate on top. I swear they were little works of art."

We went into the study and shut the door, which muffled some of the noise coming from the kitchen, but didn't do much about all the grunting and huffing as the gardeners worked outside the window. Bianca didn't seem to mind that, though. She sat in one of the armchairs and stared lustfully at one of the shirt-less gardeners as he hacked at the wisteria that choked the gutters.

"What's this?" Bianca held up one of Clara's books. "Are you actually reading these?"

"Yeah." I nodded hastily, my heart thumping. After the way Bianca had reacted last night when I'd tried to tell her about Eric, I didn't really want to talk to her about ghosts. "I thought it would be interesting to learn more about Crookshollow's history."

"Okay, sure. If you say so." Bianca gave me another odd look. We chatted and ate our cakes, but then Bianca needed to meet a client at the shop. "I'll see you on Saturday at the funeral," she said. "I'll come over early and help you do your makeup, if you like."

"Oh, yeah, thanks." The funeral. I'd almost forgotten about it. Now I felt sick all over again.

After Bianca left, I tried to get some work done, but all the numbers blurred together and every time I tapped the keyboard it was like a gunshot going off in my head. Eric started playing the violin upstairs, and I jammed a pair of headphones over my ears so I wouldn't have to hear it. I sat by the window and read through some more of Clara's book. There was a chapter on banishing a ghost from your house.

Salt is a powerful deterrent for unwanted spirits. Ancient witches used to cast their circles in salt, so that no bad spirits could enter the sacred space.

Eric was definitely classed as an unwanted spirit. Feeling rather pleased with myself, I ducked into the kitchen through the horde of catering staff busy preparing canapés. I found an industrial-sized salt-shaker on the counter, and snuck it out again under my jumper.

I pulled the top off the salt shaker. Good, it was nearly full. I went upstairs and poured a line of salt outside the attic stairwell. Then, for good measure I lined the bedroom, staircase, study and entrance hall with a salt trail. It looked like an albino snail had run amok through the house, but at least now I was safe from any more unwanted encounters with my resident ghost. I placed the empty salt-shaker back on the kitchen bench and returned to the study just as the florist arrived with more arrangements.

"I think those ones go in the marquee out back," I said, as I saw the florist—a beefy man who looked as if he belonged in a wrestling ring instead of a flower shop—heaving a giant urn stuffed with pink and white tulips out of his van. "You can come through the house if it's easier."

"What's all this white stuff?" complained the florist as he struggled through the front door with the urn, scuffing through my neatly-laid trail.

"The white stuff? It's sugar. Sorry, the kitchen has ants and I'm trying to lure them back outside," I said sweetly.

He made a face. "It's all over my shoes. These are Italian leather, you know."

"If you have a problem with it, just send a bill to Duncan. I'm sure he'll be happy to reimburse you." *He's got plenty of Alice's money to pay for it.*

～

Working was impossible. Even shutting the study door and jamming my ear buds in didn't block out the noise of the workmen preparing for the funeral. I was too jumped up and jittery thinking that an entire violin case filled with cocaine was shoved in the closet in Eric's old bedroom. And to make matters worse, I knew I'd be seeing Duncan today, and I was trying to work up the courage to report him.

My finger hovered over the CALL button on my phone. Clyde's number flashed on my screen. I knew I had to do it, but for some reason, I kept hesitating.

Could it be, sneered Devil's Advocate Elinor, *that you don't want Clyde to get the police involved and send down one of the senior lawyers to take over, sending you back to London and away from Eric?*

Shut up, I shot back. *I'm done with Eric. I'm over him. I want to get out of Crookshollow as fast as possible.*

To prove it, I punched the CALL button. Clyde's secretary answered. She informed me that he was out for a long lunch with Lila. *Of course he is.* "You could call him on his mobile phone?" she suggested.

"No, that's fine, Charlotte. Please just tell him to call me as soon as he returns."

I hung up the phone and tossed it on the desk. Spinning around in the chair, I stared up at those bookshelves, trying to divine something of Alice Marshell from the tomes she had collected and cherished. It was such a vast and fascinating collection of political writing, philosophy, science, and great literature. My gaze fell on one particular book.

Swann's Way. It was the book that had fallen on my head when Eric first surprised me in the study. Not really sure what I was doing, I reached over to the shelf and pulled out the book. As I did, a piece of paper fell out from behind it and fluttered to the floor. It was a letter, covered front and back with rows of neat handwriting.

I picked it up and inspected it. "The revised will and testament of Alice Marshell."

Holy shit.

Before I read any further, I pulled out one of Alice's ledger books and compared the handwriting. It was identical. This was the real thing, written in Alice's hand. The corners of the paper were crumpled from being smushed behind the books. I checked the date in the corner – she'd written this two years ago, and even had it witnessed by two nurses. So why was it stashed behind the bookshelf, instead of on file at the firm?

My hands trembling with anticipation, I read on.

Eric, my darling Eric. I have mistreated you. I have held you guilty for your father's sins. And now I am fading, and you are too angry and too busy being successful to concern yourself with an angry, bitter old woman who once tucked you in at night. I don't blame you. My deepest regret is that I never told you how proud I am of everything you've accomplished.

I want you to have everything. You are my son, and everything I have worked for belongs to you. Take my money and use it to fund your music, to pay for your tours, to touch more people with your beautiful mind. Don't let Duncan push you around or contest the will. I left him a nice sum when I drafted the will, but he has been stealing from my accounts for years now. He doesn't think I know, but I do. He will try to steal from you, too. Don't be hard on him, for he has looked after me well, but he's had enough of my money.

If for any reason you don't want or can't accept the money, then please take it and start a scholarship fund for music students. Let another young person full of hope and talent get the right start in life. Don't let Duncan or any of my other friends or family members get their hands on it. They have more than enough.

I love you, and I am sorry.

Alice

I set down the letter, my mind reeling. Alice Marshell had sought forgiveness in the only way she knew how, through her money. *The ledger book.*

I grabbed the black book from the bottom of the stack. It was the book I'd picked up on one of my first days in Crookshollow. I hadn't thought anything of it at the time, because I didn't know anything about Eric or his mother. It hadn't seemed important. I'd completely forgotten about it until now.

I flicked through the pages, stiff with decades of paste. It was filled with hundreds of clippings about Eric and his music, from tiny three-line reviews in underground music magazines of their early shows to big double-page spreads and in-depth interviews in the popular music press.

Even though they weren't speaking, even though he believed she despised him and all he represented, Alice Marshell had followed Eric's career. She's been there with him for every award, every platinum album, every sold-out show. She loved him. She *cared.*

Tears welled in the corners of my eyes. *Wait until I tell Eric ...*

Wait, what am I talking about? I can't tell Eric. I'm not talking to him ever again. The resolution didn't fill me with righteous anger the way it had before. *I wish it were different. Maybe he really wasn't lying about the drugs being his ...*

No, don't do that. Don't you start feeling sorry for him. So what if he had a shit life? So what if his mother tried to repair the damage on her deathbed and he doesn't know that? Everybody has problems, and they don't go drowning their sorrows in cocaine to forget them. Unless they're Eric Marshell, and then they get license to do whatever they want because they're rich and famous and have oh-so-deep and tortured artist souls ...

The righteous anger had returned. *Good.* I turned a page in the ledger. There was Eric, frowning at the camera as he posed with his violin. He was shirtless, and that dragon tattoo curled around his bicep, the piercing eyes of the beast mocking me, taunting me ...

"Is something the matter?" I jumped at the sound. It was Duncan, his rotund head peeking from around the study door.

"Oh, you startled me." I slammed the ledger shut, trapping the letter between the pages.

"You looked as if you were lost in thought," he said. "I was just wondering how your work was coming along? Many of Alice's relatives and friends will be here for the funeral. I'd really like to be able to tell them what they can be expecting from the estate."

"That's not really the way it works, I'm afraid," I said, suddenly struck by an idea. "I've actually just found something that might cause some delays."

"Oh yes. What's that?"

I handed over the letter. Duncan scanned it. I watched his face carefully, the way his eyes narrowed, and his mouth turned down at the corners. He wasn't happy.

"But this isn't legally binding, surely?" he said. "She ... she wasn't of sound mind when she wrote this. That's obvious by the fact she's accusing me of stealing from her. As if I would do such a thing! And there are no witnesses—"

"Those two nurses signed there." I pointed at their signatures. "And this document is clearly in her handwriting. In my business we call this a holographic will. It does complicate matters. I'm sorry, Duncan—"

"This is insane," Duncan mumbled. "Even in death that punk Eric is taking from her."

"What do you mean?"

"You never met him, so I can understand how you might be suckered in by the way the media portray him, but Eric Marshell was no angel. He was sulky and morose and he didn't care about anyone but himself. He never appreciated what Alice did for him, even while she was mourning the loss of her husband. Eric shunned her and everything she stood for, to go off and follow in the footsteps of the lowlife father who'd abandoned him, leaving her by herself while her mind rotted away and—" His voice cracked.

"I hardly think—" I started to say, but Duncan was on a roll. His eyes had this weird, far-off look.

"She was a saint, that woman. A saint! She never remarried, you know. She considered that once you were married, you were wed for life, even though her no-good excuse for a husband took advantage of her to fund his laziness and then ran off with his conductor. And there were men, you know. Men who would have taken care of her, who would have stood beside her. Men who would—"

Suddenly, I understood. Duncan loved Alice Marshell. He loved her more than anything, with a fierce kind of love that made him both devoted and delusional. In some twisted way, he'd taken that money because he'd felt as if it were his too, because they were one.

"Please, Ms. Baxter." Duncan's hand clamped around my arm. "You won't … turn me in, will you? I only did it for her. I needed money so I could stop working, so I could spend more time with her …"

"Duncan," I said kindly, unclasping his fingers from my wrist. I met his gaze with my own, pulling him back to the present. "I didn't mean to upset you. There is still a ton of stuff to organise before the funeral. Perhaps you should see to the caterers?"

He nodded slowly. "You're right. Thank you, Elinor. You're a kind girl." He patted me on the arm, and shuffled away, his kindly old face tight with fear.

The evening was the hardest. I sat at the desk in Alice's study and flicked through the pages of the Ghost Symphony forum on my laptop. Eric's fans were swapping stories about his life and posting outraged screen-caps of the eBay auction and arranging meetups before Saturday's funeral. I couldn't put on Eric's music, and I didn't feel like any techno, so the only sound in the house was the tick of the grandfather clock in the hall, the occasional creak of the floorboards settling, and the crashes and thumps coming from the attic, which I was trying to pretend I couldn't hear.

Bianca took me out to the local pub for dinner (and no drinking), which took my mind off Eric and Marshell House for a few hours, but then I had to come back to that big, creaking house, with the angry ghost of a drug dealer storming around the attic.

And just when I thought life couldn't get any worse, the doorbell rang.

Wondering how many more flower arrangements the marquee could possibly hold, I set down my tea and dragged my sorry body to the door. I flung it open, and was greeted by a sight that turned my stomach.

There was Cindy, looking like she just stepped off a runway, her white-blonde hair sitting on her shoulders in perfect waves. She wore a pair of tight black leggings and a printed sundress that clung to her thin body and perky breasts like ... like a blinking sign that declared nothing in the world was *ever* fair. A leather jacket was slung casually over her shoulder to ward off the evening's chill. How she looked like that after a long car ride, I just couldn't fathom. I suddenly felt extremely frumpy and unattractive in my jeans and red shirt.

"Ellie, I'm so glad to see you," she cooed, throwing her arms around me. She smelled like fresh perfume and roadside takeaways. "I'm here now, so the fun can begin. And look, I've brought someone for you to meet."

Oh. For the first time, I noticed the towering form standing behind Cindy. In the midst of Eric's drama, I'd completely forgotten about that ...

Cindy stepped aside. Damon Sputnik stood on the porch, looking even taller and more imposing than usual. He wore baggy Adidas track pants, white sneakers, and a pair of silver dog tags dangled from a chain between his impressive pecs. My eyes fell immediately on the bare, muscled shoulders bulging from his dirty white vest—shoulders so broad they could throw a girl like me around as if she were a rugby ball. His odd, abstract tattoos ran down both arms and even covered his palms and knuckles. If this was two weeks ago, his presence would have made my insides turn ... no, actually, they were still twisting. Damon Sputnik was still damn hot.

Only now, he was Cindy's boyfriend, and they were the hottest *It* couple in London. I felt my cheeks flush as I remembered how excited I'd been about our drunken snogging session only two weeks ago. How juvenile to hang so much of my hope on that one meaningless event. I was never going to have a guy like that. He was out of my league. All I got was drug-dealing lowlifes.

"Hi," Damon said in his clipped Russian accent. He managed to look both impossibly cool and embarrassed at the same time. *Of course he's embarrassed. He doesn't want to be bunking up with Cindy's chubby friend in some haunted house in the sticks. He wants to be clubbing until 5am and popping multi-coloured pills until he honestly believes he's Spiderman.*

"Nice to have you here, Damon. I'm Elinor Baxter," I said in a businesslike tone, holding out my hand for him to shake, hoping he didn't notice the dark flush on my cheeks.

"Nice to meet you," he said stiffly, shaking my hand with a firm grip. His eyes flicked briefly over me, and then darted away again. He didn't recognise me. For six months I'd been hanging onto this guy's every word and song, and he wouldn't have even been able to pick me out of a line-up.

Wonderful. I needed to feel even more like an idiot today.

"Can we come in?" Cindy's tone was chipper, but her eyes were pleading with me.

"Sure." I held open the door. Cindy strutted in, Damon behind her, holding a backpack and Cindy's stuffed-to-bursting pink Louis Vuitton suitcase. "You'll have to excuse the chaos. There's a lot of preparations before the funeral tomorrow."

I led them upstairs to the master bedroom, getting a sick sense of glee when I saw Damon's eyes bugging in horror as he took in the flower-covered wallpaper and furnishings.

"It's very ... "

"This is the best room in the house," I said, walking across and opening the drapes. "I love these gorgeous round windows, and you've got a view of both the front and back gardens, see? Now, why don't I leave you two to get naked ... I mean, unpacked. I'll just be down in the study if you need me."

"Thanks," Damon muttered, turning over a ceramic cat statue in his hands. He looked like he didn't know what to do with himself. Cindy tried to grab my arm as I left, but I darted out of reach. *Let her stew for a bit longer. She deserves it.*

Smiling to myself, I raced down the stairs and into the study. If Cindy was going to parade Damon around in front of me and expect me to act as if nothing was wrong, then I was going to take perverse pleasure in making her weekend as uncomfortable as possible. I'd *earned* that right.

I flipped idly through the heavy house keyring, searching for the smallest keys. I'd realised that some of the keys might open the desk drawers, so I was trying them all in the tiny lock. On the fifth key I had success, and popped the drawer open only to find a small flask of Scotch and two opened packets of boiled toffees. *That's a bit of an anticlimax.* The second drawer held some insurance papers I already had in electronic copy, and the third held more toffees.

I was just about to open the next drawer when I heard the door creak open behind me. It was Cindy. She pulled the door shut behind her, and faced me with a guilty expression on her face. "Elinor, I'm sorry."

I looked up from my files and beamed at her, admiring the way my grin made her face fall further. "Sorry about what?"

"Sorry for bringing Damon along and not telling you about it. I just … I didn't know how to tell you, so I didn't. That was sucky of me but … maybe I'm a sucky friend."

"Yeah, you kinda are." Cindy cringed when I said that.

"It's just … you've been so cut up about Joel and I thought your little crush would help you get over him. But of course you being you, you took it so *seriously*. It was sweet but way too intense. Damon was never going to be in for that, and I just …"

"Yes, that's fine." I made a big show of shuffling through the papers on my desk. "I'm quite busy, Cindy. So if you could leave me alone so I can get on with things—"

"Elinor, can we please talk about this?"

"Cindy, it's *fine*. Really." I looked up and grinned at her again, just to show her how fine it was. She looked stricken, desperate. I don't think I'd ever seen cool, collected Cindy look so out of sorts. She was positively *squirming*. The sight of it gave me a jolt of plea-sure. It felt good to be the one calling the shots for once.

"You have to understand," she stammered out. "I didn't intend for this to happen. I was only trying to keep an eye on Damon for you, but I think he took my hovering for interest and … well …" She giggled nervously. "Just look at him. He's *gorgeous*. I tried to be a good friend, really I did. But Damon's pretty hard to resist. And it wasn't like you were having much success with him, so I figured it didn't matter if I took a stab."

"And you thought it would be a swell idea to just bring him up here for the weekend so I could see firsthand how happy the two of you are?" I laughed, but this time it came out a little hollow. "I mean, you could have just waited until I came back to London to reveal this little secret, but instead you come up here to torture me with your happiness. What kind of friend *does* that?"

"I tried to talk him out of it, but Damon wanted to go to the funeral. A lot of record executives will be there, and it could be a really good place for him to network."

"Damon wants to network at a *funeral?*" *Wow. Subtle.* I was actually glad I hadn't landed the guy. He was starting to sound like a real winner.

"I wanted to tell you myself over a wine when you got back. But Damon was so set on coming and I couldn't tell him why we couldn't go without letting him in on our secret operation. I didn't want to embarrass you, is all. See, I do think about you." She looked at me like a hopeful puppy.

It was strange. The dynamic between us was completely altered. The old Elinor wouldn't have even confronted Cindy about this. She would have listened patiently while Cindy explained the whole thing, and by the end of it she'd have been asking Cindy to forgive her, as if she herself had been that bad friend. But the new Elinor didn't let anyone – least of all her supposed best friend – walk over her without calling them out on it.

I sighed. "I really wish you hadn't bought him with you. It was a very insensitive thing to do, Cindy. That is not necessarily out of character for you, but I would have thought my best friend would realise how much this would hurt me."

Her eyes went wide. She hadn't expected me to say that. I admit, I hadn't expected to say something like that, either.

"Luckily," I continued, (this standing-up-for-myself thing got easier the more I did it), "some things have happened over the last week that made me realise I don't want Damon Sputnik anymore. So you can have him, if he truly makes you happy."

Cindy's eyes pleaded with me. "He does, he really does. Do you mean it? Do you really forgive me?"

I hugged Cindy. "Of course I do," I said, although my voice came out stiff and formal.

"Thank you, thank you! I'll make it up to you, I promise. Back in London I will buy all your drinks for a month, and I'll iron all your fancy work blouses, and clean your goldfish tank—"

Despite myself, I laughed. "Let's just get through this weekend, shall we?"

"Of course. Hey, can you show me around this crazy house?" She linked her arm in mine. "You were right. It really is like something out of a horror film." We stepped out into the hall and Cindy scraped her ballet flat through the line of salt in front of the staircase.

"Hey." She bent down to brush off the salt. "What's all this white stuff?"

"It's salt. The catering staff are really clumsy. They've tracked trails of it all through the house." I laughed. "I'm going to be cleaning it out from my shoes for weeks. Come on, you won't *believe* the back garden. There are all these creepy statues in the flower beds, it's amazing."

SATURDAY DAWNED, a bright, cheery day, at odds with the sombre occasion. The caterers knocked on the door at quarter to six, desperate to get in to the kitchen to start their prep. I stumbled downstairs in my pyjamas and let them inside on the condition that they made lots of coffee.

My lie-in ruined, I spent an hour in the study on the phone with Gerry, our forensic accountant. I was right, Duncan had been stealing money from Alice Marshell for the last five years. Gerry estimated the amount to be more than £40,000.

"Talk to Clyde first, but you'll have to call the police," he said. "They'll need to make the arrest, and you'll need to bring charges against him. I realise this complicates your case a bit. Wasn't this man the executor of the will?"

"Yes," I sighed. "The only living named executor. Clyde will be *thrilled* to hear it." It meant the law firm had now become the executors of Alice's will. Which meant that I had a ton more work ahead of me.

I glanced out the window in time to see Duncan's car pull up in the drive. I raced back upstairs and slammed the door to my room shut. I didn't want to speak with him just then, not dressed in my pyjamas, knowing what I had to do.

This is already turning out to be a fabulous day.

I debated texting Allan and Bianca to tell them I wasn't going to attend the funeral after all. I didn't want to hear Eric's friends and family talk about how wonderful and inspiring he was, when I knew the truth. Spending the day in bed or slumped over a pint at Tir Na Nog seemed preferable to sitting down in that marquee surrounded by the cloying scent of flowers and trying to pretend I had never met this Eric person before in my life.

But despite the fact that I was never speaking to Eric again, I was still curious about certain aspects of his murder ... and his life. I wanted to see if any interesting characters showed up, especially the people from the Ghost Symphony fan forum. I needed to ask Allan about the violin. And besides, the funeral was being held *in* the house. I didn't exactly have anywhere else to go.

So I pulled on a black wiggle skirt and tailored jacket, pinned my hair back in a severe style, took a deep, steadying breath, and went downstairs to face the music.

By the time I came downstairs, the house was swarming with people. Cindy and Damon were hovering outside the kitchen, VIP lanyards dangling around their necks, trying to get the catering staff to hand them out some hot coffee. Duncan held court in the entrance hall, directing the ushers and the priest and the servers and the catering staff and yelling at the beefy dude about the flower placement. He was wearing a sombre black suit, but I noticed that his tie had a pattern of jaunty skull and crossbones. A nod to Eric, no doubt. Duncan may have been a thief, but he wasn't half bad.

He saw me standing on the staircase and rushed over, kissing each of my cheeks with wet lips. I shuddered against his touch, but tried to hide it by pulling my jacket around me and pretending I had a chill.

"Elinor, you look lovely," Duncan said. "I'm so sorry for the intrusion today, but it was so important for Alice to have her final farewell in this house."

"It's okay, really." I forced a smile. "After spending all this time here, I'm starting to feel as if I knew Alice, and her son. It will be nice to learn a little more about her life."

"I am sure you will discover some interesting things." Duncan grinned, his beady eyes flicking nervously around. "She was quite a special lady."

"She certainly seems to be. Will you be doing a eulogy today?"

"I certainly will." Duncan patted his jacket pocket. "I've got it all written down. Now, if you'll excuse me, I need to go and attend to the sound crew." He scampered toward the door, heaving his elderly frame out of it so fast that he nearly collided with Allan, who had chosen that moment to show up.

"Sorry! Sorry!" Duncan muttered, rushing off.

"Who was that?" Allan came up and clasped my hand. He was looking gorgeous, if a little strangely attired for a funeral, in tight black jeans, a leather belt with some rather painful-looking spikes extending out of it, and a black vest with ERIC MARSHELL LIVES written across the front in gothic script. His hair was gelled and spiked to perfection, and black eyeliner streaked around his eyes, highlighting their piercing blue. At the kitchen door, Cindy whirled around, her eyes bugging out when she saw the white-haired rocker. I couldn't help but feel a smug sense of satisfaction as Allan's warm hand slid into mine.

"That's Duncan. He was a close friend of Eric's family," I said.

"Where's he going in such a hurry?"

"Away from me." I grinned. "He knows I've discovered he's been siphoning money from Alice's accounts for the last five years. He's worried I'm going to call the police before his eulogy."

"And are you?"

"I haven't decided yet. I thought I'd play it casual."

Allan grinned as he leaned in to kiss me. "That's my girl."

I folded myself into the kiss, trying to force myself to enjoy the simple sensation of skin touching skin. But my mouth still burned from the memory of Eric's kiss, and although I wanted nothing more than to forget him, my body didn't want to comply. Allan pulled away, eyes glinting. He held me at arm's length and stared at my outfit in shock. "Is that what you're wearing?"

I looked down at my outfit in confusion. "Of course. It's a funeral. I was trying to be sombre."

"You look like you work in a bank." Allan frowned. "Change into something extravagant. This is Eric Marshell's funeral we're talking about. There is going to be a ton of press here. I can't very well show up with a date who resembles Margaret Thatcher."

Ouch. That comment stung. But I wasn't about to disappoint my hot drummer date. I went upstairs and turned out my suitcase, but nothing seemed "extravagant" enough.

Then I spied the shopping bag from Clara's store sitting in the corner. I'd already worn the black dress to our date the other night, but I still had the red dress ...

Do I dare? I pulled the dress out of the bag and laid it across the bed, admiring the way the red fabric shimmered in the light. I ran my fingers over the delicate beading on the corset, my heart beating nervously against my chest as I imagined wearing this decadent gown. It was one thing to see it in the changing rooms at a store, but quite another to try it under the harsh light of day. Did I really think it was an appropriate dress for a funeral?

Why not? Devil's Advocate Elinor challenged me. *This day is going to be hard enough as it is, so you might as well look as fabulous as possible.*

Sometimes, Devil's Advocate Elinor made some very valid points.

Decision made, I went into the bathroom, pulled off my

clothes, and shimmied into the dress. When I looked in the mirror, I could hardly believe the person staring back was actually *me*. The red made my eyes sparkle and my skin look luminous. I turned around to admire the corset lacing running along my back, and briefly wished I already had my back tattoo – my arms and shoulders seemed oddly bare compared to Eric and Allan and Bianca, and the corset would show off a tattoo so perfectly.

I swayed this way and that, enjoying the swoosh of the skirt as it swirled around me. Everything was nearly perfect, but not quite. I undid the bun I'd made at the nape of my neck, and brushed my hair out, letting it flow freely across my shoulders. I pulled my glasses off my nose and set them down on the vanity unit—everything would be a little blurry today, but it was worth it to make my eyes stand out. Next, I dabbed on a little mascara and eye shadow, then scrambled around in my toiletry bag to find a small necklace with a red ruby droplet Joel had given me some years ago. *Now* I was ready for a rock musician's funeral.

I jumped in fright as something metallic clanged on the attic floor above my head. So Eric was still up there. I wondered how he was coping watching all the madness from the attic windows. *No.* I shook my head. *I don't care how he's coping. I don't care about him at all. I am here to support Allan and have fun with Bianca and Cindy, and that's it.*

I grabbed my bag and fled the room. I peered over the railing and cringed as I saw Allan engaged in conversation with Cindy and Damon. "So are you the new guy Elinor has been hiding up here?" said Cindy, batting her eyelashes and touching Allan's arm in the way she did at clubs when she wanted someone to buy her a drink or dance with her or take her home for a shag. Allan was flashing her with his sexy smile and Damon was sipping his coffee and looking all Russian and stoic and *pissed*.

"I'm ready now!" I announced as I started to descend the stairs, hoping to distract Cindy before she said something even more embarrassing.

Allan looked up and he did a double take when he saw me. I held my chin high and glided down the stairs the way debutantes did in movies about the South. The corset held my back straight and my chest out, and the skirts swirled around my legs as I shimmied down the stairs. I felt like a movie star.

"Whoa, Elinor." Cindy's eyes bugged out of her head. "You know it's a funeral, not a fancy dress party, right?"

I looked down at her outfit—a figure-hugging black dress with a plunging neckline—and said, "It's also not a burlesque show, but that hasn't stopped you."

Cindy looked shocked. Damon sniggered. Allan looked like a kid staring at all the presents under the Christmas tree. I gave a serene smile and continued my descent, my chest bursting with newfound confidence.

Halfway down, something crashed above my head. My foot slipped and I stumbled, my heel catching on the corner of a step. I toppled down the remaining stairs, my dress flouncing out around me as I landed in a crumpled heap at the bottom. My knee hit the wooden balustrade and throbbed in protest.

Thanks Eric. I wanted to shout at the ceiling as my face flushed with red. *Thanks for making me look like a fool.*

Allan ran over and helped me to my feet. "Are you okay? Did you break something?"

"No. I just … tripped on my hem, I think." I brushed some salt off the skirt. "Maybe I should change my dress?"

"Are you kidding? You look stunning, Elinor. I have half a mind to carry you back up those stairs to your bedroom right now."

I blushed. "Oh … um …"

Allan looked around the hall. "I don't understand, though. It was that crash that startled you. It came from in here, not the kitchen, but I can't see anything broken or damaged."

So he'd heard the crash, too. Wonderful. That meant Eric was solid enough that the things he did impacted the real world. That could be a very bad thing—an insane drug-dealer ghost who was already upset and unstable, who could now move and influence things on the day of his own funeral. I really hoped my salt trails worked. "Oh, that wasn't in here. It's rats." I said. "There's a terrible rat problem in the attic."

"They must be pretty big rats."

"Yup." I dusted some more salt off the sole of my pump. The line I'd placed at the bottom of the stairs was now smudged and broken. I'd have to replace it as soon as I could, but I obviously couldn't do that with everyone watching. So instead I looped my arm through Allan's, and gestured toward the hallway leading out to the back porch. "Let's go."

Allan dropped a VIP lanyard around my neck, then took my arm and escorted me outside, and Cindy and Damon followed close behind. I did a double take as I saw what was out there. The gardeners had transformed the back garden, getting rid of all the choking weeds and trimming the bushes and scrubbing clean the statuary.

The garden looked every bit a feature on *Great British Gardens* —complete with neat edges, low walls, and arches bedecked with roses. The large white marquee covered most of the manicured lawn, strung with fairy lights and skull-shaped balloons and cascading flower arrangements. Inside were rows and rows of seats, many closed off with velvet ropes. Around the outside was a metal barrier, like you'd have at an outdoor concert, and security guards wandering behind it barking orders into walkie-talkies.

A lighting crew swung across the stage rig, testing spotlights, and a guitar tech wandered around in circles on the stage, strumming an awkward guitar tune and yelling "check!" into the microphone every time he went past. There were food carts and a portable bar lined up outside. It looked more like a mini outdoor festival than a funeral.

As I walked out on the back porch, I caught a glimpse of a dirty red scooter parked up beside the bushes. I sighed. "Excuse me, I'll have to get Duncan to talk to the catering staff. It looks like one of them parked this thing here where everyone coming out to the marquee can see it."

"Actually, that's mine," Allan said. "I thought it would be out of the way back here. I'll move it."

I snorted back a giggle. "That's what you drive? A little scooter?"

"Don't laugh," he said, patting the seat. "I get great mileage in this little beast."

"Seriously, you drive that?" This was not the vehicle I imagined this badass driving. "Don't you need a real car for going to the shops or transporting your drums or stashing dead bodies and things?"

"Dead bodies?" Allan's voice rose sharply. "Is that some sort of joke?"

"No," I said quickly, realising what I'd said. *Dammit, how insensitive can I be?* "I mean, it wasn't funny. I'm sorry—"

"It's fine." Allan turned away. "I'm just in a weird place today, you know?"

I rested a hand on his shoulder. "I'm sorry."

"It's fine, really." He took a deep breath, and turned around to face me, his familiar grin back once more. "And for your information, I do have a car. A little Lotus. It's currently in the workshop."

"Allan, are you going to be okay today?" I held his hand up. It trembled slightly. "You don't look great. In fact, you look a bit ill. If this is too much for you, we don't have to stay. We can go inside and—"

"No way." Allan shook his head vehemently. The piercings in his face made clanging noises as they struck each other. "The band and I prepared something really special for today. This is the last opportunity I have to tell Eric what he means to me. And besides," he said, lifting up the bottom of his vest, revealing a small flask strapped into a secret compartment on his belt. He pulled off the cap and took a swig. "I've come prepared. A little liquid courage will see me through."

I shifted nervously. "I have to ask you something, and it's a little uncomfortable, because of where we are and how you're feeling, but I have to get it off my chest." Allan looked at me, his smile frozen on his face. I hurried on, before I lost my nerve. "I saw this listing on eBay the other night for Tristan, Eric's second violin. You told me you had that instrument, so I just wondered what was going on?"

"Oh." Allan looked a bit uncomfortable himself. He stared at his feet as he spoke softly. "The thing is—and please don't let anyone else know—I'm sort of in a tight spot right now, financially speaking. I was sort of counting on the advance for the new album, but with Eric gone, that won't be coming out, so ... I was only going to sell Tristan, because I'll get Isolde whenever we find her. I'm sorry, Elinor, I know it must seem callous of me, but I honestly had no other choice."

"I wish you'd said something," I said, feeling a wave of sympathy for him. It must've been a tough decision to make, selling Eric's violin like that. Allan was going through a lot right now.

"Yeah, well." Allan shrugged, taking another swig from the flask. "A man's got to fight his own battles, you know. I have only myself to blame."

Allan offered the flask to me, but I shook my head. I was feeling nervous enough as it was. As Allan was pulling his top back down, a large crowd of people surrounded us. Camera flashes began to go off in my face. I lost Cindy and Damon in the press of the crowd. I sought Allan's arm for reassurance, but a large TV camera knocked me off balance, and I fell against him instead. He cried out as my elbow caught him in the ribs.

No. I felt my face darkening. *I don't want to be on TV looking like this.* If Clyde or any of the other lawyers saw me in this dress, they'll never take me seriously again. It had been hard encugh keeping my job after the mess with Joel's funeral. I tried to hide behind Allan, but he grabbed my wrist and pulled me forward.

'Allan, is this your new girlfriend?" A reporter thrust a tape recorder into Allan's face. He grinned and pulled me closer to him, squishing my breasts up against his shoulder. "No comment."

'Won't you say a few words, Miss ..."

"This is Elinor." Allan filled in, wrapping his arm around my bare shoulders and flicking a stray hair from my face. The cameras went crazy. My face felt like a beetroot. I stared at my shoes, wishing the earth would open up and swallow me whole.

'Say a few words about Eric!" Another reporter yelled, shoving a microphone under my nose.

"No, thanks. I need to—"

"Hey, Ellie, check this out!" Saved by Cindy. I yanked myself from Allan's grasp, and raced over to where Cindy and Damon were standing at the barrier. Damon was deep in conversation with someone, his halting Russian accent alive with unusual excitement as he discussed his latest record. Cindy jabbed her finger at one of the seats in the front row. "You're only a couple of seats away from us!"

"No way." I stared at my name printed on gold card on the black folding chair. It was true. Allan was sitting next to me, and next to him was Sabrina Slaughter, a famous singer and alternative model. All down the row I saw names of celebrities. My heart started to flutter with something that was part excitement, part dread.

After giving the reporters a few words of sorrow, Allan came to join us. The four of us got drinks at the bar and wandered around the side of the house to watch people arrive, Damon stopping every few feet to introduce himself to anyone who looked vaguely like they were in "the biz." I could already see a line of cars filling the parking spaces on either side of Blossom Road. The driveway to the house had been roped off and security staff manned the gate, checking tickets, issuing wristbands and pawing through backpacks.

Even though the funeral wasn't starting for another two hours, people had already begun to trickle up the drive and follow the signage around the side of the house to the back garden. Many of them were dressed as though they were attending a rock concert or a Victorian ball—complete with spiked hair, black lace veils and gravity-defying corsetry.

Reporters dangling press lanyards circled the house, snapping photographs of its gothic exterior and pulling groups of the more interesting-looking guests together for portraits. Down the back of the garden, where a small gate led to a path through the woods beyond, I could see pairs of people emerging—the celebrities who didn't like to use the front entrance. It was the strangest funeral I'd ever seen.

"Elinor!"

I turned and waved to Bianca, who was running across the lawn toward us, her wrist circled with a blue band that indicated she was a general admission ticket holder. She looked stunning as always in a short black dress with bell sleeves and a red-leather corset pulling in her already tiny waist. We embraced like old friends.

"I want you to meet some people," I said, stepping back and indicating Allan. "You remember Allan, the drummer from Ghost Symphony."

"How could I forget?" said Bianca, reaching in to peck Allan on both cheeks. "Nice to see you again, Allan. I'm sorry about your loss."

"And this is my friend Cindy Lawler, from London, and her boyfriend, Damon Sputnik. Bianca is a tattoo artist. She owns Resurrection Ink, just on the corner."

"Oh, we saw your place as we were coming in. The dragon in the window is just *amazing*," gushed Cindy. "Damon is into tattoos, aren't you, baby? He's thinking of getting something to commemorate his time here in England. I suggested he get a portrait of the Queen, but he doesn't seem so keen."

Damon nodded stoically.

"Well, if you're interested you should come down to the shop and see some of my work," said Bianca. "I do a lot of portrait work, so you'd be in luck if you wanted Her Highness to grace your body."

While they chatted, I glanced around the growing crowd. There were some incredible outfits around. There were recreations of monsters and mythological figures, exact replicas of outfits the band members or their models wore in music videos, elaborate Victorian and Edwardian mourning attire. I recognised a few faces from their profile pictures on the Ghost Symphony forum. A few of the ladies gazed admiringly at my gown. Even a couple of the guys seemed to be checking me out. I grinned, feeling proud that I fitted in, and then wiped the grin off my face immediately. *That's in bad taste, Elinor. This is a funeral.*

A group of girls in white makeup and skin-tight latex outfits came up and asked for Allan's autograph. Two of them glared at me while the third fished a CD sleeve and pen out of her cleavage.

My stomach flip-flopped again. I felt nervous, agitated. There was something wrong, but I couldn't quite place what it was. I scanned the crowd again, hoping for some clue to the origin of this bad feeling. But there was nothing amiss. The funeral was going perfectly so far ...

Holy shit.

My hand flew to my mouth. The movement was involuntary, caused by total and utter surprise. I leaned backward and followed the figure with my eyes as she moved through the crowd. She was wearing a simple, almost shapeless black dress, an elaborate feathered headdress, and a ring of skulls like a crown around her forehead. But that face ... it was a face I'd recognise anywhere.

It was Helen Manning.

ERIC

I watched from the window as Elinor moved toward her seat, her arm looped through Allan's as he steered her through the crowd. The train of her dress fanned out around her, as if she were a gothic bride being escorted on to the dance floor by her betrothed. She smiled up at Allan, her hair fanning her heart-shaped face. She wasn't wearing her glasses, and her eyes sparkled with newly released life. Jealousy stabbed at my stomach. *I should be the one on her arm, not him.*

Elinor looked beautiful, radiant. She made every woman in the place seem like a dog in comparison. But she was lost to me, and that made it even more painful to look at her.

I wasn't really being fair to Allan, who had been a good friend to me and did look seriously nervous and cut up about my death. But I couldn't help it; every time I looked at him, this hard ball of rage bounced around in my stomach.

He doesn't know she's your girl, I reminded myself. But I was dead. I wanted to hold a grudge. Who was going to stop me?

I crouched by the window, my new violin resting against my knee, its weight reassuring as it stayed upright, not falling through my skin as it had done so many other times since Elinor had brought it for me. I was staying solid for longer periods of time now.

I knew I shouldn't watch the funeral. It was going to be difficult to see how others saw me in life, to know I could never go back to that world. But I had a strange, nervous feeling about it, a sense of foreboding that had nothing to do with seeing my own coffin. My ghosty sense was tingling. Something bad was going to happen.

I pressed my face up against the window, but I could hardly see or hear anything through the old, smudged glass. I needed to open the window.

I stretched out my fingers across the glass, feeling the coolness of it against my palm. *Good.* I was still solid. I undid the catch and pushed at the window, but it was as if I were pushing against a solid wall. It wouldn't budge. *Ah,* I understood. It was the barrier to the outside of the house. I couldn't move any further.

I found an old, heavy wooden hat stand behind a box of books. Placing the base against the window, I pushed with all my strength. The window popped open. Now I could see and hear what was going on down there.

Elinor and Allan were now sitting in the VIP seats. I saw many other people I recognised—musicians I'd collaborated with, models and actresses I'd dated, Heather my manager who secretly hated me, important executives from my label ... anybody who was anybody was here. There was Bianca, the tattoo artist from high school who'd been kind to me whenever I came back to Crookshollow. And there—standing on the stage with a couple of old women who were friendly with my mother—was Duncan, looking self-satisfied in his perfectly tailored suit as he surveyed the gathering crowd.

Prick, I thought, as I watched him. My mother trusted him ... hell, I trusted him. And he'd been stealing from her.

Once everyone was seated and the press were snapping away madly, the funeral started in earnest. A post-punk band called

Switchblade Sawdust who've opened for us many times on our UK tours played a funeral dirge, while two coffins were wheeled up to the front by the Ghost Symphony backstage crew, all burly men straining to fit inside their sombre black suits.

I laughed bitterly as I watched that casket make its way slowly up the aisle. Was there any moment more goth than watching your own funeral unfold before you? I literally had a bird's eye view of my own death's knell as my coffin was arranged next to Mother's at the front of the stage.

I gulped. *My coffin.* It was a deep black, draped with red ribbons and a cascading arrangement of red roses. My mother's roses were white. Duncan really had pulled out all the stops. Thankfully, both caskets were closed. I guessed after being in a car accident, my body wasn't quite up to public display.

"Goodbye, Mother," I whispered as my eyes focused on her casket. She'd been a hard woman, and I hadn't always liked her. In fact, there were times in my life when I'd hated her. But she did what she thought was best, and she made her own luck. I always admired that. I was glad that at least a few of the hundreds of people who'd bought tickets for the funeral were friends of hers.

First, Duncan got up to give a short speech. He glossed over me and my career, and focused solely on my mother. Tears spilled from his eyes as he described her life after my father left, and how she'd built her fortune from nothing but hard work and intelligence, and how she'd kept up the old house, until the dementia finally claimed her.

I looked back at Elinor. She was sitting next to Allan, her long fingers folded neatly in her lap, her eyes focused on Duncan. I could see a white tissue balled up in her fist, and occasionally she would dab at her eyes with it. *What is she thinking right now? Is the crying because of me? Is she thinking about me, or are her tears because of all that paperwork she could be doing instead of sitting there in that pretty dress ...*

Wait a second.

My eyes focused on the figure sitting directly behind Elinor. Under normal circumstances I wouldn't have noticed her, especially since Elinor's beauty outshone her in every way. But now her lank blonde hair, turned-up nose and sallow skin were forever emblazoned on my memory.

It was Helen Manning. My killer was sitting right behind Elinor. My stomach twisted. *This is it. This is what you were afraid would happen.* I had to do something, but what? I couldn't even leave the house …

Do what exactly? Call the police? With what evidence, exactly? *You can't do anything, and you shouldn't try. Elinor doesn't want to see or speak to you, and you should respect that. Just stay here and watch, don't take your eyes off her, maybe everything will be okay.*

What else could I do? I sat and I watched as my killer and the woman I loved shared the same oxygen. And I waited for something to happen.

What is she doing here? Did she come to gloat over the corpse of her victim? How fucked up is that?

I snuck another glance over my shoulder. I definitely wasn't mistaken. Eric's killer was sitting *right behind me*, staring toward the front of the stage with tear-stained eyes while two musician friends of Eric's talked about his career. No matter how I felt about Eric, I couldn't just let a murderer sit there plain as day without *doing something.* Besides, if she was part of the drug plot, then she was a bad seed, anyway. Who knew what else she might do, or who else she might hurt?

But what to do? With all these cameras snapping away, I couldn't confront her here, in the audience. I had to get her away, but how ...

"Hand me the flask," I whispered to Allan, a crazy idea forming in my mind.

"Not now," he whispered back, his eyes still pinned to the stage. "All those reporters are watching."

"I'm not going to embarrass you any more than I already have. Please hand it to me. It's important."

Sighing, Allan lifted the hem of his shirt, and pulled the flask from its secret pocket in the back of his belt. Without averting his gaze from the stage, he pushed the flask into my hand.

"Booze hag," he mouthed at me. I gave him the thumbs up in return. Unscrewing the lid, I rolled my head to the side, opening my mouth as if I intended to drink. And then I flung the flask over my shoulder, aiming as best I could for Helen's lap.

"What are you doing?" A thin, high-pitched voice behind me squeaked. "You idiot! You've spilt that stuff all over me!"

Bingo.

"Oh, I'm so sorry!" I spun around, my face a picture of mock concern. I had my first good look at Helen Manning in all her glory. She had made a great effort with her outfit and her makeup was bold and colourful, her lips outlined with a deep, blood red. The dress she wore could hardly be called "sombre." Now that I was close up, I could see it had a pattern of jaunty dancing skeletons, and she had articulated skeletons dangling from her ears and around her neck, to go with that silly skull crown she wore. *Tasteful.* The front of her dress was now sopping wet, the liquid smudged across the skeletons. She reeked of scotch. I dabbed at the stain on her breast with my snotty handkerchief, but that only smudged it worse.

"Stop doing that! This is dry clean only," Helen moaned, flinging up her hands. All around us, people were turning their heads to stare. I had to move on to phase two of my plan, stat.

"I'm *ever* so sorry," I said sweetly. "Let me take you to the bathroom. I bet I can fix this."

"But I'll miss the funeral! Besides, we're not allowed in the house. The only toilets out here look like they've been imported directly from Glastonbury without being cleaned." Helen screwed up her face.

"Relax." I grinned my most trustworthy smile. "I'm Alice Marshell's lawyer. I have the keys to the house. And besides, Eric's eulogies aren't for a while yet. You won't miss anything, I promise."

"You mean ..." Helen's eyes gleamed. "I'd get to see inside Eric's house?"

"Of course. I mean, it's the least I could do after ruining your dress." I leaned closer and whispered in her ear. "If you like, I could even show you the room he slept in as a child. His mother kept it just the way he left it."

"Let's go." For someone who'd just been drenched with scotch, Helen looked as if she was going to burst with joy. She scrambled out of her chair, practically running down the aisle toward the back porch. I gulped down my fear and sauntered after her, holding up the velvet rope with the DO NOT CROSS sign so she could duck under. I didn't look up to the attic to see if Eric was watching. I was about to enter a deserted house, with a murderer. I needed all my wits about me.

ERIC

*W*hy is Elinor walking toward the house with Helen Manning?

I watched, my ghostly heart thundering against my chest, as Elinor turned around in her seat and talked to my murderer. And then she was standing up, and leading the villain through the crowd toward the house. They disappeared under the eaves as Elinor led Helen up onto the porch.

Is she insane? Doesn't she know how dangerous it is to be alone with this woman? What is she thinking?

Of course, she isn't thinking. Or, at least, she isn't thinking of what's important.

That was Elinor's problem. She was so busy trying to uncover the truth, she didn't think about her own safety. For an incredibly intelligent woman, she could be exceptionally thick sometimes.

All my hurt and anger at Elinor flew from my mind. I heard the back door open, and Elinor's voice echoed through the hall. "—if you'll just come this way, I'll show you the bathroom and we can scrub that stain right out. I have a dress you can wear in the meantime. It's upstairs in Eric's bedroom. I can't wait to show it to you."

"Oh, that would be beyond amazing!" came a high-pitched, young-sounding voice. *The voice of my murderer.*

What is she doing? The violin dropped through my knee. I was back to being see-through again. *Good.* I raced toward the attic door, flew straight through it and down the stairs. I flew into the hall, but my body slammed against an invisible wall. I bounced back into the steps, my ears ringing. *What is that?*

I tried to pass over the threshold into the hall again, but again, my hands came up against a wall of invisible resistance. It was similar to the barrier that kept me inside the house. Was it shrinking? How was I going to help Elinor?

I inspected the area around the barrier, looking for a clue. When I looked down, I noticed someone had laid a path of white powder across the front of the stairwell. At first, I thought maybe Elinor had dumped out the coke in my violin case, to make some kind of point, but when I bent down to inspect it closer, I discovered it was salt. I tried to touch the granules, but my hand was stopped mid-air.

Vaguely, I remembered a horror film I'd seen once where ghosts were unable to cross a line of salt. It looked as though Elinor had seen it, too. But, as angry as she had to be at me to attempt to trap me in the attic, I couldn't let her be alone with Helen Manning. It was too dangerous.

I took a deep breath and dropped through the floor into the ground floor below, arriving in the rear hallway just behind Elinor and Helen. I glanced around, but couldn't see any more salt trails back here. I followed them down the hall into the main downstairs bathroom. My mother had an old-fashioned laundry basket in the corner—tall and made of black wicker with a lid. It was the perfect hiding spot. While Elinor was fussing with something over the vanity unit, I flew inside the basket, so that only my eyes peeked through the slats. I didn't want Elinor to know I was there, not yet.

"Here, let's try this." Elinor dabbed something on a cloth, then wiped the front of Helen's chest. She was biting her lip in concentration. She looked so hot when she did that.

"Thank you so much." Helen looked at herself in the mirror. She made a pouty model face, which, with her heavy makeup, just made her look like a clown appreciating a Greek tragedy. "I didn't mean to snap at you before. It's just that I spent my entire pay check on this dress and the ticket and I didn't want—"

"Oh, it's perfectly understandable. I'm just glad we've managed to salvage it. Did you know Eric?" Elinor asked her.

"Oh, yes," Helen breathed. "We were friends. *Close* friends, if you know what I mean." She raised one painted eyebrow in a suggestive way. I gagged out loud. Elinor turned toward the washing basket. I quickly snapped my head back inside. She didn't say anything, so I don't think she'd seen me.

"I've been a fan of Eric's band since high school," Helen was saying. "We write each other letters all the time. I've seen every show Ghost Symphony performed in London. I'm secretary of the official fan club and vice president of the Girls of Ghost calendar committee. I just couldn't believe it when I heard Eric was dead. It felt like a part of me was dying, too. I just *had* to be here, although it's hard."

From inside the basket, all I could see was my mother's flowery towels. My whole body seethed with rage. Here was this girl who had taken my life, lying through her teeth, pretending that we were close personal friends. What was Elinor *doing?* I dared to move my head forward until I could see through the basket into the bathroom beyond. Helen dabbed her eyes with a wad of toilet paper, and Elinor patted her on the shoulder.

"Oh, of course," Elinor cooed. "There, there. I know how you feel. It's been hard on all of us."

"Oh, what do you know!" Helen sobbed. "I saw you with Allan. You looked pretty close, and he's still alive. Why couldn't it have been *Allan* who died, instead of Eric? Allan wasn't even *nice* to me, and after everything I did with him ..."

Her words gave me pause. That was an awfully weird thing for my killer to have said. Was she saying she was supposed to have killed Allan, instead of me? What the actual fuck?

"I'm not really *with* Allan, we're just friends. But while I've got you here," said Elinor, "I was wondering about something."

I watched as Elinor pulled something small out of her bra and smoothed it out on the vanity unit. The ticket stub. *Elinor, no. You idiot. You can't confront her like this, with no one watching. She's a cold-hearted killer. If she realises you're onto her, who knows what she will do!*

I wanted to rush out of the basket right then and drag Elinor away. I wanted to push Helen's head down the toilet and hold it there until she stopped struggling. But I was a ghost, what could I do? So I stayed where I was, my heart like a stone sinking through my chest.

Helen peered down at the crumpled paper. "What is that?"

"It's your ticket stub from the last London Ghost Symphony show," Elinor tapped the tiny square. "See? You wrote your phone number on the corner there."

Helen looked at Elinor with wide eyes. "Where—where did you get that? I thought I'd given it away."

"It was on the side of the road," said Elinor, her voice firm. She took a step toward Helen, her body language suddenly transforming from helpful and friendly to imposing and confrontational. *That must be a skill they teach you in Lawyer School.* "Right next to Eric's dead body."

No, Elinor, no. This was idiotic. Judging by her outfit alone, this girl was clearly insane. Panic rose in my stomach. What could I do? I couldn't warn Elinor—it was far too late for that. I couldn't call for help or attack Helen in my current state. *Maybe I'll turn solid again ... any moment now ... please ... I've never wished for a solid form as much as I have at this moment ... please ....*

"But ... that doesn't make any sense." Helen backed up against the wall, staring at Elinor with wide eyes. "How did it end up there? How did Eric get this? He was already gone when ..."

"You know how he got it. You had it on you, right before you killed him. Perhaps you tried to give it to him, and when he wouldn't take it, you went after him in your car and ran him off the road. Is that how it happened?"

"What are you talking about? Are you saying I killed Eric?" Helen's eyes filled with tears. She held up her hands in mock surrender. "I would never do that. I loved him! He meant everything to me!"

"But you didn't mean anything to him, did you, Helen?"

"What are you talking about? We were friends—" Helen's voice rose a register. She backed right up against the wall and started to slide down it, as if she wanted to curl up into as tiny a ball as possible.

"He didn't even know who you *were!* He didn't even read your letters! He rejected you, Helen. And you couldn't take it any more." Elinor towered over the shaking girl. My heart pounded faster. *Don't provoke her, Elinor! She's already killed someone. You don't know what she's capable of doing here.*

"That's not true!" Helen sobbed. Her hand reached across the vanity unit, searching for something to hold onto. A weapon?

"It *is* true. I've read the letters, Helen. I've seen the vial of blood. I know you threatened to kill him. You even explicitly detailed how you'd most like to do it. And then Eric shows up dead, with *your* ticket stub and *your* phone number beside the body." Elinor took another step toward Helen. She was so close now that she could reach down and grab the girl. "But luckily, I'm not the police. I haven't yet gone to them with what I know, and I don't intend to, as long as you co-operate with me. What I'm looking for now is a confession."

"I didn't do it!"

"I'm a lawyer. I can help you. I *want* to help you. But in order to do that, I need to know the truth. You killed Eric, didn't you?"

"No!" Helen screamed. She smashed her fist into the mirror. Glass flew everywhere, showering both girls in sharp, twinkling shards. Elinor was caught off guard. She stumbled back, her hands holding up her skirts away from the glass. Helen dropped to her knees and grabbed a large shard. Her face twisted with rage and pain.

Elinor backed up again. "Helen—" she started to say, but Helen let out a sound that wasn't quite human—partway between a growl and a screech—and lunged.

I saw that shard aimed at Elinor's throat. The whole world moved in slow-motion. I leapt out of the washing basket, and sailed across the room, not sure what I intended to do in my ghostly state, but just knowing I had to save Elinor.

Helen registered my presence. Her whole face crumpled with fear, but she already had momentum going, so she continued to sail toward Elinor with that sharp shard held high. I crashed into her, pinning her back against the tile wall, my hand clamped around her throat.

"You're dead!" Helen cried, her eyes wide with terror. "You—you're outside in a coffin right now!"

"Eric!" Elinor sobbed. Her hand clamped down on my shoulder, the heat of her touch searing my skin. "Don't hurt her. We can't prosecute her if she's dead."

"I'm not sure if I care," I snarled into the face of the gibbering, terrified girl. "She robbed me of my life. Why should I not take hers in return?"

"I didn't do it!" she sobbed. "I swear!"

"Then explain the ticket," Elinor said sternly. "How come Eric had the ticket with your phone number on it?"

"Eric *couldn't* have had it, because I never gave it to him! He'd already left the venue by the time I got backstage. I went into the dressing room looking for him, and I ended up talking with Allan. He wasn't you, but ..." She closed her eyes. "I'm sorry, I betrayed you."

"You … betrayed me?" I loosened my grip slightly. That niggling feeling in the back of my mind had returned. Helen's behaviour, some of the things she'd said … it just wasn't adding up to *murderer* in my head.

"I slept with Allan," she whispered, her eyes pleading with me. "I'm so sorry, Eric. I wanted you! Really, I did. But he was there and you weren't and he was nice to me and so we fucked in the back of his car after the show. I gave him my number, and he said he'd call me again, but he never did. I'm so sorry. I figured if I couldn't have you, he was a pretty good second choice."

Behind me, I heard Elinor gasp. "Oh, no," she whispered, her hands shaking.

"What?" I asked, and then the truth hit me like a freight train.

Allan had Helen's number. And the number had been on the road beside my body.

Allan had been at the scene of my murder.

Helen sobbed louder, struggling feebly against my grip. "Are you telling the truth?" I growled, pulling her up the wall by her dress. "Because if you lie to me, I will haunt your arse so bad, you'll wish to be rescued by Freddy fucking Krueger."

"I swear that's what happened. We went to Allan's car because there were a ton of people in the dressing rooms still and he said it was a security risk to go back to their hotel room. We were going to smoke a pipe afterward, but then this bouncer was knocking on the window waving a violin around, saying Eric—you—had taken off with the case, whatever that meant. Then Allan started cursing. He was yelling at the bouncer, 'where the fuck has he gone?' I said that you were probably in Crookshollow because your mother was sick. That's true, right? It was in the fan newsletter."

"Come on, then what happened?"

"Then Allan shoved me out the car door—I didn't even get a chance to grab my shoes from under his seat—and he sped off." Helen gulped back her tears. "I went home after that, and the next day I heard you were dead. I didn't see Allan again until he showed up here, with *her*."

"Oh my God, Eric," Elinor moaned.

I relaxed my grip on Helen. She sank to her knees, clutching her neck and crying softly.

The hot hand on my shoulder pulled me around. There was Elinor, looking frightened and shaken in her beautiful dress. She gazed up at me with wide eyes, as if begging me to say it wasn't true. But I could see that her brain was ticking away, working through all the evidence we had collected, trying to fit the puzzle pieces together in a different way.

"I just … I don't understand," I said. My voice sounded hollow. Allan was my oldest and closest friend. We'd been playing music together for ten years. He was goofy and wild, and he loved to party. He also loved spicy Indian food, Ancient Greek philosophy, and Hobnobs. We'd had fights, sure, but he'd never given any indication that he was anything other than completely devoted to me and the band. *So how could … what had …*

"He's been playing me this whole time," Elinor said, and she was looking at me with a strange, faltering expression.

"He's been playing all of us," I growled. My stomach twisted. I felt ill, which was a strange thing for a ghost to feel. *My closest friend … how could he?*

"We have to go to the police with this," Elinor said. She whirled around and addressed Helen. "This is bigger than just Eric's murder, much bigger. Will you make a statement to the police? Will you say exactly what you just told me?"

Helen nodded miserably. "Anything …" she said. And to me, "Are you a zombie?"

"Not quite, honey." Elinor gave her a sad smile, then turned back to me. I could see that brain of hers turning over, figuring out what we had to do. "Okay. This is okay. Allan doesn't know about the ticket, so he can't suspect I'm onto him yet. We just need to get through this funeral, and then we'll go to the police. We'll get him, Eric, I promise."

Her lips quivered. She was trying to put on a brave face, but she was scared. I was scared too, but not for myself. The idea of her going out to sit next to my murderer terrified me more than anything I'd ever imagined. I linked my hand in hers. "You don't have to go out there, you know."

"Yes, I do," Elinor breathed, moving closer to me. The heat of her body swirled around me. "Eric …"

"What?"

"Before I go back out there to sit next to Allan and pretend that I don't know what he did, I have to know. It's total honesty time—did you have anything to do with the drugs?"

"I swear on the grave of Edgar Allan Poe that they were not mine," I said. "My life is fucked up enough as it is, without adding drugs to the mix."

Elinor took a deep breath, her eyes narrowing. I thought for one horrifying moment she didn't believe me, that she was going to slap me and run away again. But then she exhaled, her whole body relaxing against me. "Okay, then."

"Do you believe me?"

She gave me a sad smile. "Dead men tell no lies, right?"

"Exactly. Now, please don't go out there."

"I have no choice, Eric. You're a ghost, and I have to go pretend that everything is okay so that Allan and whoever else is involved don't try to skip the country. But don't worry, I will be looking for evidence, something we can really nail Allan with. We've got a case full of drugs and the ticket, but it might not be enough to convince the police, or a jury. Especially since Allan is rich and is going to get a real shark of a lawyer." Elinor laughed bitterly. "Hell, he could probably even afford to hire my dad."

"Can't I just wring his neck until he's dead, and then kick his arse here in the spirit world?"

"There's not going to be any more death, and that's final."

Elinor gave me a weak smile. She squeezed my shoulder, and the touch sent a burst of heat through my body. I had missed her. "Let me solve this my way. The *legal* way."

"If you insist. But I don't like it."

"Neither do I. Hey, how did you get past the salt trails, anyway?" she asked.

"You didn't put any salt on the ceiling."

"Ah, *touché,* Mr. Marshell."

"So what am I going to do?"

"Go back upstairs and watch the rest of the funeral. Keep your eyes on Allan. Maybe you'll notice something I don't." Elinor dropped her grip on my shoulder. She turned away from me and started to fix her dress, pulling the top of the corset up and rearranging her breasts. I couldn't help but grin.

"Don't look at me like that," she said, swatting my arm. "Eric, this is serious."

"I know. But it doesn't change the fact that you look hot as fuck in that dress."

A blush crept up Elinor's cheeks, but she didn't acknowledge my statement. Instead, she turned to the whimpering girl slumped against the closed door, and held out her hand. "Come on, Helen. We've got to get back out there. You need to clean yourself up, and get some colour back into your cheeks. You look like you've seen a ghost."

By the time I returned to my seat, Duncan was giving the closing remarks of the second part of his long, adulating eulogy to Alice Marshell. Allan stood up as I sat down, pulling a square of paper from his pocket and unfolding it nervously. "I don't know why you were gone so long. It's been painful without you, but I'm glad you're here now. Wish me luck," he said, touching my arm. It was all I could do not to flinch away in disgust.

"Where are you going?" I didn't want to let him out of my sight.

"I've giving Eric's eulogy, of course," Allan said, looking at me strangely. "I'm one of his closest friends. I couldn't get away without saying something."

Panic seized me. I thought of Eric upstairs in the attic, listening to the man who took his life talking about their lives together. "Are you sure you're going to be okay?" I asked him. "You're so upset about Eric's death, maybe you should leave the eulogy to someone else? The bassist what's-his-name is over there. Maybe you should let him do it? Or I'll do it, if you want me to."

Allan gave me a sad smile. "You're sweet. But it's a bit late now. I'll struggle on somehow. Besides, I don't have to use many words."

Before I could stop him, Allan pushed passed me and approached the stage, just as Duncan finished speaking and walked offstage to a smattering of applause. As soon as Allan stepped in front of the microphone, the whole crowd stood up and applauded. At the back of the crowd, the fans with the cheaper tickets hooted and hollered. I clapped politely, my heart hammering against my chest as I thought of Eric up in the attic, having to listen to this.

The applause went on for so long, Allan had to raise his hands to call for silence. "Hi everyone, I'm Allan Lachlan, the drummer in Ghost Symphony, and Eric's closest friend. I'm supposed to be standing here today to talk about Eric's life and the great contribution his music has made to the world. I am not much of a speaker, and even less of a speechwriter." He paused while the audience laughed. "But I wanted to do something to honour this remarkable man. But every time I tried to think of the words, nothing sounded right. I realised that's because Eric didn't live in the world of words, not really. He communicated through his music, and so I thought a fitting tribute to him would be to perform a little music of our own." Allan leaned toward the back of the stage, and pulled out a small violin that was stashed there.

"I'm no expert on this instrument. Eric has taught me a little of the violin over the years, and the rest I've picked up through watching him at work. I thought it would be appropriate to play something for him today. This was the last song Eric ever wrote with the band before he died, and although he never titled it, we're calling it *Beautiful Mourning*. We're going to release it in his honour. I hope you enjoy it." Allan nodded off stage, and the other members of the band sauntered on, their instruments in hand. The applause grew into a roar.

The bassist drew the bow across his double bass, and a slow, haunting melody filled the marquee. Next came the guitar, filling out the sound with rich harmony. Then came the bass guitar, deep and powerful, like a thunderstorm rolling in from the hills. Allan stood under the spotlight at the front of the stage, his face bathed in shadow as he rested the violin against his neck, waiting for his cue.

I recognised the song instantly. It was the song Eric wrote for his father. The song the band had started to record, but decided to leave off the album. The song Eric said was the greatest thing he'd ever written. And here was Allan, previewing it for the world, taking from Eric the last legacy he had to give.

My blood boiled at Allan's audacity. I glanced around to see if anyone else thought it was horrible, but the crowd was completely caught up in the announcement. They were cheering and clapping louder than ever. *Of course. This is a great moment for fans of Ghost Symphony. Never mind that Eric is dead. They're getting a new song, so everything is okay.* Near the front in the press pit cameras snapped away, and a TV camera wheeled across the front of the stage as Allan placed the bow against the strings and struck his first note.

A familiar melody loomed over the marquee, the notes hanging in the air before raining down upon the waiting crowd. But where Eric's version sounded melancholy, Allan's was grim, foreboding. He strode across the stage as if it were an arena show, not the small stage in front of the coffin of his friend and his mother. I stood awkwardly as the crowd swayed and shifted around me, clutching my arms across my chest as the anger swelled up inside me, threatening to bubble over. I glanced up at the attic windows, but I couldn't see inside. Was Eric there? Was he listening to this?

Eric, if you can hear me, I'm so, so sorry. We will get him for this. I promise we will.

I focused my attention on Allan, watching his performance for any hint, any clue that might give me what I needed to nail him for his crimes. Something struck me as odd. The violin in Allan's arms looked awfully familiar. It had a plain wooden body, covered in dents and scratches. In the bottom corner the varnish had been rubbed off.

It was Eric's violin. Not Tristan, the violin that Bianca had seen on eBay only two days before, but Isolde—the violin Eric inherited from his father. Allan had Eric's violin.

The rage inside me rose to my throat, closing it tight. I couldn't breathe, couldn't think. All I saw was red. Allan pranced through the band, leaning in toward the guitarists as his fingers flew over the strings. He knelt down at the front of the stage, leaning out to play close to the fans crowded against the barrier. *He's acting like he's the frontman of the band.*

I heard something else, stray notes rising above Ghost Symphony's sound, as if they floated in the air itself.

A second violin joined Allan's. It played the same melody, but added flourishes and syncopation, creating a sweeping, intense experience that far surpassed Allan's poor attempt at emotional string-pulling.

My eyes swept across the stage, but I couldn't see any other musicians making an entrance. My gaze swept back to the house, and sure enough, through the open attic window I could just see the shadow of him, my man in black, his head bent down and his instrument pressed tight against his neck as he played with everything he had.

All the noise on the stage faded away, becoming nothing but a backing track for the true virtuoso. Eric poured everything he had into the music, his hurt and his anguish flowing out through every soulful, heart-wrenching note.

Never before had a piece of music gripped my heart and squeezed it as tightly as this. It felt as though a vice had been placed around my chest and was tightening with every scrape of Eric's bow. I held my hand over my heart, tears streaming down my face as I stood in that crowd of surging, cheering people. *I am standing with you, Eric. There is one person here who knows the truth.*

I assumed I was the only one who heard Eric's beautiful music

—I thought he was playing for himself and for me, and no one else. But as I glanced around me, I saw a few heads in the crowd turn toward the house, and then a few more. One by one, the people in the VIP area stopped cheering, their eyes trained on the attic window where the exquisite sound came from.

Soon, the whole audience had grown silent, even the photographers ceased their constant snapping. The air was filled with trembling, wrenching notes as the two violinists duelled for our attention. Allan spun across the stage, sweat pouring down his face and his clothes clinging to his body as he attacked the neck with the bow, stabbing at the notes as though he wished to murder them, too.

Fear clutched at my stomach. The air around us crackled with tension. It wasn't just me. People exchanged worried glances. The security guards moved closer to the stage. Everyone could sense that *something* was about to happen.

One of the speakers emitted a loud *POP*. No one in the crowd seemed to notice, but the sound tech on the side of the stage scrambled behind the speaker wires. When he emerged again, he was yelling something into his walkie talkie. Allan played on.

I smelled something in the air. *Fire.* Something was burning. All around me, people were whispered to each other, gazing around anxiously, sniffing the air. My stomach twisted with fear.

The second speaker exploded in a shower of sparks.

People in the front screamed and scrambled out of the way as flames licked along the front of the stage. Finally, Allan looked up and, seeing the wall of orange flames leaping from the edge of the stage toward him, dropped the violin and ran offstage.

People stampeded to the marquee exits, vaulting over the barriers and tearing through the velvet ropes. I tried to move my feet forward, but they were glued in place. The woman behind me shoved me roughly, startling me out of my stupor. I scrambled down the aisle towards the exit, glancing around me to try and find my friends. I saw Cindy and Damon up ahead, standing under the eaves of the house. Cindy's face was crumpled with fear, Damon just looked bored.

I reached them just as the flames took down the lighting rig. It crashed into the stage, bucking the metal supports. Lights burst, sparks flew, and the wooden planks of the stage flew in all directions. The fire licked at the edges of the marquee. Any moment now it would go up in flames.

The crowd scattered in all directions, celebrities, goths and paparazzi fleeing around the sides of the house, over the hedge, or down the path through the forest. Sirens wailed in the distance. Someone had called the fire brigade.

And above the chaos, Eric's final solo raged, wave after wave of bariolage rising into a soaring vibrato. The attic window was directly above our heads. Cindy yelled at me over the din of the music and the terrified crowd. "What's going on? Who's playing that music?" I shook my head. There was no point explaining. We had more important things to worry about.

"Elinor, I found you!" Bianca crashed into me, grabbing my hand and trying to pull me toward the side of the house. "We have to get out of here. The marquee is going up in flames."

I barely heard her. My mind was on Eric's body, inside the coffin in front of the burning stage. If someone didn't get his body out, we wouldn't even have a *chance* at restoring him to life. And suddenly that mattered to me more than anything else in the world. I took a step toward the burning tent, but then I saw something that stopped me.

Helen Manning came running through the orange flames devouring the marquee. Her makeup ran down her face in rivers, and her pale skin was smudged with filth, making her appear like some kind of zombie clown. Her skeleton dress flapped around her legs as she strained to push a heavy object through the cloud of smoke. Eric's coffin. She was wheeling Eric's coffin across the grass on its brass stand.

Helen saw me watching her, and tried to say something, but all that came out was a dry, hacking cough. Her eyes shut and she toppled over the end of the coffin, collapsing in a heap on the grass.

"No!" I cried, breaking free of Bianca's grasp and flying toward her. But before I could reach her, two of the security guards swooped in and scooped her up. "Take her to the ambulance," one barked at the other, and he ran off with Helen, while the first guard dragged the coffin away.

Eric's coffin was safe for now, and I heard the sirens screaming as the fire brigade pulled into the driveway and started unrolling their hoses.

"Get away!" someone screamed. "The fire's moved to the house. The house is burning!"

And suddenly Bianca was beside me, pulling me away, her voice coaxing me back to safety. I walked slowly, in a daze, not really registering that I was moving. My vision blurred, and I felt oddly detached from the whole situation, as if I were standing behind myself, looking down on the burning tent and scattering crowd. Firefighters rushed passed us, yelling instructions to each other as they dragged their heavy hoses across the new lawn.

"Is there anyone still inside the marquee?" A firefighter called out as he rounded the corner of the house, hose in hand.

"We don't think so," said the security guard wheeling Eric's coffin away. "And the only people inside the house were the catering staff, who are all accounted for."

But there was one person who hadn't been counted, because he was assumed dead. And I hadn't read enough of Clara's book to know what happened to a shade if it was touched by a fire. Eric had felt real enough when he'd touched me in the bathroom earlier, and if he was real, he could burn.

My ears buzzed with a strange, dissonant note. Everything around me moved in slow motion, the sounds dulled and muddy, as though I were moving through water. Thoughts wandered through the veil of my mind. Where were Ghost Symphony? I hadn't seen any of the band members since they ran offstage.

I swirled my heard around. I couldn't see Allan anywhere, but I had an idea where he might go.

"I've got to get into the house!" I yelled to Bianca.

"Don't be ridiculous, Elinor! The house is on fire. We've got to get to the driveway, where it's safe!"

"No, you don't understand!" I wrenched my hand from hers, and pushed my way through the stampeding crowd. I pushed over the velvet rope stringing off the area, my heels clattering across the back porch. I flung the door open, sending a billowing cloud of smoke into my face. I coughed as I took in a great gulp of acrid fumes.

Behind me, I could hear someone yelling, but I didn't turn back. I pressed my hand over my mouth, and plunged into the dark, smoke-filled house.

My eyes wept as the smoke stung them, and the smoke blinded me completely. I closed my eyes against the stinging, placed my hand on the wall and shuffled along the hall toward the staircase. "Eric?" I choked out, but my words dissolved into coughing.

My mind swirled in the blackness, struggling to think rationally. All my thoughts, my memories, were filled with that music. Eric's song pressed against my temples, the strike of the bow against the strings like a bell tolling his death. I didn't know if I was hearing the music for real, or if it was just the memory of it in my smoke-filled mind.

Get to Eric before Allan does. Get him out.

My hand brushed up against a large, moulded frame. I recognised it as the portrait of Alice Marshell in the entranceway. I turned right, and stepped into oblivion, my hands fumbling forward for the staircase. Through the dimness of my mind I remembered the fire drills at the London office, where we were constantly told that if the building was filled with smoke, we should drop to the ground and crawl. *Smoke rises. Get on the ground where the air is clearer.*

My foot hit the bottom step. I dropped to my knees, and crawled on my hands and knees up the staircase. The stairs widened out into flat, threadbare carpet. I had reached the first floor landing. Coughing violently, I crawled toward the right hallway, but I overestimated the distance and banged my head against the edge of the table. I felt woozy, sick, but I had to keep going.

Eric, where are you?

A siren rang, but it was far away, separate from the world of smoke and darkness. Sound seemed different here, distant, muddy. The siren rang out again, but this time it faded into a high screaming in my ears.

I reached the bottom of the attic stairs. I tried to call Eric's name, but my throat was so dry. Nothing came out except a dry, racking cough. This is bad, I realised, though the fog of my fading mind. *I can't—*

Then everything went black.

ERIC

Fire trucks screamed down the drive, rolling out their hoses and soaking the marquee to quench the flames. There was no one left in the back garden, so I set down the violin and folded my arms across my chest, watching and waiting to see what happened next.

You want me, Allan? Come and get me.

My hands throbbed with a strange kind of energy, like boiling water bubbling through a radiator. The fire of my anger burned inside me, brightest of all.

I don't know how I'd done it, exactly, but I just knew I had started that fire. I'd been playing, giving everything I had to that song, attempting to drown out Allan's butchery of my most precious composition. And suddenly my hands were burning, and this white hot energy flowed out of me and into the violin ... and that was when people had started screaming.

Elinor had run across the lawn below me, her red dress trailing behind her. I'd seen her flee the marquee and then disappear under the eaves of the house. At least I knew she saw safe, she was okay.

I hoped no one was hurt. Well, no one except Allan. I hope he had burned alive under the spotlight. That was *my* spotlight, and *my* song. It was my life he had stolen, and now it seemed as if he was attempting to make himself over as my protégée. Burning to death in front of the cameras was more than he deserved for what he'd done to me.

I glanced back toward the door of the attic. Smoke was curling through the cracks, reaching long tendrils across the room toward me. I sniffed the air, and could smell the dry poison of it. Below me I could hear the firefighters storming across the porch.

They're heading into the house. But why? That means the fire's reached the house.

The anger quickly turned to fear. I had grown up in this house. It held many painful memories, but some wonderful ones, also. This was where my father and I played concertos together. This was where my mother taught me to read and balance the books. If it burnt to the ground, that would be the last straw, the final piece of my life-that-was torn away from me.

Another thought occurred to me as I sat, frozen, by the window, watching the smoke curl across the room. I couldn't leave the house. The invisible barrier of my spiritual state held me prisoner within its walls. But I didn't seem to be fully ghost any longer. I had these strange moments of solidity. If I could touch objects and stand on the floor, did that mean I burned like a person?

What happened when a ghost burned to death? Was I trapped in between the realms forever? I didn't want to stick around to find out.

I used the hat stand to push the window open as far as it would go, then I crawled into the far corner of the room, away from the smoke, and waited. *Soon they'll put out the fire, and everything will be fine.*

But I didn't hear any footsteps pounding up the stairs, or any hoses washing down the walls. The air in the room was now thick with smoke. I could feel it scratching against my throat. My eyes watered. *This doesn't make sense,* I thought to myself as I broke down in a coughing fit. *I'm a ghost. I don't have lungs. Why does my chest feel tight with pain?*

I realised I had to get out of the room. Smoke rose, which meant that all the smoke pouring through the house was collecting in the attic. If I was struggling to breathe now …

I tried to drop through the floor, but I was too solid. I couldn't move through the wood. I'd have to go down the stairs and hope I could pass through Elinor's salt trails.

There was no time to open more windows. I crawled back across the attic floor and reached up to grab the door handle. The hot metal burned my skin, but I gritted my teeth and turned it, pulling the door open before dropping the handle in agony. It had been a long time since I felt physical pain, and I didn't much care for it. I was a ghost. I should just be able to float through this fire.

At the bottom for the stairs, I stepped right over the salt trail. I guess it didn't work when I was solid. I turned right, slumping against the wall as I broke down in another coughing fit. As I dived into the grey haze of smoke, I tripped over something soft and warm lying across the hall. A body. But who was it? Who would have gone up the stairs in the house?

I grabbed the body and turned it over, squinting through tear-streaked eyes as the face came into view.

No. Oh, no.

It was Elinor, and she wasn't breathing.

No. This won't happen. I won't let it. Elinor had so much to live for. She cannot become like me, floating in between the worlds, unable to be part of either. She has to live, to survive. She has to have a long, full life, even if it is without me.

I didn't even stop to think if it was the best idea or not. I pushed my arms underneath Elinor's body, and lifted her against me, cupping her knees and torso. I rose to my feet and plunged through the thick smoke toward the staircase.

I overestimated the distance, and banged my foot against the balustrade, sending a sharp flare of pain through my thigh. My foot searched the ground below me, and finally it found the first step. My stomach convulsed as the smoke filled my lungs. At any moment I expected to black out, or Allan to leap out of the shadows and finish me off.

I didn't even look at where I was treading, I just flew down the stairs two at a time. My face streamed with tears, and the smoke scraped my throat. I was dimly aware of my chest convulsing, but I didn't stop.

As my foot landed on the rug in the entrance hall, I saw a white square of light through the haze. The front door was wide open. A shadow moved across it, growling larger as it approached me.

The smoke grew thinner. My eyes adjusted to the light, and I saw the shadow was a firefighter. He stepped back as I emerged from the staircase, and he fumbled with the thick hose in his gloved hands.

"Take her!" I cried, stumbling towards him and thrusting Elinor's limp body into his open arms. "Save her, please."

The firefighter nodded. I could see through his helmet that his eyes only briefly registered my presence. His gaze was focused on the task before him—saving Elinor's life. He turned and lifted Elinor as he ran through the open front door, leaving me standing alone in the wet, smoked-out wreckage of what had once been my home.

I woke up in an ambulance. A rather handsome paramedic smiled down at me as he adjusted a bandage over my temple. "Hey, there," he said.

"Hey," I tried to say, but it came out as a croak. My throat flared with pain.

"Don't try and talk, Elinor," the paramedic said, patting my arm. "You've inhaled a lot of smoke. It's inflamed your lungs and throat badly. You're lucky; another minute inside and you might not have made it. So just lie back and let us take care of you."

I nodded, too stunned to attempt to form any other kind of non-verbal response. I felt tired all over, as if I hadn't slept for days. Behind me, a machine beeped periodically, that constant rhythm a reminder of how close I'd come to death.

I had no idea what happened inside. I remembered reaching the bottom of the attic stairs, and then nothing else. I assumed one of the firefighters had found me. How lucky was I that they had been in the house when they were.

"There you are!" Bianca stepped up into the ambulance. She fumbled for my hand against the mattress and clasped it in her own. Her fingers felt warm, reassuring. "I was so worried about you. What on earth did you go back into the house for?"

I was too tired and sore to answer, and even if I could have, I didn't even know how to begin to explain. So I just smiled weakly back at her.

"Don't worry, you're going to be just fine. We'll make sure of that," Bianca said. "I was just talking to the fireman who pulled you out, and he said that when you're better again, you'll have to thank the man in the black suit who pulled you out. He said the guy was an idiot going into a burning house like that, but he was also incredibly brave. Who was it, Elinor? Did you see his face?"

I nodded again, and closed my eyes. I was so tired, so very tired ...

THEY KEPT me in hospital overnight for monitoring. The doctor treating me reiterated how lucky I was—there was no long-term damage done. I knew I wasn't lucky. Eric had saved me. He'd carried me down the stairs and handed me to the firefighter. And the firefighter had seen him.

Despite my short stay in hospital, my room was still bursting with flowers. Cindy and Bianca had both brought bunches from Tesco's. Duncan sent some beautiful white lilies that I suspected might have been recycled from the funeral. And Allan sent some blood-red roses and a big box of Bewitching Bites chocolates. I turned his arrangement to the wall so I didn't have to look at it. I ate the chocolates, though. Chocolates should never be wasted.

Cindy seemed desperate to demonstrate she was my closest, most dedicated friend. I think she was feeling a bit guilty over Damon, which wasn't like her at all. She even went to town and bought me some clothes to wear. She reported no one was allowed in the house while the police and fire department investigated, but my clothes were probably ruined, anyway. I didn't think dry cleaning got the burnt smell out.

My dress, my beautiful red dress, was ruined. It reeked of smoke and the hem had been singed beyond repair, and the ambulance officers tore open the corset when they resuscitated me. I was grateful for their efforts, but it was still sad.

Bianca and Cindy took turns staying by my bedside, reading interesting articles from the newspaper, filling me in on the details of the funeral, and making disgusted faces at my hospital food selections.

"They've yet to determine the extent of the fire," said Bianca. "But right now it's looking as if it's nothing structural, just a bit of a hole in the wall behind the porch. The worst damage was to the marquee, and now there's a big, charred patch on the back lawn. The press are going crazy with all the stories about the mysterious second violinist. One girl even swore she saw a man in black playing at the attic window. "

"No one was hurt," added Cindy. "The band are safely back in their Crookshollow hotels. They can't go anywhere because of the police investigation, so there are hundreds of fans camped outside the hotel entrances. It's practically impossible to drive down the high street because of the traffic jams."

"Even the caskets were saved. The police weren't sure what to do with the coffins, so they interred them in the mausoleum—"

But even when they were there, my mind was somewhere else —with the one person who couldn't visit me. Where was Eric now? What did this mean? Was he still a shade? I hoped like hell Clara's book hadn't burned up—I desperately wanted to sit down with it and research, but I couldn't exactly tell Bianca to get it for me without arousing suspicion.

Luckily, neither Bianca nor Cindy mentioned the police finding a violin case full of blow inside the house.

The next morning, the doctor came back to check on me, bearing mostly good news. I was going to be fine. I needed to rest my voice for a few days, take it easy. He gave me a smorgasbord of drugs to take, and discharged me.

"Don't you worry about a thing," said Cindy, as she helped me into the passenger seat in Bianca's car. "Bianca and I have worked everything out. I called Clyde and told him what happened and that you won't be in the office for at least a week. I've called your parents and they're on their way up here as we speak. And when you get back to London, I'm going to look after you and bring you all the best comfort foods and fluff your pillows and—"

"What happened to Damon?" I croaked.

"Oh, he made a couple of good contacts at the funeral," said Cindy. "He's gone back to London to put together a demo CD. I'm free to dedicate 100% of my focus to looking after my best friend."

I nodded, groaning inwardly. I wasn't sure my weakened state could hold up to 100% of Cindy's exuberance.

"We weren't sure if you wanted to go back to London right away," said Bianca. "Or if you needed to stay here because of your work. I imagine the fire has complicated things somewhat."

I nodded. I didn't care about paperwork or the house. I cared about Eric. I needed to get back to Marshell House as soon as possible and find out what happened to him. And I had to go to the police with everything I knew about Allan, and Duncan, and …

My throat hurt just thinking about it all. I nodded at Bianca, indicating that I was going to stay.

"You can't go back to Marshell House right now, so you're coming to stay with me." Bianca grinned as she pulled out of the parking lot. "The couch folds out into a bed, and it's all set up for you. I could say it's a comfortable bed, but that would be a lie. At least Macavity will keep you in cuddles."

I mouthed thank you to them both, and settled back into the car. I closed my eyes to the world, letting my weariness wash over me and searching the darkness of my mind for some answers.

Marshell House was a mess. The whole house and surrounding garden area was roped off with police tape, and black scorch marks trailed up the exterior walls. Police officers and firefighters stalked through the site, muttering to themselves as they checked the wiring, trying to see where the fire had started. They talked in small groups or barked orders into their phones. Two guys in lab coats and latex gloves shuffled back and forth between the house and a large white van. I knew they wouldn't find anything conclusive, because the fire had started in Eric's fingers.

I talked to the inspector on the scene, and he assured me they were nearly finished. "Just give us another couple of hours, and then you can go inside and fetch whatever you need. The house is going to be fine, she's an old girl, built to last, but she's got some pretty bad smoke damage. I can get you in to find your stuff, but I definitely wouldn't recommend staying here any more. We'll also need you to come in to give a statement, of course, but it can wait until later, when you're feeling a little stronger."

I nodded, grateful I was off the hook for the moment. I was still feeling exhausted. Desperate as I was to tell them about Allan, I still couldn't speak, and the idea of writing several pages of detailed notes made my head spin. *I'll leave it until I can contact Helen Manning. The ticket stub was lost in the fire, so I need Helen if I am going to construct any kind of case. If I come forward with the drugs now, they'll just draw the same conclusion I did—that it was Eric who was involved.*

I went to Bianca's studio and watched her ink a hedgehog onto a burly biker. While she worked, I wandered around the room, fingering the different inks and tools and poring over the stack of tattoo magazines on the coffin-shaped coffee table. The beginnings of an idea were starting to form in my mind. But I needed a bit more time to think.

When we returned to the house at lunch time, the police were just finishing up.

"You can go inside," he said. "Just be careful, and stick to the front rooms for now; the fire has done some damage at the back, and it's not safe."

"Thanks," I croaked out. Bianca laid a steadying hand on my shoulder.

"Do you need me to come in with you?" she asked, her voice concerned. "I've got a client in thirty minutes, but I can cancel on him—"

"No, that's fine," I croaked. "Go ink your client. I need to see what I can save from the study, so I might be a while. I'll see you for dinner."

Giving me a final squeeze, Bianca rushed off, leaving me alone on the porch with a familiar heavy keyring in my hands. Taking a deep breath and steadying myself against the doorframe, I stepped over the police tape and stood in the entrance to Marshell House. I took a deep breath, and stepped over the police tape that roped off the front door.

It was hard to believe this was the same house I'd stepped into the previous week, with its drab Victorian wallpaper and heavy furniture. Now, every surface was charred and blackened from the smoke. The place smelled like soot. Ash sifted across the floor with every step I took. From somewhere at the back of the house, I could hear water dripping. The grandfather clock no longer ticked ominously.

I hadn't realised until I peered into the study and saw a layer of black soot covering the floor just how much I'd grown fond of the house. It really did have a kind of life force all of its own, and it had been wounded badly. I walked deeper into the house. There was more police tape on the stairs. I wasn't supposed to go up there. "Eric?" I called out, my voice barely projecting two feet in front of me. *Curse this smoke-damaged throat.* "Eric, where are you?" I tried again.

Silence.

"Eric? If you're here, I need you to give me a sign. Anything, *please*."

Nothing. Eric wasn't there. He didn't come down.

Feeling heartbroken and defeated, I slunk back into the study. There would be no answers here for me. Maybe Eric was up in the attic and hadn't heard me, or he could have been, or he was ignoring me because he thought I was flirting with Allan.

So I did what I always did when I was worried about something I couldn't do anything about: I buried myself in work. I went back into the study and started to stack up everything I needed to bring to Bianca's. Luckily, I'd locked the office doors before the funeral, so hardly any smoke had entered the room. My laptop was fine, and while the papers and ledges smelled awful, they were fine, too.

I was just collecting up the last of Eric's creepy fan mail, when I heard the doorbell ring. Thinking it must be Bianca coming back to see how I was going, I wandered into the hallway with a stack of books. "I hope you've made some room for me in that little apartment of yours, because I've got a stack of books as high as—"

I flung open the door, and leapt back in fright.

"Elinor." Allan tilted his head to the side, smiling his mischievous grin. "Can I come in?"

"Allan?" My hand flew to my throat. His name came out as a choked gasp. "What a surprise! I didn't expect to see you after you ran off after the funeral."

"That was some adventure, eh?" He gave me a crooked smile. "I'm sorry I couldn't see you afterward. I was worried about you, but I couldn't leave the hotel without being harassed by fans and media. Did you get my flowers?"

"I got them, thank you," I said stiffly, starting to close the door. "I'm quite busy, so—"

"I just have something to show you, is all. Open the door, sweets."

My heart pounded against my chest. The last thing in the world I wanted was to be alone in the house with Allan, but I couldn't let on that I knew the truth. *Take him into the kitchen, and stay close to the knives.* "Sure," I said slowly, opening the door.

Allan made a gesture over his shoulder. A tall, burly man stalked out from behind the flower bed and stepped onto the porch.

"Who's this?" I asked, my foot catching the door. Now I was scared. *Really* scared. Why had Allan brought a bodyguard with him? Did he know I was on to him?

Allan kept that grin plastered across his face. His eyes were wide as saucers. I used to think his expression was adorable, but here, in the harsh light of reality, he looked manic. *He's high right now,* I realised with horror. "This is Colin. He does sound and security for Ghost Symphony. He's cool, you can trust him." I didn't want to trust him, but Allan leaned against the door, pushing my foot back. The door flung open, clattering against the stopper. Allan and Colin sauntered inside.

The kitchen. Get them into the kitchen, where you will at least have access to a weapon.

Behind me, the staircase creaked. I whirled around, my heart pounding against my chest. In the shadow on the corner of the upper landing, I saw a flicker of movement in the darkness. I could just make out the outline of a man dressed all in black hiding in the darkness. My heart soared. *Eric.*

"What's wrong?" Allan asked, staring at the staircase as well. I quickly spun back to face him, unsure if he'd be able to see Eric in the shadows or not. *The firefighter saw him, but he might have become ghostly again. Please Eric, don't let him see you. He's on drugs. I don't know what he's going to do.*

"Oh, nothing. This old house still creeps me out," I said, my hands in my pockets. "As I said, I've got a lot of work to do, so—"

"Yes, yes, but I have something really exciting to show you. Trust me, you're going to love it." Allan held up the leather jacket he had balled up under his arm. I could see he had wrapped it around some small object. My heart sank like a stone in a swimming pool. I had a horrid feeling I knew exactly what was underneath that coat.

"Are you going to offer us a drink?" Colin asked. His voice was harsh, filled with gravel.

"Um, sure." I glanced toward the kitchen. "I've only got wine, but—"

"That's fine."

They followed me through the receiving room and into the old-fashioned kitchen. Allan leaned up against the island, following close behind me as I moved around the other side toward the stove. Colin leaned against the doorframe, blocking the exit. The only other ways out of the kitchen was the window, which was latched shut, and the door to the basement. I'd seen enough horror films to know not to run down there. *Right, I'd better try that knife, then.*

I pulled three wine glasses from the drying rack without taking my eyes from Allan. I opened the fridge wide, so the door blocked Allan's view of my hands. As I grabbed the wine bottle from the shelf, I also leaned across the bench and plucked a knife from the rack. I shoved the knife through the waistband of my skirt and shut the fridge. Allan was still smiling that maniacal grin. I unscrewed the cap and started pouring. "So, what do you have to show me?"

"This." Allan dropped the leather jacket to the floor. Clasped in his hand, the barrel pointing directly at my chest, was a pistol. I froze, my hand dropping the glass, which shattered around my feet.

A gun. It looked like an antique gun, too. The kind of gun that made an awful mess. Even though I was expecting it, the sight of that barrel pointed directly at me made me feel faint.

"Allan, what's going on?" Shaking all over, I staggered backward, my arse pressing against the bench. My hand flew to the handle of the knife in my belt. *If he comes any closer, I can whip it out and—*

"Don't try that, honey. You'll get yourself hurt." Allan waved at the security guard. "Colin, get that knife out of her belt."

Sweet holy fuck.

Colin walked around the kitchen counter, grabbed my hands roughly, and twisted my arm around. I cried out as he applied pressure to my elbow, and my fingers dropped the knife handle. "Allan, please ..." I choked out, my ruined voice trembling with fear. Tears streamed down my face.

"What's wrong, Elinor? It's unusual to see you, the unshakeable lawyer, in such a mess." Allan stepped forward, placing his fingers under my chin and lifting my head up. My chin quivered as I tried to shrink away from his repulsive touch. Allan pulled my head up, so that I looked straight at him, straight into those piercing blue eyes. "Look at me, Elinor. Now, for someone who was completely into me only a couple of days ago, you sure seem jumpy now. See, I can't help but get the feeling you know why I'm here, which is good for you, because it means you can help me find what I'm looking for."

I wanted to say something witty, like heroines in action films always do when they're facing death, but all that came out was a strangled sob.

A warm hand pressed against my chest, pushing me back. "Now, lovey," Allan's voice purred in my ear. "I don't want to hurt you, but we need some information. Just tell us where the case is, and we'll leave your pretty little self in peace."

The case. Allan meant the violin case. We were right, it *was* Allan all along. I realised with a sinking heart that I had been hoping against all the odds that it wasn't true. I liked Allan. I didn't want him to be a bad guy. But then, I had liked Joel, too. I thought of that moment on the front porch on Thursday, when Allan's lips pressed against mine. My stomach heaved.

"You are a pretty good actor, you know." I was stalling, trying to give myself time to think. "I really believed you were here for Eric's memory."

"Oh, I am. Just not in the way you assumed," Allan said. "I admit that you were a very nice distraction, and under different circumstances, I would definitely consider dating you. But unfortunately, I have some other priorities right now, and you're kind of in the way."

"You had Isolde all along, didn't you?" I asked. "That letter from Eric's lawyer was a ruse."

Allan nodded. "We removed the violin from the case in Prague. We needed the space for our own cargo. Eric took the case with him before we had the chance to swap it back. And as for the lawyer, you should know better than most that many in your professional aren't above a bribe—"

"Don't tell her shit!" Colin snapped.

"Relax, she's not going to talk."

I gulped. I *so* didn't want to know why he assumed that.

"I don't care if she's deaf, blind and mute," Colin snarled. "You don't fucking go around casually talking about what we're doing. Christ on a rope, Allan. You sound like a bad comic book villain."

"I can't help it. I'm a sucker for a pretty face. And unlike most of Eric's groupies, she's actually quite intelligent." Allan grinned at me. "That was a fine trick she pulled at the funeral, having that tape of Eric playing come on right when we did the song. You timed that perfectly, Elinor. Did you have the sound system rigged to an app on your phone or something?"

"A great magician never reveals their tricks," I choked.

"Come on, Allan." Colin urged, his grip on my arm tightening. "Let's get this over with."

"Relax, we've got plenty of time. The police are done for the day, and this far back from the road, no one is going to hear her scream. Besides, I *want* to tell her. I think she could actually appreciate the genius of our plan."

"It can't be that genius if you lost an entire case of cocaine," I shot back.

"I never said anything about coke," Allan said. "So you *do* have the case. Good, that will make things easier. Just tell us where it is and we'll be on our way."

I cringed at my own stupidity. I'd just signed my own death warrant. The only thing to do was to keep him talking. If Allan was talking, he wasn't killing. "If you knew it was in the house, why did you trash Eric's house in Devon? That was you, wasn't it?"

"We needed the police to focus their efforts elsewhere," said Allan. "With the old lady gone, our plan was to get into the house as soon as they closed the investigation here in Crookshollow, but then you moved in and made things difficult again."

"Why didn't you just come in here earlier and wave a knife around until I showed you the goods? Why the pretence of taking me out and pretending to like me?"

"I'm not really the knife-wielding type," said Allan. "It's messy and prone to backfiring. How would I know if you weren't some kind of karate master? You could've kicked my arse, gone to the police, and I wouldn't have been able to stop you. No, I planned to charm my way in, and find the case while you were sleeping or in the shower or something. It would've been much more pleasant for everyone involved, and gave me a solid alibi for my prints being in the house. But you were too frigid to even invite me up, so I had to resort to other options." Allan wiggled the pistol. My stomach lurched.

"But why use Eric's case at all? It seems ridiculously risky having him discover it. Why not hide the drugs in one of the guitar cases or—"

"Eric was nothing if not a true rock star. He didn't handle his own gear until he was about to go on stage. After Eric packed up his precious instrument, I'd take it out and place it in a secondary case, then we'd fill the case with the cash or the blow, and send it on its way. The airport staff are usually pretty lax about checking touring musicians – they figure we've been through enough airports already that someone's already done their job for them. If we ever got caught, it would be easy to pin on Eric, since he was pretty insistent on being the only one who touched his *precious* case."

"But why? Ghost Symphony were doing well. You were living the dream! Why would you throw it all away for ... for *drugs?*"

"Just because we had a few radio hits doesn't mean we're rich. Not by a long shot. There's a certain lifestyle that comes along with being in a touring rock band, and I couldn't afford to live it on my current salary. And of course *Eric* was the star. He got all the sponsorship deals and the opportunities. He had two solo albums that sold just as well as the band's material. Eric was the one invited to play with the London symphony and do guest appearances in Cradle of Filth music videos. So the rest of the band decided to supplement our incomes. Colin here was in it for the money, but me ..." Allan pressed his lips against my cheek as he jammed the gun into my chin. "I loved running a drug ring right under Eric's nose. That tickled me."

"That's ridiculous. What did Eric ever do to you? You were friends ..."

Allan snorted. "You've got to be kidding. Eric did *nothing*. That was the point. Everything was effortless to him. I was sick of having his cast-off everything—"

While Allan was talking, I was thinking. *What am I going to do? If I show them where I hid the case, they no longer have any use for me. As long as they are still talking, I'm still alive.*

But they're in the house now. If I don't comply, they could just kill me and search the place. Eventually, they'll find it buried at the back of the closet.

Maybe Allan will say something I can use? Maybe I should be listening to him, trying to talk him out of this path of action, trying to convince him to be reasonable.

Or maybe you should just offer to join him in his life of crime. You could be Bonnie to his Clyde, Devil's Advocate Elinor piped up. *After all, he is* quite *attractive.*

Shut up, I willed her. *This is no time for jokes.* I had to figure out a way to keep Allan talking. Right now that was my best option.

"—and all the women wanted him. Groupies would only deign to sleep with the rest of us if Eric had already gone home. Even my cock was a fucking Eric Marshell substitute." Allan was still railing against Eric. "And I thought, fuck this! I am an accomplished musician. I studied at the Sibelius Academy in Helsinki and have performed in front of hundreds of thousands of people. And here I was, being glossed over as I stood in the shadow of the great gothic genius, Eric bloody Marshell. Even when I was interviewed by myself, every question the reporter asked me would be about Eric. It was Eric, Eric, Eric, all the time. After ten years of it, I really hated the guy. I don't think you could understand how much."

As Allan talked, it dawned on me that I *did* know a little bit about what he was describing. I lived constantly in the shadow of others. At the law firm, I was the girl who did all the work, but was overlooked for advancement time and time again because I wasn't a size 0. The urge to define oneself, to be an individual with a unique identity, can make a person do crazy things. I was willing to get an image inked on my skin to stand out, whereas Allan was willing to break several laws in order to prove to himself that he was smarter than Eric.

"I think I get it," I choked out. *If he sees I empathise with him, maybe he won't kill me.* "You had to do your own thing."

"Right." Allan nodded. The barrel bobbed up and down. "I had to do my own thing. Sure, I could've made some solo records or designed my own brand of drumsticks, but when Colin here suggested a way to make some serious dosh right under Eric's nose, and he already had the contacts in Prague and Amsterdam where we regularly toured … the opportunity was just too good to pass up."

"Allan, this is fucking stupid," said Colin. "Let's just kill her and get out of here. We have no idea when the police will be back."

"Wait! Don't you need me to show you where the drugs are?" I was close to full-on panic now.

"I'm sorry, Elinor. You see, I've spent enough time with you over the last couple of days to know that you won't be able to live with yourself if you did that. For a lawyer, you're remarkably honest. And you're too smart. You have more than enough evidence to turn me in. So you have to go. But I'm not going to kill you here. That would create bloodstains and unnecessary questions. No, you're going to get in the car with me, and we're going to go for a little trip."

"No!"

Colin pushed me forward, so I fell against Allan. He quickly grabbed my arms and pinned them, twisting me around so I had no choice but to walk ahead of him. The gun swung up and the barrel connected with my temple. My head spun from the pain, and white stars appeared in my vision. Allan began to drag me toward the kitchen door.

"No, no, no! Somebody help me!" *Eric, where are you? Why haven't you come?*

I grabbed at the edge of the counter, but Colin prised my fingers off with ease. "Keep on screaming all you want, princess. There's no one nearby to hear you. Colin, grab that knife. We might need it."

I was dead.

ERIC

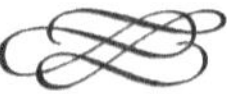

"*E*ric, help!"

Elinor's screams tore at my heart. I wanted nothing more in the world than to go to her and save her, but just as I'd started to move towards her, my foot slipped through the stairs. I was back to my ghostly form again. I could do nothing except lurk in the shadows, punching my arm through the wall every few seconds to see if I'd miraculously gained a solid form again, and listen to Allan describe how much he hated me and what he planned to do to the woman I loved.

I watched from the top of the stairs, my heart sinking, as Allan returned to the hall once again. He held Elinor against him, one hand over her mouth, and the other wrapped around her throat. Colin pulled the door open and cut down the police tape with a sharp kitchen knife, while Allan tried to push Elinor through the doorway.

She was putting up an impressive fight, grabbing the door-frame, the heavy sideboard, even trying to claw at Allan's face. But nothing could halt her inexorable journey toward the doorway. Not even me. I punched the wall again. My fist went straight through the plaster.

"Eric, please!"

Elinor's pleading, terrified voice wrenched my soul. Tears of frustration raced down my cheeks. I couldn't just stay up here and watch her. I had to try *something. If only ...*

Allan laughed. "He's dead and buried now, love. You won't get any help from Eric. Now, if you would please step out the door—"

"She's not going anywhere with you, Allan."

My voice rang out, booming down into the hall below. Allan's head whipped up, searching for the source of the sound. *He heard me.* That was a good sign. I floated out of the shadows, so that I was standing an inch above the first step.

Allan's eyes bugged out of his head as he recognised me.

I reached down, and wrapped my hand around the balustrade. The wood felt cold against my fingers. Cold and real. I stared down at Allan with cold eyes, and smiled.

"Hello, Allan," I said.

Allan's eyes fell on mine, and whatever he saw there terrified him. His skin turned as white as his hair. "H-hello, Eric," he said, his voice cracking on my name.

Elinor didn't say anything, but her eyes were wide with hope. *Just hold on, my love. I won't let them hurt you.*

"You're dead." Colin jabbed a fat finger at me. His face didn't register any emotion, but his eyes darted back and forth nervously. "We saw them put you in your tomb. This is some kind of trick. She's done it, made a hologram of him or something."

I took a step forward, landing on the next stair. Allan grimaced and stepped backward, dragging Elinor with him. "No trick," I said. "I'm dead. You killed me."

"Jesus fucking Christ," Allan moaned. The gun in his hand shook violently.

"Let her go," I said, taking another step forward. As I descended the staircase, I caught a glimpse of myself in the large mirror on the wall. I'd floated past it several times in the last week, and every time, the only thing I saw was the stairwell beyond. But this time, I met my own gaze, my eyes ringed with fire.

I don't know what had happened, but something had snapped inside me, the connection that tethered me to the world between the living and the beyond was gone. I wasn't alive again, but my essence was now firmly back in the world of the living. And I had some serious arse to kick.

"Don't come any closer!" Allan cried. "I'll do it! I'll fucking kill her." Elinor whimpered as he tightened his grip around her throat, the gun pointed at her temple.

'I don't think that's a very good idea," I said as calmly as I could, as I took another slow step down. "I'm already angry enough at you for murdering me. But if you do anything to Elinor, I'm going to be *really* pissed off."

Allan laughed. A high-pitched, psychotic-sounding laugh that made the hairs on the back of my neck stand up. "Only Eric bloody Marshell would come back as a ghost. You always had to be special, didn't you, Eric? You couldn't just die like the rest of us. Well, it's too bad, because now you have to live with watching her die, because that's what I'm going to do. I'm going to blow your frigid little virgin's brains out right in front of you. And we'll see how smug you feel then, Mr. Ghost."

"Allan, he's coming closer," Colin muttered, slinking back toward the open door.

"He's a fucking ghost!" Allan cried. "He can't fucking touch anything. How's he even going to hurt us?"

Allan cocked the trigger against Elinor's temple. She squeezed her eyes shut, and let out a strangled sob. I moved so fast I couldn't even detect it. One moment I was on the stairs, the next, I was standing beside Allan, my hands wrapped around his wrist, twisting his arm back, away from Elinor.

"Holy shit!" Allan cried out as the gun slipped from his fingers and fell to the floor. I pressed my heel against the barrel. To my surprise, as I leaned my weight on the pistol, I felt it give way beneath me, the metal making a scraping noise as it folded in upon itself. I lifted my foot, and inspected the pile of mangled metal that had once been a perfectly functioning gun. The spot where my heel had been was flat as a pancake. That gun wouldn't be firing any time soon.

"That's it," Colin moaned, "I'm out of here."

He seemed to have forgotten about the knife in his hand, for it clattered to the floor as he bolted for the door. I was faster. I slammed it shut behind him, and glared at his red, terrified face. "You're not going anywhere, big guy."

Colin backed away again, pressing his back against the locked door to the study. "Hey, man. This wasn't my idea. I was all for breaking in here, taking the goods and splitting. But Allan here wanted—"

"Shut up!" Allan screamed at him. His head darted from side to side as he tried to formulate a plan of escape. I thought he would head toward the receiving room, so I stepped toward it.

Allan's face twisted with rage, and he pounced on me, only to land in a heap on the hall rug as I swung to the side, searching for something I could use as a weapon. *The hat stand in the corner.* It was made of twisted iron, and heavy. I lunged toward it.

Allan launched himself at me, his momentum knocking out my legs and sending me flying. I crashed into the door and fell back against him. I swung my fist up and connected with his face. Blood gushed from his nose. Allan screamed and lunged at me again, knocking me to the floor and pounding my back with his fists.

While I was occupied, Colin lunged for the door, twisted the handle, and yanked it open. I scrambled to my feet to go after him, and Allan pounced on me again, his hands grabbing for my face as he tore at my eyes with clawed fingers.

Allan's momentum threw me off-balance. I staggered back, my heel clipping against the floor, and I toppled backward, pulling Allan down with me. We sailed right through the open door and clattered together against the porch.

The open door ...

My back crunched as it hit the porch. Pain exploded inside my head.

Inside the house Elinor screamed, the sound tearing through my heart. Fear welled up within me as I felt a familiar numbness start to spread up my arms, down my legs. I was outside, and the house could no longer protect me. I could feel the veil of the world slipping away. Oblivion was coming to take me at last.

Allan brought his fingers to my throat. I felt the briefest press of his hands against my skin, and then, nothing. Allan's expression turned from rage to shock as his fingers went right through me.

"Huh? What's going on?" Allan sat back and swiped at my neck again. His fingers moved through me, like a spoon through treacle. I felt the heat of his touch, but nothing more. Allan's mouth was moving, but I couldn't hear his words. My ears buzzed.

"I've got to ..." I tried to speak, but my words choked me. I gasped for air, for life. I had to cling to the life I'd been given, or Elinor would die. I poured my strength into my legs, and kicked out at Allan. I was still solid enough that I managed to knock him off-balance, and I scrambled back toward the door.

"Oh, no you don't." Allan grabbed me around the waist, and pulled me backward. His hands sank into my body, but I still had enough mass that he could pull me back from the door. "You stay out here, where you're weakest."

Faintly, I heard Elinor screaming.

My vision swam, red blotches appearing where the world should have been. Elinor lay on the hall carpet, her fingers outstretched toward me, her body pinned in place by Colin ...

Elinor ... her face swam through the pain, the vision of an angel, come to carry me off to the beyond. I reached out to her, in my mind, feeling the heat of her fingers against mine, the surge of energy that bound us together, and she pulled me up and out of myself, dragging me over into the other realm.

Then the light exploded, and consumed me.

"*E*ric, no!" I tried to struggle out of Colin's grasp, but his beefy hands held my shoulders down, while his knee dug painfully into my back. All I could do was flail uselessly and watch as Eric's body faded and faded into nothingness. Allan swiped at the fading form, throwing all his weight and anger behind every blow, but his punches fell on thin air.

Eric turned toward me, his faded mouth open in a silent, agonising scream. His eyes flicked over mine, and then he disappeared completely from view, his grey outline fading into the porch behind.

"No." Tears sprung to my eyes, tears of longing, tears of regret. *He's gone forever, and I never had the chance to tell him that I ...*

Allan continued to punch and kick the air where Eric had been. His dance would've looked quite comical if my heart wasn't tearing in two, my whole being ripping down the middle as part of me died alongside Eric.

When he was certain there was nothing left of Eric, Allan dusted off his fingers, and came back inside, slamming the door shut behind him. He stared down at me, his face bruised, his nose bleeding, his mouth twisted into an evil grin.

"Now, where were we ..." Allan sneered, as he reached for the knife.

Someone pounded against the door. Allan jumped a foot in the air. Hope surged in my chest. *Is it Eric? Has he returned somehow?*

The pounding increased.

"Elinor? Are you there?" Bianca called through the door. "I finished my client early. I thought you might like a hand with all the books. Open up, would you?"

"Jesus fuck!" Allan cried. "How many freaks are we going to have to deal with tonight?" He held up the knife, and turned the handle.

"Bianca, get help—" I cried out. Colin clamped his hand over my mouth, and the rest of my warning came out as muffled grunts.

Allan frowned at me. "We should have gagged her while we had the chance," he said. "Keep her quiet, and I'll get the door for our guest."

Colin yanked me up and turned me around, pressing the knife against my throat and shoving me back toward the kitchen so I couldn't see what was happening at the door. I tried to bite Colin's hand, but he held my neck firm, and I couldn't get any of his skin between my teeth. Allan flung open the door. The next moment, I heard a thud as something heavy fell to the floor. I started to cry. *Bianca. This was all my fault. You're completely innocent, and now—*

"Allan?" Colin called out, glancing back over his shoulder. His voice sounded concerned.

No one answered.

Colin dragged me backward, heading back toward the hall. "This isn't the time for pranks. We've been shagging around way too long. We've got to get out of here."

Still no reply from the hall.

"Move, Princess." Colin shuffled toward the door, his hand on my throat now and the knife pointing toward the doorway. I whimpered, and he pushed his hand even tighter against my face, so all I could breathe was his sweaty skin. My stomach churned. *Bianca, I'm so sorry ...*

'Allan?" Colin stepped into the hall. I saw a flash as something moved beside me, and the next thing I knew, the hand on my mouth dropped away. I gasped for air, barely noticing that I had been freed.

'Don't just stand there," said Bianca, slinging her lucky cricket bat over her shoulder as she stepped over the slumped bodies of Allan and Colin. She grabbed my hand and dragged me toward the staircase. "Upstairs, quickly, before they come to!"

She didn't have to tell me twice. I raced up the steps, two at a time, not even bothering to question why we were going up there instead of outside. Bianca had her face set in a determined look, as the cricket bat bounced on her shoulder. She clearly had a plan.

Upstairs, Bianca beckoned me into Eric's room. I sat on the bed while she slammed the door shut. "Call the police," she said, jamming a chair under the handle to lock the door.

'With what? My phone is downstairs."

Bianca rolled her eyes. "You're no use." She dug her phone out of her pocket, found a number, and pressed it against her ear, while she tapped her fingers against the handle of her cricket with the other hand. "Ted? Yeah, it's Bianca. There's been a break-in on Blossom Road, the old Marshell place. I'm trapped in a room upstairs, so you better get here fast. No, this is not a fucking joke, Ted. Get over here, *now.*" She jabbed the END CALL button on her phone.

'You talk like that to the police?" I asked.

'That's Ted. He's a friend of mine from my cricket club. He has a vicious underarm bowl, and an awesome tattoo of his pet canary —one of the best birds I've ever drawn. He'll be here any minute with some reinforcements."

"And why are we still in the house?"

"It's a defensive move," said Bianca. "Haven't you ever seen a battle scene in a movie? They're bigger and stronger and faster than us, so it's easier if we defend a small confined space, with only one way in. It's like a siege. We run into the town and shut the gates, and now they have to assault the walls while we throw stones and dung down on them. Plus, I knew you'd want to stick near Eric."

"Eric's gone," I said, and the grief rushed over me. I buried my face in my hands, my whole body racked with heaving sobs. "He's dead."

"But he's a ghost. How can a ghost die again?"

I looked up at Bianca through the gaps in my fingers. "Excuse me?"

"Elinor," Bianca dropped the bat and slid down beside me. "You honestly thought you'd be able to hide this from me? I may have only known you for a week, but it already feels like much longer. I feel as if we're old friends. And old friends can always tell when the other is lying, or when they're harbouring the ghost of a dead lover inside a big old house."

"You … you figured out that Eric was a ghost?" I lowered my tear-soaked hands and stared at her in surprise.

"Well, not *figured out* exactly. For a lawyer, you're not very good at deception." Bianca grinned. "First of all, you got really drunk at the pub and told me, remember?"

"But you laughed! You didn't believe me!"

"At the time, I thought you were just being ridiculous. But then I started going back over all the odd things you'd said and did, and I realised you must've been telling the truth." Bianca counted off all the clues on her fingers. "You seemed really interested in Eric's personal life for no apparent reason. You poured over books about ghosts and the occult. You had guy-related mood swings but wouldn't divulge any details about the guy. You seemed weirdly attached to the house. Then there was your sudden desire to buy a violin, and all the vicious rats about the place. And when that violin music started playing at the funeral … well, I'd recognise Eric's style anywhere."

"And you don't think this is crazy?"

"Oh, I think it's nuts." Bianca shrugged. "But not as nuts as you trying to take on two drug dealers by yourself. I realised at the funeral that Eric was trying to warn us about Allan, and I was at the shop when I noticed him come around the corner in a car, with that giant thug Colin behind the wheel." She patted the cricket bat. "I thought you might need a hand. Speaking of, where is lover-ghost? I thought he'd be downstairs haunting their arses for trying to hurt you."

"He was," I sniffed, pulling off my glasses to wipe away the fat tears rolling down my cheeks. "But then Allan pushed him out the door. Eric can't leave the house, or he crosses over. He faded away right in front of me. He's gone, Bianca. He's gone forever, and I never got to tell him … tell him that I …"

Bianca wrapped her arms around me, pulling my face into her warm shoulder. "Oh, Elinor. I'm so sorry."

I didn't know how long we stayed there, me rocking and sobbing as I mourned Eric, and Bianca holding me close while keeping her eyes fixed on the door. I was startled out of my stupor by a loud CRASH from downstairs. Bianca sprung to life, leaping from the bed and grabbing her bat. She approached the door and pressed her ear to the wood. But she didn't need to in order to hear the second CRASH, and the sound of someone howling in pain. *Is that Allan?* I glanced at Bianca. She checked her watch. "That's probably Ted."

"Is he—" I was interrupted by loud THUMP, and the sound of Colin's high-pitched scream.

A few moments later, Bianca's phone beeped. She checked the message. "It's Ted, and the coast is clear. Let's go."

We raced downstairs to find a tall, lanky man with black hair pulled back into a ponytail and several tattoos across his forearms directing four police officers who had Allan and Colin pinned to the rug, their hands cuffed. The first officer was barking instructions into a walkie-talkie. Allan lifted his head and glared daggers at me. Blood gushed from a deep gash above his eye.

The tall, plain-clothes man greeted Bianca with a friendly nod. "You did the right thing, hiding and calling us. These guys are clearly high as kites. I'm glad you didn't try to take them on yourselves."

"Are you kidding?" Bianca said in mock surprise, as she grinned at me. "We'd never dream of doing that!"

"We'll need you two ladies to come to the station to give a full statement. Currently, there look like several charges, including assault—"

"This is your lucky day, officer," I said, stepping forward. "You can add drug trafficking to your list of offences. These guys have been running a cocaine ring for years, and there's a mountain of blow stashed in the violin case I hid in the cupboard in the bedroom on the left up the stairs. I suggest you go and arrest the rest of Ghost Symphony, too, and bring in their stage crew for questioning."

"You bitch!" Allan yelled, before he was dragged outside by the officers.

Bianca and I watched as the police shoved Allan and Colin into their cars and backed out of the drive. Ted stayed behind with us, and he turned to Bianca. "She's in the back of the squad car. I told her to stay out of the way until we were certain things were safe. Do what you have to do, but you'd better show up at the police station within the next two hours to give your statement."

Bianca nodded. "Who is he talking about?" I asked her.

Ted opened the door, and a tiny figure bustled out, her body a blur of black hair and crocheted shawls.

"Clara!" I cried.

Bianca grinned. "I figured if anyone could help us with our ghost problem, it would be Clara."

"There's no time for pleasantries," she said, hefting a heavy black bag over her thin shoulder and hurrying up the drive towards the house. "We have precious little time. Where did he disappear?"

"On the porch." I didn't bother asking her who she meant. My heart pounded with hope. Bianca squeezed my hand. She had called Clara. Did that mean Clara was here to save Eric? But how could she? He was gone completely. He had crossed over. He was no longer a shade, stuck partway between the two worlds.

Clara bounded up the steps, and sniffed the air. "Yes," she said. "I can sense him here. We must hurry." She dumped her bag on the step and rummaged through it, pulling out a small piece of stone.

"This is Elestial quartz," she said as she placed the large stone on the porch, and scattered a few smaller stones around it. "And these smaller stones are moldavite. They are high frequency crystals—their vibrations help to locate and store energy, including the energy of a spirit. Now, link hands. I need both of you to picture Eric in your minds, as clearly as possible. Focus on the details of him—what did his eyes look like? How did his hair fall? How did being with him make you feel? I need you to bring him to life in your mind, okay?"

I nodded. Clara grabbed my right hand and Bianca's left. She nodded at us to join hands, too, completing a circle of three around the pile of stones. She lowered her head, and started to chant.

The sounds she made weren't words I recognised. At first, I thought they were Latin, but I'd taken Latin at public school and I didn't recognise the sounds. The words reverberated through my mind, pushing out my grief and fear and bringing something else to the surface. Memories. Love. My body flooded with warmth as I remembered Eric as I had known him, the brooding musician, the guy who made me smile, who loved to scare me, who taught me to play chess. I remembered the way he kissed me, and fire blazed inside of me.

The fire burned my skin from the inside, and it felt as if he really were kissing me, his tongue probing deep into my mouth. I felt the strength of his arms wrapping around my body, his hand pressing against the small of my back, pulling me in. His body pressed against mine, becoming part of me, enveloping me in his—

"Enough!" Clara cried, snapping me out of my trance. She dropped my hand, and the warm feeling in my body fled, pouring out of me into the large, clear crystal. Clara reached down and picked up the stones, carefully placing them inside a black cloth, and bringing the edges of the cloth together to create a small pouch.

Clara held the pouch away from herself, as if it contained something poisonous she didn't want to touch. "Now, where is his body?"

"In the mausoleum," I replied, jabbing a finger at the end of the garden.

"Grab my bag. We've got to hurry." Clara picked up the pouch of stones and hobbled across the lawn with surprising sprightliness. I grabbed the keyring from the hall table, picked up the shoulder bag—it was weighty—and Bianca and I followed after her.

The mausoleum was strung with solar fairy lights. They had been put up for the funeral, so that guests partying on into the night would be able to see some connection to the dead. But in the chaos of the party and the fire, no one had thought to remove them. I fumbled with the lock, searching for the right key. Finally, I found it, and pulled the iron gate open, revealing a large stone room where several coffins lay in niches on the walls. "Which one is he?" I asked.

Clara pushed past me, bending over to read the names. "Here he is," she pointed at a dark mahogany coffin resting on a lower shelf. Seeing that coffin made me pause. Were we really about to do what I thought we were about to do? Eric had been dead for three weeks now. Surely he wouldn't be himself any longer. And he would smell … I didn't want to open that coffin and see the decay of his body. I wanted to remember him as he was to me, beautiful and vibrant and alive.

If it could bring Eric back, I have to try.

"All three of us together," Clara instructed, as we prised open the lid. I stared down at the body inside, my stomach swirling with part-revulsion, part-nervous excitement. Eric appeared intact, serene. His face stared back at us with an expression of calm. He wore tailored black trousers and a black shirt, a black lace cravat at his throat. A few wounds marred his strong features —from the car accident, I presumed—and his skin was a weird pasty colour, but overall he appeared to be whole, and not filled with worms.

"Can you really do this?" I asked. "He'll actually be alive again? He isn't going to turn out like one of those characters in *Pet Sematary*, is he?"

'I've never tried this spell before, and I'm working with two amateurs, so I don't know what will happen. If we get this perfect, Eric will be as if he'd never died. But that's a big *if*. Just thank the gods he didn't decide to be cremated," Clara replied.

Clara pulled several white candles from her bag and laid them out around Eric's body, tucking them into the coffin itself. Two she placed on Eric's chest. Bianca reached across to help her, but Clara swatted her hand away. "Let me work," she snapped, as she opened a pouch of dried herbs and laid them out in a circle. Next, she pulled out several more crystals and a bunch of dried twigs and arranged them around Eric's head and hands. Finally, she withdrew a short dagger with an ornately carved handle.

"Stand over there," Clara directed me to the other side of the coffin. Bianca she placed at the top, near Eric's head. Clara whipped out her phone, opened a compass app, and readjusted some of the candles to stand at the four points on the compass. "Right," she announced, standing back and raising her hands. "We are ready."

Clara aimed the tip of the knife at the four points of the

compass, and muttered some more strange words. Slowly, she set down the black pouch of stones in the centre of Eric's chest, folding down the corners to reveal the crystals. The large quartz had a strange, white glow.

"Hold hands," Clara commanded. Bianca and I gripped each other, exchanging worried glances. Eric had been dead for three weeks now. How could this possibly work?

"Repeat the chant along with me," Clara said. "And as you do, picture a cone of white light rising up from Eric's chest and encompassing the stones. This cone will pull Eric's spirit back inside his body. Whatever happens, you must keep this vision in your mind. Let us begin." She paused, then spoke:

Shadow of chaos, death's spectre grim.
Allow my spirit once again to dwell within.

Bianca and I repeated the words, our voices blending together, echoing through every corner of the mausoleum. I focused my gaze on Eric's chest, where the crystal sat, now pulsing with a strange white light.

At first, it seemed as though nothing was happening, but then I noticed warmth spreading through my fingers, up my arms, moving across my chest. This wasn't the intense heat of Eric's touch, but a wretched, uncomfortable warmth, as if something unsavoury was crawling through me, slithering a path through my veins. I wriggled uncomfortably, trying to escape the feeling, but it only grew more intense.

"Keep chanting!" Clara ordered, her voice sounding odd, hollow, as though she were calling from the other end of a tunnel.

"Shadow of chaos, death's spectre grim—" I chanted, my voice cracking with pain. The warm slithered through my whole body, rising up my neck and flicking across my cheeks. It entered my mouth, and I gagged as a foul scent—the scent of death—reached my nostrils. Rotting, decaying flesh filled my nostrils, coming not from Eric's corpse below, but from all around me, from within me. It was my own flesh I was smelling. It was my own body that was rotting away.

It's a trick, it's part of the spell. I gagged against the loathsome odour, longing to pull my hand from Bianca's to pinch my nostrils closed. But I knew that if I broke my grip the whole spell would be ruined, and Eric would be gone forever.

"What's happening to me?" Bianca cried.

"Keep chanting!" Clara cried. "Don't break the circle!"

I closed my eyes. In my mind, I pictured a radiant cone of white light, rising from Eric's chest and enveloping the pulsing crystal. I pictured the cone pulling the energy from the crystal, tearing out Eric's spirit from where we had trapped it, blending it again with his mortal body.

"—allow my spirit once again to dwell within."

I opened my eyes. The cone was there for real, rising and falling with the rhythm of our chant. But even though our chant rose in intensity, the cone stopped moving, it even seemed to be receding back inside Eric. Whatever we were doing, it wasn't strong enough to bring the two parts of Eric's body together.

I can't lose you, Eric. I won't lose you. I love you.

A strong urge came over me, a sense that I knew exactly what to do. Without stopping the chant, without even looking at Clara for guidance, I leaned over Eric's body, pushing my head through the cone of light, and brushed my lips against his.

I love you.

"I love you, Eric!" I yelled into the light glowing from his lips. "You can't be gone. I love you."

The cone of light shot up toward the ceiling and exploded. White light enveloped us, blinding me with its brilliance. I tried to shut my eyes but even with them closed, I could see the whiteness on my eyelids. My ears rung from the explosion and I floated without feeling in the bright void, unable to move or sense a thing.

From the edge of my vision, a shape moved toward me, growing more focused as it sped through the white void. It was Eric's coffin soaring up to meet me. Just when I thought it was going to crash right into me, then there was another explosion of light, and I was standing in the mausoleum once more, the heat gone from my mind. Clara and Bianca dropped my hands.

The room came back into focus. There was Bianca, looking dazed and gripping the edge of the stone shelf for support. There was Clara, her shawls knotted clumsily around her head, her face expectant. And there was the coffin …

I peered over the edge. Eric lay inside, perfectly still. His skin still had that sickly white pallor.

No, no. It was supposed to work!

I picked up Eric's hand and lifted it to my cheek. "Eric, please. Come back to us. Please …"

His fingers were cold, limp, without life. His skin felt like clammy wax. No life flowed within his veins.

"No," I whispered. I dropped Eric's hand against the edge of the coffin.

The fingers grabbed the edge, clamping tight around the dark wood.

"Oh, my …" Clara breathed. Bianca bit her nails nervously. My whole body froze, my eyes trained on the corpse for any sign of life.

Eric's lips parted a fraction, and he emitted a sound like something slimy being sucked down the sinkhole. I hadn't realised I'd been holding my breath, but my chest heaved and begged for air. I let out the breath and sucked in another. *Please, Eric, please …*

Eric's eyes flickered open. The orbs circled the room once, looking disoriented, terrified. But then they focused in on my face, those brown pools wide and inviting, deep emotions swirling within them. An ocean of unspoken words passed between us in that one single look, a look we never imagined we'd get to have.

He's returned. He's back inside his body.

Tears of joy streamed down my face. I grabbed Eric's hand and clenched it in mine, relishing the warmth that now had now reached his palm. His fingers still felt cold, but they were warming quickly, losing their stiff, waxy feeling and giving way to supple, *living* skin.

"Eli … nor," he croaked.

"Shhhh," said Clara. "Don't try to speak. You need a few moments to fully wake up."

Eric lifted one arm, then the other, his face alight with joy as he moved his stiff limbs for the first time in over three weeks. Finally, he gripped the edges of the coffin and pulled himself up. "Oh," he breathed, clutching his stomach. He leaned forward, breaking into a retching coughing fit. A stream of pale fluid spewed from his mouth across his pants. Embalming fluid. His body was expelling what it no longer needed.

"Eric!" I threw my arms around him. He held me tightly, his whole body trembling against mine. He convulsed wildly again, spewing another stream of embalming fluid into the coffin.

"Elinor," he croaked, his hand exploring my body, touching my face, grabbing my shoulders, stroking my back.

"You're alive," I cried, burying my head in his shoulder, breathing in the scent of him.

"Thanks to you," he said, running his fingers through my hair. "The spell wasn't working, but then … I heard your voice through the void, and it pulled me to my body. You called me home."

"Oh, Eric," I sobbed, clawing at his shoulders, my chest feeling as though it might burst with happiness. "I love you so much. I can't believe you came back."

"I came back … for you."

"Let's get you back to the house," Clara said kindly. She took off her black shawl and placed it over Eric's shoulders. "Do you think you can stand?"

Eric reached across and gripped my arm with such fierceness

that I winced. Bianca stood on the other side of him, and together we helped him lift his stiff legs out of the coffin and onto the floor. We had to hold him under the shoulders while he practiced putting weight on his legs.

"Thank you," he said to me. "I think we can go to the house now."

"Of course." I squeezed his hand as we helped him shuffle toward the door. "I've kept it just the way you like it, slightly charred on the inside."

"You've done more than that. You found me," he whispered. "You were my light in the darkness."

"I don't think so." I grinned back. "I think you were mine."

ERIC

The next two weeks passed by in a blur.

One thing about coming back to life that no one ever talks about: it's like waking up with the hangover from hell. My body was filled with all the embalming fluids used to keep my corpse beautiful in death. Clara had to create several powerful expulsion charms to cleanse me of all the toxic stuff and replace my actual fluids. While the crystals and herbal sachets she placed around my body seemed harmless enough, what was going on inside of me was anything but. I'd never been to detox before, but if it hurt even half as much as having to regurgitate formaldehyde and then regenerate your own organs, then I pitied anyone who had.

I couldn't very well go to a hospital in my state. I'd be the subject of medical inquiry for the rest of my life. Bianca had graciously put us up in her tiny apartment while the repairs were being made to Marshell House. I'd instructed Elinor to release the funds from my mother's bank accounts to make it happen, and she informed me there was an army of workmen there around the clock to ensure the place would be habitable again by the time I moved in. Thankfully, although Bianca's place lacked space and light and sufficient hot water, it did have one serious advantage … the press didn't know I was there.

Elinor stayed by my side the entire time. When I was throwing up fluids, she held my hair. While my punctured organs were regrowing, she read me stories from the newspaper. Through the wall of my pain, I registered that Allan and Colin were now on trial for murder, assault, drug trafficking, and a litany of other crimes, along with the other members of Ghost Symphony and three members of our tech crew. The press were following it carefully, publishing every morsel of juicy news. Helen Manning gave an extremely emotional testimony. The outcome wasn't looking good for my band.

A police search had turned up Isolde in Allan's hotel room, amongst a lot of other damning evidence. Bianca's friend Ted delivered her to me, and she was now leaning up in the corner of the room, begging me to reunite with her again as soon as I was well.

Elinor told me about Duncan being in love with my mother, and what he'd used the money for. I decided not to press charges against him. After all, at his heart he was a good person, and he really had taken wonderful care of my mother. It wasn't as if she missed the money. Elinor grinned when I announced my decision to leave Duncan alone. "But I reserve the right to change my mind later," I warned her, wincing painfully as something inside my stomach twisted painfully. "I'm in so much agony, I can't be trusted at my word."

"That's fine, Eric." Elinor grinned, pushing her glasses up her nose. "Whatever you want."

Finally, I was well enough to start to walk around again, but Elinor and Bianca wouldn't let me leave the apartment. "We have to keep your presence a secret, until the right time," said Elinor.

Her friend Cindy popped in from London every few days to go over details—Elinor had put her in charge of my "comeback" campaign. I wasn't sure it was such a good idea, given how badly

Cindy treated Elinor. But she just smiled. "Ah, but one thing best friends do is forgive each other. The other thing they do is get even. You, my dear Eric, are going to be the most demanding, stubborn, and ridiculous client Cindy has ever had."

"I am?"

"You are. It's high time you embraced the rockstar lifestyle. Cindy will be too busy running around procuring rare French cheeses and having your suits tailored by cloistered nuns living in remote Sicilian villages to party it up with Damon Sputnik."

"You're evil," I grinned.

"I know."

The plan was to frame my death as a publicity stunt to launch the new stage of my career, and my gothic fans would eat it right up. Eric Marshell was going to be reborn as a solo artist, and he was going to be hotter than ever.

Despite all this good cheer, as my body grew stronger, I grew more anxious to return to Marshell House, or failing that, just to be anywhere that wasn't inside Bianca's tiny apartment. I was also worried about Elinor missing so much work. So I snapped at my posse and grunted whenever they asked me how I felt. I started practicing sending Cindy out for extravagant and ridiculous items, like ten pounds of pickled Swedish herring and a hand-made teddy bear dressed in an otter costume. By the end of my incarceration, I was leaving lewd drawings on the bathroom mirror and making sculptures out of my food (which was a lot more fun than eating it. Elinor was a woman of many talents, but cooking wasn't one of them, and no one could do much with pickled herring).

Finally, Clara checked my pulse and her crystals and declared that I was ready to return. Repairs on Marshell House weren't quite complete, but Elinor assured me that it was now safe to move back in. My legs still felt a little stiff, so together, Elinor, Bianca and Cindy helped me struggle downstairs, while Clara called instructions from below. Finally, Elinor settled me in the car with Isolde and we drove up the street and down the long driveway of Marshell House.

As we neared the house, I looked up at that imposing facade, the two turrets jutting out like sabre teeth, and the twin round windows like eyes glaring over the landscape. But she didn't inspire the same terror she once did. I used to dread entering her tall, floral hallways, for inside that house lurked only pain, and disappointment. But now, with Elinor beside me … I reached across and squeezed her hand.

"It looks great, doesn't it?" she smiled. "Those gardeners Duncan hired did an amazing job."

"It certainly does," I agreed.

Elinor helped me hobble up the steps and crash into the hallway. This was more exercise than I'd had in two weeks, and my body was already exhausted. She set down the keys and turned to me, looping her arm under my shoulder once more. "Where would you like to go?" she asked.

"Bedroom," I huffed, my body already protesting against all this exercise. "I want to … ravish your body …"

"Tempting as that is," Elinor said, grinning back, "I think we need to wait for you to gain some more strength. There's something I need to show you first."

Elinor helped me into the study, and sat me down in the chair by the window. She handed me a thick, black ledger book. "What's this?" I asked. "I can barely remember how to spell my name at the moment. I *really* don't want to look at numbers right now."

"This one is different. Look at it," Elinor said, flipping through the pages and shoving it into my hands.

I glanced at the old news clippings of my father's disappearance. "I've already seen those," I said. I had many of the same clippings in a box under my bed upstairs. "My mother must have been cutting them out and keeping them."

"What about these?" Elinor grabbed the book out of my hands, flipped to a page toward the back, and turned the book back around so I could see.

It was a picture of me, taken five years ago during Ghost Symphony's first European tour. I was sitting beside a fjord in Norway, my violin resting across my chest. I was looking forlornly at the camera while grey clouds gathered in the background. I remembered the shoot well—about two minutes after the picture was taken, the heavens opened up and drenched everything.

Elinor flipped the page. There were more clippings about the band, GHOST SYMPHONY NUMBER 1 AGAIN. LATEST GHOST SYMPHONY ALBUM NOMINATED FOR GRAMMY, ERIC MARSHELL VOTED SEXIEST MAN OF THE YEAR. All the press about me, all the cheesy photo shoots and gripping exposés and news articles and revealing interviews ... she had kept it all.

I couldn't believe it. My mother had never said anything to me about my music. *Never*. As far as I'd known, she still hated me for choosing the same career as my father. And yet, all the time, she'd been doing *this*.

For the first time since my mother died, pain welled up inside me. I stared down at those pages with a tremendous sense of loss. Here she was, the mother I thought I had lost forever. She had been right here this whole time, and she was just too proud to tell me how she really felt. And now it was too late, for her and for me.

Tears pressed against the corners of my eyes. I blinked them away.

"Thank you," I said to Elinor, closing the book. I closed my eyes, suddenly feeling very tired.

"I'm sorry I didn't show it to you sooner," she said. "I found it the first day I was here. I didn't understand the significance of it before now."

"That's okay."

"And that's not all." Elinor handed me a letter. "This is a will written by your mother. It's what we in the lawyering business call a holographic will. She had it witnessed by two of her nurses. It's completely legally binding, Eric, and Duncan is not going to contest it."

As I read the words from my mother—the apology I'd long wished to hear while she was alive—tears streamed down my cheeks, thick and fast. I placed the letter down and wiped them away. "I'm sorry. This is supposed to be a happy day, and here I am—"

Elinor patted my knee. "Eric, you've quite literally been through hell, and come back to tell the tale. This is a happy day, because you are alive again, and you're back here at last, and you have all your mother's funds behind you. You can do anything you want now."

"We'll set up the scholarship fund. I want all the money to go to other kids like me, other young Eric and Erica Marshells. All I want to do is play music," I said. "And make love to you."

She laughed, and squeezed my hand. "That's perfectly fine by me."

"Here she is." Elinor handed me the case.

My fingers brushed over the dark wood, touching all the familiar scratches. Reverently, I lifted the lid. Inside, nestled in a bed of crushed velvet, was Isolde, my old friend. I ran my hand along her length, admiring her smooth curves, her sensuous form, the elegant curl of her scroll. It was as though I were seeing her for the first time. Already, the music hummed against my skin, begging to be released.

I let out the breath I didn't realise I'd been holding.

Elinor sat down opposite me. "If you don't feel up to it, you don't have to play," she said.

"That's where you're wrong."

Gingerly, I lifted Isolde out of the case and settled my chin into the rest, holding the position I'd practiced ever since I was a boy. Having her back in my hands was like coming home. I couldn't believe I'd been given this second chance at life, that I had many more years ahead of me to make music.

I drew the bow across the strings. The note rang out, perfect and true. My fingers moved over the strings, slowly at first, then with more confidence, the memory of my songs still coursing through me. The song rose from the ashes of my death, a phoenix rising anew. Sweeping notes and dazzling arpeggios rung throughout the house, breathing life into it, into me.

The song pulsed and swelled, plunging me deeper into its spell. I stood, drawing strength from its beauty. My legs shook a little, but held firm. I took a tentative step across the rug, and then another, and before I realised what was happening, I was dancing, swooping and twirling in time with Isolde's music.

Elinor laughed and clapped as her gaze followed me across the room. I dipped and turned, flying through the song as my fingers danced over the familiar notes. As I met her eyes again and felt the connection sizzle between us, and Isolde's grip felt warm and familiar, I knew no song I'd ever played before had been as joyous as this one.

AFTER DINNER, Elinor helped me into some black pyjamas decorated with tiny grinning skulls she'd found in the village. (The doctor's orders were to keep me warm at night, and Elinor loved to follow rules, even though the flannel pyjamas were completely ridiculous and if any of my fans saw them they would totally ruin my goth cred). She tucked me into bed in my old bedroom, then climbed in beside me, naked, the warmth of her body searing me through the blankets. She touched my cheek. "You must be tired."

"A little. I tell you, being resurrected is hell on the nerves."

She laughed, her eyes boring into mine. Her hair splayed out across the pillow, a halo around her face. Suddenly, I didn't feel tired at all. My whole body lit up like a Christmas tree.

"So …" I raised one eyebrow playfully. "How do you feel about being ravished by a man in black?"

"I think that would be very lovely," Elinor grinned, smothering my lips in hers.

I wrapped my arms around her body, enjoying the sensation of touching her for real. Her lips against mine tasted sweet and rich, her skin like honey. She fumbled with the buttons on my pyjamas and pulled the shirt open, pressing her hands against my skin. Fire raced through me where she touched me. I shrugged off the grinning skulls and pressed my chest to hers. At last, we were skin against skin, an blazing inferno of desire.

"You're so solid," Elinor cooed, trailing her fingers across my chest.

"That's not the only part of me that's hard," I growled. Elinor grinned wider, and moved her fingers down, running them along the waistband of my pants, before running them down and freeing my cock. She wrapped her fingers around it, moving them slowly while I twitched in her hands. The sensation of her skin against mine sent a shiver of delight through my body.

I pulled her close, kissing along her collarbone, trailing my tongue across her sensitive skin. "I want to kiss every inch of you," I murmured against her skin. "I can't believe you're real."

She moaned in reply as my fingers found her nipples. I stroked them softly, then twisted them until she mewed with delight. Her grip around me tightened, and it took everything I had not to explode right then.

I lay her back against the sheets, removing her hand from my shaft. There was so much I wanted to do to her – *for* her – first.

I kissed and sucked and nibbled every inch of her, exploring her glorious body with all of my senses. She smelt of fresh spring flowers, her taste was sweet and warm and utterly intoxicating. Her nipples hardened in my mouth like tiny stones, and she moaned and writhed beneath me, begging me for more.

Between her legs, I worshipped her, giving her the attention a goddess deserved. Her sweet scent filled my nostrils, and I drowned in the joy of her. My tongue worked her until she could take no more. Her thighs clenched and her back arched as her orgasm tore through her.

Seeing Elinor lying in her ecstasy sent me ever closer to the edge. My cock pressed against her leg, begging for release. I dragged her toward me, sliding my body between her legs. Her eyes met mine, languid and heavy-lidded. She wrapped her arms around my neck.

"I love you," she said.

"I love you." I slid up into her, and my body body shot with fire. We moved together, our bodies one. She felt so good around me, like the first notes of a new song, wrapped in all the promise of tomorrow.

Time stood still as we devoured each other, our kisses ravenous as our bodies flowed together. Every tiny movement, every scrape of her nails against my skin, every tiny gasp from her gorgeous lips held me deeper under her spell.

Elinor dug her nails into my shoulders, and the pain made me remember that I was alive, and I was here making love to Elinor Baxter, and I could make love to her again and again for the rest of my days and each time it would feel amazing. Because I had been given a second chance at everything, and damn if I was going to screw it up again.

My muscles tightened as the ache inside me grew larger, consuming all of me. Our bodies climaxed together, hot skin shuddering against each other, two souls entwined in a precious moment. We collapsed together, our bodies spent, blankets strewn around us.

Even though the night was silent, with Elinor's head resting on my chest, music danced through my body. The song of my life had many more movements to go, and I intended to enjoy each and every one of them.

IN BETWEEN MAKING love and sleeping, Elinor told me all about her previous boyfriend and her outburst at his funeral. "So much of what I was feeling wasn't about you. It had to do with Joel and how I still blamed myself for being sucked in by his bullshit. He made me feel foolish, and I hate that feeling. And with you ... I felt so out of control, as though I were slipping back into the same trap again. I am so sorry, Eric."

"Of course that's okay." I embraced her. "I just wish you'd told me, because I could have been more patient. I mean, not terribly patient, because I did want to rip your clothes off you pretty much from the moment I first saw you, but ..." She pressed her lips to mine, and I ran my fingers down her naked back as I kissed her deeper, enjoying the way her tongue entwined with mine.

"Did I mention I was sorry? I just got so sick of always been pushed around and walked over. I didn't want to take that from you. I didn't want you to see me as weak."

"You're not weak. You're not that person anymore, babe."

"No." She grinned, moving in for another kiss. "I'm not."

Later that day, we put our clothes on again, and Elinor twirled around the living room in a new version of her red gothic dress, sent over from Clara as a present. Bianca came over with a box of cupcakes from Bewitching Bites. She set out tea for us on the back porch, while I enlivened the mood with a couple of jigs on my beloved violin. While I played, I looked out over the back garden, and the patches of charred earth where the fire had been worst. I thought how lucky we had been to escape that with our lives. The fire could have so easily got out of control.

"To Eric." Elinor held up her teacup. Laughing, Bianca reached over and clinked cups.

"Why are we toasting me?" I demanded, pointing my bow at them with disdain. "If it wasn't for you ladies, I wouldn't be here to toast with tea at all, which is a completely ridiculous waste of tea if you ask me, since you've spilt it everywhere."

Bianca made a face at me, but Elinor said seriously, "You're alive, Eric. You're real. I can *touch* you. That alone is worth toasting, without any of your other accomplishments."

"But it was an incredible thing you guys did for me. I just lay there and let you do all the work. You should be toasting yourselves." I smiled. "I do kind of miss that electric shock feeling whenever we touch, though."

"I don't!" Elinor hugged me again. "Now I know that when I touch you, we both feel the same."

"Ah well, then." I held up my cup. "I can drink to that!"

We toasted together and sat back in silence, enjoying our tea as a crisp breeze blew the fallen leaves across the porch.

"So what happens now?" Bianca asked, looking from Elinor's face to mine. "Are you going back to London?"

I stared at Elinor as I dragged the bow over the strings slowly. We'd avoided talking about the future while I was recovering, but it was playing on my mind. How would I live without her when she returned to London? Should I go with her? But how could I leave the Marshell House?

"Of course she is," I said, at the same time, Elinor said. "I don't think so."

I whirled around to face her. "What are you talking about? Of course you're going back. You have your career to think about. I'm in London a lot anyway, in the studio and doing press and such. We'll find a way to make it work."

Elinor toyed with the tulle on her skirt. Finally, she said, "Oh, I know we will. But there's just one thing I have to do."

"And that is?" I raised an eyebrow.

Elinor whipped out her phone.

"You're not going to play some of that godawful house music again, are you?" I groaned. "I have literally just come back from the dead. I can't deal with a seizure right now."

She shot me a dirty look, then held her phone to her ear. "Hello, Clyde. It's Elinor Baxter. I'm sorry to be disturbing you on the golf course … yes, it's going very well. I've not only completed Alice Marshell's estate, but I've also solved a murder mystery and uncovered a drug ring. I think I've done the firm proud … Oh yes, well, see about my return … it turns out I'm not going to be back in the office on Monday. I'm tendering my resignation, effective immediately."

She what? I dropped my bow in surprise.

Elinor watched me as she listened to the man yelling on the other end, a big grin spreading across her face. "Oh, no. I don't have a competing offer. Well, at least, not one you can match. I've decided to take up an apprenticeship as a tattoo artist. I'm going to be starting as soon as I've moved up to Crookshollow."

Bianca laughed. I gasped. Is Elinor sick? Has sitting next to me for the last two weeks made her crazy? Did the fumes from the embalming liquid addle her brain?

Elinor's boss sounded equally miffed. I could hear him yelling and spluttering from across the table. "I'm sorry that you're upset, but I'm sure Lila will take your mind off it. Toodles!" Elinor hung up the phone, cutting off her boss mid-rant. She tossed the phone down on the table and leaned back in her chair, grinning madly. Her eyes sparkled from behind her black glasses.

"Elinor Baxter. I am speechless," Bianca said. "And to think I've been interviewing pimply-faced schoolboys for the apprenticeship all week."

"So you'll take me?"

"Of course." Bianca grinned, extending her hand across the table and shaking Elinor's firmly. "Welcome to Resurrection Ink."

"Well," Elinor prodded me. "What do you think?"

"About you moving to Crookshollow?" I leaned over to her and picked her off the chair, sweeping her into my arms and planting a hot kiss on her yielding lips. "I think we'd better hurry up and get the house repairs completed."

Elinor wrapped her arms around my neck, raising one eyebrow. "So you're asking me to move in?"

"I am. I mean," I gestured towards the house, "she's a little run-down in places, and there are a few holes due to age and arson. It's been recently haunted, but we fixed that. I think it's got real potential, don't you?"

Elinor giggled, pointing to the large burned hole at the back of the dining room. "Absolutely. It's got great indoor–outdoor flow."

"Excellent amenities," added Bianca, pointing to the mausoleum.

"A menagerie of delightful pets," I added, indicating the stone gargoyle sitting on the edge of the fountain.

I spun Elinor around, admiring the way the corset accentuated her luscious curves, and her bare shoulders revealed the line of her neck as she threw her head back to laugh with abandon. My whole body felt light and free. Elinor was coming to live with me. We were going to fill Marshell House with books and music and games and children. And there would never be a day in my life that went by when I wasn't grateful for the second chance I'd been given.

I set Elinor down again, and she reached across the table to snag one of the cupcakes Bianca had brought. "Remember what I said," Bianca told her. "You can't be a tattoo artist until you have your own ink."

"I know, and I've decided what I want."

"Please say it's a leprechaun," said Bianca. "I'm actually getting quite good at them. I think it might be my new specialty."

Elinor laughed. "No leprechauns. I want a pair of beautiful wings, spreading out from my shoulders down my back, ready to unfurl and fly away at any time. Because I feel as if this house has allowed me to fly away from the things that were holding me back. Finally, I feel free."

"We'll start first thing tomorrow," said Bianca, licking icing off her fingers.

"Not so fast." I grabbed her. "Ever since I met you, I've been yearning to feel your skin against mine, and my yearning has not yet been sated. I don't think we're planning to leave the bedroom for at least a month."

"A month?" Elinor gave me a breathtaking smile. "I'd better limber up then." And with that, she broke away from me and ran across the lawn, heading down to the crooked path heading into the forest, her voluminous skirt billowing out behind her. I grinned and chased after her, enjoying the way the wind whipped my hair around my face and the long grass shifted against my black pants. *God, it feels good to be alive.*

At the gate, Elinor paused and waited for me, her brilliant eyes gleaming. The red shirt swirled around her legs, accentuating her foxy curves. She had never looked more beautiful, or more like herself.

"Did I tell you how gorgeous you look in that dress?" I said when I caught up to her, my eyes wandering over her body.

Elinor leaned in closer, pressing herself against me, enjoying the heat of my flesh against her bare shoulders. "This is a ghost story, remember. I needed my voluminous gothic gown."

Beautiful, unpredictable Elinor. I loved her already, more than she could ever know. I bent down and placed my lips against hers, relishing the flicker of hot energy—a remnant of the afterlife she had saved me from—that passed between us as my mouth devoured hers.

THE END

Want another story from the world of Crookshollow? In book 5 of the *Crookshollow Gothic Romance* series, bakery owner Belinda Wu saves an injured raven, who turns out to be a shapeshifter on the run. Is Cole just the man she needs to save her from her own problems? Read Watcher now

Want free books, exclusive giveaways and exclusive sneak peeks at upcoming Steffanie Holmes paranormal romance books? Sign up for the mailing list to get the scoop.

Anna

It's been five months since my boyfriend was tragically killed in a climbing accident. I didn't think I was over him … until Luke walked on to the archaeological site.

Tall, dark, sexy, tattooed, funny, dangerous. Everything I want in a man.

But he's hiding something. He acts strangely in the moonlight. He won't tell me anything about his life. And I caught him trying to destroy an important find.

My body aches for him, but my heart tells me I'm not ready to make myself vulnerable again, especially not for a guy who isn't being straight with me.

If only …

Luke

Anna Sinclair – archaeologist, geek girl, totally and utterly delectable.

I knew from the moment her intoxicating scent wafted across my wolf senses, she's meant to be mine.

And that knowledge is *terrifying*.

The last thing I expected was to find my fated mate on an archaeological site. Whenever I'm near her, all I want to do is claim her.

But she's broken. The last thing she needs in her life is a werewolf out for revenge. I'm here to destroy the site, to keep my family's past buried forever.

If Anna finds out the truth, she'd never speak to me again.

But I can't deny the bond between us. **I'll do anything to make her mine.**

Digging the Wolf is a standalone paranormal romance by USA Today bestselling author Steffanie Holmes. Read if you love archaeological mysteries, badass wolves, a broken heroine, and a hero so hot he'll have you howling for more.

START READING NOW

Luke whirled around, the light of his torch temporarily blinding me. "Anna, you startled me."

"I might say the same thing," I said, suddenly nervous. It had been curiosity that compelled me to follow him into the caves, to see why he was sneaking around the site at night after explicitly warning us not to. But now that I was here, confronting him wearing only my pyjamas, thermal underwear, boots, and jacket, I realised just how dangerous this situation could be. I barely knew Luke. Just because he was gorgeous didn't mean he didn't have some nefarious purpose. As far as I knew, the guy could be unstable. And I was alone with him, without my hard hat, in the dark, in an unexplored section of the cave. No one else knew I was here. If he killed me now, they wouldn't ever find my body.

I'd just made all the mistakes I'd promised myself I'd never make.

"I asked a question," I said, trying to stop my voice from wavering. Luke stared at me with wide eyes. His mouth moved, but no sound came out. Fancy that. I'd actually rendered him speechless.

"Luke?" I prodded, careful to keep my voice stern. No sense in letting him sense my fear.

"I'm just … checking up on some of the details of your excavation." Luke nodded firmly. "Frances's notes weren't very expansive. I thought I'd come here and try to get a sense of things *in situ*."

"This area of the cave hasn't been explored," I said, my voice shrinking in the cavernous space. "That fact was in the notes you were reading. It's dangerous to come here by yourself, especially at night, especially if no one knows where you are."

"You know where I am," he growled, those fierce green eyes flickering over my body. With a flush, I remembered that I was wearing my hideous pink thermal leggings underneath my Snoopy pyjama pants. Could this day get any worse?

"We shouldn't be in the caves at night," I repeated nervously. "I believe a certain ranger told me it's against the rules."

"Do you ever do anything that's against the rules?" he asked, closing the gap between us in a heartbeat. He still hadn't touched me, but my body flooded with warm, pulsing energy. How was it he could make me feel this way? Especially when I'd just caught him red handed doing something he shouldn't.

"I … er …"

"I thought so." Luke stepped closer. "Anna, I can explain. I—"

"Argh!" I screamed as something swooped down from the darkness and flapped beside my face. I dropped my torch as I flung my hands up to protect my eyes from the screeching bat. My stomach turned as the bat's furry body slipped through my fingers and scrambled into my hair, its wings twitching as it tangled itself deeper.

The torch clattered on the rocks below, bouncing down the steps and plunging into the pool. The light went out.

"Fuck," Luke swore. "Stand still!"

"I can't stand still. There's a bat in my hair!" I wailed, flailing my hands around my head. I turned to run back down the fissure, but instead I crashed into Luke, sending his torch flying from his hands. It hit the rocks with a crash, and the light flickered out, plunging us both into complete darkness.

Tears welled in my eyes. The bat's feet scrabbled against my head, yanking my hair so hard the entire side of my scalp felt as though it were being pulled off. Luke's hands battled in my hair. He swore again as the squabbling intensified. Finally, the bat released me, and I heard its wings flapping away into the darkness.

"Ow." I touched the side of my head. My scalp felt tender. But at least it was still there. Luckily, I'd already had a tetanus shot.

"Anna, are you okay?"

I nodded, biting my lip. After a moment of silence, I realised how stupid that was. "I'm fine," I said, my voice cracking.

"I can tell. Here, hold on to me," Luke ordered. I reached out, grabbing for his elbow, but instead, my fingers brushed the fabric of his jeans. I felt the button on his fly. Shit. I'd grabbed him right—

"If you wanted an excuse to grope me, you just had to ask," he said, laughing.

"Shut up," I shot back, heat flaring in my cheeks. I was lucky it was so dark, he wouldn't be able to see how beet-red I must be. I reached up, clamping my hand around his forearm. The warm sensation raced through my fingers, down my whole arm, lighting all my senses on fire.

Woah. The heat was intense. It wasn't just my hormones on overdrive. The heat penetrated every layer of my body, spreading through my limbs and circling through my head. My chest swelled with intense emotion. I gulped back the urge to … I'm not sure whether I wanted to cry or laugh or kiss Luke or push him away or beg him to marry me. The intense sensation swirled around my head, and in the darkness, it was even more disorienting. I squeezed Luke's arm tighter, reassuring myself that he was there, and that I was standing upright still.

"Luke," I asked, tugging at my hand. "I feel—"

"I know." His deep voice came through the dark. Confident, reassuring. "Don't think about it right now, Anna. We need to focus on getting out of here. Can you follow behind me?"

"I ... I think so."

Luke's fingers closed around mine. The warmth in my body surged. Slowly, Luke felt his way back up the fissure, squeezing his way between the gap. I kept close at his heels, my other hand feeling my way along the rocks, re-establishing my bearings. Every few moments he squeezed my hand. I squeezed back, assuring him I was fine.

"You're good at this," I remarked as we emerged onto the site and Luke picked his way carefully around the quadrants without disturbing any of our cuttings.

"I can see well in the dark," he said, then sucked in his breath, as though he'd said something he shouldn't.

"That's interesting."

"Is it?" He slid down a rocky ledge, then turned to grip my waist with his strong hands. Before I could say anything, he'd lifted me down, and crushed my body against his powerful chest. My face was millimetres from his. His hot breath warmed my lips. The energy between us sizzled. "I can think of much more interesting things right now."

Kiss me, my body screamed. In the dark, my senses worked in overdrive, assailing me with Luke's intoxicating masculine scent, the sensation of his fingers gripping me, the press of his bulge against my thigh.

"Luke—" I murmured, not sure whether I was protesting or begging.

"Anna." His husky voice grated against my ears. His breath caressed my cheek. And then, he pressed his lips to mine.

Want more? Read Digging the Wolf *if you love archaeological mysteries, badass wolves, a broken heroine, and a hero so hot he'll have you howling for more. Now FREE from your favourite ebook store!*

ABOUT THE AUTHOR

Steffanie Holmes is the author of steamy historical and paranormal romance. Her books feature clever, witty heroines, wild shifters, cunning witches and alpha males who *always* get what they want.

Before becoming a writer, Steffanie worked as an archaeologist and museum curator. She loves to explore historical settings and ancient conceptions of love and possession. From Dark Age Europe to crumbling gothic estates, Steffanie is fascinated with how love can blossom between the most unlikely characters.

Steffanie lives in New Zealand with her husband and a horde of cantankerous cats.

STEFFANIE HOLMES MAILING LIST

Want to be informed when the next Steffanie Holmes paranormal romance story goes live? Sign up for the mailing list!

Come hang with Steffanie
www.steffanieholmes.com
hello@steffanieholmes.com

Dear Fae,

Don't even THINK about attacking my castle.

This science geek witch and her four magic-wielding men are about to get medieval on your ass.

I'm Maeve Crawford. For years I've had my future mathematically calculated down to the last detail; Leave my podunk Arizona town, graduate MIT, get into the space program, be the first woman on Mars, get a cat (not necessarily in this order).

Then fairies killed my parents and shot the whole plan to hell.

I've inherited a real, honest-to-goodness English castle – complete with turrets, ramparts, and four gorgeous male tenants, who I'm totally *not* in love with.

Not at all.

It would be crazy to fall for four guys at once, even though they're totally gorgeous and amazing and wonderful and kind.

But not as crazy as finding out I'm a witch. A week ago, I didn't even believe magic existed, and now I'm up to my ears in spells and prophetic dreams and messages from the dead.

When we're together – and I'm talking in the Biblical sense – the five of us wield a powerful magic that can banish the fae forever. They intend to stop us by killing us all.

I can't science my way out of this mess.

Forget NASA, it's going to take all my smarts just to survive Briar-wood Castle.

The Castle of Earth and Embers is the first in a brand new steamy reverse harem romance by *USA Today* bestselling author, Steffanie Holmes. This full-length book glitters with love, heartache, hope, grief, dark magic, fairy trickery, steamy scenes, British slang, meat pies, second chances, and the healing powers of a good cup of tea. Read on only if you believe one just isn't enough.

Available from Amazon and in KU.

Art of the Hunt (Alex & Ryan)

Art of Temptation (Alex & Ryan)

The Man in Black (Elinor & Eric)

Watcher (Belinda & Cole)

Reaper (Belinda & Cole)

Wolves of Crookshollow series

Digging the Wolf (Anna & Luke)

Writing the Wolf (Rosa & Caleb)

Inking the Wolf (Bianca & Robbie)

Wedding the Wolf (Willow & Irvine)

Fallen Sorcery Fae (shared world)

Hollow

Witches of the Woods

Witch Hunter

Coven

The Curse (coming in 2019)

Want to be informed when the next Steffanie Holmes paranormal romance story goes live? Sign up for the VIP Readers Club at https://www.subscribepage.com/briarwoodprequel *to get the scoop, and score a free bonus epilogue to enjoy!*